Uprising
Jonathan Kinkaid in the West Indies

By Michael Winston

Copyright 2011

*An adventure in the continuing saga of
Jonathan Kinkaid of the American Navy*

For Mom, an unsung hero

Preface

On November 16, 1776, the American brig-of-war *Andrew Doria*, commanded by Captain Isaiah Robinson, entered the roadstead of the Dutch free port of St. Eustatia and rendered honors to the flag of Holland that flew over Fort Orange. The commander of the fort, Abraham Ravené, was at first reluctant to return the salute, but the governor, Johannes de Graaff, ordered him to do so, making history and bestowing upon St. Eustatia the distinction of becoming the first foreign power to officially recognize the sovereignty of our fledgling nation.

Only seven miles square, the "Golden Rock," as she was called in those days, was once the richest territory per square acre in the world. Far from British blockades and with sometimes as many as two hundred ships in her spacious roadstead, the island provided the perfect location for the duty-free transshipment of goods. It was especially important to the continuation of American resistance to the Crown, as a port where practically anything needed to supply an army or a navy, to carry on a war effort, could be bought or traded from sympathetic countries. Benjamin Franklin even had his mail sent through "Statia."

After an official reception, the *Andrew Doria* returned to America, her hold filled with badly needed arms and ammunition. When the infuriated British learned of this activity, they sent Admiral Rodney to loot the island, burn ships, and destroy the harbor, ending the contraband trade from there.

With the advent of slavery and the colonizing of the Caribbean came native uprisings, mercilessly put down with cruel vengeance. The jungle island of Dominica was no exception. Located midway between the Leeward and Windward Islands, it is the largest, wettest, and to this day least-developed island in the Lesser

Antilles, populated by the once-cannibalistic Carib Indians, wandering descendents of the Arawak tribes of South America.

In the summer of 1979, a week before Hurricane David devastated the island, a sure-footed guide in "treads" led me into the wet rainforest of Dominica. We climbed up a narrow ridge, to where a mountain with three peaks touches the clouds, then down into the steaming Valley of Desolation, at the end of which is Boiling Lake. In spite of her primitive beauty, Dominica remains largely undiscovered by the rest of the world.

Jack Blackstone is representative of the various brigands and buccaneers who made their settlement kingdoms throughout the islands of the Greater Antilles. Made of deserters and shipwrecked sailors, runaway slaves, and escaped criminals, these outlaw groups in their fast and well armed ships might be called pirates one year and allies the next, for English, French and Spanish governors often employed the violent services of pirates by issuing letters of marque, turning cutthroats into mercenaries at the stroke of a pen.

In this second book of the series, Kinkaid is given command of the lightly armed brig, *Swift*. His mission, threefold: to deliver a diplomat bearing a copy of the Declaration of Independence to the island of St. Eustatia, to assist a major of marines with a secret assignment, and to gain information of any pirate activity in the Caribbean that might interfere with American shipping between St. Eustatia and American shores.

Contents

I Reunions

II Presents of Departure

III Men's Gifts

IV Greetings…

V …and Farewells

VI Pirates or Patriots?

VII Mad Doctors and Bad Cooks

VIII Uneasy Passage

IX Uprising

X The Prize and a Proud Name

XI Ally to Enemy

XII Cannonballs Will Do

XIII Big Guns of Hurricane Hole

XIV Just Desserts

Reunions

It was early summer and the two weeks spent with Elizabeth were a joy. Her father, the elder John Whipple, was most kind and understanding and had insisted that Kinkaid use the family's guest cottage on the grounds of the estate. Mrs. Whipple had apologized about the smallness of its rooms, but compared to life aboard ship, his new quarters, filled with overstuffed furniture and Persian rugs, provided an atmosphere of luxury and ease that Kinkaid had slowly and grudgingly allowed himself to enjoy and appreciate, finding he had little choice, a beached naval officer, told only to "await further orders." The war had seemed far away, but now the blowing curtains reminded him of sails, especially since receiving orders from the Marine Committee, telling him to report to the Commander of Naval Forces in a week, which likely meant a new assignment that would bring an end to idle living and an uncertain future.

The war seemed far away and it was to the sounds of neighing horses and quacking geese that he arose, not the creaking of rigging or lapping of waves against a hull. Instead of salty sea air, pleasant aromas from the fields and barns drifted in through the open windows. In the front were spacious green lawns under towering oak trees, full of playful squirrels by day and hooting owls in the evening. In the back was a pond ringed with cattails, where red-winged blackbirds chattered and mallards grazed the duckweed with their tails in the air.

The best part, of course, was being so close to Elizabeth. They rode together along the wooded trails of the estate. They took long walks around the pond. Deliciously alone and together in their perfect, unblemished world, living a life of peace and contentment that every sailor dreams of. They attended the theater together and any number of teas and soirees, making it plain that they were a couple, and a striking couple at that. Even with an aversion for false pride, he would have confessed to some smug conceit in being seen by her side, finding genuine pleasure and contentment by consenting in good grace to every social engagement, every invitation, happily attending even the dullest party simply because she was there and he with her. She was a marvel in company, comfortable and confident; he could only admire her innate wit and verbal dexterity. She could graciously draw out the shy or just as gracefully silence the boor, as if she occupied her own quarterdeck of social activity on a ship-of-the-line in a worldly fleet. So adept was she at handling her cultural milieu, constantly aware of the various signals hidden in one guise or another that he found himself teasing her, pronouncing such fanciful titles upon her as "Commodore of the Social Tea" or "Winner of the Order of the Soiree." Of course, she returned the jests, referring to him as "my hero" or "my attentive admiral." He didn't even mind when Elizabeth wanted to show him off to all her friends after that Boston newspaper article told of how the dashing First Lieutenant Jonathan Kinkaid of the frigate *Randolph* "with bravery and fortitude," had taken those prize ships whose cargoes of war munitions were even now benefiting General Washington's army along the Delaware. Kinkaid thought the glorified account had too blithely glossed over the human tragedy that he remembered only too well. To his mind, he deserved no distinction—he was merely a survivor—and so the story not only embarrassed him but brought up feelings of sorrow and guilt. Adding to his guilt, while promising a marked improvement in his finances, was learning that a hefty sum of prize money awaited him as his share from the sale of those ships and cargoes, to be paid if and when the courts ever finished adjudicating the proceedings.

In the meantime, the Whipples had refused to accept even a modest rent, and a good thing too, since most of Kinkaid's meager salary went toward social entertainment and fashion—suits, shirts, stockings, and shoes, for he soon learned that going with Elizabeth meant going in style, and style could be expensive. She always wore the latest trends from Paris, and her hair, though not as elaborate as in the salons of Europe, was always fashionably done in natural ringlets and ribbons. For Kinkaid, it was more a matter of keeping up with her, for dressing with impeccable taste and flair did not come naturally to him. At least with his slim frame and erect bearing, he made any suit look good, as long as it was properly fitted, a process he found tiresome.

Yes, the war seemed very far away and Kinkaid could not remember his days before Elizabeth, when he thought of them at all, as anything but dark and dreary, empty and bereft of the secrets of love, as so much time wasted. For now he could not measure his joy and contentment or, indeed, imagine life without her. There was no end to the topics they discussed, and their time spent in silence seemed full beyond understanding. And irrespective of the fact that the world seemed to be coming apart at the seams, there was strength in the knowledge that somebody in this crazy world cared if he lived or died. With his heart so full, his views of others became less critical, more tolerant, more accepting. Love seemed such a wonderful thing, an ending to war, he thought, if only everyone could find it. And so it was with such idealistic thoughts that First Lieutenant Jonathan Kinkaid stepped into the Office of the Naval Department on Wharf Street in Boston.

"Lieutenant Kinkaid reporting as ordered."

The young yeoman at the desk rose to attention. "Good morning, Lieutenant, you are expected. Please have a seat in the waiting room, there. The Commander should be with you in a moment, sir."

Kinkaid sat there still, in the stuffy room, almost an hour later, hot and sweaty in his new uniform, his neck itchy from the stiff collar, feeling thirsty and drowsy. There were no paintings of ships at sea on the bare walls, no crossed anchors on the door, nothing to indicate that this was indeed the Naval Office, nothing to attract the eye or break the monotony of the surroundings, and he found himself wondering whether his quarters on the estate had already infected his mind with the need for opulence and comfort, that anything less would seem a torture to him.

But those apprehensive and overblown thoughts were interrupted by the sound of the opposite door opening, and out stepped an elderly, eagle-faced gentleman with neglected sideburns and an unkempt mustache. Affectionately nicknamed "No-Nonsense" Nathanson by his peers for his modest and practical nature, the Commander's dark-blue uniform had the golden epaulets of rank on the shoulders but boasted no medallions or frills.

"Good morning, Lieutenant Kinkaid," came the sonorous greeting.

"Good morning, Commander," replied Kinkaid as he rose stiffly from the straight-backed chair.

"Sorry to have kept you waiting for so long."

"Quite all right, sir," replied Kinkaid, glad at least that his wait was over.

"I detest anyone wasting my time, and so I detest almost as much wasting another's. My only excuse is that I've been waiting for someone else to arrive. Please, come this way, Lieutenant."

The high-ceilinged room was darkly paneled with built-in bookcases. The windows were heavily draped, and the air was cool. The Commander's heavy oak desk sat on a maroon rug in the middle, and on the right, in an overstuffed chair, almost unnoticeable, sat a blond-haired, middle-aged gentleman wearing a fashionable gray suit, hands clasped calmly in his lap.

Nathanson made the introductions. "Lieutenant Kinkaid, I'd like you to meet Mr. Simpson, from the Foreign Affairs Committee of Congress."

Simpson stood up gracefully, as though he were unraveling from his compact position in the chair. Of average height, he was pale and handsome, with a clean-shaven face. "Most happy to make your acquaintance, Lieutenant," said Simpson, his enunciation perfect, his handshake firm, but there remained a certain calculation in the sky-blue eyes.

Nathanson sat in his chair behind the desk and motioned to the couch. "Please, sit down, Lieutenant."

"I must say that I have heard good things said about you, sir, very good things indeed," proclaimed Mr. Simpson.

Kinkaid could not think of a proper response to the flattering statement, and as he sat down he was suddenly aware of the tall and stately grandfather clock that stood solidly behind him, ticking away the seconds. Surely the man was about to persuade him of something after such a statement, for Kinkaid could not, aside from the superfluous oratory of the newspaper article, imagine what good things, from whom these good things had come, or how they happened to make their way to this Mr. Simpson. Kinkaid could only conclude that the man was, after all, a diplomat, accustomed to such outpourings of flattery, and so, before the clock ticked away too many more seconds, he decided upon the obligatory, "Most kind of you, sir."

"If only all our naval officers were made of the same fine stuff as yourself," continued Simpson relentlessly.

Kinkaid wanted to stop the man. This Mr. Simpson could know nothing of Kinkaid's person or history; how could he stand there and tell him how fine he was? This was becoming uncomfortable.

"You see, Mr. Weatherby and Mr. Cutler have been quite generous in sharing with me the extent of your brilliant…"

So that was it. Mr. Simpson had apprised himself of the story told by the two boys, probably so awed by having someone from Congress interview them that they had embellished and bedazzled the man with outlandish tales of victory and glory at all costs. Hearing this, Kinkaid could scarcely follow the rest of what Mr. Simpson was saying.

Recognizing that Kinkaid may have been taking what he was saying with a grain of salt, Simpson said something that both surprised and gladdened him. "…and you may be interested to hear that I happen to know the whereabouts of a certain gunnery officer."

"Mr. Hill?" asked an astonished Kinkaid.

"The very same." A genuine, almost boyish smile broke the artful countenance of Mr. Simpson.

"Where is he?"

"My yeoman will provide you the address before you leave," Nathanson assured him.

"Is he all right?"

"I should think, in time," answered Simpson.

"I thank you. That is—"

"It seems it is your enemy whom you should thank, Lieutenant," said Nathanson. "The very captain responsible for sinking your *Randolph*."

"Captain Wilkinson." Of course Kinkaid was happily surprised to hear that Hill was alive, that he had not perished aboard the prison hospital ship in New York harbor as he had feared, yet he was not surprised to hear that the captain of the British frigate *Gaspee* and his surgeon, Dr. McKay, were involved. True gentlemen in the highest sense of the word.

Simpson stepped to a large globe that rested in a stand behind the Commander's chair. "I'm happy that we were able to provide you this good news," he said, placing one hand on the sphere. "However, my reason for joining this meeting with your superior is over quite another matter, as you may well expect."

"Of course, sir."

Simpson casually gave the orb a shove, sending it slowly turning on its axis. "There is a small island in the West Indies…St. Eustatia. Perhaps you have heard of it?"

Kinkaid said the name to himself. "Also referred to as Statia?"

"One and the same. A most unique and special island."

"A Dutch free port, as I recall," said Kinkaid, his memory jogged.

"Excellent businessmen, the Dutch; they've proclaimed the island neutral of all international conflict and have decided to charge no customs duties…with the result that it has become the preferred port of exchange for a host of nations. The English, French, Spanish, Danes, to name only a few, trade and store their merchandise there."

"As do we," knew Kinkaid.

"Indeed, Captain," noted Simpson as he paced around the desk, Kinkaid's ears pricking up at the title, an unwarranted title. "In fact, without the trade that goes on between the island of St. Eustatia and the Colonies, we would have very much less than we do now in the form of arms, munitions, powder, all sorts of military and seagoing hardware and supplies. The British are becoming aware of this illicit trade and have taken measures to put a stop to it. In fact, they have recently imposed an embargo on all…contraband, as they like to call it." Simpson looked Kinkaid in the eye and emphatically affirmed, "To state the obvious, these shipments are essential to the Colonies. They simply must continue. The British mean to impose fines, seize ships, take entire cargoes. In short, Lieutenant, they mean to ensure a halt to this indispensable trade."

"As if the incessant piracy along the Virgin coasts weren't enough of a hindrance to our shipping," complained Nathanson.

"If I may ask, sir, what is the Dutch government's position?" asked Kinkaid. A naval officer must always apprise himself of his likely friends and enemies.

"Make no mistake, England has a mutual assistance treaty with the Netherlands in force as we speak," explained Simpson. "Officially, of course, The Hague condemns all smuggling, not wishing to arouse the enmity of the British Empire or, perhaps closer to the truth, do anything that might restrict their own trade. But as a seagoing nation in their own right and especially after having thrown off the Spanish yoke, they would very much like to see British sea power destabilized…which is why they unofficially support us. In fact, as evidence of that support and in spite of their mutual assistance treaty, when England asked the Dutch for troops against us not a month ago, they declined to provide any."

As Kinkaid found himself wondering why he, a lowly lieutenant with negligible seniority, should find himself in such a high-level discussion with one of Congress's inner circle of advisors, Mr. Simpson went to the crux of the matter. "We have an assignment for you. Actually, a number of assignments, to be correct. Commander?"

Nathanson stood up, his arms behind his back, head held high, strong chin jutting out. Kinkaid could easily imagine him standing on a quarterdeck, a fair wind blowing in his rugged face. He looked out the window. "There is a ship over there across the inlet, Lieutenant, a brig called the *Swift*. Even now she is being modified, all her rigging upgraded, her timbers reinforced, ports cut for twelve guns—six-pounders, I believe. She is to be your ship, to be sailed in approximately two weeks' time, depending upon how quickly you can raise a crew to man her, for the islands of the West Indies, namely this island of St. Eustatia. You will take aboard with you a number of important cargoes, the first of which will be our recently appointed Consul to St. Eustatia, Mr. Simpson here, who will be carrying a copy of our Declaration of Independence."

Simpson met Kinkaid's eyes for a moment in recognition.

"You will also be carrying various items of baggage belonging to your commander of marines, uh…"

"A Major Bauer was chosen for that assignment, Commander," Simpson informed him. "Training has already begun."

"I see," acknowledged Nathanson. "Now then, Kinkaid, you will be expected to assist this Major Bauer in the accomplishment of a special assignment that will be revealed to you after Mr. Simpson is delivered to St. Eustatia."

"For security reasons," explained Simpson, adding, "The major will have your orders."

"A third and periphery concern will be to keep your eyes and ears open for intelligence of any pirate activity in the area," continued the Commander, "although this is not to be your major concern, nor will you be expected to seek out such bandits. Keep in mind that your primary goal is to deliver Mr. Simpson, which will necessitate avoiding situations that might hinder that mission."

"Of course, sir," said Kinkaid.

Nathanson, anticipating the concern any ship's captain might have in carrying as a passenger a member of a Congressional Committee, said reassuringly, "If you are concerned about having a civilian aboard of Mr. Simpson's authority—"

"Please allow me to assure you, Captain," interjected Mr. Simpson, "that all decisions concerning the running of your ship shall remain yours and yours alone."

"Thank you, Mr. Simpson," replied Kinkaid. "However, I should correct you. I am a lieutenant, not—"

Nathanson cleared his throat and said, "Given Mr. Simpson's status and mission, we felt it only fitting that you should hold the rank of captain, effective immediately."

"I am honored, sir," returned Kinkaid too somberly in his attempt to keep his surprised delight under control.

Nathanson smiled affably. "Mr. Simpson insisted."

Simpson ignored the comment as if more important matters were to be discussed, declaring, "Our primary intention is to provide evidence to the Governor of St. Eustatia that we are a sovereign nation and, as such, have as much right to legally trade anywhere in the world as any other recognized nation. Therefore I will deliver, in person, the document that declares us free of British subjugation. I will also ensure that members of the international press are informed of my diplomatic mission, which will be to influence the governor to continue official or unofficial trade with us."

"I understand, sir," said Kinkaid. It seemed all that was left for him were questions pertaining to the readiness of his ship, certainly more important to him at the moment than a diplomatic mission in which he had very little to do other than to safeguard the simple delivery of Mr. Simpson to his destination, and whatever happened after that they weren't telling him. Kinkaid knew that Elizabeth's father, prominent in the shipping business in Boston, could have been of great assistance in helping him to gather a crew, but believing that he had imposed upon Elizabeth's family enough, he was reluctant to ask the man for further favors.

"As for a crew, I am not familiar with the situation here in Boston."

"Commander Nathanson will be able to point you in the right direction," stated Simpson with a ready answer.

"Most assuredly," asserted Nathanson. "In fact I believe we have just the man for your first lieutenant—one of your own shipmates, the officer who brought the *Nancy* in, a fine bit of seamanship, by all accounts."

"Midshipman Saddler?" Kinkaid almost choked on the name.

"The very man who made it possible for Washington to continue the fight for these last couple of months," said Nathanson in admiration. "Why, without those supplies, General Washington might have had to retreat into the Carolinas. *Lieutenant* Saddler now, of course, a fine young officer, none more deserving of a promotion, I should think."

"Indeed," added Simpson.

"The two of you should make a formidable team," judged Nathanson.

The last man on earth Kinkaid wanted on his quarterdeck was Saddler, the man he had persuaded Captain Mallory to send off on the British prize ship *Hermes* to escort the munitions transport *Nancy* back to American waters. At the time, Kinkaid wanted only to save an old boatswain's mate from an unjust punishment, possibly saving his life, not to make a hero out of the bullying, self-centered midshipman.

Kinkaid's first impulse was to refuse the appointment outright, but he could think of no good reason that he could tell these men why he would not want the man who had saved Washington's army as his first officer. Besides, they had promoted the less than brilliant, overbearing midshipman to lieutenant and as man of the hour it was only to be expected that an important assignment would be forthcoming. Under the circumstances, the only comment

Kinkaid could offer was, "I'm sure Mr. Saddler will be...adequate for the job."

"Then that's settled," said Nathanson, "We'll leave it up to you to round out the crew at your pleasure, keeping in mind that *Swift* should be ready in a fortnight. I'll make the appropriate inquiries concerning crew for her, and you will report to me as soon as you are ready for sea. If there is anything you need or if anyone gives you any trouble with your supplies or stores—bad meat, foul water, anything at all—make sure I know about it. This is a priority mission, Captain, and so you will inform me immediately of any unnecessary delays."

"Of course, Commander," said Kinkaid, knowing the interview was over. "Ah, if I may, sir, would you consider a request?"

"I'm feeling most agreeable at the moment, Captain. What did you have in mind?"

"If possible, sir, I was thinking of a promotion for one of my midshipmen," put forth Kinkaid earnestly. Aware that his petition should be backed up with the appropriate facts, Kinkaid continued, "Midshipman Weatherby, sir. If you read my report you will see that—"

"Of course I read your report, Captain. Carefully, as a matter of fact." The gruff answer left no doubt that Nathanson had indeed read his report. "You must think highly of this Weatherby, and that is as much of a recommendation as I need. Of course he'll be *acting* lieutenant...at least until the papers are official."

"Thank you, sir." That was certainly easy, thought Kinkaid. Weatherby was young, true, but he was also exceptional, brilliant in all areas, and could easily fill the duties and responsibilities of any position aboard ship. In addition, the promotion would put Weatherby above any petty recriminations that Saddler might wish to foist upon the boy.

"Very well, then," said Nathanson, extending his hand. "Allow me to wish you well, and be sure to see my yeoman for those names...and where you can find your shipmate."

It was late morning and a woman was busy setting up her flower stand as the streets came alive. Two gentlemen were having a late breakfast at a café on the corner and others were hurrying by on various errands, but he scarcely noticed any of them, his mind preoccupied with thoughts and questions concerning his meeting with the Commander and that Simpson fellow. But they noticed him and made way for the determined young officer, a man obviously going about important military business, for he certainly appeared commanding in his stiff-necked uniform coat, forcing the proud and erect bearing. He had been made the captain of his own ship and had been given an important, though relatively simple assignment—taking a diplomat to the West Indies—yet nagging at the back of his mind was the fact that he had not been given the full extent of his mission. Actually, the Commander had referred to it as the major of marine's mission, in which he was expected to assist. Of course he would follow orders, strive to do his duty to the best of his abilities, but he could not help but feel that perhaps he might fulfill those duties better with more information.

There it was now, a big brick building; the faded sign under the second-story windows read "Boston Military Hospital."

"Yes, we have a Mr. Hill here," said the elderly nun at a rickety table. Less a reception area than a large and dingy room, she sat busily folding rags by the light of the window as an attractive, middle-aged woman in a calico dress entered behind him.

"Good morning, Mrs. Waverly," the nun greeted her.

"And a fine morning to you, Sister Katherine," answered Mrs. Waverly as she closed the door and placed her parasol in the stand.

"This gentleman is here to see Mr. Hill. I thought, since you…"

Mrs. Waverly smiled and said, "Of course, I'll be happy to show him to Mr. Hill's room, Sister Katherine. This way, please," she said to Kinkaid as she turned and walked briskly down the dark and dusty corridor.

Kinkaid could only hurry to catch up.

She turned and asked, "And who might I tell him is calling?"

"Lieutenant Kinkaid," he answered, forgetting his recent promotion.

"Why, you are all I've heard about since that Admiral Nathanson inquired as to Mr. Hill's condition."

"Commander Nathanson," Kinkaid corrected her.

"I beg your pardon?" she asked with raised eyebrows.

Kinkaid could readily see that this dignified woman was seldom, if ever, questioned, and instantly regretted the correction. But now he had to finish the business as he tagged along, hat in his hands. "Nathanson, ma'am. He is a senior captain, not an admiral. The Continental Navy has no admirals...though I can see how you would—"

"The Navy has no admirals?" she said, cutting off Kinkaid's attempt to mollify her. Then her mouth curled up in a wry smile. "From what Mr. Hill tells me, one would think *you* are an admiral."

"Perhaps some day, ma'am...if my luck continues," he stammered.

She turned and gave him an inquiring look, as if attempting to fit him into the heroic vision of Mr. Hill's portrayal. Then, as if unsatisfied, she strode down the corridor, saying, "Yes, well, come along, then."

Her action and comment brought to his mind a curious and unsettling idea. Here he was, the captain of a ship, in control of a virtual arsenal of firepower, his every order and command unquestionably obeyed, and he had been instantly reduced into subservience by this strong-willed woman, leading him down the hall as if he were an obedient puppy.

But his attention was soon taken by curiosity of a different sort as he followed her down the corridor, open doors on either side. His natural instinct was to look into the stinking and squalid rooms as he passed, but after seeing a number of ailing men looking back with hopeful expressions that perhaps they would receive a visitor, or worse, hopeless expressions that their suffering was in vain, he felt embarrassed, and resolved to keep his eyes directly ahead.

Mrs. Waverly finally reached the last door and after motioning for Kinkaid to wait, stepped in.

"Good morning, Mr. Hill," she announced pleasantly, pushing aside a clean but faded curtain.

"And a good morning to you, Mrs. Waverly," came the familiar voice.

"I hope you are well-rested."

"Enough to feel like taking a stroll," he assured her.

"Perhaps a bit later," she said, tucking his sheet under his arms. "At the moment, you have a visitor."

Kinkaid entered the room with some apprehension, remembering the horrifying condition Hill had been in when he last saw him aboard the British frigate, *Gaspee*. Now, Hill was swathed in gauze from his waist up, except for his right arm, with only two slits revealing the sparkling eyes and pale mouth of the man he had served alongside only a few months earlier.

"Kinkaid!" exclaimed Hill cheerily, raising his head and showing a crooked smile.

"Now, you mustn't become overly excited, Charles," Mrs. Waverly chastised him. "You don't want to injure yourself." She turned to Kinkaid and said with a charming smile, "You may speak with him for a few minutes, but I don't want you to be tiring him out too much."

"Of course not," he promised.

Kinkaid waited until she left the room, then, bending low, could only think to say, "I see you have a tyrant for a nurse."

Hill laughed weakly and said, "Aye, Glenda keeps me on my toes." Then, lowering his voice to a whisper, added, "If I don't behave myself, her tongue-lashing is worse than a cat-o'-nine-tails. But a lovely lady. Husband was killed a year ago; she's been volunteering here ever since. Looks in on me most every day, she does."

Hill was obviously better now than before; at least he was out of his terrible pain and delirium, but what of his wounds? Not wishing to add to his depression by asking for what might be bad news, Kinkaid decided to wait and speak later with Mrs. Waverly.

Hill noticed the blue breeches, red lapels, and waistcoat Kinkaid now wore and remarked, "The uniform suits you."

"It's the new regulations." Leave it to Hill to speak of uniforms. "I was surprised to hear that you were…here."

"Dr. McKay petitioned Captain Wilkinson to keep me aboard, pretending to be one of their crew. Then they signed me into a British hospital in the city. Wilkinson must have had some pull because there was a prisoner exchange, and he was able to get me right there at the top of the list," explained Hill. Then he began to cough.

"Shall I call for Mrs. Waverly?" asked a concerned Kinkaid.

"No. No, please, she'll only make you leave. I'll be fine." He managed to get the coughing under control. "What about the boys? Are they well?"

"Cutler and Weatherby are the same foolish rascals they always were," answered Kinkaid with a grin. "And Weatherby is now a lieutenant."

"Well, good for him, though I've a mind you had a hand in that development, not that the lad don't deserve it. Brilliant young man; knows everything there is to know about gunnery, always grilling me. That boy could come up with the confoundest questions." Hill coughed again and groaned in pain, his eyes watering, then said, "Don't worry about me, sir. I understand it was touch and go there for a while. Can't say as I remember much about the *Gaspee*, but according to the best estimates of the medical staff around here, I'll be shimmying up a mainmast before the summer is over." He seemed out of breath as he finished the sentence.

"I'll keep you in mind, then, if I happen to need a good gunnery officer," gave Kinkaid, relieved to hear what Hill was telling him, though he could not be sure it was the truth. And other than a few volunteers, he had to wonder what Hill meant by medical staff.

"Have they given the hero of the *Randolph* a command, then?" asked Hill.

"As a matter of fact, I've been assigned a brig—the *Swift*."

"Then congratulations are in order," granted Hill, a crooked smile evident.

Knowing Hill would want to know, he added, "Twelve guns...six-pounders, I'm told."

"Not bad, and a good name," said Hill. Not wanting to comment on her light armament, Hill added the caveat, "I hope she's fast enough to stay out of trouble."

"I doubt she'd come close to the *Randolph*, in spite of her name," admitted Kinkaid.

"Aye, the Randy was somethin', wasn't she? Do you have a crew yet?"

"So far I have a first lieutenant, specially picked by the Naval Office...Mr. Saddler."

"Saddler?" growled Hill. "I heard he was promoted to lieutenant after he brought the *Nancy* in. It didn't surprise me; according to the papers, her capture made all the difference to Washington's army. Well, you could always toss the bastard over the side on a cold, dark night."

"I'll be tempted, I'm sure," joked Kinkaid.

"So you'll be heading out to sea again, I'd expect, the way things are heating up. I suppose you'll be taking the boys with you?"

"Yes, and O'Toole, too."

"Never hurts to have the Lord's messenger on your side. Why, it'll be like old times," Hill pointed out. Then as both men's thoughts turned first to the loss of *Randolph* and then to the fact that Hill would not be joining them, Hill coughed and inquired, "Do you know where you're headed?"

"Running a diplomat to the West Indies."

"Sounds pleasant enough," observed Hill with a sigh of fatigue.

Mrs. Waverly swished into the room at that moment, as if in anticipation of Hill's ebbing strength. "I hope you had a fine visit, sir, but Mr. Hill needs his rest now."

"It was good to see you again," said Hill, reaching up with his unbandaged hand. "And good luck to you...out there."

Taking his hand, Kinkaid said, "Don't worry about me, Hill. You just take care of yourself, and I'll be sure and look you up when I return."

"Godspeed, Kinkaid."

Once back at the front table where the elderly nurse still toiled, Kinkaid asked, "Is Mr. Hill being properly cared for here? I mean, is there a doctor or..."

"Mr. Hill should be up and about in a few weeks, according to Dr. Astor, who comes in every afternoon," answered an annoyed Mrs. Waverly. "Infection was the greatest danger when he first arrived, but now that it is under control, I'd say that in a couple of months' time you will be able to take him out on one of your silly seagoing adventures...and perhaps the next time you will take better care of him," she answered, rebuking and comforting Kinkaid in the same breath.

"Yes, ma'am, and thank you," stammered Kinkaid, uncertain if he should remain serious or laugh with relief. Judging by the severe look on Mrs. Waverly's face, he chose the former course, but he could not have been happier if Nathanson had made him an admiral.

A young boy stood on the corner outside the hospital, hawking the morning news. Kinkaid reached into his pocket and tossed the youth a six-pence, telling him, "Keep the change," then playfully tousled the boy's hair as he passed.

"Why, thank you, sir," exclaimed the happy youth, chasing after him, "but you forgot your paper!"

"Haven't the time to read it," Kinkaid tossed back over his shoulder.

No, no time for bad news, not on this day. He was captain of his own ship, Hill was alive and recovering, and with the exception of Saddler being assigned as his first lieutenant, there was the added bonus of having old crewmates aboard in key positions. Plus he was in love. What more could a sailor ask?

Yes, it had been a satisfying and profitable day, and he found himself whistling a tune as he sauntered happily back to the Whipple residence, a dozen Tiger lilies under his arm that he'd purchased from the woman at the flower stall.

II
Presents of Departure

Though certainly not a new ship, Kinkaid had to admire her lines as he approached *Swift* from the dock. She presented a graceful hull: black, with a blue stripe running across her gunports, and with her raked masts, her name fit her perfectly.

At the moment, however, her decks were cluttered with stores, cordage, tubs of oakum and nails, canvas, spare spars, four new short-barreled swivel guns, parts for last-minute modifications, and some heavy oak reinforcing timbers that Boatswain O'Toole and Jake Rafferty, the carpenter, kept measuring and scratching their heads over. On the dock lay a heap of rotten rigging and cordage, blocks and pulleys that O'Toole had insisted be exchanged for new materials.

Already stowed below were hundreds of gallons of fresh water, casks of rum, pipes of wine, oil, vinegar, candles, barrels of oatmeal, peas, beans, rice, dried fish, salt pork and beef, pickled pig's heads, bacon, cheese, tea, coffee, brown sugar, molasses, and ship's biscuit by the hundredweight. There were bushels of oranges, lemons, and fresh vegetables such as onions, turnips, beets, cabbages, and potatoes, as well as many loaves of fresh bread, none of which would last long. On each side of her long deck in neat rows sat six six-pounder, cast-iron cannons, measured by the weight of the 3.494-inch-diameter ball they fired, their barrels five feet long, each resting in its own red-painted wooden truck. Stowed in her hold and magazines were tons of shot, powder, and wads for the guns and over a hundred French muskets packed in oil-soaked rags.

Kinkaid moved aboard immediately, almost unnoticed by the few men already aboard, his extra uniforms and meager belongings crammed into a small ironbound chest. There was little time or need for ceremony with so much to be done, what with the daunting tasks of readying the ship for sea and finding a complete crew for her—hopefully men who could be counted on, men who knew at least something of the seagoing trade. Of course, there was also the hope that whatever men he found would agree to work for him, a young, unknown captain of little seniority. A full and able crew was one thing; earning their respect would be another. He tried not to dwell on his doubts—whether he would be up to the responsibilities of command, whether he would be wise enough or inspire loyalty. Even if all these things fell to him, there was always the element of luck, good or bad, that could bring ruin to the most brilliant captain or make a hero of a fool. But mostly he found himself too busy to contemplate the unknowns of the future.

It was almost noon. The weather was cool and cloudy with a light drizzle falling when there drew up to the dock two lorries with heavy-duty cargo beds and massive wheels, each pulled by stout horses and each driven by equally stout men wearing the green jackets with white facings of Continental Marines. Each lorry carried a wooden box of considerable size, each massive box surrounded by various smaller boxes, all bearing in black stencils the label "1st Marines." This must be the remainder of the "various items of baggage" referred to by Commander Nathanson, realized Kinkaid, watching from the rail.

Driving the first wagon was a compact, tobacco-chewing sergeant whose face reminded Kinkaid of an English bulldog. Behind him, sitting proudly astride the largest box, was a thin, dark-skinned Indian, dressed in fringed buckskin, with a long-handled hatchet in his belt. The only regulation uniform item he wore was the hat with the left brim turned up, but even that he had modified with the addition of three turkey feathers stuck into the cockade. A fat, pink-skinned corporal drove the second lorry, looking too out of shape to be a marine.

"Ahoy on the ship, there!" called out the tough-looking sergeant, jumping down from the wagon as it swayed to a halt. "Special cargo to be loaded by order of Major Bauer, Commander of Marines!"

O'Toole soon had a working party out, and the marine sergeant and his overweight corporal stood by and watched in smug amusement as the sailors struggled to move even the smaller boxes along the beds of the lorries. The Indian seemed to care little about the proceedings, instead sensibly finding shelter out of the rain under the eaves of a nearby warehouse.

The larger boxes gave not an inch, and so O'Toole called the men off and disappeared below, soon returning with some thick new rope with a hook on the end and the heaviest double-shiv block and tackle he could find. He supervised the rigging of the massive device to the upper mainmast spar and then tied a stout harness around the first box, the ends of the harness joining with an iron ring on top to which the hook was attached.

O'Toole stood by the mainmast with his hands on his hips, looking up to where the spar extended from the mast, as seven sailors took a strain on the thick hemp rope that hung from the spar, cutting by four the power needed to raise the immense weight.

"Ready!" O'Toole called out. "Altogether now, pull! Easy…easy…" Ropes and harness strained and creaked with the tension and the spar lowered and bent somewhat from the effort, but inch by inch, the heavy cargo lifted from its bed.

"Nice and slow…steady…don't let her swing!" cautioned O'Toole. "Mindful of the wet deck, now!"

At first standing quietly next to the lorry, the burly sergeant suddenly became animated and began shouting orders and making obnoxious comments to the sailors on the ship as the box began to move, fussing over it like a mother hen over her flock. .

Two big and strong gunner's mates—Aaron Tripp and Joseph Treadwell—tended the line that swung the spar. The two looked like Vikings with their massive shoulders, immense arms, and long hair; Tripp's was straight and in a ponytail while Treadwell allowed his curly locks to blow free. Both men were assigned to the number-one gun, and because both were big-boned and fair-haired and where one went the other was sure to be near, the crew had taken to calling them, aptly enough, "The Travelin' Brothers."

As they swung the first box over the ship's rail, the agitated sergeant shouted, "You damned fools! Ease off there!" But the sailors were too preoccupied with their task to pay much heed to the thundering sergeant on the pier. "Are you idiots deaf and dumb, to boot?"

The angry exhortations drew Kinkaid's attention and it immediately occurred to him that either of the titanic sailors could have lifted the short sergeant off his feet or crushed him if they'd a mind to. But no such thoughts plagued the arrogant marine's agitated mind at the moment as he continued to shout, "Ease off there, I say! That's no side o' beef you're yankin' on!"

"Damned lubber," Kinkaid heard O'Toole growl from the waist.

Kinkaid could see that his boatswain was simmering over the heedless comments from shore and so he decided to make for the dock and have a word with the sergeant, perhaps distract him so that O'Toole could do his job.

But the overwrought sergeant paid no heed to Kinkaid's approach; instead he persisted in berating the two sailors who were now bringing the box to a halt over the deck.

"Hold everything!" the sergeant shouted. "I'll come over there and show you where I want them!" he bellowed, leaving his fat corporal standing beside the lorry while the Indian remained calmly smoking his pipe under the shelter of the eaves, seemingly aloof to the drama.

"I am Captain Kinkaid, sergeant, captain of this ship," Kinkaid said with authority as the sergeant almost ran into him.

The leathery sergeant stopped, and then turning his head and spitting on the dock before giving a sluggish salute, he looked up at Kinkaid and said in a gravely voice, "Sergeant Anders, Captain. But if you don't mind, sir..." And he began moving in the direction of the gangway.

"Sergeant Anders!" bellowed Kinkaid. "I have yet to dismiss you!" He could not abide such insolent behavior.

The sergeant stiffened at the rebuke, spun around, and came to attention. "Pardon me, sir!" And while he stood there, he kept glancing in the direction of the box already being lowered to the deck, his eyes darting back and forth.

"Just what is in those boxes, Sergeant?"

"You're gonna have to ask the major 'bout that, Captain, 'cause I've orders to keep that information to myself and tell no others, not even you, with all due respect, sir," asserted the obstinate marine, a hefty wad of tobacco poking his cheek out, a look of supreme joy on the man's tough and craggy face.

Kinkaid took no pleasure in the bald exercise of his rank at the moment. The sergeant evidently was entrusted with the mysterious cargo, and so, in spite of the fact that he was gloating over the fact that he knew something the captain of the ship did not and that the scarcely hidden smirk was of itself insubordination, Kinkaid checked his anger and said, "You may carry on, Sergeant."

With that, Anders gave a quick salute, said perfunctorily, "Thank you, sir," and was off down the pier, shouting to the seamen on deck, "Steady there, sailors! Let her down easy!"

Kinkaid determined to keep the incident in perspective as he followed the trotting sergeant toward the gangplank.

Anders strode onto the ship and headed directly for the mainmast where Tripp was releasing the shackle from the harness, the first big box already firmly on the deck. Treadwell and the other sailors were running lines through cleats on the deck, passing them over the box and tying their ends to more cleats on the other side, securing the heavy thing for sea.

Anders frowned and looked as if he were about to complain about something when O'Toole, having held his tongue long enough, warned him, "I'll be tellin' the men how to set it down, mister. And I'll be decidin' where they set it on my deck, and this one here, she's gonna sit right where she is 'cause that's where I want her to sit." It was an invitation to a fight if there ever was one, and Kinkaid edged closer to O'Toole.

Anders glared back, hands on his hips. "You mean this deck?" he asked and spit a long brown stream, jumping back as the foul juice hit the deck with a splatter, spraying all over the boatswain's white canvas pants.

O'Toole took a step in the burly sergeant's direction, as if he were about to physically pounce on the man as the marine bent to inspect the boxes for chips and dents.

Both men were of similar character, and so it was fortunate that Kinkaid had decided to stand behind O'Toole and was able to grab him by the arm and say quietly, "Might be better to turn the other cheek this time, O'Toole." Kinkaid knew that the sergeant had little idea as to how proprietary O'Toole was when it came to the top decks, and knew as well that it would not be conducive to morale to have the two butt heads before the ship even left port.

O'Toole hesitated a moment, warily eyeing his captain. Then he smiled shrewdly and answered, "Aye, I get your drift, Captain. A time to refrain from embracin'."

"That's the spirit," encouraged Kinkaid, recognizing the quote from the Bible. "To every thing there is a season." As O'Toole ignored the sergeant and turned back to supervise the hauling aboard of the second big box, Kinkaid thought to add a word to help put a positive slant on things. "We were fortunate to get new cordage, blocks, and pulleys. Those old ones might have killed somebody."

"Aye, Captain," growled O'Toole, but still mindful of the obnoxious sergeant, grinned slyly and whispered, "The season for killin' will surely come later."

Kinkaid laughed, but knew there was some real animosity directed toward the oblivious Sergeant Anders.

When all the boxes were safely aboard and properly secured, the Indian and two marines reported aboard with their baggage and had their names added to the ship's roster by the studious Mr. McBride, the purser.

"Name, rank, and position," said McBride.

The Indian said his name was something like "Maunk Chaunk."

McBride asked the Indian, "Spell that, please," only to have him stare blankly back.

Sergeant Anders explained, "We call him Monk Chunk, spelled just like it sounds."

"To be listed as..." McBride wanted to know.

"He's our scout," gave Anders.

"A marine?" asked McBride.

"Algonquin. You might say he is attached to us."

McBride carefully spelled out the Indian's name on his roster, exactly as it sounded, listing him as "marine scout," leaving out the fact that he was an Algonquin Indian, since he was required only to list a man's name and duties on his roster.

The overweight corporal was next. "Corporal Courtney Stockton, sir. I'm the troop's supply sergeant."

McBride, ever the perfectionist, had to ask, "So, are you a sergeant or a corporal, then?"

"Well, technically, he's a corporal, now," broke in Anders. "Was a sergeant till last week. You see, there was this, uh, discrepancy in the amount of blankets and boots we was issued by the commissary." Anders and Stockton exchanged knowing winks as the Sergeant continued, "Never could get that straightened out—to Stockton's misfortune, I might add—but he's still our supply sergeant...even though he's a corporal now." Anders seemed to take great pleasure in his explanation, adding, "No such thing as a supply *corporal*, you see."

"I'll list him as a corporal, then, with supply sergeant duties," said McBride in his businesslike way.

30

"That's it exactly," said Anders facetiously before letting loose another jet of brown juice onto the deck.

Kinkaid resolved that he would have a talk with the marine commander about his sergeant spitting on the boatswain's deck.

A week passed in frantic activity as modifications and fitting-out continued. With the search for qualified crew remaining a high priority, Kinkaid had O'Toole draw up a public announcement that *Swift*, a fast and graceful ship, was soon putting to sea, her destination the warm waters of the West Indies, and that she was seeking the employment of able seamen who would likely find "fortune and honor in the service of their country."

It soon came out that O'Toole had employed the hidden talents of the young midshipman, Mr. Henry Cutler, in the writing of the advertisement. Of course he had taken to the task with his usual fervor, embellishing its promises with flowery language about the glories of the naval service and the romance of the sea, and then ensuring that the handbills were posted in various pubs and public places throughout the town.

In addition to six "volunteers" found at the city jail—"petty criminals, sneak thieves, and embezzlers," O'Toole had called them, "but good enough to stop a ball for the cause, Captain"—a few experienced hands were brought in by Cutler's handbill effort. But mostly the crew was filled out with ex-soldiers who might have thought riding a ship to war less strenuous than marching, landsmen of dubious ilk, and a few boys thinking adventure at sea a way to fame and fortune…or at least an escape from home and dreary chores. Of course, his young midshipmen were aboard, including the newly promoted-to-lieutenant (acting) Mr. William "Billy" Weatherby—brilliant, blond, square-jawed, and handsome—who was appointed as gunnery officer. Aware of his prodigious knowledge and curiosity, and inspired by the sight of the boxes of books Weatherby brought aboard, Kinkaid had also made him ship's schoolmaster. He was in charge of teaching what he could to the other "young gentlemen" aboard, one of whom was

Weatherby's best friend, the bright-eyed and ever-cheerful Mr. Midshipman Cutler with his freckles and curly brown hair. A piano player and man-of-words, he was in charge of sail details. The two young men were forever playing jokes and pranks on one another. There were also two new midshipmen: the dark and nervous Mr. Anthony Briggs, and the tall, pale and overly serious Mr. Ephraim Malakiah Lofton, with his drooping eyes. There were carpenters, cooks, coopers, a moody-looking chaplain named Carlton, and the silver-haired Dr. Grafton, a surgeon who seemed at first glance too old to withstand the rigors of going to sea. The purser, Mr. McBride; a quartermaster, Mr. Johnson; and a lean sailing master, Mr. Thorne, were all signed on, 111 men in all.

The man assigned to be Kinkaid's steward and cook was a rough and burly man by the name of Raymond Roach. The name was a bit disconcerting, though Kinkaid told himself that he would simply have to eat the man's food, not think of his name while doing so. It was readily apparent that Roach knew nothing of the proper way to brew coffee. Even after Kinkaid had shown him how it was done, the results remained less than satisfactory, either too weak or too bitterly strong. With hands that resembled sledgehammers, Roach was totally lacking in finesse and seemed bereft of a sense of discrimination, of proportion.

One day at breakfast Kinkaid asked him, "Were you always in the cooking business, Roach?"

"Skinned and tanned hides, Captain," he answered, setting a plate of ham and eggs on the table, "up in the New York woods."

"So, how did you end up here in Boston?" asked Kinkaid, noting immediately that his eggs were too hard this time. Better than too runny, like yesterday, he thought, trying to see the positive side.

Roach's low brow furrowed as he shook his head and said, "Couldn't stand the smell, Captain, but mostly it was the thought of those poor animals. So I thought I'd try my luck goin' to sea, and, well, here I am, sir."

Kinkaid could certainly understand how anyone would find the smell of a tanning house offensive, but it struck him as incongruous that a rough man like Roach would have tender feelings for animals...though it was the fact that Roach was to be his steward and cook that concerned him most at the moment.

"So, you never worked as a cook?" asked Kinkaid, taking a bite and crunching down on a piece of eggshell.

Roach's wide face grew wider still as he laughed and answered, "Never cooked much but beans and oatmeal, sir. Maybe a johnnycake here and there."

The fact that Roach seemed unaware of why his captain was inquiring about his cooking skills only added to Kinkaid's doubts, and his first impulse was to curse Mr. Thorne for not selecting a few likely candidates and allowing him to interview them and then choose his own steward. Yet he could only blame himself, he knew, as he picked eggshell off his tongue. He had not given the prospect much thought and had left the assigning of a steward to Mr. Thorne with no further instructions, and so now he could only console himself with the thought that Roach might improve his kitchen skills with time and practice.

Sergeant Anders received a message from the Marine Committee one day and left the ship "for procurements," as he explained it, soon leading back two squads of stern-faced marines with a young drummer boy marching proudly alongside. The twenty-man group quick-marching in a double row to the drummer's beat looked smart in their new uniforms: green jackets with white facings, beige breeches and hats with one side turned jauntily up with a cockade of red ribbon. The white linen of canteen and haversack straps crisscrossed their chests. Cartridge cases and bayonet scabbards hung from their belts, and each man carried the heavy, 1763 model French musket of .69 caliber.

"Column, halt!" barked Anders. "Column, left face!" The men turned in unison, facing the ship. The only movement came from the young drummer with a peach fuzz mustache, whose head followed his eyes to the top of the mainmast, his lower jaw remaining behind, his mouth open in awe.

"Private Kirkpatrick, how would you like a cannonball shoved down yer gullet?"

"No thank you, Sergeant!" returned Kirkpatrick, slamming his mouth shut and staring straight ahead.

"At ease, men," said Anders. "You will provide this gentleman your name and rank," pointing to Mr. McBride, who was standing at the gangway with the ship's roster. "And remember when you go aboard that we are all on the same side; sailors and marines are brothers, especially out at sea. 'Course, when we get on land we're in charge, but out here you will remember—and I know I won't have to remind any of you—that you will take orders from ship's officers the same as you would from me or the major. And let that be the last thing I have to say about that."

It was comforting to overhear the Sergeant remind the men of shipboard discipline, and Kinkaid could not help but notice that Sergeant Anders conducted himself quite professionally with his men while they waited for McBride to add their names to the ship's roster. Without being obvious, he also had to admire the look of the young but weathered marines, a strong and eager lot they seemed.

At the head of each column was a corporal. Corporal Irwin Decker looked hard all over. A powerful man with wide shoulders and a slim waist, even his face had a hard, unforgiving look. Stubborn and unyielding, the others called him "Bull" Decker. The other was Corporal Jacob Bentkowski, soft spoken and gentle, as big and strong as Decker but rounded off at the edges. His twinkling eyes indicated a keen and curious brain to go with his brawn.

Anders spoke quietly with his men in a friendly fashion as they waited, telling them what they might expect aboard a naval vessel. He appeared particularly solicitous to their young drummer with the downy face, Private James Kirkpatrick, who seemed in awe of the ship, fascinated by her tall masts, crisscrossed with spars and rigging, and her clean decks with neatly coiled lines laid out between rows of red trucks and black cannons.

When McBride finished, he showed the men to their berthing space, forward, just behind the forecastle, which O'Toole called, "boatswain's country."

By the end of the week, the ship's roster had been filled, the bulk of the stores had been taken on, and various details were completed to make the ship ready for sea. The special modifications that reinforced the main deck were still in progress, however, and, according to the carpenter, Rafferty, might go on into the following week, there being still a pile of heavy timbers lying on the dock, some sawed into pieces with strange angles at the ends.

Kinkaid was on the quarterdeck that afternoon, watching as Rafferty worked the end of a recently sawed wooden block with an adze on the pier. O'Toole stood nearby, leaning one foot on an already adzed block, lending moral support, it seemed. The young officers were gathered on the starboard side of the quarterdeck—all but Briggs, who had been detailed to deliver the ship's daily readiness report to Mr. Simpson as he had requested—and Lieutenant Weatherby was holding a class on keeping the quarterdeck log.

Since learning from Boatswain O'Toole that Cutler had been the composer of the flowery handbill advertisement, Weatherby was taking advantage of his position at the moment to tease his friend, asking, "Mr. Cutler, why is it important to write only the facts of the matter in the log?"

"Uh, to keep the Captain apprised," answered Cutler uncertainly, his answer sounding more like a question.

"Yes, Mr. Cutler, that is one reason, of course," gave Weatherby, but not ready to let his friend off the hook, in fact, having to make a show of no favoritism, continued, "but perhaps you could elucidate?"

"Well..."

Noting that the gaunt and lanky Mr. Lofton was rolling his eyes in disgust, Weatherby, determining that Cutler had had his chance, gave in to Lofton's silent pleading. "Mr. Lofton?"

"By adhering strictly to the facts, one avoids unintentional deceit," answered Lofton in his droll and confident way. "After all, the quarterdeck log, indeed any ship's logs, are legal documents and, therefore, should remain free of untruth and mere opinion."

"Mr. Cutler, I hope you will take note of Mr. Lofton's clear and correct answer."

"Aye, Mr. Weatherby," returned Cutler dutifully, but by the way he was grinding his teeth he was clearly miffed by the rebuke.

"Very well, then, that's enough for today. Same time tomorrow. The subject will be signals, and I hope everyone will come prepared with the proper answers."

Cutler's embarrassment was still in the air, but the formality of the classroom gave way to familiarity as Mr. Lofton approached Cutler to comment on his handbills, in part to assuage Cutler's peevishness, but more in an attempt to ingratiate himself with Weatherby and Cutler, two veterans of the *Randolph*.

"I must say, I do admire your skill for turning a phrase, Mr. Cutler. To 'serve for the glory and the greater good,' and 'just deeds shall just rewards return.' Inspiring prose."

But Cutler's defenses were aroused and, not at all sure if Lofton's comment should be taken as compliment or insult, he decided to take no chances, giving back, "What would you have me say? Tell them they'd end up feeding the fish?"

Lofton, determining that he had been misunderstood, turned up his nose and coldly observed, "To each man his fate, and some will feed the fish," before strutting away, his dignity offended.

Weatherby overhead the remark and, taking some responsibility for his friend's discomfort, asked, "What's all this talk of feeding the fish, Hank? It is the enemy who should be consulting such philosophies, and where did you learn to write like that, anyway?"

This time Cutler was embarrassed in a different way as he relaxed and admitted to his friend, "Probably absorbed it from my father."

"I knew your father was in the printing business but didn't know he was a writer."

"Well, he belonged to a group in our town calling themselves the 'Author's Club.' Always had a secret project he was working on, but I think more in idea than in reality. In fact, I don't believe they ever wrote more than a few poems among the lot of them. But they gathered in the café downstairs almost every evening to talk and argue about writing and books and authors, quoting from Shakespeare, Milton, and Homer, until mom sent them packing."

Cutler was not known as a garrulous boy, but, once started, could tend to go on. "Every one of them, bad actors. Why, I remember one time—it was in the fall because the farmers were bringing in the hay…"

This time Weatherby was saved from one of Cutler's long stories by the sight of a naval officer staggering toward the ship under a heavy burden. "Talk about bad actors," he said.

Kinkaid also noticed the lieutenant from the quarterdeck as he approached and then stepped onto the gangway.

The lieutenant swung the heavy sea bag off his shoulder and, placing it alongside his leg, came to attention, thrust his chin out, brought his hand up in a stiff salute, and gave the traditional, "First Lieutenant Saddler requesting permission to come aboard, sir."

Kinkaid answered with the traditional response, "Permission granted," and returned the salute. There were two things that Kinkaid remembered about the man—his bulbous nose and his pompous air—and it appeared that Mr. Saddler still carried both. But then Kinkaid forced himself to think along more constructive lines. He would have to give the man a chance; they would have to work together for the good of the ship. Hopefully, the events of the past could be put behind them as the misfortunes of youth; perhaps the responsibilities of Saddler's new rank and position would serve to mature the man.

Saddler saluted the flagstaff aft, then crossed onto the quarterdeck. "Good afternoon, sir," he said somberly. "It shall be an honor to serve with you once again. And allow me to add my congratulations upon your appointment as captain."

Kinkaid could see that Saddler was also making an effort.

"And my congratulations to you, Mr. Saddler, upon your promotion to lieutenant," answered Kinkaid. A stilted reintroduction, but so far, so good.

"Thank you, sir."

"Mr. Cutler, please show the first lieutenant to his quarters. As Mr. Simpson will be occupying my cabin, I shall be in the First Officer's cabin, and so Mr. Saddler will find his berth behind Mr. Thorne."

"Aye, sir," answered Midshipman Cutler without enthusiasm, leading the way while Saddler followed behind, attempting to engage Cutler in conversation.

Kinkaid then went into the waist to find out how things were progressing below. O'Toole was standing by the after stores hatch as a working party passed crates of lemons to men on the deck below, who in turn passed them down to the lowermost level of the ship.

"Is Mr. Johnson down there?" Kinkaid called out.

"Aye, Captain," O'Toole informed him. "Shall I have him come up, sir?"

"No need. I'll come down."

Making his way below, Kinkaid was startled by a commotion coming from the crew's galley.

"Damn your eyes, you stupid nigger!" came the angry shout, followed by the clanging of pots and pans. "Those are turnips, not beets, you dumb blackie!"

Kinkaid strode toward the doorway in time to see the head cook swatting with his hat at a young black man cowering in the corner, his hands raised over his head to fend off the blows. Kinkaid had heard some of the crew refer to the big head cook as "Hairy Hyde," the name appropriate enough as the man's arms and neck were covered with thick black hair.

A cook's helper stood behind Hyde and quickly wiped the smirking grin off his face when he noticed his captain in the doorway. "Attention!" he shouted, coming to attention himself.

The startled Hyde jerked abruptly around and blurted out, "Afternoon, sir!"

The young black man also sprang to attention, knocking a pot off the wall that came clanging down onto the brick deck under his feet.

"What is the problem here, Hyde? Why all the shouting?"

"I told Smith to fetch a bushel of beets, and he brung turnips, sir."

Kinkaid asked Smith, "Can you tell the difference between beets and turnips, sailor?"

"Sorry, Cap'm, suh," answered Smith apprehensively.

The crate at Smith's feet was plainly marked "turnips" on the side, but inside were indeterminate orbs covered in dirt. It was obvious that Smith could not read and had made an understandable mistake.

"Then it would seem a simple solution for Smith to return these turnips and bring up some beets," suggested Kinkaid.

Hyde took in a deep breath and almost sighed, but, containing himself, answered, "Very good, sir. You heard the Captain, Smith. Go find some beets."

Smith saluted the Captain, picked up the crate of dirty turnips and left.

Smith may have been guilty of poor performance, but Hyde's treatment of Smith had seemed out of proportion to his mistake. "Punishment for dereliction of duty is a prerogative of the captain," Kinkaid reminded him.

Hyde wiped his hands on his filthy apron before answering sourly, "Aye aye, sir."

Kinkaid would have left the galley, but, angered by Hyde's hesitant and surly acknowledgement, turned to add the forceful reprimand, "And I will have no such disparaging language aboard my vessel. Do I make myself clear?"

"Quite clear, Captain," came the quick and unequivocal response.

Leaving the galley, Kinkaid then made his way beneath the main deck, where Rafferty and his carpenter's mates were struggling to place a heavy timber against the inner starboard hull. With sawdust in the air and working amidst a clutter of beams and woodworking tools, the deck covered in sawdust, they were still installing reinforcing timbers under the heavy boxes on deck.

Taking a narrow ladder down one more level, Kinkaid finally found his quartermaster in the candlelit hold standing between crates of lemons, taking an inventory of stores coming aboard. Still somewhat out of temper from his encounter with the head cook, Kinkaid sounded more abrupt than he intended when he asked, "How are we doing, Mr. Johnson?"

Johnson looked weary and haggard and rubbed his forehead as he glanced at his notebook, bushy eyebrows rising. "We took on just today a full load of fresh water, fresh vegetables, bread, and cheeses. These lemons are almost the last of our stores—a good thing, too, as they'll stay fresh longer. The trim looks fine and all's we've left is to take on the livestock. Don't ask me what the carpenters are up to. Still a hell of a mess up there, sir, and always in the way," he complained.

"I know, Mr. Johnson; can't be helped," gave Kinkaid, well aware of the fact that the carpenters thought that it was Mr. Johnson and McBride and their never-ending working parties that were always in *their* way.

Returning to the deck, Kinkaid found Mr. Thorne, the wiry sailing master, going over some new charts that had just been delivered to the ship. Approaching him, Kinkaid asked, "Excuse me, Mr. Thorne, but didn't you say Mr. Simpson would be coming aboard today?"

"Oh, sorry about that, Captain," answered Thorne, his leathery face prematurely wrinkled from the elements. "Change in plans, sir. Mr. Simpson will be reporting aboard, I believe, tomorrow instead," he added, shaking his head.

"Why do you say you 'believe' he will be reporting aboard, Mr. Thorne?"

"Well, sir, as you are aware, we have received many reports from Mr. Simpson informing us as to when he is expected aboard, and then he changes the time once again. Now I am told he will be arriving with the commander of marines tomorrow morning. Meant to tell you earlier, sir."

As the honored guest and the very reason for the cruise, Mr. Simpson had been kept up to date on a daily basis concerning the readiness of the ship for sea. The ship would certainly not sail without him, but Kinkaid could not help but feel annoyed that the man felt free to change his decisions at a whim, especially after sending repeated and insistent requests to make the ship ready at the earliest possible date. In fact, Mr. Simpson had sent so many messages that Kinkaid had told his officers to simply pass them on to him at their convenience; with so many charts to find and organize, with their first lieutenant reporting aboard only now, and having to assist in assigning the crew their duties and berthing spaces, it was no wonder that the harried sailing master had forgotten to pass on the information.

"I know you've been busy, Mr. Thorne. Did he give a time when he wishes to board?"

"His message only said 'early in the morning,' Captain."

"Very well, then. Thank you, Mr. Thorne. Where is Mr. Weatherby?"

Little redheaded Rudy, one of the messenger boys, ran below to find the lieutenant. Meanwhile, Kinkaid found himself thinking about what Mr. Johnson had told him. If all stores were aboard and with only the livestock remaining to load, they were ready for sea, awaiting only the arrival of Mr. Simpson and the marine commander the following morning. The remaining carpentry work could just as well be completed at sea.

"You asked to see me, Captain?" reported the fair lieutenant.

"I'll not be aboard tonight, Weatherby. The first lieutenant will be in charge. I will expect you to assist him with his inspection of the ship in the morning. Mr. McBride will accompany you. Check with Mr. Johnson as well, and make sure that everything is secured below. I shall return before breakfast, but if there are any problems, you'll know where to find me...and do not hesitate, understand, Lieutenant? Any problems at all that may delay our departure or interfere in any way with the workings of the ship and you will immediately send for me."

"I understand perfectly, sir," said Weatherby, a barely concealed smile turning up the corners of his mouth. Of course he knew exactly where the Captain would be.

In spite of the fact that Kinkaid liked and appreciated the intelligent and efficient young Weatherby, he felt some annoyance with him at the moment, too obviously taking pleasure in his captain's private affairs. "Now please go and inform Mr. Saddler of my plans and tell him that he is in charge until I return."

The grin left Weatherby's face, hearing the name of the first lieutenant. "Yes sir."

As Weatherby left the quarterdeck, Kinkaid found himself questioning his prerogative to leave the ship on this last night. But in spite of his guilt over duty, he knew he would not disappoint his Elizabeth by remaining aboard. After all, the ship was ready for sea, and he would not miss spending the last evening with her. He would at least say good-bye.

They sat in the gazebo in the back garden. The late afternoon sun fell warmly on the couple, setting in a golden sky of orange-tinged clouds, its burnished rays shining on Elizabeth's face, bringing out the freckles that ran across the bridge of her nose.

"Jonathan," she said sweetly, "I know that you're worried about your ship's readiness, not to mention the fact that, well...this is your first command..."

Sometimes Elizabeth could be too insightful, thought Kinkaid, knowing exactly what she was about to say.

"And I am so happy that you have taken the time to be with me before you leave; it really does mean the world to me, but I do wish you had allowed my father to help you in some way, with your ship, that is. You know he really—"

"Of course, you're right, Elizabeth," he had to admit. "I only thought to save him the—"

"But now you see that you were simply being stubborn," she said, love in her voice.

"Well…just because I'm here, with you…" he tried to defend himself, "well, he's been so kind to me already and—"

"And why shouldn't he be? You're a man he can admire, an up-and-coming naval officer, practically a hero already," she said with mock seriousness.

"More a lucky sailor," laughed Kinkaid.

"Well, no one could possibly question your luck with women," she observed with a knowing look, poking him in the chest with her finger.

"You have me there," admitted Kinkaid, catching her hand and holding it to his chest, his emotions making him feel light and forgetful of his ship for the moment.

Suddenly she grew very serious in the way only a woman in love can, a woman who knows her man is about to go far away, face unknown dangers, perhaps never return. "Jonathan," she said, coming closer, her eyes looking up into his. "I do have you, don't I?"

"You do, Elizabeth," he said, the only answer he could possibly give. "You know you do," the only true answer.

"So you will at least accept my father's parting gift."

"Well, of course, I would be honored to accept anything your father gave me. But what…?"

"Now, don't get too excited," she chastised him with a playful warning. "They're not giving away daughters around here just yet, you know."

"I'm sure your father has spoiled you, given you everything," charged Kinkaid, trying to sound serious.

"And what is wrong with that?" she posed whimsically.

"Actually, there is one thing that he neglected to give you."

She looked at him quizzically for a moment, turned her head in thought, then asked, clearly puzzled, "I can't, for the life of me, imagine what that could be."

Whereupon he suddenly pulled her over his lap, saying, "A sound spanking at least once a day!"

"Jonathan!"

Their fun and laughter was cut short by the voice of Chandler, the butler. "Miss Whipple. Sir. Dinner is being served."

It was somewhat of a shock to have been interrupted, and Kinkaid's first thought was one of guilt, hoping that the butler would see the incident as something innocent and playful. While Kinkaid told himself that he had meant it in only that way, feeling suddenly childlike and free in Elizabeth's company, there were other, not-so-innocent feelings, strong feelings of lust that surprised him and found him arguing with guilt.

But the ever-discreet Chandler stood smiling affably in the doorway while Elizabeth took Kinkaid by the hand and said, "Shall we?"

Elizabeth's father had brought up the morning newspaper article describing the fact that *USS Swift* was soon to depart on a diplomatic mission to the West Indies. He didn't mention the fact that Kinkaid had not asked for any assistance in making his ship ready for sea—relying mostly upon official naval channels which tended to be thin on materials and scarce on manpower—while both knew that Mr. Whipple was in a position to provide practically anything the young captain might have required. Kinkaid knew that he had made an error by not including the man in his activities, but this was in hindsight, and there was little to be done about it now. He was consoled by the fact that his feelings for Elizabeth had grown day by day, and those feelings had been returned. Having lost his own family years ago when he was only a boy, joining another had not been easy, and the days spent with

Elizabeth were filled with many revelations about giving, acceptance, and love.

These thoughts were with him during the pleasant dinner, although he could not completely forget about the ship waiting for him. He wondered if she would be ready for sea without his presence and without his worrying about every last detail. He worried about those last stores, about crewmen who might want to slip away before she sailed, about something, anything, that could not be overlooked but might be if he were not attentive enough.

Elizabeth's mother, Martha, noticed the distant expression on his face and remarked, "I see our sea captain is already far away over the ocean somewhere."

"Please forgive me, Mrs. Whipple," he apologized, smiling uncertainly.

But Elizabeth came to his rescue, saying, "Jonathan, tell Daddy about the dream you had last night."

"Well, I dreamt I was at sea and had forgotten to bring an anchor," he admitted. After all, it was only a dream.

"Father, didn't you used to have dreams like that?" asked Elizabeth.

Mr. Whipple chuckled and said, "It's only natural, wondering if you might be forgetting something important before a cruise. I never could find the mainsail in my dreams. Why, I'd spend half the night looking all over the ship for one, in the forecastle, the hold, down in the bilges. Most distressing."

Only fanciful dreams, of course, but indications of some anxiety over the prospect of simple oversights causing disaster later, knowing that even a small mistake at sea can lead to greater trouble later, the loss of a ship, even the end of a career. Elizabeth was, of course, aware of his preoccupation with the ship, but as the daughter of a man in the shipping business, was more than understanding.

After dinner, Elizabeth's father gave a nod to Chandler, who was standing by, waiting for the moment. The butler went to an ornate bureau that stood solidly between the dining room windows and took out of a lower drawer a polished wooden box. Bringing it over to the table, Mr. Whipple set it before Kinkaid and said, "Captain, I'd like you to have these as a token of my respect for you and the cause for which you go into harm's way."

Raising the lid, Kinkaid found, resting within red felt pockets, a matching pair of dueling pistols. He took one out and hefted it in admiration. Though somewhat ornate, they were beautifully balanced, and the feeling of guilt over excluding the elder Whipple from the preparation of his ship was greater than ever. Kinkaid could only say, "Thank you, sir. I am deeply honored."

Later, when alone, the couple spent the evening talking quietly in the salon. After some stilted conversation, Kinkaid had to recognize what they were both thinking, that this was the last evening they would spend together for some time, perhaps forever. He had asked that she not come down to the pier when the ship left. After all, he reasoned, it would not be proper for the crew to witness the weakness of their captain, a man in love. In truth, Elizabeth trusted Kinkaid's crew more than he trusted himself. But if her naval captain were somehow fearful of showing some emotion as the ship departed, then she would abide by his wishes.

Soon it grew very late and the more they talked the less they found to say, until they sat staring into one another's eyes. Kinkaid wanted to kiss her, yet feared that if he did he would not want to stop, that his passion might overwhelm him. Elizabeth must have sensed this, for she stood up, causing Kinkaid to stand up with her and, leaning forward at the waist, kissed him sweetly. She then stepped back and, her eyes misting, softly said, "Goodnight, Jonathan."

Perhaps because it would be too difficult to say goodbye or perhaps to prove to himself that he had regained his senses, Kinkaid said, "Elizabeth, please don't bother seeing me off in the morning…I shall be leaving quite early and…"

She smiled, making a show of strength, resolving not to cry, at least in his presence. She wanted to ask him to make sure he returned but couldn't say the words, couldn't bring herself to voice the doubt.

True to his word, Kinkaid was up before anyone else in the household, shaving and then dressing in his second-best uniform, hours before breakfast would be served, the sky still dark. Of course, Elizabeth, suspecting this, dressed hurriedly and met him as he was about to go out the door. While glad that she had gone against his wish of the night before, he was relieved that she did not ask him to remain for breakfast. She did, however, place into his hands three small books, saying, "If by chance you find yourself with an idle moment, perhaps these might keep you company."

"I see that you intend to complete my education," said Kinkaid, placing the books into his leather satchel.

"When you return," she promised, coming close. They held one another for a moment, and as the coach arrived, they kissed one last time. "Take care of yourself, my Jonathan," she whispered before letting him go, and then watched from the doorway as the driver flicked his reins and the coach pulled away, the sky in the east already glowing with the light of day.

It was with some anxiety but mostly excitement that Kinkaid returned to his ship that morning, the box of pistols tucked under one arm, the satchel with Elizabeth's books and a few personal items under the other, and an old and decidedly plain sword at his side that he had spontaneously bought in a pawnshop on the wharf. With a silver guard and pommel roughly depicting a lion's head, it was nothing fancy, but having splurged on a pair of silk stockings and a new uniform it was all he could afford, and with a diplomat aboard, Kinkaid decided he'd better be prepared for a formal occasion. The moment he came aboard, however, he felt relieved that all stores had been taken on, that the ship was properly trimmed, and that First Lieutenant Saddler had seemingly taken charge effectively and reported that the ship was ready for sea.

Roach, receiving no word of his captain's return, had prepared nothing for his breakfast. When the burly cook inquired as to what he would like, Kinkaid realized that he was so excited to be leaving with his own ship under him, so ready for adventure, that he had completely forgotten about breakfast. So he asked for a simple meal of bread and jam, just to be practical, two slices of which he wolfed down with a cup of weak coffee, so impatient was he to return to the deck.

Yet there was little to be done once he arrived there except wait, for it was apparent that Mr. Simpson's idea of early was not the same as the Continental Navy's. Kinkaid could not help but think of the wasted hours as so many miles of ocean not covered. That he was unable to take advantage of the favorable winds offered at the moment was a most unacceptable state of affairs to a sailor.

It was almost 9 A.M., with he and all his officers and the marine contingent still waiting patiently on the deck, when the Honorable Mr. Simpson finally arrived in a gilded coach.

Mr. Simpson was immaculately dressed in a dark-blue, perfectly tailored suit, which made Kinkaid feel somewhat shabby with his worn, everyday uniform coat on. Accompanying Mr. Simpson was the Commander of Marines, Major Bauer, a tall and powerfully built man with a long nose and a lantern jaw, with the silver epaulette of rank on the right shoulder of his distinctive green uniform and a huge sheathed knife hanging from his belt.

Sergeant Anders brought the marines to rigid attention as Mr. Simpson was formally piped aboard. Brief introductions were made on the quarterdeck, and then Major Bauer made a quick inspection of his troops before asking in a quiet voice, in stark contrast to his dangerous looks, to be shown to his quarters, whereupon the messenger boy took him and his small bag directly below.

Mr. Simpson, in contrast, seemed in no hurry and had brought with him a particularly large trunk, which Kinkaid knew would never fit into the cramped captain's cabin where Simpson would be quartered.

"We've been blessed with a beautiful day for our departure, I see," stated Mr. Simpson, looking appreciatively around at the deck of the ship that he would call home for some unknown period of time, the man apparently oblivious to the fact that he had kept the ship waiting. Under his arm he carried a package, neatly wrapped in brown paper and tied with string. But Kinkaid's attention was on the dock as he watched Tripp, Treadwell, and two more of O'Toole's deck hands straining mightily to carry Mr. Simpson's heavy trunk across the gangway. "I realize the trunk is quite large, Captain," allowed Simpson.

"It won't fit into your cabin, sir," stated Kinkaid matter-of-factly.

"Anywhere will be fine…as long as it remains dry. If you don't mind, Captain."

Kinkaid was about to inform Mr. Simpson that the hold was already packed full with essentials for the long cruise, that there was little room left for even a gentleman's trunk, especially a very large gentleman's trunk. But before he could open his mouth, Simpson handed him the package, saying, "And this is for you, Captain."

Was this a present to appease him, to make amends for his tardy arrival or large trunk? Kinkaid was about to voice a protest when Simpson added, "It's from Commander Nathanson."

Kinkaid, unsure what to do with the package, tucked it under his arm and stammered, "Uh…thank you, Mr. Simpson."

Simpson, smiling, had expected as much and suggested, "You might want to open that, Captain. It's for the ship, actually."

"Very well, then." Whereupon Kinkaid broke the string, opened the paper and found inside a neatly folded flag.

"It's the new design of the Continental Congress," explained Simpson.

The hands finally had Mr. Simpson's heavy trunk aboard, and they grunted as they set it down on the quarterdeck. O'Toole then gave Kinkaid a jerk of his head, wondering where he was supposed to put the thing, knowing as well that it would be impossible to place it in the captain's cabin.

"Anywhere in the hold, O'Toole," said Kinkaid. A working party would have to be called to move certain provisions to make room for the ungainly trunk. But, after all, Mr. Simpson was a diplomat and Kinkaid's chief cargo, so he would have to accommodate the man and his baggage.

"If you could ensure that it is accessible…please," asked Simpson.

"Make it so, O'Toole."

Kinkaid had little Rudy, the messenger boy, run the new ensign up to the mainmast spar. Under other, less hurried circumstances, it would have been fitting and proper to conduct a ceremony of sorts with the raising of the ensign, but, because of Simpson's late arrival and the urgent need to get out to sea before the winds died away, there would be no pomp or fanfare. The officers and men on the quarterdeck, however, watched in interest as the bright new flag rose up the mast, and as it caught the breeze and fluttered out, all could see that its colorful design had the cross of Saint George in the upper corner on a field of alternating red and white stripes.

"Most striking, Captain," remarked Weatherby.

Mr. Thorne, the practical sailing master, interrupted their admiration over the new ensign by dutifully reporting, "All hands are aboard, Captain. The wind remains favorable out of the northeast, and all lines are singled up."

"Very well, Mr. Thorne," returned Kinkaid, and then, turning to his first lieutenant, Kinkaid said, "Mr. Saddler, take us out, if you please."

III

Men's Gifts

The Continental Navy brig-of-war *USS Swift* was a hermaphrodite brig. That is, she carried two masts and upon those masts was a mixture of sails. Besides her two jibs, her foremast held three ship-rigged square sails with the addition of a rectangular sail rigged sloop-like behind them. The mainmast had two fore-and-aft-rigged sails, a triangular topsail above, and a large rectangular mainsail, her main driver, below, its heavy boom extending over the quarterdeck a dozen feet beyond the stern rail. Additional staysails could be hoisted between the topmasts for added speed. She was sleek-hulled, her masts raked back at an angle, and could sail closer to the wind than a strictly square-sailed vessel. In addition to the twelve six-pounders on her main deck, four two-pound swivel guns had been mounted on the gunwale, two at the bow and two on the slightly raised quarterdeck, quite modest armament in comparison to the average British man-of-war.

Captain Kinkaid was on the quarterdeck of his ship this morning—the beginning of a bright summer day, the second day out of port—looking up at the clean white sails, hands clasped behind his back. Each sail was bellying out gracefully, each trapping the power of a strong and steady breeze. He noted no luffing, no waste of efficiency. Satisfied with his practical inspection, he took a moment to enjoy the scene, taking note of the way the billowing sails mimicked the cottony clouds above, how they caught the wind and propelled the ship—an amalgam of wood, cordage, and canvas designed to interact with wind and waves, crew and creation, combining into a living, breathing thing that found its nature on the open sea. He smiled and then self-consciously scanned the deck to see if anyone had been watching. If they had, they were quicker than he, for all he saw were barefoot men busy with the running of the ship, now headed due south and rolling easily with the long Atlantic swells, the wind tugging at the crests of blue-green waves. Lines creaked in their blocks, the wind hummed in the rigging, and there was a gentle splash from the bow wave forward, sending up occasional sprays that landed on the foredeck; sights, sounds and rhythms welcome and soothing to a sailor.

Lieutenant Weatherby had become seasick soon after the ship made the Atlantic and had been joined at the scuppers by the Honorable Mr. Simpson, who looked most undignified heaving his guts over the rail that first day. Weatherby soon got over it, accepting the characteristic weakness as the passing phenomenon that it was with him, a day or two of activity usually enough to dispel the illness, but Mr. Simpson had not been seen on deck for the rest of the day and now into this one.

Kinkaid strolled up and down his twelve feet of deck on the windward side of the quarterdeck, the proper place for the captain. The other officers of the watch, along with First Lieutenant Saddler, were on the leeward side. It was something new, being captain, master of all before him, and the thought of it was both satisfying and anxiety producing.

The first order he had given was to have his first lieutenant take the ship out. Saddler was certainly a capable seaman, with some years of experience at sea, but sailing a ship and handling men were two separate realms. As first lieutenant, Saddler would have to deal directly with the other officers in their various divisions, his judgment not always observed by the Captain. But to be fair, Kinkaid would have to give the man the leeway to make mistakes. All in due time, thought Kinkaid, for he too had something to prove to the men serving under him. So far, they had turned out in good time to their drills and sail evolutions and seemed eager enough. But at present, Kinkaid was most bothered by the fact that he was carrying cargo of which he knew nothing.

"Mr. Briggs, I'd like you to inquire as to the health of Mr. Simpson," requested Kinkaid of one of the new midshipmen, Mr. Briggs, a black-haired and darkly complected young gentleman. Kinkaid found himself wondering if there was any Spanish blood in his line. "Please convey my regards and inform him that perhaps some fresh air may be of some benefit to his condition. And you might bring him a plain biscuit—tell him it is sometimes agreeable to a queasy stomach."

"Aye aye, sir," answered Briggs, who immediately turned for the after hatch.

"And have Mr. Weatherby report to the deck, as well!" Kinkaid had to call out.

"Yes, sir, right away, sir!" shouted Briggs, his head disappearing over the coaming of the after hatch.

"That boy needs to calm down," said Kinkaid to himself.

Mr. Thorne was on the quarterdeck and, witnessing the exchange, ventured, "Eager to please, Captain."

The remark recalled Kinkaid's own first time at sea, only fifteen and fearfully in awe of Captain Davenport, a huge man with a full beard and a cruel streak. After a week at sea, the mere sight of the bullying seaman had made young Kinkaid a nervous wreck, and he had been only too thankful to take his leave of the unhappy ship some three months later.

Though it was true that there was little room on the main deck because of the two large wooden boxes tied down to half the cleats, Major Bauer was exercising his marines in what space they could find between the guns. They were having a bit of trouble keeping their footing, all of them except the Indian, who seemed excused from the exercises and sat between the first and second guns, smoking his pipe while sewing a new pair of moccasins.

Sergeant Anders was up front, wavering to the heave and roll of the deck, his cheek bulging out, first on one side, then the other. If he was susceptible to the nausea of seasickness, it certainly did not hamper his desire for tobacco. Kinkaid had spoken to Major Bauer about the rough sergeant spitting on the deck, and so every few minutes Anders staggered awkwardly to the rail and spit a brown stream over the side.

Corporal "Bull" Decker was the most enthusiastic, exercising with unmitigated vigor and occasionally shouting encouragement to flagging spirits. Corporal Bentkowski was by far the funniest, the way he playfully swayed and balanced himself in the middle of the waist while the others gave him plenty of room to flail about without stepping on them. And there was the heavy-set Corporal Stockton, huffing and puffing, his belly bouncing up and down, struggling to keep up.

Corporal Bentkowski took to gently taunting him, "Don't worry, Stockton, if you fall overboard, the whales will take you in as one of their own!"

Decker joined in with, "Hell, if we run out of stores, we'll eat you. Should last a year or two!"

But Kinkaid noticed that none of the marines joked or made fun of the Indian scout they called Monk, who ignored the banter, concentrating on his stitching. He kept to himself and could often be seen gazing solemnly out to sea, as if mesmerized by the never-ending expanse of ocean that stretched to the horizon on all sides of the ship.

Kinkaid doubted if any of the marines had ever been to sea before, yet knew it would not be long before they would be walking in step with the pitch of the deck, getting their sea legs. But at the moment the group of them was something to be amused over, and there was O'Toole and Rafferty and a few veteran sailors forward, chuckling at the unintentional antics of the "lubbers." Major Bauer ensured that his men ignored the comments of the sailors, though Kinkaid saw the compact Sergeant Anders give O'Toole a glowering look under his fierce and overhung brow.

Here was Weatherby. "You wanted to see me, Captain?"

"I take it you are pleased to be gunnery officer, Mr. Weatherby?"

"Most pleased, sir. An honorable duty, following in the tradition of Mr. Hill," declared Weatherby, who had visited the recovering Hill just two days before the ship had departed. Of course Weatherby was just as pleased at being made lieutenant, but would never say so, suspecting Kinkaid had much to do with it.

"I'm sure you will make Mr. Hill proud," grinned Kinkaid, intending a vote of confidence, but then immediately judged from Weatherby's expression that he was ready and eager to carry out his assignment with a businesslike assurance. "Have you assigned your gun crews, yet?"

"All assigned, Captain."

"Very well, then," gave Kinkaid, not surprised. "As soon as those marines are finished doing whatever it is they are doing on my deck, I want you to call out your crews and practice loading and running out the guns. Only dry runs for now; keep it slow and make sure each man knows what his job entails. We're not looking for speed just yet, but efficiency…the basics. Don't bother sanding the decks, and I certainly don't want any powder involved. Plenty of time to get to that."

"Of course, Captain. We'll save that for quarters drills later," allowed Weatherby, his blond hair spilling out from under his hat, blowing over his ears.

"You might pick a couple of experienced gunners; spread them out to help show the others how it's done," suggested Kinkaid.

"The Travelin' Brothers, sir," answered Weatherby.

"Traveling brothers?" asked Kinkaid.

"Tripp and Treadwell, Captain," said Weatherby. "Course, they're not really brothers, but we call them that because they're mates and because of…"

"…their names," concluded Kinkaid, impatiently. "Very clever, Mr. Weatherby."

"Yes, sir," answered Weatherby, and suspecting that his captain may not have thought the shared nickname all that clever, gave a reassuring, "I'll make sure every man knows his job, Captain."

"I'm sure you will, Mr. Weatherby," granted Kinkaid, "and I'll trouble you to ask the Boatswain to come up here. I'll have a word with him if he's free."

"Of course, Captain," said Weatherby. Then, casting his gaze behind Kinkaid, asked, "The men were wondering, sir; if could you tell us what are in those boxes?"

"No, Mr. Weatherby," answered Kinkaid, irked by the reminder, "I cannot."

Just then the young Briggs ran up, stood rigidly at attention and gave a stiff salute. "Excuse me, Captain. Mr. Simpson sends his compliments, sir. He appreciates the dry biscuit, sir, but says he is not ready to come up on deck at present, sir."

"Very well, Mr. Briggs. Thank you. And Mr. Briggs, kindly watch your sirs, if you will."

"Yes, sir," stammered Briggs, the rolling deck causing him to step out of his at-attention position.

"We needn't be so formal while under weigh, Mr. Briggs. That is, you may remain at ease when addressing me."

"Thank you, sir," said Briggs, relaxing his shoulders a bit

"What is your assignment?"

"I'm in charge of the forward magazine, sir, directing the powder monkeys. Mr. Weatherby had us attend a class, uh…whereby he instructed…well, sir, myself and Mr. Lofton and—"

"Why don't you join Mr. Weatherby, then. We won't be breaking out any powder just yet, but make sure you know about the necessary precautions and where your station is."

"Yes, sir."

Mr. Thorne was standing beside the helmsman when Briggs lost his balance as the quarterdeck rose on a high roller, causing the young midshipman to trip over Mr. Thorne's feet. "Oh, I'm terribly sorry, Mr.—"

Thorne caught the boy by his shoulders and, steadying him, condescended to add, "Be sure to give your attention to Mr. Weatherby's instructions, Mr. Briggs, and in time you should know everything about proper powder room precautions and gunnery."

"And from there," added Kinkaid, "we'll move you on to learning something of each and every man's position aboard ship."

"Yes, sir," said Briggs, still standing halfway between attention and at ease, the former winning the contest.

"Attend to your duties now, Mr. Briggs."

"Aye aye, Captain," answered Briggs, saluting again before hurrying off after Weatherby, who was calling out the men for mock gunnery drills.

For a moment Kinkaid felt as if he were in charge of a kindergarten class, so rudimentarily would this young crew have to be trained. And he hoped that they would catch on fast, faster than his cook, Raymond Roach. The man seemed incapable of taking instructions, and Kinkaid had thought seriously of replacing him if his meals did not improve. Kinkaid did not think himself overly fastidious; he did not even have any special needs or dishes that Roach would have to cook, but it seemed to him that the captain of a ship should have a decent meal three times a day, without having to worry about each one before it came. At least he had a base of men whom he trusted, which gave him confidence, and for this he was thankful. But he would have to be patient and take things slowly until the men were familiar with their assignments, even the bumbling Roach.

As first lieutenant, Mr. Saddler would be in charge of instructing the midshipmen each day at noon, holding classes on navigation and seamanship, though Kinkaid knew that Weatherby was probably Saddler's superior in all these things, especially nautical mathematics. If Weatherby were not careful with his duties as ship's schoolmaster, if he showed off too much in front of the first lieutenant, then he would be inviting the same troubles he'd had before—when Saddler was senior midshipman on the *Randolph*—in spite of the fact that Weatherby was now also a lieutenant. Saddler would ride them hard, of that Kinkaid had no doubt, but that was as it should be. There was no room for slackers aboard ship, especially in the midshipmen's quarters, where it was expected that every man do his job and be familiar with the other man's work as well in case of death or accident. After all, these were ship's officers in the making, but Saddler lacked patience and was wont to bully, and so Kinkaid would watch his progress most of all.

"Those special reinforcements are all finished, Captain," reported Rafferty, the Irish carpenter, a short, squat man with an ugly and pockmarked face. A long scar ran down his left cheek, next to a large, bent nose that had been broken several times. His greasy hair, held back with a red bandana, was liberally sprinkled with wood chips.

"Any problems with the installation?"

"All kinds of problems, sir," returned Rafferty, scratching his head. Then he simply stood there, looking at Kinkaid.

"Yes, well, what kind of problems, Rafferty?"

"Well, sir, those precut timbers didn't fit at all like we was led to believe. Had to cut 'em all over again. Found some rotten knees and futtocks as well." Again Rafferty stood there after his negative report, waiting.

"Are you telling me this ship is not seaworthy?"

"Oh, she's plenty seaworthy, Captain," he answered with a crooked grin. "It's just that with the ship in the water we couldn't take the chance on replacin' knees or futtocks."

"Yes, I understand that, Rafferty," said Kinkaid patiently. "We certainly don't want to tear the hull out of her, now, do we?"

Rafferty, seemingly satisfied that his captain understood the danger of destroying hull planks by attempting to tear out rotten ribs while under weigh, grinned widely once again and answered, "No, sir. A hull comes in mighty handy, 'specially at sea, Captain." The carpenter, by his expression, seemed at first inordinately pleased with his joke, and then just as suddenly seemed to change his mind as he closed his eyes, turned his mouth down, and gave a sour look.

Kinkaid forced a smile while coming to the conclusion that Rafferty's conversational style would demand a measure of tolerance. If he wanted a full report from his carpenter, he was going to have to work for it. "So I assume you were able to find another way of dealing with the problem?"

"You could say that, Captain."

"I could say what, Rafferty?"

"Well, sir, we did a right fine job there." Rafferty hesitated again, waiting for his captain to ask him about his fine job, no doubt.

Kinkaid decided to experiment, to hold back a response, to wait the man out.

Rafferty stood there a moment and then began fidgeting. Finally realizing that his captain was content to wait for his complete report, he gave in. "We braced 'em up real good, sir, solid as can be. Should hold up those heavy wooden boxes on the deck with support to spare, I'd say," claimed the carpenter, "whatever they be."

"Good job, Rafferty. Thank you," offered Kinkaid, and although impressed with the carpenter as a man who took pride in his work, he was relieved to bring the awkward conversation to an end.

Mr. Simpson had insisted that the contents of the boxes should remain a secret until they were at sea, referring to them only as "Major Bauer's cargo." He had also refused to explain what the special reinforcement beams were for. Though Kinkaid could very well guess their purpose, he also thought that a captain should not have to guess about cargo on his own ship. And now Simpson was remaining below, in fact had not been seen on deck since they left port, adding to Kinkaid's annoyance. His impatience was getting the better of him, and he had concluded that if anybody might know what was in those boxes, it would be his boatswain, striding up to the quarterdeck now, his long white hair tied neatly in pigtails.

"O'Toole, what the hell is in those damned boxes?" he asked irritably as soon as O'Toole was within earshot.

O'Toole, taken aback at first, rubbed his stubbled chin and said, "Don't rightly know, Captain. Nobody told me." Then, the pugnacious chin jutting out, added, "That little bast...uh, that sergeant knows...excuse me, sir, but he—"

"Well then, take a guess," insisted Kinkaid sharply, his patience at an end.

O'Toole was able to shake some of his agitation before answering, "Well, sir, if you take into account those shorin' timbers we just put in and you add to that the shape o' those boxes, and then you add the considerable weight of 'em...well, I'd say we've got us a couple of mortars on board 'ere, Captain."

"Thank you, O'Toole, that is the same conclusion I am coming to."

They both stood looking at the two large boxes for a moment before O'Toole asked, "What are we going to do with a couple of mortars, Captain?"

Not wanting to admit that Major Bauer and Mr. Simpson were withholding that information and therefore irritated by the question, Kinkaid decided, "O'Toole, come with me. I may be needing your assistance with Mr. Simpson."

"Aye, sir. Be glad to help."

"Mr. Thorne, you have the deck. I shouldn't be long below."

"Aye aye, sir," said Mr. Thorne. "I have the deck."

Already the belowdecks were beginning to smell of sweaty bodies and rotten food, odors of no comfort to a queasy stomach. There was no answer when Kinkaid knocked on the door of the captain's cabin, and so he opened it and peered in. The smell of vomit was overpowering and made Kinkaid wince. Simpson was in the cot in a fetal position, facing the hull, a faded gray blanket twisted about his form. Below him on the deck was the bucket he was using, the source of the vile smell.

Kinkaid knocked on the doorframe. "Mr. Simpson...sir."

Only a groan came from the unmoving form.

"Mr. Simpson, you need to get out on deck," said Kinkaid encouragingly. "Get some fresh air."

Simpson sighed and then rolled over, pale as a whitefish, drool running down his chin.

"Did you manage to eat the biscuit Mr. Briggs brought you?"

Simpson held out a shaky hand holding a half-eaten biscuit.

"Very good. Now you just need to get out of that cot, up on deck. I know it seems difficult at the moment, but once you get out there, up in the fresh air, it's going to do you a world of good, trust me, sir."

Simpson rose slowly from the cot, moaning in misery, eyes rolling. Kinkaid removed the blanket twisted around his body and helped the man as he swung his legs out.

"O'Toole, give me a hand," directed Kinkaid. "That's it, up we go. And have somebody take care of Mr. Simpson's bucket, would you?"

"Right away, sir," agreed O'Toole with a sour face as the odor hit him.

He was right about hauling Mr. Simpson up on deck, for after a half hour of sitting against the bulwark at the stern in the sun and taking in the fresh air of the open deck, the man was actually beginning to look around and take an interest in his surroundings.

Mock gunnery exercises were taking place on deck, with Weatherby and O'Toole taking the men through numerous dry runs to familiarize them with their duties. Bauer had moved his marines to the bow and the staccato sounds of musket fire could be heard as they practiced their marksmanship by firing at wood chips tossed over the side.

Kinkaid noticed that one of the crew's cooks, the young black man who had mistaken turnips for beets, had approached Weatherby and after a short conversation, the man picked up a bore swab and took his place at one of the center guns.

"Isn't that one of the ship's cooks?" asked Kinkaid of Mr. Saddler.

"Uh, yes, Captain. Venture Smith," answered Saddler. "I don't believe he's been assigned to gunnery duty, sir. Shall I inquire of Mr. Weatherby—?"

"No, that won't be necessary, Mr. Saddler," said Kinkaid.

It was a small thing, but Smith had been assigned to the ship's galley and assigned duties were not to be so easily changed, therefore, after the hour-long exercise Kinkaid decided to ask Weatherby about the matter.

"Smith volunteered for gunnery duty, and I saw no reason to reject his request, Captain."

"And what of his previously assigned duties?"

"I spoke to Hyde, the mess chief, and he informs me that as long as Smith is there to help prepare meals and clean up afterwards, he…well, he doesn't care if he wants to shoot guns too." Weatherby decided to leave out the fact that Hyde had really said, "I don't care if the useless blackie blows himself up," instead adding, "He also mentioned that he would just as soon replace the man, Captain."

"And why is that?"

"The man shows little interest or skill with food, sir."

"I see," gave Kinkaid, pondering Weatherby's answer and thinking as well of his steward, Roach. Still, it seemed to him that Weatherby should have asked him about any reassignment first, but rather than reproach Weatherby, Kinkaid surmised, "So it is for the good of the ship that he has taken it upon himself to be reassigned."

"The boy is quick and has vigor, Captain," answered Weatherby without hesitation.

Perhaps it was because of Roach and the fact that Kinkaid had resisted the impulse to change his steward's assignment and disturb the routine. Or maybe it was because Kinkaid needed to assert his dominance, feeling that some of his power as captain had been usurped by Bauer's orders, keeping secret his assignment and the contents of those ungainly boxes. Or maybe it was the fact that

Weatherby had seen no need to inform him of the incident. In fact, it was a combination of factors that made Kinkaid noncommittal.

"I shall give the matter my consideration, Mr. Weatherby."

"Thank you, sir," said Weatherby.

Later, Kinkaid walked over to where Mr. Simpson still sat. He had his faced turned up into the sunshine, and his eyes were closed in reverie.

"Mortars, huh?" was all Kinkaid said.

"You opened the boxes?" Simpson asked and opened his eyes to see them still sitting there.

"It's easy enough to assume, sir," explained Kinkaid.

"Well, you are correct," admitted Simpson. "Four-and-a-half-inch mortars."

"And for what purpose, may I ask?"

"They are part of Major Bauer's baggage, Captain," said Simpson calmly, squinting up, "and he has explicit orders not to discuss his assignment. He is free to discuss them with you only after I have departed the ship."

"I see," replied Kinkaid. "Which is the same time that I am to open my orders, the very ones Major Bauer is carrying for me."

"Precisely, Captain. You are to engage in a special mission, assisting Major Bauer...after I have left the ship."

"Involving mortars."

"Major Bauer thought they might come in handy. Commander Nathanson agreed."

"And you are to have no knowledge of my orders."

"You are catching on, Captain Kinkaid," remarked Simpson. "In fact I would go so far as to say that no one has any knowledge of your orders—an important precaution. It helps protect certain interests and is all done in the name of the American cause, as you shall see. I can, however, assure you that you will have at least some discretion in carrying out your assignment. You will have to trust me, Captain."

It seemed apparent to Kinkaid that these "certain interests" that needed protecting were, in fact, Mr. Simpson himself. Whatever

Bauer was supposed to do, with Kinkaid's assistance, was not to be associated with Mr. Simpson or his mission of diplomacy.

Major Bauer was also a mystery, remaining aloof, occasionally speaking quietly to his sergeant. He occupied himself with either exercising his men or sharpening that big knife he always carried in a sheath on his belt that he could toss, twirl, and catch like a circus performer, so adept was he with the heavy-bladed weapon. And he had vacated the officer's cabin that he had been assigned, preferring to "roost with the men," as he put it. A practical move, considering that the big man would have had to practically fold himself in half to fit into one of the officer's cots, and so he would certainly find more room to stretch his bulk in the 'tween decks. But Kinkaid now saw even less of the man, reinforcing the notion that he had been left in the dark over important orders, making him feel…distrusted, not to mention that it precluded making any intelligence plans until after Mr. Simpson left the ship. Of course, Kinkaid could not blame Major Bauer; after all, the man was only following orders. Nonetheless, it was all quite maddening.

Simpson finally stood up and stretched. "You know, I'm beginning to feel better already."

"I'm certainly glad of that, sir," gave Kinkaid, unconvincingly.

Kinkaid was thankful that the passage off Cape Hatteras was an unusually smooth one. Of course, he had skirted it by a wide margin, but the habitually stormy area was unseasonably calm and did not interfere with the progress of his crew's exercises. Gun drills and sailing evolutions were the order of the day, and from after breakfast to before sunset the men were busy practicing endless variations of ship maneuvering in between calls for general quarters. As exercises on the guns progressed and more steps were added to the training process, it was becoming apparent that the crew was slowly but surely beginning to work as an efficient fighting team. And for the last two days, as live-fire exercises were begun, the young black ship's cook continued to join gunnery exercises, now at the number-twelve gun, the last one on the starboard side, right on the quarterdeck.

Weatherby, noting Kinkaid watching the exercises with interest, especially how quick and nimble Smith was at his gun, smiled and provided the information, "I thought you might like to know, sir, that he's named his gun 'Troubadour'."

"For her sweet voice, I suppose?"

"Claims it works on him like a lullaby, Captain," answered Weatherby, grinning.

"Then let us hope his aim is as sweet as her sound."

By the end of the week, the gun crews were familiar with the procedures and rhythms of loading and firing, and Kinkaid felt it was time to fire at a target. The secret out, he decided one afternoon that he would have the boxes removed from around the mortars and use the wood for target practice, to be replaced by protective tarps—but not without vehement protests from Sergeant Anders, who complained that they would become rusty if exposed. Kinkaid took the precaution of asking Major Bauer about the guns and was assured that they were well greased and protected from the salt air.

Kinkaid was standing on the quarterdeck, watching O'Toole help Rafferty remove the boxes. Sergeant Anders was standing behind the ship's bell, his eyes filled with dark malevolence.

Rafferty had just pried the lid off the first box, unaware that Anders was not ten feet behind, glowering at the two of them. Kinkaid heard Rafferty say to O'Toole, "You'd think we was violatin' the man's daughters."

"Maybe these *are* his daughters. They're almost ugly enough," came O'Toole's retort, bringing a laugh from the carpenter, both unaware that the sergeant was moving up behind them.

Kinkaid was standing on the quarterdeck, not twenty feet behind Anders, and saw the whole thing developing. He was about to open his mouth in an attempt to stop the attack when he saw Major Bauer come from behind the mainmast. Bauer had been wise enough to keep his eye on his hot-tempered sergeant and was making to head him off. Anders was almost behind O'Toole now, raising his fist in the air, intending to deliver a blow from behind, his concentration total, to the point that he did not notice Major Bauer coming from one side. The major merely stuck his boot out, catching Sergeant Anders in mid-stride, sending him sprawling onto the deck at the feet of O'Toole and Rafferty.

"Look at 'is face, will ye," goaded Rafferty, "redder than an English lobsterback!"

Anders's face was fiery red from rage and embarrassment, and he reached for a belaying pin in a rack surrounding the mainmast as he stood up. But Bauer stepped forward and held the man's arm, saying quietly to the three of them, "That'll do. Save your fighting for the English."

Anders glared at O'Toole and then stomped off toward the forecastle, muttering obscenities.

O'Toole and Rafferty shrugged and went back to work removing the boxes from the mortars.

O'Toole was right about one thing. The mortars were certainly ugly things, black and squat, and the sight of them led to murmuring and speculation about the use for which they were intended. But Kinkaid soon had any idle hands put to work on more productive things. By nailing the two boxes together, end-to-end, Rafferty soon fashioned a nice target to shoot at; in fact, it looked like a miniature ship. When it was finished, Rafferty added a spar to the middle, making a small mast to which he attached a red flag. By late afternoon, it was ready to be lowered into the sea, the red flag fluttering gaily in the breeze. This done, the crew was called out for live gunnery exercises.

"Fire!" yelled Weatherby.

Six six-pounders crashed out, belching rings of smoke that curled back over the windward transom, their shot splashing the makeshift ship a bit but otherwise leaving it untouched.

"Mr. Cutler, back the tops'ls; bring us about!" shouted Kinkaid. "Starboard side, Mr. Weatherby! Time us, Mr. Saddler."

"Aye, sir!"

Cutler was doing an adequate job of supervising the sail-handlers, but his men could still improve upon their speed aloft and in lining the spars—though this was something that would improve with more practice as the men gained confidence in being up so high, over a swaying deck. But he had to be pleased with the way Cutler had taken charge of his assignment, the young, freckle-faced midshipman scrambling up and down the risers like a monkey and by his courage setting an example. All the while he praised and encouraged the new men at their dangerous task instead of arrogantly shouting and complaining about hesitant performance in the tops. Cutler instinctively recognized that slow and steady would win their confidence more than pushing and forcing a man beyond his capacities, resulting perhaps in needless injury or even death, his patient style less than appreciated by the unforgiving Mr. Saddler.

The tall and lanky Mr. Lofton seemed an effective midshipman, quick and adept at his studies. And while he took every order and assignment with ponderous gravity, his no-nonsense approach met with respect on the part of those seamen under him, those men even now hauling round the bowlines as the helmsman spun the rudder for a quick turn into and through the wind.

Weatherby was having the starboard side guns loaded and run out as the eager Briggs directed the shot and powder carriers from below. The gun crews moved almost in unison now—not quite, but better than before.

The ship came around on the opposite course, running slightly against the wind, the breeze over the port beam this time. The target box was closer now, and Kinkaid would give Weatherby the chance to aim and fire each gun in turn.

"As she bears, Mr. Weatherby!" said Kinkaid. "Fire as you please!"

Aaron Tripp stood next to number-two—the first gun on the starboard side, aptly named "Wet Willie"—blowing gently on a smoldering wick as Weatherby strode up behind the gun and took aim. He waited for the hull to rise up before giving the order, "Fire!"

Tripp touched off the piece with a roar, and there was Treadwell, already swabbing out the bore as it slammed back against its train tackles while Weatherby moved to the next gun, number four, named "Wandering Willie" for its notorious inaccuracy, having too much windage or space between the ball and the bore.

Weatherby was learning of such idiosyncrasies and continued down the line, always adjusting his aim from the fall of the last shot. He scored a hit with gun six, "Fritz," its crew letting out a hearty cheer. Then another good hit with gun eight, "Boomer," smashing away one wall of the box. Gun ten, "Nina," with the short Stevens her captain, scored a direct hit, blasting the box apart, splinters flying, causing a delighted Weatherby to rouse all the crews to a cheer as little remained of the target but the thin mast, still flying the red flag.

"Well done, Mr. Weatherby!" observed Kinkaid appreciatively. "Compliments to your crews!" He was glad to praise the men. And Weatherby—he was a natural at gunnery, just as he was at anything he undertook.

Weatherby returned a dashing salute to the quarterdeck as the high-spirited men beamed and slapped one another on the back.

There was still one cannon loaded, however, one cannon that had not been fired on the starboard side, number twelve, right on the quarterdeck: Smith's Troubadour.

"Clear that last gun," ordered Kinkaid.

"Aye aye, sir!" Weatherby turned to Smith. "Last gun…"

"Mr. Weatherby, suh?"

Smith whispered something in Weatherby's ear, causing Weatherby to smile. "Smith requests permission to discharge Troubadour at what's left of the raft, Captain."

Kinkaid looked off the starboard quarter and could see that a raft of timber still floated flat upon the sea, enough to stubbornly hold the red flag aloft, a small enough target. Kinkaid answered,

"You'll have your chance, Smith. Mr. Saddler, take us about! Mr. Cutler, hands to the braces!"

"Aye aye, Captain," answered both officers, Cutler with a grin.

The entire ship was watching the figure of Smith at his gun as the ship made her circling turn. It did not escape Kinkaid's attention that Stevens, the captain of number-ten gun was, by his sour look, not impressed with Smith's bravado as he took his place behind Troubadour.

But Smith ignored him with an expression of serious intent on his face as the flotsam drew near, the timbers riding on a carpet of foam as a wave passed beneath, some fifty yards away.

"Here it comes, Venture!" shouted Matthew Edwards, Troubadour's loader.

"I sees it," said Smith quietly. "You best step aside, now, Matt."

Smith bent his knees and leaned his frame against the truck of the gun, aiming along the barrel as he blew on his slow match, right arm behind his back. The dark timbers of the shattered box were hidden in the trough of a wave almost abeam now, only the tiny flag barely visible, waving mockingly above. Smith waited, judging the rise of the ship with the action of the waves. Just when it seemed that the raft would pass unmolested, Smith touched off the gun.

A loud crack and a cloud of white smoke swirled over the quarterdeck, then a geyser of water in the middle of the raft, sending up a shower of splinters, the red flag spinning off into the air as the mast was shattered, followed by the excited whoops of the crew, while Matt the loader joyously twirled his red liberty cap over his head, leaving Stevens scowling with contempt.

Weatherby awarded the beaming Smith a hearty, "Well done!"

"She do like to put them to sleep with her song, Mr. Weatherby," Smith answered proudly as both men turned in the direction of the quarterdeck.

The puff of smoke had hit Kinkaid squarely in the face, stinging his nostrils and eyes before dissipating in the fresh breeze, and he was still blinking the tears away when he said to the cocky cook's helper, "That was some fine shooting, Smith."

Smith bowed and said, "Thank you, Cap'm."

"Secure the guns," said Kinkaid with a sense of satisfaction. "Helmsman, steer us south."

A moment later, Hyde, the head cook, poked his head over the coaming of the after hatch and shouted, "Smith, get your arse down here! We've dinner to prepare!"

Another week of easy sailing continued, the sea changing from the brown-green of the northern waters to a bluer hue as the temperatures rose, the days increasingly filled with sunshine. The exercises continued as well, the men becoming familiar with their day-to-day duties and their special assignments when they beat to quarters. First Officer Saddler faultlessly made his daily inspections of the ship, held classes with the midshipmen, and made his daily reports. There seemed to be no ill will among the officers, though Kinkaid was still eating in his cabin or sometimes with Mr. Simpson and had not yet paid a visit to the wardroom. He was concerned that Saddler and the others might think he was spying, so he would wait a few more days. Roach had improved but little, his offerings remaining uneven to say the least, but Kinkaid was too busy with the ship to pay much attention to what he was coming to accept as a minor annoyance. The crew was generally well-behaved, although it later came to Kinkaid's attention that the gun captain of number ten, the short, wiry Stevens, had had some harsh words with Smith, the two almost coming to blows but for the intervention of their respective crews. Sergeant Anders and O'Toole were at least avoiding one another, and so far no one had been arrested. The midshipmen were turning in their daily position reports, showing the ship making good speed, and Weatherby held regular evening classes to help prepare them for their lieutenant's test.

There were always tasks to complete, drills and exercises to keep the men busy. But even so there was free time, the crew spending it in various ways—some reading, some sleeping, some writing letters that would probably never leave the ship until they arrived back in their own port (when there would be no need to send them), others carving pieces of wood or whalebone that they had procured from the fishermen of Boston.

Kinkaid had finally gotten around to the books that Elizabeth had pressed into his hands the morning he left. She had included a book of verse by Johnson entitled *The Vanity of Human Wishes*; one of John Trumbull's recent political satires, *Elegy of the Times*; and a Bible. The satire he thumbed through quickly and put aside. The Bible he had always found inspiring, preferring to open it at a whim to find answers to unasked questions. The book of verse pleasantly surprised him with its sensible philosophy and ideas, which he sometimes tried on Mr. Simpson at dinner or pondered while strolling the quarterdeck.

The crew had taken to inventing amusement to help pass the time and quirky words began to spring up here and there, growing out of routine and boredom, mere nonsense really, their meaning not always clear, sometimes changing with each situation. And of course, Kinkaid seemed to be the last to know about them. One morning he overheard O'Toole berating Hyde for tossing two rounds of cheese over the side, whereupon the cook explained, "Those cheeses were exceedingly scuptious, Boats."

Later, when Kinkaid was in the waist with Mr. Saddler and the midshipmen as they took the noon sighting, he stopped O'Toole and asked him, "What exactly was wrong with the cheese this morning?"

O'Toole looked askance for a moment and then smiled, answering, "Oh, you mean 'scuptious,' sir."

"Scuptious?"

"It's not proper English, Captain."

"I assumed as much."

"Actually, somebody made up the word, sir," admitted O'Toole.

"I see," said Kinkaid, still feeling unsatisfied.

"I find little profit in it, myself, sir."

Kinkaid hated to ask, "And what does this made-up word mean?"

"Something unpleasant, it would seem, sir." And then, as if to ensure that the important part of his captain's question might be answered, O'Toole added, "I checked on the cheese meself, Captain, and I can readily verify that some o' those cheeses were most definitely turning green and unpalta…unpata…"

The far from erudite O'Toole had boxed himself into a corner from which he was having difficulty extricating himself, and so Kinkaid finished the sentence, "…and scuptious."

"That's it, Captain," grinned the boatswain, recognizing that it was not the state of the cheeses but the invented word that was the object of Kinkaid's inquiry.

Of course, it was only a matter of time before someone referred to Rafferty as having a "scuptious" face. One sailor was even heard to say, "You know, when you look 'scuptious' up in the dictionary, there's a picture of Rafferty, there. Yeah, that's right." But the word quickly met its demise when O'Toole heard one of the waisters refer to Rafferty as "Seaman Scuptious." O'Toole liked and respected Rafferty, so he had it passed among the crew that henceforth the word was off limits, that the next man heard using the word, even if not about Rafferty, would answer to the tough boatswain. O'Toole had also heard a rumor that the midshipmen were referring to the brooding Mr. Lofton as "The Undertaker" behind his back, but what happened between the midshipmen was none of his concern.

Next, anything to do with the word "wonder" became the thing. The word "wondiferous" was quite popular and could be applied to anything that one liked or admired. "The contradiction of 'scuptious'," whispered Weatherby mischievously to Briggs.

Weatherby had the afternoon watch and was standing on the quarterdeck, gazing to the west, his attention on the colorful sunset. Midshipman Cutler came up on deck to relieve him, and Kinkaid overheard Weatherby give his report.

"Good evening, Mr. Cutler. The ship is on a course of due south, making all of four knots. Studding sails have just been set and..." Weatherby held his arms out, dramatically presenting the western horizon, "please allow me to present you this spectacular sunset."

Whereupon Cutler declared, "Why, thank you, Mr. Weatherby, the sky is a veritable wonderama. You are relieved."

The temperatures continued to rise on a daily basis, then, at the end of the week, sometime during the night, the wind died. Completely. One bright and hazy morning, the crew came out on deck to find the sails hanging limply from their spars, the ship immobile on a flat sea. They were in a dead calm, with no steerageway, drifting idly under a blazing sun in a cloudless sky, and with no wind to mitigate it, the heat and humidity soon became intolerable.

"Is this normal?" asked Mr. Simpson that noon, wiping the sweat from his brow.

"The doldrums, sir," explained the spare-framed Mr. Thorne laconically.

"So there is a specific name for the phenomenon," surmised Simpson.

Mr. Thorne merely gazed at the man as if unable to fathom why anyone would wish to waste energy to pursue the question, or any other question, under such sultry conditions.

"An area avoided by the wind," explained Weatherby, a young man having many interests and always ready to share his varied knowledge. "Usually in the middle of a circular system, like here in the mid-Atlantic. Mr. Thorne's chart shows us to be at the edge of such an area, called the Sargasso Sea. If you look out there, Mr. Simpson, you will see some extensive patches of kelp, or seaweed—"

"Couldn't we have avoided it, then?" asked Simpson, appearing irritated by Weatherby's detailed explanation.

"Difficult to tell when it's going to happen, or exactly where it's going to be at any given time," put forth Mr. Saddler, just finishing his morning inspection. As first lieutenant, he was always making an effort to come up better than Mr. Weatherby, a never-ending and mostly unprofitable undertaking.

Kinkaid had overheard the conversation and, detecting the frustration in Mr. Simpson's question, felt the need to respond with an explanation of his own. "We might have kept closer to American shores, Mr. Simpson…good, steady winds there you can rely on, mostly. But that's where the British are patrolling. Even had we been able to evade their ships, the route, being out of our way, would have delayed us as well. I thought to chance a straight run, a good notion this time of year, I believe. These doldrums usually occur later in the year."

"But how long will this last? I mean we can't stay out here in the middle of nowhere all day."

The men on the quarterdeck looked askance at the clearly agitated Mr. Simpson when he made the remark, Thorne raising his eyebrows.

"All day, sir?" said Kinkaid with a bemused smile. "This could last a number of days. Even a week or more would not be out of the ordinary."

"A week or more?" exclaimed Simpson, clearly distressed. "Well, this simply cannot be. You have to do something, Captain."

"Do something?"

"We cannot afford to drift idly about while the world is at war. Don't you understand, Captain? Each day that goes by without trade between our country and St. Eustatia means the loss of countless tons of precious war material, supplies that keep armies in the field, ships such as your own at sea. My mission is most urgent, Captain; there must be no delay."

Kinkaid thought for a moment. The wind was still nonexistent, and he knew it was unlikely to pick up as evening fell. There was only one course of action open to him if he were to take Mr.

Simpson's urgings seriously. And the man was certainly to be taken seriously, his argument well made and valid.

"O'Toole, let's have both boats over the side and fully manned. We'll tow the ship from here, due south, into the nearest wind. Rig lines from the foremast through the anchor ports. Mr. Saddler, make a schedule so that the men are relieved every hour, and ensure they are provided with adequate water." At least it would be something; better than waiting, though it was going to consume large quantities of their water and likely wear the men out.

"Aye aye, sir," came the responses and the movement to action.

The two boats were soon put out—lines running from the forward deck through the anchor ports on either side and thirty yards over the still ocean to each boat—and the oarsmen bent vigorously enough to their task under the hot sun. Kinkaid watched the weak wake trailing behind them over the glass-smooth surface of the sea. Saddler was in one of the boats and made sure the men kept at it, not hesitating to point out when he thought a man was not giving his best effort. He also had to ensure that they kept rowing in the proper direction, for it was hard work just keeping both boats pointed straight ahead. At every stroke, the boats would pull against their dead weight, lifting the tow cable out of the water for a moment, and then turn slightly one way or the other, the cable relaxing back into the sea before the next stroke, which lifted the cable once again, its length dripping water. Then there was the effort required to remove the pods of drifting kelp that periodically blocked the path of the boats.

The rowing continued on throughout the day and into the night, each sweat-soaked crew being relieved after the stipulated hour, the spent crews returning thirsty and exhausted. Saddler finally had Mr. Lofton relieve him in the evening, and then Mr. Cutler took over for the midwatch.

Kinkaid came out on deck that night, finding it too hot to sleep below. With all fires extinguished because of the heat, he'd had Roach make him a sandwich since he had skipped dinner, it being too hot even to eat. Now, with his appetite returning with evening, he was munching the sandwich on the quarterdeck, under a clear, star-filled sky, when Mr. Simpson joined him.

"It's marvelous...the effort your men are making, Captain," ventured Simpson, leaning against the stern rail, feeling some need to acknowledge their labors since it was at his urging that the men toiled so.

"They're good men," acknowledged Kinkaid, his mouth full.

"Yes, they are," agreed Simpson. "I just wanted to express my gratitude and hope that they understand how important— "

"They are simply doing their duty, Mr. Simpson," explained Kinkaid. To his mind, the men did what they were told. There was no other way to run a ship. The men didn't expect gratitude, and he doubted whether they cared to "understand" the importance of their duties.

"And their duty is whatever you decide it is," replied Simpson.

Kinkaid turned his head at the curious statement and offered, "It's simply the way things are out here, Mr. Simpson," as he gazed out onto the dark ocean, the moon perfectly reflecting off the still water, the stars blinking up from below as if the ship were held suspended in the middle of the universe.

"The way it must be," added Simpson.

"Well, yes, until a better system proves itself," affirmed Kinkaid. "Out here, away from man's laws, a ship must be a law unto herself."

"Those laws embodied in her captain."

"I would hope so," noted Kinkaid, taking the last bite of his sandwich, a recipe that even Roach could not abuse.

"I see that it is because of the dreaded idea of someone else taking charge—"

"You mean a mutiny," offered Kinkaid, Simpson seemingly reluctant to say the word.

"Yes...mutiny, that makes the rule so strong, the reason why a captain's word is law. The idea that, since we are far from the conventions of civilization, and with conditions likely to change at any moment and men being as they are, such a policy is the only reasonable way to ensure rule of law."

"I believe you have stated it quite well, Mr. Simpson."

"Yes, well...the idea is a good one when her captain is a fair and decent man. Like yourself, Captain."

"Thank you, but I don't believe I quite understand—"

"What would happen, I wonder, if a ship full of men went to sea without a captain, without any one person in command?" asked Simpson.

"A curious idea, Mr. Simpson," observed Kinkaid, puzzled by the question yet willing to ponder the possibility.

"Let me assure you, Captain, that I ask it purely out of curiosity."

"Then you are not thinking of throwing me over the side," deduced Kinkaid, trying to keep a straight face.

"Even if I were strong enough to toss you over the side, you would be able to swim back to the ship easily enough, at the speed we're moving," laughed Simpson.

"Then I should worry once we are under weigh again?"

"I'm sure you could swim back to Boston. Probably arrive with a terrible cold, however."

"Maybe not...if I had a plank to keep me afloat and drifted with the Gulf Stream."

"The what?"

"The Gulf Stream. A warm current of water that moves up from the Gulf of Mexico, right up the east coast."

"Did we pass through it?" asked Simpson.

"Practically followed it most of the way down here...until two days ago. Did you notice the steam rising during the night?"

"Yes, now that you remind me."

"Like a warm bath from the second day out."

"You are always aware of the state of things around you, I've noticed," observed Simpson, adding, "You might be interested to know that Benjamin Franklin happens to take an interest in sea temperatures."

"I remember that being mentioned in an article I was reading about his ideas for watertight bulkheads in ships," recalled Kinkaid.

"A man of boundless energy and curiosity, to be sure," said Simpson in admiration. "I don't know how many languages he speaks."

"You know the man personally, then," surmised Kinkaid.

"We've shared many a stimulating conversation, and I've sorely missed having dinner with him since he left for France. Not only is he our most able diplomat, but he somehow finds the time to pursue science and write and invent, as well. But as I was saying about ocean temperatures, he showed me a number of thermometers that he took with him aboard the packet when he left for France. Said he was going to keep a careful record of the temperature of the ocean from our coast to the shores of Europe to prove his theory of ocean currents. I'm sure Mr. Franklin would be interested in hearing your own theories on the subject. It seems you are able to know the temperature by sight, Kinkaid."

"Purely an occupational hazard. I can't claim to have formed any theories on the subject. But what is your theory concerning this question of a ship with no captain?" asked Kinkaid, his curiosity still aroused by the idea.

"I was merely thinking of a ship as a smaller version of a country or even the world at large. I suppose, given time, one man would emerge as the leader, dominating the others either through sheer physical power or possessing some force of character that the others would naturally tend to admire or respect."

"Is that the way men become leaders in the world?"

"Often, yes. But if we are talking about ships' captains, then you know as well as I that they are often chosen not for any special talents or abilities, at least in the Continental Navy, but more often by their power to influence members of Congress…which, now that I think of it, is how we will most likely elect our own country's leaders in the future."

"Just as I have been chosen to command this vessel," observed Kinkaid, aware that there were at least a dozen or more captains with more seniority and experience at sea than he. He was out here primarily because Mr. Simpson had requested him, probably because he thought he possessed some superior talents or abilities.

"Hopefully, fate would always decree that the best man will also be the luckiest, though sad to say such is seldom the case."

"I would have to agree with that, Mr. Simpson," allowed Kinkaid with a knowing smile. "Given the vagaries of fate, the wise man is as likely to stumble into a pile of cow dung as the fool."

"I suppose it is because of the existence of the dung of this world that we recognize luck for what it is. Of course, the fool has the advantage of not recognizing the dung, avoiding the unnecessary embarrassment, perhaps even baking a row of pies from the discovery."

"Then his embarrassment only comes later…and at a greater price," added Kinkaid, not to be left in the dust of a quicker wit than his own.

Recognizing one another's contributions to their shared nonsense, Simpson laughed and said, "A most sage observation of the human condition; however, this human is about out of discourse and philosophy at this time of the night. Hot as it is, I believe I will try to capture some wisdom in my dreams…so I will bid you goodnight, Captain."

"And a good night to you, sir."

Morning came and Mr. Saddler took his place once more in one of the boats. The men still toiled diligently, and there remained not a ripple on the surface or a puff of breeze on a sail. After dinner, Saddler had Mr. Briggs relieve him while he went to eat, but not before warning Briggs to make sure the men did not slack off, in spite of the unrelenting heat. Even then, Mr. Saddler went below only for a moment to gulp a bite, then soon came back up to watch the progress from the forecastle, seeming not to trust Mr. Briggs to the task of pushing the men.

"Hot, hard work," observed O'Toole toward two in the afternoon, after insisting that he take his turn as an example to the men. He was mopping his brow, a few stray gray hairs plastered to his forehead. Though many of the men were suffering from bad sunburns, they were still giving their best, only a few complaints so far, but even those were of good nature.

"When is it the officers' turn, did you say, Boats?" joked the big Treadwell, his voice carrying easily to the quarterdeck over the dead calm.

"On the third Sunday in April, after services…but only in a leap year," ventured the boatswain's mate, Rikker.

"I say we go fishin' and catch ourselves one of those big whales, put a harness on him and make him pull us to the islands," suggested Tripp, the other half of the Travelin' Brothers.

"Aye, the islands," came in Rafferty, taking up the idea, "where rum flows like water and the women run naked."

"Yeah, Jake, they may be naked," returned Rikker, "but when they see your ugly face they're gonna be runnin' all right…for the hills in fright."

"They may not like my ugly face, I'll grant ye that," admitted Rafferty through the laughter, "but when I shed my clothes, they'll surely come a runnin'," he bragged, and the men laughed again, this time too heartily for the ponderous and duty-filled Mr. Saddler.

"Silence on those boats!" shouted Saddler to the men from the deck. Briggs made the mistake of smiling at the rebuke and drew one himself. "Mr. Briggs, if you are unable to stop this insolent behavior then perhaps you will have to take a turn at the oars yourself!" Just when Kinkaid was beginning to enjoy the banter.

The men kept at it into the evening, inspired by a few songs led by Boatswain O'Toole—Saddler at least not considering those insolent—then again throughout the night, their strokes slowing in spite of Mr. Lofton's exhortations, a midshipman resolved to following the pattern of duty almost as rigidly as Mr. Saddler.

By morning each watch in turn sat hunched tiredly on their hard seats. They kept doggedly at it as the sun rose high in the sky, then past the noon hour, and now it was almost one o'clock in the afternoon and the hottest part of the day. The men were quiet, out of jokes, out of songs, just barely keeping the oars dipping, though they were still moving steadily, and the ship still made a wake, no matter how weak. Saddler again commenced to stir the men to more vigorous action until Kinkaid approached him on the quarterdeck.

"Mr. Saddler."

"Sir?" the man turned abruptly, not realizing Kinkaid had approached him, so intent was his concentration on the men.

"I appreciate your efforts at keeping them at their job," began Kinkaid with the compliment, appropriate enough.

"Thank you, sir," answered Saddler, and thinking the conversation over, turned back as if to say something encouraging to the men once more, to get them to move the oars with a bit more energy, have them dig a bit deeper into the still pond, to show his captain that he was, indeed, keeping them at their job.

"Yes, well, I think they've done magnificently," continued Kinkaid, more to distract Saddler from saying anything more to the men than to compliment them, though in truth they had physically borne the burden.

"Aye, I'd agree, sir," affirmed Saddler, as if in accepting the compliment he were accepting it for himself, since the men could only have done magnificently, in his mind at least, by making them do so with his unflagging vigilance.

"Yes, very good then, let's stand them down, now...for an hour. We'll have a nice swim, a half hour for each watch, then we'll begin towing the ship again," said Kinkaid, finally reaching the point that he wanted to make, and almost immediately realizing that his statement still came too abruptly for the unrelenting and single-minded Mr. Saddler.

"Pardon, sir? A swim?" He turned to look at his captain, as if not comprehending what he had said.

"Yes, it's the hottest part of the day. I'm sure a good swim will serve to refresh the men, wash away the sweat." It seemed ridiculous trying to explain the simple concept of taking a swim in the terrible heat, yet Mr. Saddler seemed to require one.

"What about sharks, sir?"

"Mr. Saddler, swimming in the ocean is merely a suggestion, not an order," Kinkaid explained tiredly. "Those men who choose to swim may be permitted to do so. Those choosing not to swim may rest or fill their free time as they may. I, for one, intend to take a swim. If you are worried about sharks, then have some of the marines on deck with their muskets."

"Yes, sir, I'll do that, sir," said Saddler.

"Secure the rowing!" shouted Kinkaid to the men in the boats.

With that, knowing that an example would have to be set, Kinkaid stripped off his shirt and shoes, then his pants. Naked, he opened the starboard side rail and jumped into the ocean, surprising Saddler and everyone on deck, including the men in the boats who were only now hesitantly bringing their oars in.

The water was as cool and refreshing as it looked. He rolled on his back, looking up at the ship and the many heads turned his way. Saddler was hurriedly getting some of Bauer's marines out, fearful of losing him to sharks. It was a good feeling, Mr. Saddler worried about his captain, thought Kinkaid, smiling. He could see Mr. Simpson standing up from his piece of shade behind the mainmast shrouds, an amused look on his face; even the aloof Indian, Monk Chunk, looked up with apparent interest.

"Well, is anyone going to join me for an afternoon swim?" Kinkaid said loudly to the foolish looks.

A barefoot Smith was sitting on the starboard bulwark, a length of small stuff in his hands with which he had been practicing knot tying. He was showing off his expertise to the marine drummer, Private Kirkpatrick, who took an eager and active interest in anything having to do with how the ship was run. Smith, seeing that his captain was swimming in the ocean and calling for others to join him, handed his line to the young marine private, stood up on the rail, leaned his body to the side and slipped gracefully into the blue-green sea with nary a splash, clothes and all, leaving a startled look on young Kirkpatrick's face and drawing peals of laughter from the waisters. Not to be outdone, the sweating men in the boats quickly stripped off their clothes and jumped in with loud shouts and big splashes, followed by Weatherby and Cutler. Mr. Briggs would have joined them but for the fact that he had the quarterdeck watch.

Threatened with the possibility of the entire crew jumping overboard, First Lieutenant Saddler scrambled to picked up the captain's speaking trumpet and announced, "Starboard watch only! Larboard watch in thirty minutes!"

"C'mon Kirkpatrick! C'mon in!" shouted Weatherby in encouragement to the young marine drummer.

"Yeah, c'mon Jimmy! The water is supremious!" added Cutler, employing his latest invented word.

Thus encouraged and excited by the two boys, Kirkpatrick threw away all caution and leaped in between the two, promptly disappearing beneath the surface. He finally came up, thrashing, choking, and desperately flailing his arms.

Weatherby and Cutler came to Kirkpatrick's aid and held his head above water as he coughed and churned the surface until he found a grip along the ship's ladder.

"What's the matter?" asked Cutler.

"I forgot I couldn't swim," admitted Kirkpatrick, still choking and sputtering water.

Within five minutes, all those of the starboard watch that could swim were splashing in the water alongside the ship. A few non-swimmers had even tossed spars and empty barrels over the side to hang on to while four of Bauer's marines stood by with loaded muskets in case of sharks. And they eventually took their turn when O'Toole rigged a line from a mainmast spar so the men could go swinging out over the water before dropping into the cool blue ocean. An adventurous Corporal Decker was the first to try the device, his heavy body landing next to Cutler, sending up a tremendous splash and a big wave that rolled over Cutler's head.

"Wondiferous!" shouted Weatherby as he came flying through the air next, landing with a smaller splash beside Cutler.

Major Bauer came in too, as an example to his marines. Corporal Stockton and Bentkowski took their turn as well, though Sergeant Anders was not to be seen on the deck.

The thoughtful Lofton had been watching the antics of the crew for some time when finally came the larboard watch's turn, and not being able to wait any longer, he went to the side ladder and calmly lowered himself into the cool sea. Although he never became very playful, preferring to bask quietly on his back, he at least seemed to enjoy the cool water while retaining that ever-grave look on his face.

The Indian was last in and proved not only a graceful swimmer, but was remarkably fast as he thrashed the water with long strokes of his arms while he kicked with his feet, the sight drawing incredulous stares from the others.

The stiff Mr. Saddler and the dignified Mr. Simpson remained standing on the deck, fully clothed, sweat pouring off their faces, somberly watching the men as they splashed and played in the water.

If it was sharks that kept them out, their apprehensions were in vain, for no sharks appeared. There was a scare for a moment as a series of fins broke the water, but it turned out to be a school of friendly dolphins. They came up beside the men, even allowing themselves to be touched. Some of the men took to diving beneath the surface, playfully acting like dolphins themselves, while the smooth, intelligent creatures with perpetual smiles cruised gracefully around them. Even the staid Mr. Lofton allowed himself a moment of awe and wonder at the beautiful and gentle creatures who seemed to enjoy the company of humans, a crooked smile turning up the corners of his mouth, the first smile Kinkaid had ever witnessed from the droll young man.

An hour or so later the sun had fallen a little from the sky, the air just a degree or two cooler. The men were back in the boats and rowing with some increased vigor, talking and joking quietly once more, their smiles and renewed energy showing that the swim had been invigorating and, therefore, worthwhile.

O'Toole, returning aboard after his stint at the oars, strode up to the mainmast, took out his pocketknife and stuck it forcefully into the mast. He spoke quietly with Rafferty for a moment, and then turned for the forecastle, leaving his knife buried in the mast.

Simpson had witnessed the peculiar act and, concluding that O'Toole must have forgotten his knife, decided after a few moments to retrieve it for the crusty boatswain, but was halted by Kinkaid with the explanation, "It's to coax up a wind, Mr. Simpson. An old sailor's superstition."

Their rowing was interrupted only briefly that afternoon when a sea turtle was sighted and, with Mr. Saddler belowdecks, a bored and weary Rafferty spontaneously decided to cast off his boat's towline and give chase, ignoring Mr. Cutler's not very convincing pleas to refrain from the action. Rafferty, having instigated the chase, suggested to Cutler that, "The officers might look forward to a sea turtle stew," the argument effectively putting off Cutler's mild protests to the contrary. It was a foolish thing to do, a complete waste of time and energy, for they never came close to catching the animal, becoming fouled in a large mass of kelp instead, which the turtle made for before diving below.

Mr. Saddler was back up on deck as the boat was returning to its position and began shouting at Mr. Cutler for allowing the transgression, his emphatic threats carrying to where Kinkaid was having a less-than-satisfactory supper. Saddler wanted the men arrested, including Mr. Cutler and especially Rafferty. When Cutler offered the poor excuse that, "Rafferty thought a sea turtle soup would be welcomed in the wardroom, Captain," Kinkaid felt that the incident was not so much an act of blatant insubordination as it was merely evidence of the giddiness that fatigue could bring about, and so played the matter down as best he could. Mr.

Saddler's expression could not hide the fact that he was disappointed in his captain's decision to let the incident go. The men returned to their position in front of the ship and once again took up their oars and continued their monotonous task of pulling the ship over the still waters, into the evening and, once more, all through that night. And the night was a torture.

Kinkaid turned in that evening only to find his closet-like cabin fouler and hotter than the night before, when he had slept little, tossing fitfully on the lumpy chaff mattress. Now here he was once again, sweat dripping from his body, barely able to breathe the rank air, an odorous mixture of body sweat, rotting bilges, and decaying food. He lay there for perhaps five restless minutes, his skin prickling from the heat, before deciding to haul his mattress out onto the quarterdeck. Other sailors had done the same and the gun deck was cluttered with prone bodies, but the quarterdeck, as if sacred, still provided ample room. As he lay down, the sky full of bright stars above him, the night air cool on his sweaty skin, he almost said aloud the word that the sailors had been bandying about recently. "Splendiferous!" he thought to himself.

In the morning, two boats were still in front of the ship, twenty oars still dipping into the calm sea, an untiring Mr. Saddler still encouraging the men at their thankless task, though even his efforts were becoming half-hearted.

Kinkaid was standing in the shade of the mainsail after a barely palatable breakfast of ham and eggs swimming in a pool of grease. Feeling irritable from the heat and lack of sleep, he had sworn at Roach, who merely hunched his shoulders at the remark and slinked away. Now Kinkaid was watching the group of dolphins playing astern. He had a bucket next to him and was dipping a cup into it and pouring it over his head, neck, and arms. That's when he felt it, the first sign a chill on his bare arms. They were wet and sweaty, and at first he thought they felt cool from the water. But there it was again; this time goose bumps rose on his forearm. Then the boom creaked. Just once. He looked out over the water to where he had spotted the dolphins and saw tiny ripples on the surface. The ripples came toward the ship and as they did, a breeze shook the sails, only slightly…but there it came once again, another puff.

"Mr. Saddler, bring the men in. O'Toole, haul in the tow cable; secure the boats."

"Be a pleasure, Captain," answered O'Toole happily as he yanked his pocketknife out of the mast where he had left it. Then he folded it smugly and returned it to his pocket, convinced that his act had brought the wind.

"Have the hands aloft, Mr. Cutler. Stand by those lines."

"Aye aye, sir."

By the time the ship's boats were secured, *Swift* was moving once more, slowly and fitfully at first, but under her own power at last, with all sails set. Kinkaid stood on the quarterdeck, the cool breeze blowing on his face, the happy gurgling sound of a ship under weigh as the ship and sea came to life as one. Only moments before, the sun had been something to avoid, regarded as an enemy, sucking life and energy out of the crew. Now that very same sun shone happily upon the ship, playfully throwing shadows of mast and rigging across her decks, where men were smiling and joking once again.

By noon a fair and steady breeze was blowing, the sails were filled, and *Swift* was once more riding the whitecaps as the school of dolphins rode the bow wave. Weatherby and Cutler were hanging over the bowsprit, watching the animals in awe and fascination as they leapt and cavorted. They invited the young Kirkpatrick to have a look, and he crouched on the spar between them—three laughing boys, Weatherby, Cutler, and Kirkpatrick, momentarily forgetful of the distinction between young gentlemen and marine drummer boy.

The trade winds remained steady out of the northeast for the next three days, and *Swift* made good use of them, continually heading due south. On the fourth day after the calm, Kinkaid thought he saw a flight of pelicans some distance off the port beam and recalled that pelicans rarely strayed far from land.

Mr. Simpson had mostly recovered from his seasickness since the calm. During the first two weeks at sea, Kinkaid had scarcely seen the man, Simpson rarely coming out on deck, but since the day of the swim the two had been regularly taking their dinner together. Some of those dinners provided strange and varied conversations of the kind that Kinkaid was most unaccustomed to.

"So, Mr. Kinkaid, how is it that you came to the sea as a profession if the people who raised you ran a farm?" asked Simpson, busy separating a forkful of sweet potato from its charred skin after finding the tough beef boiled flavorless.

"I think it was more running away than any decision to pursue one career over another," responded Kinkaid, somewhat surprised at his own answer. Simpson had a way of making him say things that he had never told anyone else, not even Elizabeth. "I was attending school in Philadelphia and sometimes during breaks would find myself down by the docks, watching the ships. They seemed so…majestic." Kinkaid stopped as if embarrassed by his words.

"Please, go on, Captain," encouraged Simpson.

"Well…a ship's hull, the way it curves, has a certain grace and beauty…and with its masts and confusion of lines and rigging, its sails billowing out, taking power from the wind…I don't know, at times it seems almost magical."

"You sound like a poet when you talk of ships, Captain," smiled Simpson. "I find it interesting how people are led into one line of endeavor or another. I'm coming to believe that men are born into what they will later become, that there is very little leeway for outside influences to change what, in essence, a man is."

"You believe in predestination, then?" asked Kinkaid, intrigued by such ideas.

"Not exactly. I do think that men are born with a certain basic disposition that remains with them, but at the same time there are always outside influences at work that offer a choice as to how a man will react to those influences. And because of that, I believe that men have the power to change the world as they know it—individual men, as well as groups of men acting in concert. In the age of kings, it was always the man at the top who would decide the course, but in the future I believe it will be a society of men who will decide what road a nation takes. I find it immensely exciting that more men are finding such ideas intriguing."

"But will a group of men always decide better than a single man?"

"Ha, good point, Captain. No, I'm not that naive. But at least men can argue among themselves, persuading one another of the correct course."

"Yes, I would think a single man is too easily led by narrow considerations."

"Precisely," added Simpson. "Too often pertaining only to his own welfare."

"Do you believe most men think only of themselves?"

"Look no further than yourself for the answer to that question, Captain. Do you not consider the welfare of your men, even if only for the sake of running an efficient war machine? And what about the case of the mother who runs out to shield her child from danger? Or the soldier who takes a bullet, saving a friend's life? I would like to think that most of us are capable of thinking of the other, sometimes even putting the other first."

Kinkaid thought of what Simpson had said. "You seem to live in a world of ideas, Mr. Simpson. Only a man with the luxury of leisure is able to live in such a world. Most of us cannot afford to think too largely."

Simpson looked up, nodding, "True, most men generally don't have the time to think about certain things, even setting aside the larger issues of philosophy—too busy putting food on the table for their families. And some men get into a lot of trouble when they start thinking too much."

"I have noticed that powerful men tend to worry when good working men think."

"That can certainly be dangerous," agreed Simpson. "Yes, it seems that the powerful are the most threatened by new ideas. Intelligent men, well spoken, loving of their families, but without imagination. Men who are not interested in anything different than what they already know; fearful, even, of anything new, creative, or innovative."

"You mean Tories?" asked Kinkaid.

"One might call them Tories in our country, I suppose, but they have always been with us, in one name or another, since the beginning of time. Conservative types…concerned mostly with keeping what they have, even at the expense of others or at the expense of anything that might interfere with business as usual. Quite intolerant—selfish, believing they know what is good for all simply because it is good for them, capable of the most outrageous partisan intrigues."

"A diplomat, I suppose, might find such types quite irritating."

Simpson laughed. "It comes as an occupational hazard to deal with highly opinionated men, Captain, but I see my work as a great challenge. In fact, I believe I have a gift of sorts. 'Blessed is the man who finds his gift,' is how my father used to put it. I like to think that my gift is to bring order out of chaos, agreement out of misunderstanding, peace out of strife."

"And how do you do that?"

"With words, sir, simply with words. You see, words are quite powerful; that is something I learned early on, something I paid attention to, exactly as you pay attention to the set of your sails or the morale of the men. There, you see what I mean—for each of us, a natural bent leads us to different vocations."

"But I don't see how merely words—"

"The words have to be true, first of all. Words bereft of truth have no soul, no ring to them. But in their proper use, an atmosphere is created, as an artist painting a masterpiece or a composer writing a symphony…one is creating a vision, a cooperative, inclusive mood, all with the use of words instead of paint on a canvas or notes on an instrument."

"Isn't that manipulative, forcing one's viewpoint upon another?"

"I think of it as using the power of benevolent influence to create an atmosphere in which parties are willing to listen to the others' point of view, to point out the benefits of compromise and cooperation. All life influences its surroundings while it reacts to them, whether it be over food or a mate or territory, or a clash of wills among men or nations."

"Even a tree struggles to gain light over its neighbors."

"Precisely. And, like the tree, I prefer to use the subtle approach. When that fails, armies and navies are called in."

"As a warship is designed to force its viewpoint with the might of its cannon."

"There you have it. And though it is sometimes necessary to use brute force, I look upon its use as the failure of diplomacy."

"Might does not make right."

"Of course not. Do not forget that, ultimately, it is the value of the ideas behind the force you wield that determines right or wrong. The greatest force in the world is worse than useless if it has the wrong idea."

"But who is to say which idea is right or wrong?"

"Well, that is why men must argue reasonably."

"And that is why there are diplomats."

Simpson laughed. "Your insight astounds me, Captain."

There was a knock at the door.

"Come," said Kinkaid.

It was the serious Mr. Lofton. "Lookout reports land off the larboard beam, Captain."

"Very well, Mr. Lofton. Please inform Mr. Thorne as well. Have the watch call me when it is three miles off, unless sails are spotted first."

"Aye aye, sir," said the midshipman before scrambling back up the ladder to the quarterdeck.

Kinkaid resisted the impulse to rush up on the deck at the news. He did not wish to appear overly excited at the sight of land. A captain must show some decorum, some confidence in his navigational abilities. Besides, the land would not go away, and nothing could change which island it was; even three miles off might not be close enough to positively identify it.

Kinkaid's chart showed that they were most likely off the eastern shores of Puerto Rico, but he would wait for the sailing master, Mr. Thorne, to confirm how accurate his navigational calculations were and hope his estimated position was not ridiculously off. There was also the chance of the crew perhaps losing some faith in a captain who could not keep track of where the ship was.

Though somewhat distracted from the conversation, Kinkaid sat with Mr. Simpson for another half hour before excusing himself and returning to his own tiny cabin. He needn't look at his chart; he knew exactly where he had placed them, and in a few moments Mr. Thorne would verify their actual landfall. He thought back over the last twenty-three days and tried to determine if there might have been some conditions that he had overlooked—perhaps the currents were not as strong or the winds were too favorably estimated—but he could not, in all honesty, think of any factor that could throw his calculations very far off course. For most of the journey, he had headed the ship due south, taking into account the steady trade winds from the northeast and the currents heading up the east coast.

There came a knock.

"Yes?"

It was the scrawny Lofton again, reporting from the quarterdeck. "Ship on the western horizon, sir."

"Very well," said Kinkaid, "I'll be right up, Mr. Lofton."

"Aye, sir," said Lofton, then pointed aft. "I'll…inform Mr. Simpson as well, Captain."

"Did Mr. Simpson ask you to inform him if we spotted a ship?" asked Kinkaid, not at all sure what was bothering him.

"Uh...no, sir. Mr. Simpson did, however, specifically ask the quarterdeck watch if we would inform him the moment you were called out on deck, sir," said Lofton nervously.

"And why wasn't I informed of this?" asked Kinkaid, irked enough that his quarterdeck watch was being employed by a passenger, even Mr. Simpson, but doubly peeved that his officers had not apprised him of the fact.

"Well...sir, Mr. Simpson suggested that—"

"Mr. Simpson suggested that I not be informed about something that has to do with the running of this ship?" Kinkaid's anger flared abruptly at the thought of it.

"Not exactly, sir..." Lofton looked terribly distressed at the moment.

"Very well, Mr. Lofton," said Kinkaid, knowing it would do no good to grill the flustered midshipman any more than he already had. He did, however, hope that Mr. Lofton got the point. "Is Mr. Thorne topside?"

"Yes, sir," answered Lofton, then blurted out with an effeminate wave of his hand, "He says your navigation is astonishing, sir...put us no more than a couple of ship lengths off. Fine work, Captain."

It was uncharacteristic of Mr. Lofton to become so excited, thought Kinkaid. Even so, Kinkaid could hardly believe his ears, and almost let out a sigh of relief.

"Thank you, Mr. Lofton," he said calmly, as if unconcerned with what anybody thought of his navigational abilities. "You may report to the quarterdeck that the Captain will be up directly."

"Aye aye, sir," answered Lofton brightly, and then turned to go. "Oops! Sorry Mr. Simpson, sir, didn't see you there!"

How long had Mr. Simpson been standing outside the door?

"You seem to be one of those blessed men, Captain," said Simpson reflectively, "for you have evidently found your gift."

"And you yours, good sir," said Kinkaid, a frown on his face. Having berated Midshipman Lofton for not informing him about Mr. Simpson's request, he was now forced to remind the diplomat,

"In the future you will kindly inform me first if you wish to give any orders to my crew."

"You are, of course, correct," answered Mr. Simpson, showing a serious face. "Terribly sorry, Captain." Both knew the conversation was little more than a formality; both held back a knowing smile. Then Simpson pointed to Kinkaid's telescope resting in its cradle on the wall and asked, "May I, Captain?"

"Of course. Bring it along."

Though it was late afternoon, the sun still shone brightly, and both men squinted from the glare off the ocean as they came up on deck.

The first lieutenant was looking up, watching an intrepid Midshipman Cutler as he climbed the shrouds of the foremast peak, his curly locks blowing in the wind, the strap of a telescope looped over his neck, the heavy instrument dangling at his waist. Weatherby was just below him, standing on the starboard bow rail, one hand in the shrouds, the other shielding his eyes from the glare, gazing toward the distant ship. Midshipman Lofton and Mr. Thorne were on the quarterdeck and Rafferty was at the wheel.

"Why does Rafferty have helmsman duties?" asked Kinkaid loudly enough to be heard by all, taking his place on the windward side of the quarterdeck. Mr. Simpson was looking at the distant ship through the telescope.

"He volunteered for it, sir. Traded places with McKinley," offered Mr. Saddler.

"First Smith and now Rafferty. Is there no one on this ship that is satisfied with his duties?" asked Kinkaid and instantly regretted the question. Of course none dared answer, and Kinkaid had not expected an answer, but now the question hung in the air, and Kinkaid realized that he had made everyone uncomfortable, especially Rafferty, standing stiffly at the wheel.

"Do you enjoy driving the ship, Rafferty?" he asked the man.

"Very much, thank you, sir," replied Rafferty, bowing slightly.

"Carry on, then."

"Thank you, sir."

He had to ask the question that everyone was waiting for: "Now then, where are we?"

Mr. Thorne had been waiting anxiously and exclaimed, "Captain, I have to give it to you. Right on the penny," he said in admiration. "That landmass off the starboard bow is Puerto Rico, and right there in front of us, under that big cloud there, just like you—"

"Culebra."

"Aye. Culebra, Captain."

"What is that ship there?" asked Kinkaid, diverting successfully and happily from the topic of navigation. There was, of course, immense satisfaction in knowing that his navigation had been so accurate. It would soon get around the ship that the Captain had brought them to exactly the point he intended over a distance of more than fifteen hundred miles—and there was some satisfaction in acting as though it was something that concerned him little.

"Cutler is just in the top now, sir," reported Lofton.

Kinkaid looked up to see Cutler sitting on the royal foremast yard, his arms wrapped around the very top of the mast, the wind blowing at his hair and shirt, the telescope up to his eye. Kinkaid had to admire the boy's courage; he doubted that he could have climbed up there as fast and was thankful that he would not have to find out. No use in hailing him; if Cutler had anything to report, he would report it.

Weatherby was coming from forward and said, "She looks to be an old Spanish galleon, sir."

"She's Spanish!" came Cutler's shout a moment later.

That Weatherby, eyes like an eagle.

"We'll follow her, Mr. Lofton," said Kinkaid. "Rafferty, bring us a point to starboard."

"Aye aye, sir."

It was not long before her full hull could be seen. High and stately, she was built like a castle upon the sea, once a fortress of firepower that proclaimed the might and glory of a vast Spanish empire.

Simpson had the telescope braced through the ratlines and asked, "Do you think she's a pirate ship, Captain?"

"Not likely," answered Kinkaid. "I'd guess she's carrying sugar and silks, not cannons."

"How can you tell that from here?" asked Simpson, handing Kinkaid the telescope.

"I don't need a telescope to tell me that pirates value speed and maneuvering in their ships," answered Kinkaid, taking the telescope from Simpson and having a look. The old galleon's rows of gun ports had been boarded up, but her sides still had the checkerboard look of gun ports, meant to frighten would-be attackers. Her sails were stained and patched, and even from this distance he could see that her hull was fouled with algae and barnacles. She was coming down the coast of Puerto Rico on her slow way down the island chain; it would be better yet for them if she was going around the island.

"Why are we going to follow her, Captain?" asked Mr. Simpson.

Mr. Lofton stiffened at the question. To his mind, no one would ever ask the captain of a ship to explain an order. Mr. Weatherby and Mr. Lofton gave one another a quick glance.

"Why, just look at her," said Kinkaid, "the way she sails with confidence, closely along the shore there. She may be old and slow, but that Spanish trader knows ever reef and current, every safe passage between these islands."

"Of course," realized Simpson. "She'll show us the way."

The sun was low in the western sky by the time they had taken their station astern of her. Some of her officers and crew could be seen watching curiously from her high quarterdeck as the *Swift* luffed her topsails to keep from overtaking the tattered and sleepy merchant that dragged a carpet of green algae behind her. The name painted on her stern in faded gold letters read *San Ignacio*. She headed straight for Culebra, then, to Kinkaid's satisfaction, turned abruptly south, through the passage between the two islands, toward Vieques, a dark smudge on the southern horizon. Just as he'd hoped.

The setting sun sent long shafts of light over the mountains of Puerto Rico, bouncing off the clouds, painting their undersides whiter than white against the dark-blue sky. In an hour, the blue of the sky had turned a majestic purple and a quarter moon rose off the port beam, making it easy to keep the crawling merchant in sight. Finally, just after the midwatch, she turned to starboard, continuing her journey around the big island. It was two in the morning, and as the ships steered clear of Vieques, Kinkaid ordered their new course.

"Steer us south by east, and a half east," he said tiredly to the helmsman, Treadwell. "I'm going below for a spell. Mr. Weatherby, ensure the next watch wakes me when we're in view of St. Croix."

They were now in the Caribbean Sea and after three more days of easy and uneventful sailing, the *USS Swift* found herself off the roadstead of the busiest and richest harbor in the world.

IV
Greetings…

"There she is, the Golden Rock," declared Simpson. His nose was peeling, but his ruddy color gave him a healthy glow. Both men stood at the rail that morning: Kinkaid in his new uniform, Simpson wearing a teal-blue suit. Simpson's ungainly trunk had already been hauled out of the hold.

It was always a thrill to enter a strange new port, and Kinkaid felt it today as he gazed out upon the limestone cliffs along St. Eustatia's northern shore. She was little more than a bump on the Caribbean Sea, or more precisely, a cone—and a beautiful cone at that, formed by an ancient volcano, her flanks wrapped in dark-green vegetation, the entire island ringed with white sand beaches and blue-green waters. Frothy breakers surged just offshore, warning of reefs where the water was turquoise blue and menthol green, colors calming to the eyes. Seagulls were wheeling and squawking overhead and pelicans dove from the sky with half-closed wings, their rocketing bodies gaining speed just before they plunged headfirst into the deep, sometimes coming up with fair-sized fishes in their long beaks, then jostling them down their gullets.

Looking over the side, Kinkaid could see a sandy bottom interspersed with reefs. The leadsman in the chains was reporting a depth of eight to ten fathoms, yet the reefs appeared to be passing directly under the keel, so crystal clear were the waters here.

Though they were still too far out to see the harbor itself, two ships could be seen leaving the roadstead, their crews hauling up mainsails as they cleared the breakwater. As *Swift* drew nearer, many masts could be seen towering above the line of land ahead, where pastel-colored houses dotted the hillsides. Soon a view of the harbor revealed a veritable forest of masts. There must have been thirty or more large merchant ships anchored in the roadstead, another dozen close to or right up next to the land. A few ships were lying careened on the beach, their hulls being scraped of seaweed and barnacles. Beyond the many hulls was the town of Orangestad, a haze hanging over the houses from breakfast fires. There was Fort Orange on the right, overlooking the harbor. The Dutch flag fluttered lazily from the flagpole, over parapets of gray stone.

"Bring us right, helmsman. We'll go around that ship anchored there," ordered Kinkaid as they entered the roadstead. "Mr. Saddler, prepare the ship to render honors to the flag of Holland. Mr. Weatherby, stand by for a thirteen-gun salute. Mr. Cutler, at the ensign."

With those orders the first lieutenant, with Mr. Simpson looking on expectantly, called out the crew, all in their best uniforms. Bauer and his marines were lining up on the port side to the sound of the drummer, facing inboard, the brass buttons on their jackets bright and shiny in the hazy morning sunshine. Weatherby's gun crews were an active contrast to the rigidity of the marine line as they prepared the charges on the starboard side.

"Guns are ready, sir!" hollered Weatherby in the waist.

"Stand by!" Kinkaid waited for almost two minutes, until they were abreast of the fort. Now he could make out the dark forms of men on the parapets without the telescope.

"One-second intervals, Mr. Weatherby!"

"Number-one gun, fire!"

As soon as the first gun fired, its crew scrambled to reload.

"Number-two gun, fire!"

At Weatherby's command, each gun in succession fired its wad, the echo of their booms resounding off the walls of the fort until, the final gun crashing out, Kinkaid gave the order, "Dip the ensign, Mr. Cutler."

After the squeaking of the pulley, there came only stillness and silence upon the deck of the *Swift* as every man waited in anticipation, intently watching the fort. Nothing. Men on deck turned their heads back and forth from the fort to the quarterdeck as Kinkaid stood rigidly waiting. One minute passed. There was no return salute of cannon, not even the acknowledgment of their dipped flag. Mr. Simpson stood solemnly at the rail throughout the exercise, and now he was fuming—the whole purpose of his coming was for recognition—their salute a humiliating waste of gunpowder. But he said nothing. There was nothing to be done except to carry on.

"Secure the guns, Mr. Weatherby."

The first gun boomed out from the fort, a flash and a puff of smoke high on the parapet, then another, and another. "Count them—that's three!" shouted Simpson, looking up excitedly, happily relieved. "How many do we get, Captain?"

"We should get thirteen in return."

The flash, then the puff, and then a second later the boom; nine, ten, eleven, silence. The flag on the parapet dipped. Cutler raised the ensign once more, answered by the flag on the fort doing the same. That was all, eleven. Two short of thirteen.

"All right," exclaimed Simpson, beaming with elation, "we'll accept eleven."

"Better than none at all, sir," observed Mr. Saddler.

"Secure from salute, make ready the anchor detail," ordered Kinkaid, back to business. "Helmsman, take us over there, behind that big schooner, the one with the red railing."

"Look, sir," observed Mr. Cutler excitedly, "those are American colors they're showing. And there too."

It was true; there must have been four or five American ships in the harbor, and since the official salute they were running up their colors in a show of recognition and support.

"It seems that our arrival has been anticipated," pronounced Simpson, grinning broadly.

They passed three merchant ships close by, all anchored, all swinging their sterns toward the town, their anchor lines angling into the sandy bottom. Men on those ships had come out onto their decks, curious to see the American warship. Kinkaid brought the *Swift* past the last schooner and then pointed her directly into the wind.

"Drop anchor and back the tops!" he ordered, and Rikker hammered the block holding the chain, sending the anchor careening noisily over the side, hitting the water with a loud splash, the heavy chain rattling afterward. As it settled to the bottom, the ship backed away, the wind pushing against the backed sails. The anchor line was then secured to a cleat so that the ship tugged against it with some force, digging the anchor into the sandy bottom. Then, as the sails were taken in, more of the heavy hawser was paid out and finally the cable secured. Now the *Swift* tugged gently against her own anchor line, her bow pointed in the same direction as all the other ships anchored in the bay, facing into the gentle breeze.

"Look, sir, a boat is putting out from shore," noticed Weatherby, pointing.

It was a small white pinnace with blue trim that had put up her sail and was heading directly for the ship. As she approached nearer, the red, white, and blue Dutch flag could be seen flying from her stern.

"Prepare for an official greeting," said Kinkaid, and the deck was suddenly a flurry of activity as side boys and officers took their places at the rail. Major Bauer once more had his marines in a double-row formation in the waist by the time the boat drew alongside.

There were five men in the boat: three sailors in blue-and-white-striped shirts with white duck pants and hats and two gentlemen wearing suits. The gentlemen stood in the waist; one was tall and fair, the other was short and dark and held what looked to be a bullwhip rolled in his hands. Drawing abreast, the sailor at the tiller gave orders and the other two released the halyard, setting the sail flapping free, and then passed securing lines to the waiting sailors on board *Swift*, who quickly made them fast alongside. O'Toole began his piping as the head of the tall gentleman in the beige suit came even with the deck.

Reaching the deck, he then turned to assist his stout companion up the ladder before announcing in English, "I am Mr. Vanderveer, personal aide to Governor Johannes de Graaff." The handsome, blue-eyed man spoke with the trace of an accent, bowed and extended his hand, his blond, wavy hair gleaming in the sunshine, his face darkly tanned. "In the name of the governor, allow me to welcome you to the fair island of St. Eustatia, gentlemen."

Kinkaid stepped forward and shook Mr. Vanderveer's hand, introducing himself as, "Captain Kinkaid of the American Navy brig-of-war *Swift*," and then turning, continued with his officers, "My first lieutenant, Mr. Saddler.

"A pleasure, Mr. Saddler," said Vanderveer, shaking hands and drawing an awkward bow from the stiff first lieutenant.

"My gunnery officer, Mr. Weatherby."

"Mr. Weatherby, you seem quite a young man to be shooting those big cannons."

Weatherby, though sensitive about his boyish looks, forced himself to smile affably at what was obviously meant as a compliment. "Thank you, sir."

Finally, Mr. Simpson stepped forward and Kinkaid knew what was expected from him.

"Please allow me to introduce Mr. Simpson, ambassador to St. Eustatia, representing the Congress of the American Colonies."

"I am deeply honored, sir," said Mr. Vanderveer as the two shook hands. Then Vanderveer introduced his portly companion in the tight-fitting black suit.

"This is Mr. Horvath, who will assist you with your revictualing. He speaks perfect English."

Horvath bowed with a quick jerk of his large head, his thin and greasy hair wetly plastered to his forehead. A tight collar squeezed his neck, making his face red, and he seemed to be sweating profusely in spite of the cooling sea breeze coming into the harbor.

"A pleasure, sir," said Kinkaid, shaking the man's limp and clammy hand.

"The pleasure is all mine, Captain," answered Horvath in a squeaky voice.

"Mr. McBride, you will speak with this gentleman about our needs: fresh water, meat, fresh fruits and vegetables, tobacco, as many chickens as our cages will carry, and some eggs would be nice, too."

"I've got my list, Captain." McBride knew what the ship required.

But they also needed to be frugal. The coffers of the Continental Navy were not exactly overflowing, and so, stepping closer to his purser so that Mr. Horvath could not overhear him, Kinkaid whispered, "I trust you will make some good bargains."

"I'll be sure and put that on special order, Captain," answered the savvy McBride.

Mr. Vanderveer and Mr. Simpson had been talking quietly, and now Mr. Vanderveer instructed his oarsmen to take Mr. Simpson's trunk with them. The three proved no match for the heavy trunk, but with Tripp, Treadwell, and Rikker pitching in and with a nervous Mr. Simpson looking on, they finally managed to get it aboard the tiny pinnace.

With that, Mr. Vanderveer announced, "Gentlemen, I have been instructed by His Eminence the governor to invite Mr. Simpson, and all of you who have come such a great distance to visit our fair island, to an official reception this evening at Government House."

"We are deeply honored," answered Mr. Simpson.

"Of course, you are invited, Captain, and all of your officers, as well."

Kinkaid had wanted only to deliver Mr. Simpson, restock his depleted stores, and get back to sea, eager to learn of the orders from Congress that Major Bauer carried for him. "I will have to see to the readiness of my ship, of course. And then there is the matter of—"

"Captain, I'm afraid I must implore you," said Vanderveer, interrupting him from his excuses. "You see, I had hoped you would be bringing a few of your dashing young officers with you…like Mr. Weatherby here. There is a shortage of young men on the island and the ladies…well, they shall require suitable dancing partners this evening." Vanderveer smiled, the epitome of charm and gracious sincerity as he played on Kinkaid's guilt.

"I would not wish to be blamed for such a tragedy, Mr. Vanderveer. I shall be honored to attend," said Kinkaid, playing the gallant gentleman and thinking there was something too perfect about Mr. Vanderveer and that perhaps there was more to learn than what met the eye. Not surprised by the impression made by his young gunnery officer, he added, "And I promise to bring Mr. Weatherby and perhaps a dancing midshipman, as well."

"Splendid, Captain," said Vanderveer, detecting the note of flippancy in Kinkaid's remark but gamely ignoring it. "The ladies will be forever grateful. I shall return for you, then, at seven o'clock, on the dock." Then he turned to Mr. Simpson, telling him, "We shall all be looking forward to seeing you and your distinguished guests later this evening, Mr. Simpson."

After more bowing and shaking of hands all around, Mr. Vanderveer climbed back down into the newly painted pinnace with Mr. Simpson's huge trunk weighing it down, leaving Mr. Horvath standing on the quarterdeck. And now the pinnace pushed away, raised sail, and turned back toward the shore from whence it came, if a bit less nimbly now, the handsome and charming Mr. Vanderveer standing in the waist, waving cheerfully back to the ship.

Kinkaid was only too aware of the noticeably uneasy Mr. Horvath standing at the rail, sweating in his tight black suit as he kept shifting the whip he carried from one hand to the other, clenching and unclenching his fists and wiping his palms against his breeches. Perhaps the man suffered from a nervous disposition or perhaps the gentle roll of the deck affected his stomach. Regardless, he was obviously suffering from the heat.

"Something refreshing to drink, Mr. Horvath?"

The man spun around as if startled and blurted out, "No thank you, Captain. I'll, uh, get something ashore."

"Very well," answered Kinkaid, feeling snubbed, "then I shall see that you are returned to shore forthwith."

"Thank you, Captain," he answered, "and let me assure you that I will do everything within my means to see that all your needs are met. And the rum will be the best, sir. Prime Jamaican."

"I am sure it will be satisfactory," answered Kinkaid, and with his civil duty done, Kinkaid turned away, almost bumping into Roach, who was coming up on deck with his list of things to procure for his pantry. Revictualing was something Kinkaid wanted to have done sooner rather than later, he reminded himself, and so, turning to the duty boatswain, he gave his orders.

"Mr. Cutler, Mr. Horvath here, along with Mr. Johnson, shall accompany you and a ten-man working party to the shore. You will be in charge. Ensure that all supplies reach the ship in good order and without undue waste of time. Use both ship's boats and please see that there is room for my steward."

"Aye aye, Captain," returned Cutler with a salute, looking too happy to suit Kinkaid's mood, forcing a reminder.

"Major Bauer, if you could spare a few marines to accompany and protect the working party ashore."

"Certainly, Captain," gave Bauer, recognizing as well that the shore provided not only replenishment but trouble. There was always the danger that some sailors, thinking they had found a paradise on earth after weeks at sea, might grant themselves liberty, and so a few armed marines would add a discouraging factor.

"Who is the off-duty midshipman for the eight-to-twelve watch?" asked Kinkaid.

"That would be me, Captain," answered Mr. Lofton.

"Can you dance, Mr. Lofton?"

If Lofton thought the question strange, he gave not a hint of it, answering, "Passably, sir."

"Then you shall accompany myself and Mr. Weatherby ashore this evening. Dress accordingly and see to it that my gig is ready before seven o'clock…and I want the oarsmen presentable."

"Yes sir," answered Lofton unemotionally, betraying neither trepidation nor expectation, answering just as he answered every order.

The two ship's boats were soon packed full of men and they headed to shore, the uncivil Mr. Horvath in the bow of the first boat. In the second boat, with the marines, was Roach, crammed uncomfortably onto the stern seat next to Cutler at the tiller.

All that afternoon, both boats plied their way back and forth, piled high with mounds of fruit and vegetables, sides of beef and pork, casks of rum, and rounds of cheese and loaves of bread. For hours and into the evening, the working party took their dinner in shifts, other men volunteering to take the place of those who became fatigued simply to get on the shore, to stand on its firm ground, to breathe and smell the land air.

Mr. Simpson had been standing impatiently at the rail since six-thirty, a leather pouch over his shoulder, watching as Mr. Lofton gathered the oarsmen for the captain's gig. He had to admire the six sailors, looking impressive in their blue tunics and white duck breeches with red stripes.

They soon had the boat lowered and were waiting alongside the ladder when Kinkaid came up on deck at a quarter to seven. There was Weatherby and Mr. Lofton, too, and Mr. Simpson was pointing up to where the white carriage was leaving Government House.

Kinkaid wore his new uniform with his sword, something at least to dangle at his side, adding to his recognition as a naval officer.

"I believe destiny calls," said Mr. Simpson.

Mr. Simpson was eager to be off, but Kinkaid had his instructions to pass on. "Mr. Saddler, you will be in charge of the ship. No one, other than the working parties, is permitted ashore. You might periodically ensure that the men are properly attendant to their duties…and allow no one on board in my absence. Expect my return around midnight, I should think, give or take an hour."

In other circumstances, Kinkaid might have permitted liberty to a ready and willing crew after weeks at sea, but, uncertain of the situation, and with Bauer's intentions still unknown, his instinct was to be wary. He decided that celebration would have to come later, when they might have something to celebrate—an unruly crew upon an unknown shore was not worthy of the risks.

"Aye aye, sir," acknowledged the first lieutenant.

"And double the watch," added Kinkaid. "Instruct them to take particular note of any ships coming into or leaving the harbor…and should any British warships be spotted offshore, you will inform me with all haste. Is all that clear?"

"Yes, Captain," Saddler assured him.

Stevens and Tripp stood in the waist, waiting to help the others down while Rikker took his place at the tiller. Kinkaid motioned for Mr. Simpson to go down the ladder first. Mr. Lofton and Weatherby were next, and as Kinkaid's hat reached the level of the deck, O'Toole piped his captain ashore, the shrill announcement carrying over the water.

"*Swift*, departing!" announced Mr. Saddler.

Once in the boat, Simpson gave Kinkaid a half-concealed smile and said, "You didn't expect an important guest such as myself to go ashore unescorted, did you, Captain?"

Kinkaid smiled politely. "I am only too happy to be your escort, Mr. Simpson."

"Well, I am grateful," said Simpson. "I know you would rather be reading your orders right now, finding out what Major Bauer is up to. But they will keep and, who knows, you might even enjoy yourself."

The truth of which Simpson spoke was, of course, undeniable, but Kinkaid also recognized another truth, that his orders could only be read when his duties to Mr. Simpson were complete.

Apprised of his future, he might better make use of the present, yet he had to accept that his duty to Mr. Simpson was not yet complete and that a few hours more would not matter. Besides, it might behoove him, no matter what his future assignment might entail, to gain some information from shore. And so he maintained, "That is not as important as the present success of your mission, Mr. Simpson."

They were nearing the dock, where Mr. Horvath stood at the landing in his black suit, whip in hand, wiping his brow with a handkerchief as the open carriage with the gaily-fringed top emerged from a street leading from the center of town and then turned onto the dock along the shore. Presently it drew up to the stone landing and waited as the boat arrived at the bottom of the landing.

Also waiting were a couple of rough-looking men sitting at the top of the steps as Kinkaid and his party climbed out of the boat. One wore a gold hoop earring and had a poorly rendered tattoo of a shark on his forearm, both men easily recognizable as sailors by their tarred bellbottoms and canvas hats. They made way for Kinkaid and the others as they climbed the stairs to the dock.

Mr. Horvath was drinking from a coconut that a young black man had expertly cracked open for him with his machete. He drained the husk, dropped the empty shell at the native's feet, and began to walk away when the native touched his arm, pleading, "Only a pence, sir."

Horvath spun around, crying, "How dare you!" and swung the butt of his whip against the side of the native's head, staggering the man, who now crouched fearfully at Horvath's feet, arms outstretched to ward off the next blow.

"Mr. Horvath!" called out Kinkaid as the man drew back his whip to strike again.

Horvath immediately brought his arm down and composed himself, saying, "These insolent savages need to be taught to keep their filthy hands off of gentleman."

"Be that as it may," answered Kinkaid, looking coldly into Horvath's eyes, "I would hate to trust in provisions we acquired through violence."

"I merely wished to report to you directly, Captain," answered Horvath in appeasement, putting on a pleasant tone, "that all stores required by your ship have been provided, though some hard-to-find items, such as fowls and eggs, are still being collected…and all at fair prices, I might add."

"Well, then…thank you, Mr. Horvath," answered Kinkaid, wishing only to forget the incident, mindful of their mission and determined that a fool like Horvath would not interfere with it, while equally certain that he disliked the man.

Mr. Vanderveer pretended not to notice the ugly scene as he stepped down from the coach, extended his arm toward the carriage, and greeted them all cordially once again, this time wearing a smartly cut maroon suit. "Good gentlemen, if you will accompany me, please."

After weeks at sea and unaccustomed to the stability of solid ground, Kinkaid walked with a stagger toward the coach like a drunken sailor. His instinct was to reach out his arms to steady himself, but he checked the impulse by pretending to adjust his hat. Once all were in the coach, Mr. Vanderveer gave the driver a word and they were off, moving briskly along the busy dock, alive with late-afternoon color and activity.

Torches attached to the pilings illuminated the way, revealing fishermen in multicolored boats hauling out their evening catch or repairing nets, others calling out to flirtatious girls in bare feet. Fruit and vegetable vendors had their carts piled high along the road and were bringing in more loads of coconuts, mangoes, and bananas for the ships, and there was Cutler and the working party, with the marines pitching in as well. At the end of the dock a quartet of drums and a wooden xylophone played a lively rhythm while a couple gyrated to the happy beat.

If Kinkaid had looked back, he would have noticed a battered ship's pinnace with a full moon painted on its bow putting out with the two rough-looking men aboard. She was quickly under sail and made for the mouth of the roadstead, the loathsome Mr. Horvath standing above the landing, watching them depart.

The coach entered a crowded main street of fancy restaurants and smart shops filled with the latest fashions, jewelry, chocolates, and liquor. Everything about the place—the streets and shops, the roads and sidewalks—was clean, bright, and colorful. And was that red, white, and blue bunting flying from the windows and terraces of the buildings? And what was this, people waving and cheering? Yes, it was true, the townspeople had actually turned out on the streets to welcome Mr. Simpson to the island. And now the bells of the church were ringing. The community had gone to a lot of trouble to make them feel welcome, and Mr. Simpson could not stop smiling as he waved back to the friendly crowds lining the sidewalks, the people in back craning their necks to watch the coach pass.

"A great day for you, Mr. Simpson," observed Mr. Lofton.

"Not for me, for our country," Simpson asserted. "The first official salute of the American flag, symbolizing the recognition of our nation's sovereignty by a foreign power."

"This day will go down in the history of both our nations," declared Vanderveer, smiling and waving from the carriage.

Kinkaid felt foolish waving back at the crowds as if he had done something to warrant the excitement.

Weatherby, however, had little trouble catching the festive atmosphere, and he was grinning happily back at the faces they passed.

Mr. Simpson, of course, was in his glory, and sensing Kinkaid's discomfort, joked, "Have no fear, Captain, I will be sure to spell your name correctly in my memoirs."

The crowds thinned as the carriage continued up the hill, passing fine stucco homes painted in pastel shades of blue and green, pink and yellow, and then winding through an area of parks and gardens of aloe and palms before opening to a high vista above the harbor where the vast Caribbean Sea shimmered below.

Finally, they arrived at the big white building from which Simpson had seen the coach depart, where the air was cool with a fresh breeze.

"Here we are, gentlemen," said Vanderveer, stepping out of the coach, "Government House."

Six formally dressed men lined the sidewalk that led from the entrance gate to the portico and massive wooden doors of the brightly whitewashed mansion. Hibiscus bloomed along the walls and sidewalks, and bougainvillea trailed from rows of columns and planters. The dark and heavily timbered doors were intricately carved with scenes of the town, ships in the harbor, and important events from the island's history. Under the portico, waiting expectantly on the steps, was a small group of distinguished men.

Mr. Vanderveer addressed the man in the middle, a pink and portly gentleman with thinning hair, wearing an off-white suit. "Governor de Graaff, I have the pleasure of introducing Mr. Simpson, representing the Continental Congress of the United States of America. Mr. Simpson, I present His Eminence, Governor Johannes de Graaff, of the neutral Dutch colony of St. Eustatia."

The two men bowed and shook hands, and then Simpson introduced his naval escort. "Captain Kinkaid…Lieutenant Weatherby…and Mr. Midshipman Lofton of the American Navy."

After more bowing and hand shaking, the group went inside, where waiters greeted them with trays of champagne. Fashionably dressed men and women were here and there in small groups, talking and drinking and laughing. Somewhere among the corridors came the strains of chamber music.

Mr. Simpson was soon off with the governor, being introduced to important guests.

Mr. Lofton was taken aside by a man in a dazzling white suit and his rather plump wife, wearing a pink crepe dress of many layers, who smiled politely at every dull comment Mr. Lofton made.

And Mr. Weatherby was soon making small talk with a slim young woman in an elegant, long white gown. She was radiantly beautiful, with a petite nose, large blue eyes, and thick, dark hair done up in the European style. A dainty pink coral necklace matched her earrings and set off her tawny skin to perfection.

It was dark and smoky in the crowded foyer, and so Kinkaid, his duty to Mr. Simpson apparently complete and his presence largely ignored, went out through tall French doors to the courtyard, where wide stone paths crossed, dividing rows of flowering shrubs. In the center was a pool with pink water lilies where red swordtails and brightly colored guppies swam. Hummingbirds were darting in and out of the bushes, busily drinking the sweet nectar, and martins were flying overhead.

In one shady corner of the courtyard was a post with a number of limbs jutting out, each holding a parrot—six in all, each of a different color combination, a spectacular living display. A loveseat was positioned so that those seated there would have a view of the birds and the garden. Two couples were standing before the parrots, enjoying the sight, and Kinkaid found himself thinking how much Elizabeth would have enjoyed such a garden; how wonderful it would be to have her with him in this tropical paradise. Sighing, he drained his glass and decided to take a closer look at the parrots.

"Oh look, Chester, it's a naval officer," said a woman in a full, peach-colored dress that swished as she walked. She was followed by her escort, a young man who did not look as happy to be here as she obviously was. "Are you from one of the ships in the harbor?" she asked boldly, a blond lock dangling artfully over her forehead.

"Yes, ma'am," answered Kinkaid, his empty champagne glass in one hand, his hat under his arm. "From the *Swift*." He couldn't tell as he bowed if it was her perfume or the scent of the many flowers blooming in the courtyard that wafted his way.

"Oh, isn't that the one from America?" she asked, turning to her escort.

"Captain Jonathan Kinkaid," he said, extending a hand to the gentleman.

"Pleased, Captain," said the calm man who spoke like an American. "I am Chester Murray," he said, returning a firm handshake. "Allow me to present my fiancée, Duchess Catherine Cronenberg."

Kinkaid bowed, while the duchess curtsied and said excitedly in her Southern accent, "Have you ever been to a nicer party? Why just look at this place. Chester, I can't recall ever being to a nicer party back home, can you? It is so lovely, wouldn't you agree, Captain?"

"Most lovely, ma'am," agreed Kinkaid.

"We both seem to be out of champagne, Captain," observed Murray, taking Kinkaid's glass. "You won't mind if I leave you here with the fine Captain, will you dear, while I find us more refreshment?"

"Don't be silly, Chester. Of course not," she said, her own glass spilling over its rim.

When Chester had gone to find a waiter, the duchess said blithely, "So tell me, Captain, what is it like commanding a warship? I would think it must be very dangerous, what with the British out in such force these days and with the pirates as well."

Kinkaid had to laugh. "I'm afraid I've not yet had the honor of meeting any British ships or pirates either, at least not so far on this cruise."

"Chester tells me the British will be here with many more ships in a couple of weeks. You'd better be careful," she added with a flirtatious smile before draining her glass.

"That is interesting news," allowed Kinkaid. Any news at all at this point would be interesting, even coming from a lovely, if somewhat inebriated, duchess. "Though I doubt that I will be lingering for that long."

"Oh, that's too bad. Chester and I are getting married here in three days' time and afterward will be staying with the governor's family for a week more. I simply adore the islands. If you are still here, I think it would be simply marvelous if you came to visit. I have two sisters and—"

"Here you are, Captain. Replenishments all around," announced Mr. Murray, seemingly coming out of his gloom. Passing him one of three full champagne glasses, he added, "By all means, Captain, you are most welcome to visit with us at the governor's estate after Catherine and I are married. She is related, you know…a very old Dutch family. Though her parents moved to Charleston…in South Carolina."

"Yes, I know Charleston somewhat," said Kinkaid amicably. "A fine Southern city. Please allow me to offer my congratulations upon your marriage; however, due to time considerations, I'm afraid I must regretfully decline your gracious invitation."

"Ah, we understand perfectly," granted Murray. "Of course, a naval captain's time is not his own, what with one's country at war."

"Sad but true," said Kinkaid. He was happy to change the subject and, though anxious for some information, tried to sound casual when he asked, "I understand that there has been some increased British activity in the islands."

"Oh my word, yes," replied Murray. "Why, the British are positively steaming over this event. In fact, I'm surprised there weren't British warships waiting for you…they've been following American ships right into the harbor, you know."

"You don't say," said Kinkaid, encouragingly.

"Governor de Graaff has sent protests to the West India Company while the British call for his ouster. Though he doesn't seem to take their threats very seriously, I must say."

"What kind of threats?"

"Why, the British have just declared an embargo of all goods deemed useful to a war effort, and that seems to include almost everything, including the obvious arms and munitions. They want to stop food, clothing, rope, lumber—anything that will keep a ship afloat. It was just in the papers the other day. King George says that the Royal Navy will henceforth show 'more vigilance and less reserve' in their prosecutions of the contraband trade."

Although it sounded as if Mr. Simpson had arrived in the nick of time, it remained to be seen what his efforts might accomplish, if anything. "Yet everyone here seems calm enough," Kinkaid observed.

Murray shook his head. "Oh, they are quite accustomed to hearing the British rattle their sabers. Of course I'm not privy to official policy, Captain, but in my humble opinion, I sincerely doubt that the governor will pay much heed to such pressure. His priority is to keep the trade going."

"Governor de Graaff is one of the richest merchants and planters on the island," intoned the duchess.

"That's right," affirmed Murray. "He owns most of the privately held land and owns or controls upwards of sixteen merchant vessels, all doing a brisk trade. No, he is unlikely to go along with any policies that might interfere with the interests of St. Eustatia, even if it does come from the British Empire."

"Well, it would seem that he is taking quite a risk," said Kinkaid, "although I saw as many British merchant ships in the harbor as those from other nations."

"One of the reasons why the governor does not take the threats seriously is that their government says one thing while their businessmen do another. And closing down this port interferes with the commerce of all nations. The British may send their warships, but they will not dare to start more international conflict; they have their hands quite full the way it is. Of course, there are British loyalists here on the island, plenty of them. But they are also businessmen and dare not take sides. And on a day such as today, especially since the governor had the commander of the fort recognize your flag, they will be lying low. The governor has many friends and relatives in important political positions here, and he controls the Island Assembly as well."

"It seems the governor is a very powerful man, then," gave Kinkaid.

"Quite," agreed Murray, looking about and speaking low. "In fact, I would think the only way to stop him would be for The Hague to call him back and throw him out. But that is unlikely to happen. Oh, they may make a show of censuring him to appease the British, but it means nothing. There is simply too much duty-free money to be made by all to risk instability here." The sound of a servant ringing a bell carried across the courtyard.

"Oh, they are calling us to dinner, Chester," said the duchess, tugging at her gentleman's arm. "Won't you join us at the table, Captain?"

"I would be delighted," answered Kinkaid chivalrously, the champagne beginning to go to his head.

With that, the duchess took Kinkaid's arm and, with Chester Murray taking her other, the three of them marched off to dinner. And what an affair it was: ten courses: lobster, grouper, onion soup, tender roasts, imported game birds, chicken pies, fresh-baked breads, peas and beans and stuffed cabbage, flower salads, scalloped potatoes, yams, and sweet potatoes. Served with white wine, then red wine, the alert servers coming by the moment one's glass ran dry, it was fare fit for kings.

Mr. Lofton sat some ten places to Kinkaid's right, next to a young woman with a long nose who chattered on and on as she ate, while Lofton nodded his head agreeably and gave quick fake smiles that threatened to crack his rigid face. It was a strange and amusing sight, especially since Mr. Lofton could have saved himself the trouble, for the young lady never glanced in his direction but kept her attention on the food on her plate or on the fork or spoon as she raised it to her mouth. She turned it this way and that, as if inspecting each and every morsel, before taking it into her mouth, stopping her chattering only long enough to chew her food vigorously before chattering on again and then bringing up a new morsel to inspect. A middle-aged gentleman with a thick black mustache sat low in the chair on the other side of her, and after introducing himself to Mr. Lofton as Captain Clancy, completely ignored both Mr. Lofton and the talkative woman, only occasionally speaking quietly with the matronly woman to his left.

With so much wine and food, and the hot and humid air made more hot and humid by the press of bodies, Kinkaid soon felt drowsy enough to take a nap right there at the table, before even finishing his dessert, a magnificent light torte topped with tropical fruits and shredded coconut. All that kept him awake was the constant banter and gossip of the duchess next to him.

"The man in the blue silk suit across from you is the Marquis de la Renier," pointed out the duchess, ever with a glass of wine in her hand. "He is a very rich French trader and has dealings with my husband-to-be."

The beautiful young woman who had greeted Weatherby in the lobby was sitting next to the Marquis; Weatherby sat on her other side and they were talking animatedly, Weatherby looking dashingly handsome in his uniform, with his tanned face and charming smile. "And is that his daughter sitting next to my lieutenant?"

"*Mais oui, monsieur,*" answered the duchess. "Marie de la Renier. Quite beautiful, is she not? And your lieutenant…well, they do make a handsome couple, don't they?"

"They do indeed, Duchess," agreed Kinkaid politely, though the conversation—indeed, the evening—was beginning to bore him. He knew only too well that Mr. Simpson had been right; he would rather have remained aboard and learned what mysterious assignment he was supposed to assist Major Bauer with. Instead, here he was, stuffing himself with food and wine, enjoying himself, while British fleets might be sailing in his direction, perhaps to trap his tiny ship in a neutral harbor for the rest of the war.

The duchess, as if detecting some flagging of Kinkaid's attention, leaned over and whispered under her hand, "Though it is rumored that he has dealings with the British as well as the Americans."

"A dangerous business, it would seem," answered Kinkaid conspiratorially, playing along with the duchess's game.

It was only when Kinkaid thought he could sit no longer or consume another morsel that one of the servants opened a set of immense doors behind him, rang a bell, and announced that the men were to retire for brandy and cigars at the bar.

Mr. Lofton was the first to excuse himself from the table; while no connoisseur of brandy or cigars, he was only too eager to escape the talkative young lady seated next to him.

Rows of tall windows reached to the ceiling on the far wall of the darkly paneled room, opposite the long, marble-topped bar, revealing a spacious terrace beyond. As Kinkaid strolled toward the open doorway, he was presented with a magnificent and awe-inspiring panorama of the harbor, filled with merchant ships and bathed in the rays of a red sun setting low in the western sky, its warm glow reflecting off the mirrors and dark wood, causing even the palest merchant to look healthily tanned. There, on the left, below Fort Orange, was *Swift*, her sails neatly furled, riding gently on her anchor cable.

Kinkaid looked about, hoping to find Mr. Weatherby among the men filing into the room, but he was nowhere in sight. Mr. Simpson was there, talking with a group of men, the governor among them, and Mr. Vanderveer, all lighting cigars. He decided to join them.

Simpson noticed his approach and said gaily through the smoke, "Ah, here is the very capable naval officer who brought me here."

"Captain Kinkaid," said the governor, his eyes glazed, his skin flushed. Governor de Graaff possessed a deep voice and spoke slowly, deliberately. "I must congratulate you on your, ah...ability in avoiding the British warships that recently have made a habit of patrolling the waters near our peaceful island."

"Thank you, Your Eminence, but we were fortunate to find no ships to hinder our entrance to your harbor," came Kinkaid's honest reply.

"Be that as it may, there are, ah…more than a few American ships fully loaded in the roadstead at the moment, fearful to venture out without an escort. Why, Captain Murdock," said the governor, turning to the stout man next to him, who was puffing on a big cigar, "perhaps you would like to tell the American Navy captain of your, ah…little adventure."

The man with the heavy sideburns cleared his throat. "Pleased to meet you, Captain. I'm Captain Murdock of *Prudence*, out of Baltimore. I was chased right into the roadstead by that little sloop," he related, pointing out to sea with his cigar. "At first I thought she was a pirate vessel—though the British are bad enough. Another few moments and we would have been a British prize, my ship and cargo lost, myself and my crew in a stinking hellhole somewhere."

"Captain Kinkaid," petitioned the short, black-mustached Captain Clancy who had sat next to the chattering young lady, "with all due respect to you, sir, why didn't they send more ships?"

"Well, that is assuming the British fleet is really out there waiting for you," interjected Mr. Simpson in Kinkaid's defense, his voice low and calm. "Have you any evidence that there is a larger force out there? You say you saw a sloop, Captain. If all of you banded together and left the harbor at once, why, you would be able to beat her off with your little popguns."

"We've talked about it, all right," said Murdock, "and if we have no other choice, that's what we'll have to do. Of course we'd be fine as long as she was the only British ship out there. Sitting here in port with a full load of wine and sugar isn't filling my owner's coffers. Perhaps if Captain Kinkaid would join us…."

"I'm afraid you misunderstand, gentlemen. I have no orders to escort civilian vessels," Kinkaid told them as Mr. Lofton joined the group, "and even if I had, I doubt that the small vessel under my command would ensure your safety."

Kinkaid's statement brought disappointed looks, and Captain Clancy spoke up, pleading, "If only to see us thirty miles from here, to give us a fair chance, sir. Even then we would have to stick together and watch out for pirates that are rumored to work out of the Virgins."

Kinkaid considered the man's appeal. Mr. Simpson had been delivered, and he knew that his orders included apprising himself of any pirate activity in the Virgins. They were only three days' sail from the Virgin Islands, and a chance to help these men and fulfill that requirement was enough reason. "Very well, then. If you want to leave, let's do it now."

The men, taken unaware by the sudden offer, stood looking at one another for a moment. Even Mr. Lofton betrayed his surprise by raising his dark eyebrows.

"Right this moment, sir?" asked Murdock.

Kinkaid merely looked him in the eye.

"I see you are a practical man, Captain," said Murdock. "Yes, of course, as the night falls; why wait for a British fleet to show up?" Then, jabbing his cigar toward the other captain, "Clancy, are you prepared to leave the harbor tonight?"

"I've been ready to leave for the last week," he said assuredly.

"I'm certainly ready," agreed Murdock. Turning to Kinkaid, he asked, "How far will you see us then, Captain?"

"You say there are pirates operating from the Virgins?"

"We've heard that the Royal Navy has been chasing a pirate ship about the Virgins for some time now," explained Murdock. "Haven't been able to find her base of operations, it seems, though I think their ships are too slow to catch her."

"Aye," intoned Clancy, "they ought to get that little sloop after her; she seems quick enough."

"Then we'll see you as far as the Virgins," said Kinkaid.

"Let's go then," said Clancy, emphatically. "I'll inform the captain of the *Brunswick*."

"And I'll tell Captain Harper on the *Mary Belle*," pronounced Murdock.

"Tell all the American ships that are ready," enjoined Kinkaid. "We leave tonight. If there is a fleet out there, we may have to turn back. If not…."

"We're on our way!" rejoiced Murdock. He looked around, and then added, "Well, what are we waiting for?"

Kinkaid turned to his midshipman and said, "You might see to our transportation, Mr. Lofton."

"Of course, Captain. I'll have a coach ready, sir," answered Lofton before leaving the room.

Governor de Graaff had followed the developments and said jovially, "Well, well, Captain Kinkaid, it looks as if you are causing my, ah...fine party to disband before the dancing begins. Where will the ladies find partners?"

"I must apologize, Your Eminence, but allow me to assure you that the ladies are missing nothing by my absence...except perhaps stepped-upon feet," answered Kinkaid, trying his best to be charming.

"A man of action who can't dance? An unlikely excuse, Captain," gave de Graaff, smiling knowingly. "Of course, I understand your urgency, sir, but what if you run into the entire British fleet out there?"

"One can only hope, sir, that favorable winds will blow," said Kinkaid, at a loss for a better answer, and hoping the comment did not sound condescending.

The governor laughed, "Good answer, Captain. Very good, yes indeed." The other men also laughed with the rotund man. Then de Graaff's face grew serious and he said, "Captain, ah...I believe I owe you an apology."

Kinkaid was bewildered. "An apology, sir?"

"Ah...for the delay in responding to your salute. Most awkward of us," said the governor. "Commander Ravené, as a military man, ah...reluctant to stir the wrath of powers greater than his own, may have been momentarily blinded to the, ah...larger picture."

"That is most gracious of you, Your Eminence," was all Kinkaid could think to say, thoughts of preparing his ship for sea distracting him from a conversation with one of the most powerful men in the western hemisphere. At the moment, he was more concerned with whether he had an adequate fresh water supply and essential provisions.

"The applause from the people of St. Eustatia after our, ah…demonstration, confirms that we remain on the correct road…that of ensuring free commerce among nations," continued de Graaff.

"Hear, hear, Governor," chimed in the cigar-chomping men around him.

"And Captain," continued the governor, "as a token of our, ah…appreciation, I would like you to take back with you a half-dozen cases of champagne."

"You are too kind, sir," said Kinkaid.

Governor de Graaff gave a nod, eliciting from Mr. Vanderveer, "I'll see to it right away, Your Eminence," before he approached a waiter and whispered something in the man's ear.

With that, Kinkaid thankfully found himself left out of the conversation as the governor and the men around him turned their attention to matters of trade and international affairs. The two American sea captains were saying their good-byes, and Mr. Simpson excused himself from the circle.

"Captain, it appears that duty calls you away," said Simpson.

"No use in wasting the night," said Kinkaid.

Simpson, seeing through Kinkaid's pretended regret, answered, "As resourceful as I know you to be, Captain, I'm sure you will put the darkness to good use."

"And I hope your mission here is not too trying, Mr. Simpson," Kinkaid teased him.

Simpson suppressed a smile and pulled at his chin, saying, "Other than the fact that my cheeks are in pain from smiling too much, I think I shall get along quite nicely here on this lovely shore. And if the food is any indication of things to come," said Simpson, patting his stomach, "I shan't even feel deprived of the culinary delights of your chef."

"If you make a habit of attending feasts like this, I'll have to find a bigger ship to carry you back in."

"You've discovered my weakness, Captain, but seriously, I would like to thank you for all you have done to afford me not only a safe passage but also a very pleasant one. It has been an honor to make your acquaintance and I wish you the best of—"

"You do have a silken tongue, Mr. Simpson," said Kinkaid with a smile and a handshake.

"Damn you," he said, dropping the diplomatic veil. "In all sincerity, Captain, be careful out there, will you?"

"At the moment, I'd be happy to find that gunnery officer of mine."

"I think he's been kidnapped, Captain," said Simpson with a knowing grin. "However, I believe if you were to make a reconnaissance of the courtyard...do you know where the parrots are?"

"I believe I do."

"Godspeed, Captain."

It was, in fact, near the parrots where he found Weatherby and his enchanting new friend, the two occupying one of the loveseats. Weatherby stood up when he saw his captain approach and made introductions.

"Marie, this is Captain Kinkaid. Captain, please allow me to introduce Marie de la Renier."

Rising from her graceful curtsy, Marie said musically, "So very pleased to make your acquaintance, Captain Kinkaid."

"The privilege is all mine," returned Kinkaid with a bow. Then, turning to Weatherby, he said stoically, "We are returning to the ship, lieutenant. I'll give you a moment. Meet you in the foyer."

If Weatherby was surprised or disappointed he hid the fact, answering, "Thank you, Captain. I'll be right there."

Mr. Lofton had dutifully brought a coach around to the front gate. Since it was filled with six cases of fine French champagne, three on the floor and three on the seat, there was room for only two, and so Mr. Lofton, as junior officer, sat outside next to the driver on the way back.

Weatherby seemed detached, pensive.

"So, I take it you enjoyed yourself at the party, Weatherby?"

"The party? Oh, yes I did, indeed, Captain."

"And I see you made a new friend."

"Of that I'm not so certain, sir," answered Weatherby, gazing out at the moon rising over the harbor.

"Well, I am quite familiar with the feeling of uncertainty," said Kinkaid, content to know that he would soon no longer be in the dark concerning Major Bauer's mission. But aware that duty had interfered with Weatherby's social agenda, Kinkaid thought to offer his love-struck gunnery officer a word of encouragement. "We must return for Mr. Simpson, regardless, following the completion of our duties and, afterwards…well, a day or two of liberty would seem in order."

"She will be leaving after attending a wedding next week. Her father has business in America," answered Weatherby wistfully.

"You didn't find out where?"

"She wouldn't say, sir."

"Afraid you might come looking for her?" teased Kinkaid.

"Perhaps she just didn't care for me, sir," he answered with a brave and uncertain smile.

Weatherby was smitten, that was for certain, his heart left with a beautiful young woman on this faraway island, without even knowing where she might take it.

V

...and Farewells

Briggs was climbing out of the ship's boat when the coach arrived at the dock, a tense expression on his face.

"Any problems, Mr. Briggs?" asked Kinkaid, somehow knowing there was, striding quickly toward the boat where Rikker and the oarsmen waited.

Running alongside, Briggs saluted and blurted out, "Mr. Saddler's compliments, Captain, and I was just coming to inform you that a British sloop-of-war is out beyond the breakwater, sir."

"Only the one ship?"

"I believe so, sir."

"I wasn't asking you about your religion, Mr. Briggs," said Kinkaid impatiently.

"No, sir," returned a stung Briggs, explaining, "It's just that I was the only one to see her, Captain, and I didn't see no other ships, sir."

"Rikker, we've got some boxes to load!" Kinkaid called out to the boatswain. It would not do to insult the Governor of St. Eustatia by leaving his gift of French champagne on the dock.

"Right away, Captain!" answered Rikker.

"Could you estimate her strength, Mr. Briggs?" asked Kinkaid, heading toward the ship's boat.

"I'd say she's a small sloop of about ten guns, sir. And perhaps a long swivel. Though I could be wrong, sir. She was passing pretty far—"

"A small sloop of about ten guns, then," said Kinkaid, interrupting Briggs from his doubts.

"Yes, sir," answered Briggs, more confidently.

"Back to the ship," said Kinkaid, champagne and men squeezed into the ship's boat.

Rikker took the tiller and roused the oarsmen, "Give a good pull, now, mates!"

As the boat surged forward, Briggs said, "And sir?"

"Yes, Mr. Briggs?"

"Well, sir, there's been a problem, Captain."

"A problem?" asked Kinkaid impatiently, his thoughts on the enemy sloop and the readiness of his ship.

"It's Rafferty, sir," said Briggs, reluctantly. "He's been arrested."

"Over what?"

"Well, sir," stammered Briggs, "with all due respect, Captain, I'd rather Mr. Saddler tell you. He's the one had him locked up, sir."

"Very well, Mr. Briggs, I shall allow the first lieutenant to tell me why Rafferty has been arrested."

"Thank you, sir," said Briggs with evident relief.

If Briggs knew something, then it was somewhat irksome that he did not want to tell it, but the fact that Rafferty had been arrested might be the least of his worries. At least one British enemy ship was waiting beyond the roadstead, his own ship about to meet her, perhaps the same ship Captain Murdock spoke of, the one that chased Murdock's ship into the harbor. Her timing seemed impeccable, yet if she were indeed small, with only ten guns, and alone, she would pose little trouble to the *Swift*, escorting five merchants with a few guns of their own, a respectable show of strength. But if she was the vanguard of a larger force....

Kinkaid, aware that the young and eager Briggs might have some anxiety over not providing more information concerning Rafferty's arrest, thought to ask him, "Are you of Spanish descent, Mr. Briggs?"

"My mother is Sicilian, sir."

"I see. I'll wager she's a good cook, then."

With that the young Briggs came alive. "Oh, she's the best!" he exclaimed. "Why, father says her cooking is what it must be like in heaven."

"Mr. Briggs?"

"Sir?"

"You forgot to address me as 'sir' a moment ago."

"Oh, sir…oh…I'm terribly sorry, sir. I—" Rikker had been following the conversation and was holding back a grin.

Kinkaid hid his smile and suggested, "Why don't we call things even, Mr. Briggs, and perhaps we can be more thrifty with our 'sirs' in the future."

"Thank you, sir. Thank you very much…sir."

Kinkaid turned in time to catch a glimpse of Rikker giving Briggs a wink of encouragement.

"Boat ahoy!" hailed a voice from the ship.

"*Swift* returning!" called out Mr. Lofton in reply.

O'Toole was waiting at the ladder with his boatswain's pipe as they pulled alongside.

"Mr. Saddler, call out the crew. We're putting to sea," said Kinkaid firmly as he bounded up the ladder, even before O'Toole finished his piping. "O'Toole, get the boat in and set the anchor detail." Then to the ship's boy, Rudy, he said, removing the cumbersome sword from his side, "Take this back to my cabin."

Three voices acknowledged.

Saddler, however, seemed agitated. "I sent Mr. Briggs the moment we spotted her, Captain."

The response puzzled him, but he chose to ignore it. "Did we manage to take on any fresh food? Water?" asked Kinkaid, annoyed. Of course he sent Mr. Briggs the moment he saw the ship, thought Kinkaid, and then it occurred to him that it might just as well be true that Mr. Saddler did not send Mr. Briggs the moment he saw her.

"Yes, sir," answered Saddler quickly, as if he were glad to change the subject, adding to the evidence against him. "We've just completed bringing aboard a goodly load of fresh food, sir.

Bread, meat, lots of bananas and coconuts, and some green things called...."

"Mangoes?" said Briggs, as he was untying the lashings from around the boom. The deck watch went below to rouse out the men from their hammocks, the officers from their cots.

"That's it, I believe, sir." confirmed Saddler. "Mangoes."

"Very good, Mr. Saddler," said Kinkaid, and then asked, "Did you see the sloop of which Mr. Briggs speaks?"

"Uh, no, I did not, sir," answered Saddler, warily. "Briggs said he saw the ship just as it was passing behind the headland to the east there. By the time any of the other of us looked—"

"Where were you when Briggs saw the ship?" asked Kinkaid.

"Sir, I was attending to a question of discipline—"

"There she is, Captain!" shouted Weatherby at the rail, telescope in hand, as the crew turned out in rapid fashion. Rikker took over the helm as some of Cutler's sail-handlers helped manhandle the ship's boat into her cradle, and then Mr. Lofton and O'Toole went forward to organize the anchor detail. Bauer's marines were forming up in the waist, equally ready to render passing honors or to fight.

"Is she coming into the roadstead?" was Kinkaid's first question, striding along the deck in Weatherby's direction. She had every right to—any ship did in a neutral port. If she did, it would give the opposing forces a chance to size up one another. Only if both left the harbor at once would there be a fight, but then there was the rule that prohibited enemy ships in a neutral harbor from leaving at the same time.

"Anchor detail set. Ship manned and ready, sir," reported Mr. Thorne.

"Let's go, then. We're playing the mama duck tonight," said Kinkaid, taking the telescope that Weatherby offered him.

The British ship was still two or three miles out, definitely a sloop, the kind used to scout for bigger, slower ships. She was small and lightly built and could not have been heavily armed.

"She looks to be able to out-sail *Swift* on many points," observed Kinkaid, looking through the telescope, the sloop's hull just visible as she rose up over a roller. Especially with the mortars on board, Kinkaid thought; their only use at the moment was in cluttering up his deck and cutting the speed of his ship by a third. He steadied the telescope against the main shrouds and continued his careful observation of the distant sloop as she skimmed over the waves. He counted five gunports. Ten guns.

"Her weight of cannon seems her only disadvantage," provided Weatherby.

"Not a big difference," said Kinkaid, yet he knew that a ship with her speed, captained with experience and run by a well-trained crew, could be more than an equal to *Swift*.

"Unless our consorts decide to scatter at the first sign of a fight," Saddler pointed out.

Kinkaid looked around the moonlit harbor, noting the American ships hoisting their anchors, unfurling sails. To go out with a show of strength seemed the easy choice, but what if his next assignment was precluded by capture, caused by a foolish decision? More and larger ships might be right behind her, just over the horizon. He thought to ask for Major Bauer, anxious to review his orders at last, but put off the idea. He was going out regardless, to beat off the sloop and give the merchants a good start toward home, no matter what his orders might call for.

"I'd judge that her present heading will take her across the bay, sir, but not into it," offered Weatherby.

Kinkaid, turning his telescope back toward the sloop, said in a low voice, "You're right, Mr. Weatherby…as usual."

"Sir?" Weatherby asked.

"I said you're right. She must be making a long-range recon of the roadstead." Still looking through the telescope, Kinkaid asked, "Mr. Weatherby, did your mother ever accuse you of being perfect?"

Without hesitation, Weatherby answered, "My mother believes I *am* perfect and would never think otherwise, Captain."

Kinkaid knew by the wry smile that Weatherby was being facetious.

"I admit I am a spoiled child, sir. My father, however, once told me: 'Never envy superiority in others or be ashamed of it in oneself.'"

"Profound advice," admitted Kinkaid, noting a luff in the sloop's topsail. She was preparing to tack. "And I can see how such a statement has found its embodiment in you."

"Why thank you, sir, that is—"

"Barely a land breeze, Captain, here in the harbor," noted Mr. Thorne, interrupting their banter. "Might be a while before we catch some air."

"I want us after her before we lose our sea room," said Kinkaid, bringing the telescope down. "If she comes too close, we dare not fire upon her and break the neutrality."

"That would certainly throw a damper on Mr. Simpson's plans," observed Saddler, quite unnecessarily.

A jib was running up, along with a topsail, and *Swift* began moving forward.

"Mind your helm. A bit of right rudder, there. That's it, steady now," said Kinkaid to Rikker at the wheel.

The anchor line came in faster than the men could haul it in, so Kinkaid had the ship fall off, and she drifted to a halt while they caught up the slack. Now they came to the chain, and O'Toole had the cable cleated off, the sails were refilled, and the ship surged forward, breaking the anchor out of the bottom. Then came the sound of the capstan winch, clanking round and round.

"What's the matter, Treadmill, you gettin' dizzy?" joked Rikker as they bent their backs to the task.

"Just don't care to dance by myself," came Treadwell's retort.

"More muscle and less wind outta the both of you!" came Mr. Saddler's complaint.

Finally came the report, "Anchor secured!"

"Secure special sea and anchor detail!" ordered Kinkaid.

The sun was just touching the western horizon as the ship headed toward the mouth of the roadstead. At least three ships were forming up behind them; two others were still hauling up their anchors. It would be a clear night, with a half moon to brighten the sails of the enemy ship.

"Let's go to quarters!" announced Kinkaid as the ship cleared the harbor. "Mr. Weatherby, load guns with shot!"

All hands were already standing by in anticipation of the order as Kirkpatrick rolled his drum with a flourish. Weatherby took his place in the waist and the gun captains began shouting and organizing their crews.

"I understand that our carpenter has been arrested," said Kinkaid to his first lieutenant, handing the telescope off to Briggs.

"Well, sir," began Mr. Saddler somewhat hesitantly, "that is the matter of discipline to which I was attending when Mr. Briggs made his report."

"And so you may have been...distracted for a moment."

"Perhaps a moment, sir...by Rafferty. The man was technically off the ship, then disobeyed a direct order...and then had the temerity to argue the point with me, Captain." As if the explanation wasn't enough, Saddler added, "I believe he intended to go ashore, sir. Couldn't understand why the crew wasn't granted liberty."

Briggs remained standing at the quarterdeck rail, pretending not to hear the conversation, dutifully watching the enemy sloop through the telescope, occasionally glancing astern at the five American merchant ships that followed and began to form a ragged line.

Saddler sighed before continuing, "When the vendors came out—"

"We had visitors?" asked Kinkaid.

"Some vendors, Captain," explained Cutler, who had been watch officer at the time. "Selling trinkets and souvenirs to the crew. As far as I know, none of them came aboard, sir."

"And?" asked Kinkaid, eager to arrive at the crux of the matter.

"Well, I saw Rafferty get into a boat with one of them, Captain," explained Saddler.

"One of the females, sir," added Cutler, suppressing a smile.

"And so you arrested him," said Kinkaid.

Briggs interrupted, reporting urgently, "She looks to be coming about, sir."

A sporadic sea breeze began to fill the sails as *Swift* cleared the roadstead, making for the open ocean, and Kinkaid could see that the sloop was backing her head sheets now, intending to close and have a look at the six American ships boldly leaving the harbor at once.

"Thank you, Mr. Briggs. Keep a close eye on her."

"Aye aye, Captain," answered Briggs, intently peering through the telescope.

Mr. Saddler went on with his agitated explanation. "I ordered Rafferty to come back aboard, sir…after informing him that he was off the ship without permission. He…well, he pretended like he didn't hear me, sir. Just kept…whatever he was doing with that…woman."

"Guns manned and loaded, sir!" came Weatherby's shout from the waist.

"Very good, Mr. Weatherby!" answered Kinkaid. "We'll keep our ports closed for now!"

"Aye aye, sir!"

"You mean he was having intercourse," said Kinkaid irritably. Cutler and Briggs were both trying to keep straight faces.

"Perhaps, sir."

The sloop was clearly turning in their direction now, but still a mile out, Briggs still watching her intently.

"How far away from the ship was this boat with the…vendor and Rafferty in it?" asked Kinkaid, continuing with the tiresome interview.

"Right alongside, sir," offered Cutler, also watching the enemy sloop.

"That is correct, sir...the boat was tied to the stern rail," admitted Saddler.

"So, Rafferty was in a boat, tied to the side, having intimate relations with a female," said Kinkaid.

"Which made him technically off the ship, sir," explained Saddler.

The tiresome comment made Kinkaid ask, "Mr. Saddler, how is it that you know that Rafferty 'intended to go ashore'? Those were your words, were they not?" he reminded him.

Saddler, unsure how to answer the first question, answered the second after a moment's hesitation. "Yes, sir, I believe those were my words, sir."

Swift was clear of the roadstead now, her sails catching the steady breeze of the trades as evening fell, with the sloop on a reciprocal course. Kinkaid was impressed with her quickness in coming about, her crew well-trained and efficient. The distance between her and *Swift* was closing fast now.

"Very well, then," said Kinkaid, finding the admission enough and other matters more pressing. "Do we have any other problems? I don't believe anyone has yet told me if we have managed to take on any fresh water."

"Sorry, sir," said Saddler, relieved to be done with his explanation and hoping to leave his embarrassment behind. "We do indeed have water, sir, clean and fresh."

"Good. That is something, then," said Kinkaid. The sloop was within a half-mile now and, apparently satisfied, turned back into the wind, her actions once again quick and nimble.

"There she goes! Running away again, Captain!" reported Briggs.

It was obvious to all that *Swift* was no match for the sloop's speed, weighed down by the mortars as she was.

Finally Saddler asked, "What about Rafferty, sir?"

The heedless and impatient question from his supercilious first lieutenant removed even the slightest consideration Kinkaid might have entertained regarding punishing Rafferty, even for insolence.

Keeping his eye on the enemy sloop, Kinkaid said firmly, "Release him."

It was an awkward moment for Saddler, and he paused before answering, "Very good, sir," making an effort to hide his disappointment.

Grins and winks passed slyly between Mr. Cutler and Mr. Briggs, enjoying the comeuppance of their overbearing first lieutenant.

It had been unfortunate to have to question his first lieutenant's judgment in front of the young midshipmen, allowed Kinkaid, and to subsequently rescind the arrest of Rafferty. True, the carpenter may have shown some insolence in ignoring the first lieutenant, but for Saddler to put words into the carpenter's mouth simply to spite the man was going too far. Rafferty had demonstrated no intention of leaving the ship, besides the fact that intention in itself could never serve as grounds for accusation or punishment. Besides, the argument could just as easily be made that Rafferty was "technically" on the ship by being in a boat tied alongside. The entire incident was an unnecessary and ill-timed distraction at a time when Mr. Saddler, in charge of the safety of the ship, should have chosen as his primary concern the fact that an enemy ship had been sighted. By his poor judgment and abuse of authority, Saddler had brought the situation upon himself and would have to deal with the consequences, hopefully learning a valuable lesson. The incident closed, Kinkaid turned his attention back to where it belonged.

Their small convoy was soon far from the roadstead, heading north by west, *Swift* in the van and still keeping the sloop at bay. Occasionally, as if testing their vigilance, she would veer to one side or the other, forcing Kinkaid to position *Swift* between her and the merchants.

"I doubt we could ever catch her," observed Mr. Lofton.

"At least we have her on the run," said Cutler cheerfully.

And Kinkaid would just keep her running until the merchants were well away and gone. A simple thing, and there was no real sense of danger. Of course, it was possible that the lightly armed sloop could turn on them suddenly, so he would keep the crew at their battle stations. The sky was turning almost purple now as the sun dipped below the horizon and a few stars began winking in the eastern sky.

Weatherby was still watching the sloop intently. "She's not pulling away from us, sir, though I believe she could if she wanted to," he surmised, standing at the rail. Indeed, the chased sloop seemed unworried, confident of their speed advantage, for she was allowing *Swift* to come ever nearer, most likely curious as to her size and armament. After making one more scan of the horizon, Weatherby added, "Though, it's nice to see that there isn't anybody else out here with us, Captain."

"Why, Mr. Weatherby," said his friend, Cutler, "that is most unsociable of you." The comment was jocular, the antithesis of the previous conversation over the arrest of the carpenter, and a welcome change.

"I simply prefer to choose with whom I socialize," said Weatherby, following the offbeat line.

Mr. Lofton, standing near the quarterdeck rail, had overheard the exchange and could not overcome the temptation to add, "And I can tell you that when Mr. Weatherby chooses them, he chooses by far the prettiest ones."

"Then I shall expect a full and detailed account of your adventures ashore, Mr. Weatherby," insisted Cutler, intrigued. "A pretty report, at that," he added, playing with the words.

The thought crossed Kinkaid's mind as the two friends bantered back and forth that a quick blow from the sloop, if damaging enough to the *Swift*, would leave the merchants vulnerable. They were far away to the west now, but still within sight and easy enough for the fast sloop to catch.

"A pretty maiden for a perfect man," tossed back Weatherby, enjoying the game.

"Mr. Weatherby, the perfect *lieutenant*, I hope," interjected Kinkaid, attempting to bring some military reminder into the situation. "Tell me now, what are the men on the sloop up to?"

Weatherby squinted his eyes in her direction once more, Briggs still peering through the telescope.

"She's turning, sir!" came the simultaneous replies.

"To your stations!" shouted Kinkaid. "Weatherby, starboard side! Run out your guns!"

She had decided to chance a quick attack, hoping to hit a mast or a rudder and disable *Swift* with a lucky blow. She spun around easily and would soon pass off *Swift*'s starboard side, flying with the wind. Cutler ran to his station in the waist with Lofton, their sail-handlers ready for imminent action.

"They're running out their guns, sir!" yelled Briggs.

She would sail by quickly, about one hundred yards off the starboard beam if she maintained her present course—long enough range to make gunnery challenging but hits effective.

"She should have halved the distance before pulling her trick," O'Toole could be heard to say, encouraging the gun crews in the waist, ready to give back what they were about to receive.

"As she bears, Mr. Weatherby!" said Kinkaid.

Weatherby was keyed up and ready at the first gun, Wet Willie. He checked the quoins to ensure the proper elevation and waited a moment as the hull rose.

"Fire!" bellowed Weatherby, and Tripp touched off the gun, the report splitting the air, the deck trembling from the discharge, an instant later the splash, twenty yards short.

Kinkaid could see the officers on the tiny quarterdeck of the enemy sloop and the men at their guns, too, over her low railing. Briggs had guessed correctly; she only carried ten main cannons, probably six-pounders or less, and a long swivel gun on her quarterdeck.

"Fire!" Another crack, jet of flame, and puff of smoke. No splash evident, an overshot. Weatherby had the range now.

"A bit of right rudder, helm," ordered Kinkaid. A gentle curve to starboard would keep the fast-moving sloop broadside long enough for Weatherby to finish his work.

"Fire!" This time a ragged hole punched through the sloop's mainsail.

"A hit!" exulted Smith beside Troubadour.

"Lower your sights, Weatherby!" shouted Saddler.

"Fire!" The fourth gun roared, throwing sparks and wood chips up from the sloop's forecastle, scattering a gun crew there.

"That's it!" hollered Mr. Thorne.

Kinkaid's stomach tightened when he saw the first puff of smoke belch from the sloop, then a dark object zip over the water, the ball slamming into *Swift*'s side, the concussion felt through the deck beneath his feet, followed an instant later by another landing right alongside, the splash slapping Kinkaid in the face.

"Just pebbles!" shouted Smith. "C'mon Mr. Weatherby, let's give it to 'em!"

"Fire!" continued the relentless Weatherby, refusing to be distracted by the enemy's gunnery as another ball crashed into *Swift*'s bulwarks. Nina, Stevens's gun, returned the favor and scored a hit at her waterline.

"Mr. Saddler, find Rafferty and get below to check on the damage!" ordered Kinkaid over the roar. "Quickly, and I want a full report as soon as you're finished! But be thorough!"

"Aye aye, sir!" returned Saddler, heading for the belowdecks hatch.

The enemy sloop was also making a slight turn to starboard to keep their guns abeam, and the two ships closed to eighty yards as Weatherby came to the last gun, Smith's Troubadour. Instead of aiming the gun himself, he pulled Smith by his shirtsleeve behind the barrel.

Smith sighted and fired at the same time the enemy sloop fired her swivel gun, Troubadour's ball slamming into her quarterdeck bulwark, downing a couple of men and bringing a hearty cheer from *Swift*'s gun crew as the distance between the ships grew, quickly and inexorably.

"Bring us about!" bellowed Kinkaid. "After her!" He would keep *Swift* between the wolf and the sheep. He turned to shout a word of praise for the gun crews when he saw a stunned group of seamen standing over a fallen form amidships.

It was Mr. Cutler, his torso a bloody mess, lying in a pool of blood. Weatherby ran to him, knelt, and lifted Cutler's body onto his lap. Cutler gasped, opened his eyes, and seemed to say something in Weatherby's ear.

Kinkaid made his way toward the two. Dr. Grafton was just running up. So was O'Toole.

Weatherby held Cutler, his head down, rocking a bit. Cutler's face was pale, his unseeing eyes staring up into the tropical night.

Dr. Grafton bent over him a moment, closed the boy's eyes, and stood up. "I'm sorry, Captain," he said quietly.

Oblivious to the examination, Weatherby continued to hold his friend, slowly rocking in shock and grief.

Kinkaid stood over the two, placed a hand on Weatherby's shoulder and watched helplessly as the enemy sloop sped away to the northeast under the half moon, her wake reflected in the sparkling sea. His instincts screamed out to do something, to fix the situation, to make things right again. But there was nothing to be done. He looked into the face of O'Toole, trying not to show on his face the agony that he felt inside, only to see tears coursing down the hardened boatswain's cheeks as those watching turned away in sympathy and pity.

Kinkaid could only say, "Let's get these two below," as the ship made her turn and sailors scrambled to sheet home the sails and brace them on the starboard side.

Dr. Grafton waved his loblolly boys over. They patiently took Cutler's body out of Weatherby's arms, leaving a great spread of blood on the sandy deck. Then they carried him below as gently, as reverently, as was possible. Weatherby remained kneeling on the spot, his shirtsleeves and pants wet with Cutler's blood, stunned. Finally, he allowed O'Toole to lead him toward the after hatch.

The short, vicious battle was over as suddenly as it had begun, and Midshipman Henry Cutler, Billy Weatherby's good friend, a young man with whom he had shared many an adventure, was dead.

O'Toole followed the shattered body of Cutler and the shocked Weatherby below while Kinkaid returned to the quarterdeck. The watch remained quiet and solemn as they continued to beat after the sloop, but she veered off and was soon far away.

"Bring us about. Head us west," he ordered. Then he simply stood there on the quarterdeck as if dazed, staring out, unseeing, as *Swift* turned back toward the convoy, safe and on its way home.

Mr. Saddler reappeared and gave his report. "Three hits along the lower hull, sir, only one serious, right along the waterline aft. Rafferty is already tending to it, and I've men at the pumps."

"Good," was all Kinkaid could say, Saddler's words barely comprehensible to him.

"Thank you, Captain," continued Saddler, oblivious to the tragedy. "Their gunnery was lucky, but I'd say they got the worse of it, Captain."

"It would seem so," answered Kinkaid, then added bitterly, "except that Mr. Cutler was killed."

"What? Oh, sir…I didn't know…," stammered the confused Saddler.

Kinkaid fought to collect his thoughts. He felt a sudden and overpowering urge to sit down and knew he sounded tired as he gave his orders.

"Keep us after the merchants. We'll see them through to the Virgins. And keep an eye on her," he said, jerking his head in the sloop's direction, barely visible now under the half moon.

It was doubtful that the sloop would pursue. Weatherby's gunnery had achieved some good hits on her. She had taken her chances with a sudden attack, but, realizing her hits were not sufficient to cripple *Swift*, would be licking her wounds, finding refuge, and attending to repairs.

"I'm going below. My regards to Major Bauer; have him report to my cabin at his convenience."

"Aye aye, sir," mumbled a subdued Briggs.

Roach was waiting by his cabin door.

"Can I get you anything, sir?" he asked meekly. "A cup of coffee, a sandwich, perhaps?"

"Just some light, if you please."

He slumped on his cot behind the small table, thankful to be off the quarterdeck, with at least a few moments of privacy, some time to collect his senses. He sat in the dark, numb and unthinking, until his eyes adjusted to the darkness, and he could make out the form of the table in front of him. Roach returned with the lit candle and set it on the table.

"Thank you. You may retire, Roach."

"At your service, Captain," said Roach before closing the door quietly behind him.

An unwelcome thought assailed Kinkaid as he sat there: that he had been somehow responsible for Cutler's death, that if he had strictly followed orders and not volunteered to escort a group of frightened captains concerned only for profits, Mr. Cutler would still be alive. He only half tried to push the thought aside, for there was a strange feeling of relief in blaming himself. Yet he could not help but realize that as a commander of men he could never profit by second guessing himself; if he sought to remain an effective commander, he would have to accept that men might die with every order he issued. And now a curious thought crossed his mind as he gazed into the flame: a young life was much like a candle, burning brightly with optimism and confidence, never realizing its own fragility, and that a sudden gust, a twist of fate, could very easily and cruelly snuff out its existence.

There came a knock at the door.

"Yes," was all he said, still gazing into the flame.

The tall, lantern-jawed major of marines ducked his head through the doorway. He was cleanly shaven and immaculate in his green uniform.

"Captain," he said in his soft-spoken way. In his hand was a sealed leather pouch.

"Please be seated, Major." At any other time, Kinkaid would have told the major that he had been waiting in some anticipation for this moment, but now it vaguely occurred to him that perhaps he had called for the marine commander more because it provided an excuse to be away from the quarterdeck and a distraction from the oppressive remorse that clung to him.

Bauer placed the pouch on the table where the thick candle burned low. "Bad business tonight, sir," said Bauer with sincerity as he sat down.

"Yes...well...war is bad business," said Kinkaid grimly, defensively, while trying to remain aware that it must have been difficult for the major to have been called to his cabin at such a moment. "The Dutch seem to have the right idea. Free trade for all, stay out of fights, make money. Tonight we managed to trade the safety of some merchant cargoes for the life of a fine young man."

"Hardly a bargain, Captain," agreed Bauer, glancing at the unopened pouch on the table, reminding Kinkaid that the man had also been waiting for some time to fulfill this requirement.

Kinkaid picked up the pouch. He broke the seal and took out two papers, both folded in half. One was a letter, addressed to the Captain of the *Swift*. He held it up to the candlelight.

> You are hereby ordered to make for the island of Dominica, avoiding all shipping, if possible, and especially avoiding any and all British warships. You will go to the harbor marked on the chart provided. There you will be met by His Excellency, Dr. Karza Pitt-Pouliessier, whom you will assist, in any manner within reason that he deems necessary, in the fulfillment of his aims, that is, the overthrow of the British-held island of St. Kitts by means of native uprising.

Major Bauer shall be in command of land operations, and you will discuss with him how your ship is best to be employed. It is hoped that the island will be rid of British influence by this action, at least temporarily. However, should the British repel the native forces, you will be expected to disavow any link to the endeavor and keep in mind that Dutch neutrality is not to be in any way jeopardized. In the unfortunate event that you are captured or detected assisting in such an uprising, the Continental Congress will deny your orders and actions.

Following the successful conclusion of this assignment, you shall return to St. Eustatia and bring Mr. Simpson home, if his mission to the island has been completed to his satisfaction. You will then proceed along the trade route followed by American shipping from St. Eustatia to the Virgin Islands, gathering any intelligence of British shipping or pirate activity in the area. To engage or attack enemy ships, privateers, or pirates shall be left to your discretion, bearing in mind that the return of said intelligence is to be of paramount concern.

You will destroy these orders as soon after reading them as is practicable.

At the bottom was the stamp of the Marine Committee, but no signatures. The other paper had a hand-drawn chart on each side. One was the island coast of Dominica, showing a bay on the northwest side of the island. The other was a chart of the harbor of St. Kitts, marking various reefs and rocks surrounding the outer beaches on both the west and east sides of South Friar's Bay.

"There we have it, Major," said Kinkaid with a sigh, the orders confirming his guilt in the first sentence, telling him that he was to avoid all British warships. Perhaps if he had known of those orders only an hour earlier, Mr. Midshipman Henry Cutler might still be alive.

"I can see why Mr. Simpson would not want to be associated with these orders," Kinkaid added sourly. "We want to help the Dutch, but in so doing not link them with our cause," he said, dropping the papers on the table. "So this is to be a native uprising. I admit it makes good sense. I especially enjoy the part about my actions and orders being denied." He was irritated by the world at the moment and nothing seemed quite real or valuable.

The orders themselves were something to be irritated about as well. They in essence told Kinkaid to do something, yet at the same time to be careful of doing too much. Exactly the kind of orders a military man detests, though he tried his best to understand the viewpoint of the men who had formulated them.

"Of course, if the British suspected that the powers on St. Eustatia were assisting us in any way, or that a ship bearing diplomats was involved in fomenting uprisings...well, we certainly wouldn't want to be the cause of a war between England and the Netherlands, now, would we?"

"I realize the thing sounds rather vague, Captain," admitted Bauer, "but the details have been left to us."

"Well, that is refreshing," said Kinkaid cynically.

"I'm afraid it's all we've got. We did promise the Dutch we would try and do something." And then Bauer hit home. "It's only what's expected, Captain."

Bauer had stated it clearly, unmistakably—they had orders that they were required to carry out. Although Bauer had not intended the statement to be insulting, the words hit Kinkaid like a slap in the face, bringing him to the realization that he had been defending his hurt feelings with anger, that he had been taking his guilt and frustration out on the major, knowing as well that he would have had very little patience with a subordinate who indulged himself so.

"You're right, Major," he gave, collecting himself, trying to overcome his depressed mood. "Tell me about this island of Dominica."

Bauer noticed the effort and said, "Assigned to the British since the Treaty of Paris in '63. Other than a few banana plantations, there is little there of value to a foreign power. The British military maintain only a minimal presence because of those plantations, perhaps an armed supply ship. They've built a small fort in the town of Roseau, not so much to defend the town or the island from foreign invasion, but to protect British operations and troops there from the local population, the Caribs. The Indians have the run of the island and have always given visitors considerable trouble. The British concern themselves only if the banana shipments are threatened. It is the largest island in the Lesser Antilles, the wettest and the least inhabited, actually nothing but mountains and jungle, so I doubt we will run into any British warships there as long as we stay away from Roseau, quite far from where we are to rendezvous with the Doctor."

"And these Caribs…the same people that this Doctor is in charge of?" surmised Kinkaid.

"That is correct, sir."

"So what is the plan for this…uprising?"

"Well, Captain," said Bauer, spreading open the chart of St. Kitts harbor. "I've studied these maps and figure we could bring the Doctor and his Indians to the northeast shore, here. From there, they head south along this road. It's only about four miles to the edge of town, where they can begin their attack from out of the forest at a prearranged signal. Their objective will be the British garrison."

"Where most of the troops are likely to be."

"Yes, but I see that as an advantage. The garrison consists of only two barracks buildings with a parade ground between. It has no wall around it, and we should be able to surround it and take the soldiers prisoners before they can know what's happening." Bauer's gentle voice and quiet manner bespoke an inherent confidence, and Kinkaid could see why men might eagerly follow this stout and fearless major into battle.

"What about shore defenses?"

"We know that there are at least four large-caliber pieces located in strong redoubts above the warehouses along the dock, here. They are dug into the hillside and point out over the harbor, so they present no threat to a land attack from the other side of town and once taken from behind they can be used against any ships in the harbor. What we don't know, and this is critical, is if there is a battery or any guns at all up along this ridge overlooking the harbor."

"Well, it's a likely spot for a battery," said Kinkaid. "It would command the town, the bay, and the garrison."

"And could make mincemeat of any Indian attack; command of that ridge commands the island."

"And a reconnoiter from the sea is out of the question."

"It would give away our presence, not to mention risking the ship." Bauer smiled wryly and said, "I know the adage, Captain, that a ship is a fool to fight a fort, so I certainly would not ask you to risk your ship against shore batteries."

"I am glad you appreciate that, Major," said Kinkaid.

"Which means that my marines and I are going to have to go up there and take any guns we find."

"And that is where the mortars come in handy."

"A man directing their fire from this ridge will be able to drop explosives onto any positions we might find without their being seen. Now, I'd like you to station your ship in the same cove where I will land my men…of course you will have to fix your position with anchors and possibly lines to the shore…."

"And secure all sails," observed Kinkaid, appreciating Bauer's grasp of the situation, though still not liking the position of vulnerability that acting as an anchored mortar platform would demand.

"Who will be in charge of the mortars?" asked Kinkaid, already knowing the answer.

"Sergeant Anders will be the only marine to remain aboard ship. He knows their powder requirements, fuse settings, range capabilities. I would like as many of my men as possible with me in the event we have to assault a strong position, so, if you are agreeable, there is plenty of time for Anders to apprise your best gunners of their duties." Anticipating Kinkaid's concerns, Bauer added jocularly, "Anders is no lover of sailors, but I think I can persuade him to share some of his expertise with the lower classes."

145

"Of course, Major, and I'm sure my men can handle the guns—with the sergeant's help, that is," gave Kinkaid. "And we'll need a good spotter."

"Since you mention it, Captain, I can tell you that both Mr. Midshipmen Briggs and Lieutenant Weatherby have taken a keen interest in the weapons and would probably be equally capable in the capacity. Especially Mr. Weatherby. Fuse settings, arc of shot flight, ranging mathematics...I've never heard so many questions. I might also mention that Weatherby is the only sailor on board your ship that Sergeant Anders has anything good to say about."

"I'm quite aware of Mr. Weatherby's tenacity...and charm," said Kinkaid, forcing a grin. "So you are willing to place the responsibility in his hands, then?"

"I would trust either man, certainly, sir."

"Well, Briggs is an eager midshipman, but Weatherby has the best vision...and possesses sound judgment." Suddenly Kinkaid felt the full burden of leadership. A spotter, detected by the enemy, could be in serious trouble. Yet there was no denying the facts; Weatherby it would have to be. He would not allow the death of Cutler to paralyze his decision-making, but he was not about to send Weatherby up there alone, either. "I'll send Briggs with him, as well as O'Toole and a couple of his hands."

"Excellent, Captain," said Bauer appreciatively. "We'll need a line of communication between the spotter and the ship, regardless."

"The thing I worry about is warships in the harbor. They might hesitate to fire into their own troops, into the town, or upon the garrison, but once they begin to receive fire from shore batteries, you can be certain they'll turn everything they've got against you."

"Quite possible, Captain. We'll have to work fast and hit them hard before they hit us."

"Perhaps we might come up with a way to distract or reduce the naval threat," answered Kinkaid.

"Any ideas would be welcome, sir."

"What do we know about the terrain along this escarpment?" asked Kinkaid. "The chart shows the area to be wooded, but if you say our intelligence is dated, they could very well have cleared this area by now."

"True," Bauer had to agree. "We won't know how close we can get to any fixed positions without being detected until we actually get up there on those heights."

"I assume our attack would be made at night and in a coordinated fashion."

"We've trained in night operations, Captain. I believe we would have a decided advantage in the dark."

"What about civilians?"

"They should not concern us, Captain. The civilian population has little choice but to accept British presence, and there are indications that they would welcome the defeat of an occupying force."

"Then we will have to trust that this Doctor will keep his natives in line."

"I would hope so, Captain, his group will have to come through the town of Basseterre before they can attack the garrison."

"And this Dr. Pitt-Pouliessier? Have you met the man?"

"I have not," admitted Bauer. "I know very little about him, except that he is an escaped slave, originally from the island of Martinique. But we have reports that he has been able to set himself up with a considerable force and in a relatively short period of time. He must have some force of character."

"And he is certainly opposed to the British?"

"Not exactly, sir," said Bauer grudgingly. "From what I gather, he is opposed to all colonizing of the islands, except by himself of course. But if we can help him take St. Kitts, which is the nearest British base to St. Eustatia, well, you can imagine, sir, the benefit to our cause."

"But what is to stop this Doctor from one day taking St. Eustatia by the same means?"

"It's certainly a shell game, Captain," Bauer had to admit. "However, such speculations are best left to the politicians. I am only a marine with a mission to accomplish."

"What happens when it's over?"

"We're to turn the island over to the Doctor and his band of Indians."

"And if the Indians decide to leave?"

"Well, the natives on St. Kitts have always maintained a guerrilla element. They could be trained to man the batteries. Regardless, it will take some time for word to reach England and for them to send a force to retake the place."

"And in the meantime, St. Eustatia continues a brisk trade in contraband."

"While expressing shock to learn of the native uprising on St. Kitts," grinned Bauer.

"I suppose time is as much as we can expect to gain from such an endeavor, lacking a sufficient force to leave behind."

"Believe me, I made the suggestion, sir," said Bauer, adding, "Have you ever tried to argue a point with a committee?"

"I suppose it's a matter of resources," granted Kinkaid, leaning back from the table. "Well, your plan is straightforward enough, given our lack of recent intelligence. The natives of this Doctor's army will certainly bear the brunt of the attack, and if there are batteries along those heights, their control would seem to be the decisive factor."

"And the fact that they will never be expecting a mortar attack from the sea," observed Bauer. Kinkaid hated continuing to carry the mortars on board and Bauer knew it, adding confidentially, "Once they have fulfilled their purpose, you are free to dispose of them as you may, Captain."

"Most generous of you, Major," said Kinkaid, looking him in the eye, "Since I'll need all the speed I can muster to get us out of there should we be detected."

Bauer nodded his head in agreement, saying what Kinkaid would not voice. "All would be lost if we lost *Swift*, Captain."

As instructed, Kinkaid held the letter with his orders over the candle, allowing the paper to burn until the flame reached his fingers.

Later that evening, Kinkaid received a report from Mr. McBride about the stores the ship had taken on. Most everything had been delivered, but three hundred loaves of bread were stale and weevil-infested and the rum that Mr. Horvath had promised would be "prime Jamaican" turned out to be one-third water.

"I tested the rum on the dock beforehand, Captain," McBride assured him, "but he tricked me nonetheless. I'm sorry, Captain."

"You couldn't very well test every barrel," allowed Kinkaid.

"The workin' party was more than willin' to try, Captain," laughed McBride, adding, "If it's any consolation, sir, it'll mean using less of our fresh water supply."

"That is something, at least."

"Perhaps we shall require the services of Mr. Horvath in the future," McBride reminded him.

"And we'll be sure to ask him about our rum, then," said Kinkaid, though caring little for such concerns at the moment.

Swift had caught up with the merchants during the night and the convoy was on a course of north by west. The morning dawned bright and sunny like the days before, belying the unhappy event taking place in the waist.

The crew was turned out for the service. O'Toole had stitched a canvas bag around Cutler's body, and Chaplain Carlton said a few words from the Bible before commending the young officer to the deep. Three marines stood behind the plank and, at Major Bauer's order, fired their muskets in salute as the small wrapped body went sliding into the ultramarine depths, sinking with the weight of shot sewn into the bag. Then the men recited the Lord's Prayer in a low and mumbling monotone. It was a sad and solemn affair, with Weatherby merely saying at the end a barely audible, "Good-bye Hank. I'll miss you, my friend."

The ceremony concluded and the men drifted away, all except for Weatherby, who Kinkaid noticed approaching one of the marines who had served on the honor guard. Weatherby spoke with the man for a moment and then asked Major Bauer to join them. Bauer listened to what each had to say and then nodded his head, whereupon the marine handed Weatherby his musket.

O'Toole was amidships, and Kinkaid heard him call out to the young lieutenant, "Thinking of joining the marines, Mr. Weatherby?"

"No, O'Toole," answered Weatherby, bringing the weapon up to his shoulder and sighting along the barrel of the long, heavy gun, "but one never knows when a good shot might come in handy."

The young marine drummer, Kirkpatrick, stood nearby, watching Weatherby in admiration.

VI

Pirates or Patriots?

"There they are, sir, the Virgin Islands," said Weatherby, who was at the rail as Kinkaid came out on deck. "We're full and by. Wind steady from the north, northeast. Course north by west, a half north."

It was the morning of the third day with the merchants. The convoy maintained a nice, disciplined line, sailing to windward, with *Swift* in the van. The sky was brightening in the east, and it looked to be the beginning of another fine day. Off the bow, a hazy line of dark blue was just visible on the horizon to the northwest; some towering thunderheads hovered above, contrasting sharply with the blue line of land. The crew had finished breakfast, and the cooks were tossing the garbage over the stern, attracting a flock of seagulls that swooped down with cheerful cries.

Boatswain O'Toole was standing next to the main starboard ratlines with a group of seamen, Smith and Kirkpatrick among them, demonstrating how to wrap standing rigging to protect it from weather and wear. "Worm and parcel with the lay, but always serve the other way," he could be heard to say as he bound spun yarn into the hollows between the strands of the larger rope, prior to applying a protective coat of tar.

Mr. Briggs was on the quarterdeck, as was the sailing master, Mr. Thorne, who was beginning to sport a beard, and was standing by with his charts of the area in a leather folder. Kinkaid thought he heard the chirping of a cricket from belowdecks—a very loud cricket—as the businesslike Mr. Thorne began giving his navigation report.

"That one just north there is Virgin Gorda, sir," said Thorne, the chart spread before him. "Part of this chain of islands here. Behind them is the Drake Channel and on the other side is the larger island of Tortola. And way up there, off to the right of Virgin Gorda, looks like a peninsula, that's Anegada, a bad place for a ship to get caught when the winds are out of the northeast, Captain. More than a few ships with broken backs lying off her reefs, I can tell you. I hope those merchants know enough to steer clear of her on their way home."

"Ship ahoy! Two points off the port beam!" came the shout from the mainmast lookout, followed by another loud chirp from below.

The topsails of the sighted ship could just be seen off the headland of Virgin Gorda. Weatherby watched her for a moment through the telescope before reporting, "Two-masted schooner, Captain. No colors visible." He handed the telescope to Kinkaid.

Kinkaid quickly found her. She was coming between an island and something less than an island, a tall rock surrounded by reefs, both landforms part of a chain of islands that extended some twelve miles to the southwest. The schooner was coming out of the long Sir Francis Drake Channel between the island chain and the larger island of Tortola to the north. The schooner had all sail set and was broad-reaching with the wind off her port beam, showing good speed, a froth of foam under her bow. She was still too far away to tell if she was armed, but she was making a slight adjustment to port, a small turn that did not escape Weatherby's eagle eyes.

"On a course to intercept, Captain."

"Must find our little convoy interesting," gave Kinkaid, still keeping his telescope on her. There were no colors that he could discern as yet, just a long, white wind pennant. She made her turn and steadied on a course of north by east, and now her hull could be better seen: a muddy red with a black stripe running round her bulwarks. She seemed about the same size as *Swift*, perhaps only slightly smaller, and if she carried a deck of guns, she did not advertise the fact with painted gunports. It annoyed him that the strange sound of the cricket, or whatever it might be, was distracting him. Did no one else hear it?

First Lieutenant Saddler was coming up now after making his morning inspection. "All's well, sir," he said, unaware of the developing situation, "and the men have finished with their breakfast, Captain."

"Very well, Mr. Saddler, call the crew to quarters. Mr. Weatherby, load, but do not run the guns out."

Saddler followed Kinkaid's line of sight to the distant ship before quickly giving his orders that had the crew turn out in fine fashion to the boatswain's pipe, and in less than three minutes came the first reports of readiness, drowning out, temporarily, the sound of chirping from below. Rikker took the helm.

"Guns ready, Captain!" gave Weatherby in the waist.

"Sail crews standing by, sir," reported Midshipman Lofton, having taken over Mr. Cutler's duties.

"Pumps manned, all fires extinguished, deck crews ready, all hands at their stations, Captain," Saddler passed on.

"Very well, Mr. Saddler."

Another very loud screeching came from below and Kinkaid had to ask, "What is that damned racket?"

The men on the quarterdeck turned, surprised by their captain's outburst. Weatherby merely smiled and explained, "Why, that's Roach's canary, sir."

"Roach has a canary?" While Weatherby's answer explained the strange chirping sound, it struck Kinkaid as incongruous that a rough seaman like Roach would have a canary.

"Bought it from one of the vendors, Captain," provided Mr. Thorne.

Kinkaid would keep on his same course to wait and see what developed. *Swift* carried only tops and jibs to keep just ahead of the merchants, the slower ships plowing steadily along behind her, and in a half hour the strange schooner was about a mile directly ahead of *Swift*. She was obviously a fast ship and presently enjoyed the advantage of the weather gauge.

"She's coming about, sir," reported the alert Briggs.

She pointed only momentarily in *Swift*'s direction as she made her turn, showing no threat but apparent interest. She had made her observations and seemed satisfied with going back the way she had come, which made her all the more curious to Kinkaid. He was still unable to detect any colors other than that long white wind pennant flying from her mainmast, which told him nothing.

"Back the tops and loose courses. Helmsman, bring us two points to larboard. We'll let the merchants pass," Kinkaid decided. He would follow behind, heading slightly in the schooner's direction, ensuring that she wasn't tempted by a stray merchant at the end of the line—such as Captain Murdock's ship, *Prudence*, packed full of French wine and Caribbean sugar.

To the north was a long line of thunderheads, their underbellies visible now, dark and foreboding, their edges hardening, curling in on themselves. A long flash of lightning lit the inside of a cloud momentarily, but no sound of thunder came as yet. A front, possibly containing some nasty weather; some rainsqualls, at the least, might be in the offing.

"She's going behind that big rock there, sir," said Briggs, diligently keeping up his reports as the merchants made their plodding way past the slowed *Swift*. The schooner was going back through Round Rock Passage, the opening between small Ginger Island and the aptly named Round Rock, where she was first spotted.

The crew had been at quarters for almost an hour now, the schooner out of sight. She was either far off to the west and no threat at all or could just as well be lurking nearby behind one of the islands.

Swift was within a mile of the opening of the Drake Channel when Weatherby called out, "There she is again, sir!" Perhaps it was only happenstance that she had seemingly been hiding behind the rock; anyway, she was coming out once more, toward *Swift*.

154

The schooner was indeed acting most curiously. She was no real threat to the convoy, not now. Even if she were fully armed, *Swift* was a match for her, though the schooner would be faster because of the mortars. However, if she were persistent, she might follow them, and if bad weather separated the line, it was possible that she could board and make off with one of the merchants. But Kinkaid was keeping *Swift* between the schooner and his consorts, giving them more time, and it looked as though the merchants would clear the area before the approaching weather front reached them. If *Swift* could just keep the schooner busy for another hour, block her inside the channel she was in, the merchants would be far to the north, safely on their way home.

Swift was barely making headway, her mainsheet shivering noisily in the gusty wind, her bow pointed almost directly at the schooner as the last ship in his flock passed off the starboard side. Kinkaid could see that Captain Murdock and other men on the deck of *Prudence* were also watching the unknown ship with interest. Then came a rumble of thunder as a dark line of clouds spread over the larger island, dropping a sagging curtain of rain over Tortola, darkening the sky and forming a misty haze that spread out on both sides of the storm. The clouds flashed with lightning and threatened to blot out the sun that still shone brightly in the eastern sky.

"There she goes again, sir," exclaimed Briggs, as the schooner once more turned away, back through Round Rock Passage, back into the channel. The first of the merchants in the line was nearing Anegada, the others following closely behind, and after steering clear of her dangerous reefs they would head directly north to American waters. If the schooner were to give chase, she would have to decide quickly...and she would have to pass *Swift* first.

Swift was still on her very slow heading of north by west toward Virgin Gorda, and Kinkaid too would have to decide soon on a new course. He could turn north and back toward the convoy, following it around the islands and out into the wide Atlantic, protecting their rear, or he could turn another point in the direction of the schooner and the smaller chain of islands, give the schooner chase, drive her farther from the convoy, watch her reaction, maybe find out what she was, what she intended. The first of the rainsqualls was bearing down now, and the merchants looked safely on their way.

"Rikker, steer us directly toward the schooner. Mr. Lofton, all sails; let's see if she runs!" he said and noticed a barely perceptible smile pass between Lieutenant Weatherby and Mr. Briggs.

Swift heeled onto her new course as the sail-handlers went to work, adding speed in spite of the mortars, with unsteady winds directly off the starboard beam, broad-reaching toward the middle of the island chain. Kinkaid could not help but feel a thrill of excitement as the ship bounded over the waves, the roiling waters surging alongside, a foamy wake left behind as they gave chase.

The schooner had to know that she was being chased, but so far gave no sign of concern. Kinkaid was surprised at how closely she allowed *Swift* to approach. In fact, the schooner's sails were slacked, her tops noticeably luffing. She was making no effort to out-distance *Swift*, even slowing, bringing some anxiety, what with the quick turn of the British sloop and the resultant death of young Cutler just days before. Kinkaid remained vigilant, as did the entire deck.

A long bolt of lightning flashed a mile ahead, a white, jagged ribbon running from the sea to the clouds above, a deep-throated boom coming a few seconds later. Menacing clouds rolled overhead, and gusts of wind tore over the tops of the waves, forming dark ripples on the surface as *Swift* drew within long-gun range of the schooner.

"She's turning to larboard, Captain," came Weatherby's report. "She'll be running with the wind along the inside shore of that island." No sooner had she completed her maneuver and began her run, just as Weatherby had predicted, when a rainsquall moved over her, hiding her from view.

"Keep us on the same course. We'll go through that passage as well," ordered Kinkaid, handing the telescope back to Weatherby.

"Don't let her surprise us, lookouts!" came the warning shout from Mr. Saddler.

A sudden gust struck *Swift*, heeling her sharply as large drops of water began pelting the sails like a drumbeat. Another flash and a sharp crack of thunder close off the starboard bow made the deck watch jump.

"Mr. Saddler, get at the binnacle and take some bearings. I want to know exactly where we are in five minutes. Mr. Thorne, let's try to keep the chart dry."

"Aye aye, sir," came the replies.

"And get a leadsman in the chains," ordered Kinkaid, knowing they were moving too fast for a leadsman's depth sounding to be of much use, but at least they would know if they were over dangerously shallow water. They were too close to islands to take any chances, and he didn't know these waters, not like the captain of that red-hulled schooner apparently did. A reef just below the surface could easily tear the bottom out of *Swift*. With the storm coming on, the seas had begun to throw up whitecaps and the waters turned dark. Under these conditions, it was impossible to judge depth by sight. Now a solid wall of water was coming in torrents, lighting and thunder crashing all around, visibility down to only tens of yards, the surface of the sea a roiling misty gray, the rain pounding on the deck.

"Rocks just ahead!" screamed the lookout.

"By the mark nine!" came the leadsman's cry. Either the waters were quite shallow here or they were over a deep reef.

"Damn," said Kinkaid spontaneously. The schooner was losing them and *Swift* was in danger. "Mr. Thorne…"

"I'd say come to larboard, Captain," suggested Thorne immediately. He had been closely following the chart since the pursuit began, Saddler supplying him with dead-reckoning bearings taken from various headlands of islands as they could be seen.

"Make it so, helmsman," said Kinkaid, trying to hold in his mind's eye his sense of direction, imagining from his earlier view

Round Rock just ahead. "Make it two points." Then to the sailing master, "Where are we, Mr. Thorne? Exactly—show me on the chart."

"Rudy, bring us a lantern," asked Mr. Thorne of the messenger boy.

The sun was long gone now, the *Swift* under slate black clouds and the waters just as dark. Mr. Thorne had to take the chart out of his jacket, where he had it rolled up and protected from the driving rain. They held their coats over it in the shelter offered by the mainsail, while little Rudy held a cabin lantern.

"I make us right here, sir," said Thorne. He looked up as if to confirm his position by sight, a drop of water falling from the end of his nose onto the chart. He was pointing at an area where two chains of islands merged at the opening of Round Rock Passage.

The rains had abated momentarily, just long enough for Kinkaid to be able to see the black, wet mass of Round Rock just off the starboard bow, beyond which was the wide Sir Francis Drake Channel, the dark mass of Tortola beyond, mostly hidden behind a line of heavy squalls charging their way.

"Bring us to a heading of north by west, a half west," said Kinkaid calmly to the helm.

"Aye aye, sir."

The line of dark and threatening clouds overtook them by the time *Swift* steadied on her new course, bringing wind-driven rain that churned the waters, blowing whitecaps into sheets of foam and surrounding them with crackling lightning that jarred the nerves.

The last they had seen of her, the schooner had all her sail piled on and was heeling under the gusts. Kinkaid had little choice but to do the same if he wished to keep after her. It would be easy enough for her to hide behind a squall, then duck into one of the many coves along these island shores, with *Swift* passing by and losing her.

Kinkaid barely noticed as the watch changed, new men coming up from below to take the place of those thoroughly soaked. When he turned and looked, there was Rafferty standing at the helm, his hands firmly on the wheel, grinning a wide-toothed grin, a stubbled chin thrust defiantly into the storm as if reveling in a contest with the elements. The dark mass of Round Rock was just visible, passing a hundred yards off the starboard beam.

Roach came up on deck, bringing with him Kinkaid's oilskin coat. Only now did Kinkaid think of it, so intense was his concentration on keeping after the elusive schooner, but it occurred to him that his coat would have been more useful had Roach brought it up when the rains first began. Roach, as if reading his captain's thoughts, said meekly, "Can I bring you a cup of coffee, sir? Something to nibble on, perhaps?"

Kinkaid was thankful for the dry coat, late or not, and though Roach's coffee was never quite right and his meals uneven, at least he was still trying. Kinkaid tugged the bulky coat on over his wet jacket and mumbled, shivering, "Anything would be fine, Roach, thank you."

"Coming right up, Captain."

The rain seemed to abate, fooling the deck into thinking that the storm was finally passing, but in a few minutes another heavy downpour hit with sudden violence, gusty winds whipping the sheets, driving rain across the deck, soaking the watch. Rain splashed in Rafferty's face in spite of the broad-brimmed hat that he wore, momentarily wiping away that defiant grin, his eyes squinting into the maelstrom. The already drenched officers scurried to find some shelter behind the mainsail, to get out of the wind as much as possible. The crashing thunder was beginning to get on everyone's nerves and visibility was down to a few hundred yards, but Kinkaid was relieved to see that they were now in the passage between Round Rock and Ginger Island, the water deepening once more.

And then, as suddenly as it had come, the heavy rain was gone, though thick black clouds still billowed overhead, promising more rain, lightning, and thunder.

Throughout the showers and the wind, the lightning and the thunder, Weatherby remained standing stubbornly at the rail, the telescope even now still in his hands. The lens kept fogging over, and he constantly had to wipe it clean, though by now he had given up, the device useless under the conditions. But as the rains tapered off and the air cleared somewhat, Weatherby's vigilance paid off as he pointed forward, the schooner just close enough now to make the telescope unnecessary. "There she is, sir, still heading away, now south, around that island there!" Her dim shape was just visible in the misty distance, heading south between Ginger and Cooper islands.

O'Toole muttered, "Flying nothing but that wind pennant…a ship with no country. And you know, Captain, I'd say she waited for us."

"Probably wondering why we can't catch her," said Kinkaid, pleased to have found her again, but frustrated by his inability to give her a serious run.

"A safe bet, Captain," agreed Mr. Thorne. "We carry more sail than her, though she's a mite smaller, so our speeds should be about equal." He had neglected to add, "but for the mortars," knowing his captain's feelings on the subject.

"Bring us left, helmsman, head us due west," ordered Kinkaid as *Swift* passed between the two islands of Ginger and Round Rock, another squall hiding the schooner once again. Kinkaid still shivered in spite of the relatively dry coat, for his clothing underneath remained wet, the chill penetrating to his bones, the wind stubbornly whipping at his pant legs and collar.

"Seems to be leading us along, sir," ventured the first lieutenant through chattering teeth.

"Uses the islands as well as the weather to his advantage, sir," said Mr. Thorne.

"A savvy captain," gave Kinkaid, wary of the line of foam off the port beam as *Swift* steadied on her new course, evidence of a hidden reef. That schooner certainly knew these waters, the way she was dancing about so close to islands, rocks, and reefs.

Roach appeared once more on deck, a mug of steaming coffee in one hand and a bundle wrapped in a towel in the other. Inside was a thick and hearty roast beef sandwich. Kinkaid tore at it with relish and then gulped at the steaming liquid. It didn't matter that it was bitter; it was hot and warmed his insides. Only then did he realize that the men would be suffering as well, in need of warmth and sustenance after the long hours without, and a twinge of guilt overcame him. He put it quickly aside when he realized that the reason he had not thought of the men's suffering was because he had given such little thought to his own.

"Mr. Briggs, see that the cooks get something hot up to the men on deck," said Kinkaid as he watched the schooner once more disappear into the mist. Roach remained topside, pleased to see that his captain was enjoying his offering. Curiosity getting the better of him, Kinkaid decided to ask, "Roach, I understand you have a bird."

Unhappy in his role of captain's cook, increasingly wary and morose, Roach seemed to come alive. "Ah, Ellie's a lovely thing, sir. Yellow and happy as the sun." Then caution took its place, the man quickly adding, "But she'll be no bother, Captain. I cover her at night, an', well, she's quiet as a mouse an' happy with crumbs…"

"I'm sure she'll be no bother, Roach," allowed Kinkaid.

"Thank you, Captain," said Roach appreciatively. Another lightning bolt struck nearby, its boom sounding like a cannon shot, and Roach quickly retreated below.

The winds were abating somewhat now, the gusts less extreme. The rain continued, but only a light drizzle. Ginger Island was passing some two hundred yards off the port beam, a gentle swell splashing against the black rocks along her shoreline. Rafferty looked like a statue, clinging to the wheel, unmoving, staring stubbornly ahead. Kinkaid thought to pass a hand over his face to break his spell, but dismissed the temptation. He had slowed his devouring of the sandwich, savoring the dry beef, the moist bread, the hunger he did not know he had until he had begun eating.

"There she is again, just going around that next island, sir!" shouted the ever-vigilant Weatherby in the waist, seemingly oblivious to the elements. The black and red hull of the schooner looked gray behind the rains.

"That would be Cooper Island, sir," added Mr. Thorne, glancing at the chart under his coat, wet hair plastered to his forehead. The schooner was indeed turning right, heading around the end of Cooper Island, the line of islands appearing through curtains of rain, Tortola just barely visible. "Salt Island would be on the other side, sir."

"Bring us to larboard, Rafferty. Keep us after her," mumbled Kinkaid, his mouth full.

"By the mark twelve!"

"Leading us on a merry chase, Captain," observed Saddler, still at the binnacle and still shivering.

Was she going to weave in and out of these islands all afternoon? By the time *Swift* had reached the end of Ginger Island, the schooner was already around the end of Cooper Island, turning to starboard and once more out of sight. Still determined to follow, Kinkaid brought *Swift* on a southerly heading with the wind at their backs as the next line of squalls hit, bringing yet more rain, more thunder and lightning. Everyone was already wet to the bone, so another dunking didn't much matter. Mr. Thorne was rolling the chart up once again, tucking it away under his jacket, the men quiet on the quarterdeck in their misery. Even Roach's canary was silent now.

The sandwich finished and the coffee gone, Kinkaid turned his thoughts to the fact that the crew had been suffering out on deck for the last three hours with little to protect them from the rain and still with nothing to warm their insides. Never could he recall a drearier or more uneventful pursuit, the schooner seemingly playing with them, leading them on a twisting, turning, follow-the-leader chase.

The last of the rain squalls finally passed overhead as *Swift* also turned to starboard, clearing Cooper Island, the schooner still maintaining her distance, still zigzagging between the islands, still leading them on. The lightning and thunder were slowly trailing off to the south, though the rains remained light and sporadic, the skies dark and cloudy. Now, finally, the cooks were bringing up hot soup and bread from below, passing it down the line of men on the decks who wolfed the food down greedily.

It was late afternoon and still the strange chase continued, the schooner going around Salt Island, then Peter Island, then turning to starboard again between Peter and Norman islands, always just ahead, weaving in and out, keeping her distance, and just as well ensuring that *Swift* didn't lose her.

"Like a dog leading its master," remarked Mr. Thorne.

"Yes," agreed Briggs, "but leading us where?"

"To trouble most likely," guessed Saddler.

Early evening came, and the sun even peeked out now and again as the clouds began to break up. The watch changed again, allowing the men the chance to get below, dry out, and put on some warm, dry clothes. The rains had finally stopped, and the wind was mitigating as the schooner headed toward the larger island of St. John, finally turning into a large, shallow bay with a meandering shoreline—Coral Bay, which gave Kinkaid reason to hesitate.

"She's letting herself get trapped, Captain," observed Mr. Thorne, his chart out once more.

"She must feel safe or she would have outrun us, sir," added Mr. Saddler.

As tempting as it was to follow, there was too much intention on the part of the wily schooner to follow her into the bay. Her captain obviously knew every rock and reef in the area and had been in control of the chase from the beginning, his ship acting too much like bait.

"Let's get out of here," said Kinkaid instinctively. "Take us north into the channel again," he said to the helmsman as he checked the chart. He would break off the pursuit now, as the light was failing.

Once out of Coral Bay, Kinkaid turned the ship east and then north, taking *Swift* around the easternmost headland of St. John, through gusty winds that the storm had left in its wake, and finally bringing *Swift* to Haulover Bay as the sun was setting.

Now she swung from her anchor cable, bow into the stiff breeze that was blowing off the channel. It was not exactly a sheltered anchorage, but would have to do for the moment.

"We'll have a proper dinner," announced Kinkaid. "Give the men a chance to dry out and warm up."

Roach prepared boiled potatoes and cabbage that evening—overcooked and mushy, though the beef was acceptable. But Kinkaid had had enough of beef, his sandwich having been full of the dry stuff, and he had also tired of complaining about Roach's food. It would do no good anyway and perhaps even make his cook more nervous, resulting in the next meal being worse than the one before it. Besides, learning more about that schooner was foremost on his mind.

When Kinkaid returned to the deck, he found Weatherby there, on duty as officer of the watch, talking with Major Bauer.

"Good evening, gentlemen. Weatherby, have the messenger inform Mr. Briggs and Boatswain O'Toole to meet me in my cabin in ten minutes."

"Aye aye, sir," said Weatherby, passing the word to the messenger. Then, "Sir, I suppose you will be going ashore tonight?"

"Quite possible, Lieutenant," answered Kinkaid, well-aware that Weatherby was always cognizant of the tactical situation, his quick mind often ahead of his own thinking, and equally aware that the young lieutenant would be feeling left out.

But it was the marine commander who interjected. "Sir, if I may. My men are—"

"I'm sure your men are well-trained for such a reconnoiter, but there are other considerations, Major."

"I understand, Captain," allowed Bauer. He would need every one of his marines later, to storm an island.

"Mr. Saddler, you will be in command of the ship. Mr. Weatherby, you shall remain, as well; I prefer my ship with a gunnery officer aboard while I'm ashore."

"At your service, Captain," came Weatherby's stoic reply.

Kinkaid returned to his cabin where O'Toole and Mr. Briggs soon joined him, the chart of the island spread out before them.

"If the chart is accurate, we won't have to go far through the woods, probably only a few hundred yards, before we come to the bay on the other side of this rise. O'Toole, you'll pick five oarsmen who can handle themselves. We'll go in with pistols and blades. We'll wait another hour; make sure it's dark."

"Very good, sir."

Kinkaid waited in his cabin, sipping a bitter cup of Roach's coffee, pondering what he might find ashore, trying to rest, to relax, allowing the time to slip by, waiting for the tropical night to fall. When he came up on deck, he found O'Toole passing out pistols and cutlasses to the shore party, Smith, Rikker, and Rafferty among them.

Briggs had tucked a saber into his belt and was hefting a pistol, sighting along the barrel, when Kinkaid asked him, "Have you ever fired a pistol, Mr. Briggs?"

"I'm not a bad shot, sir," answered Briggs without hesitation.

"Well, we're not going in for a fight," he reminded them, "just to have a look, so there will be no shooting except on my order."

"Aye, Captain," came the acknowledgement.

The Indian scout, Monk, stood by the rail, dressed in buckskins, hatchet in his belt, a black stripe running across his cheeks, looking sinister.

"Captain, my scout has eyes like an owl," Bauer made his appeal. "If there's a trail in there somewhere, Monk will find it for you."

"Does he understand English?" asked Kinkaid.

"As well as you and I, sir," Bauer told him, admitting, "except he doesn't like to speak it."

"Then how will I understand him?"

"You'll understand him, sir," Bauer assured him.

Turning to his first lieutenant, Kinkaid said, "Mr. Saddler, if we are not back by first light, send an armed party after us."

"Aye aye, Captain."

"Your scout is welcome to join us, Major," he decided.

The clouds were blowing away to the south now, revealing a clear night sky filled with stars, the moon high over Tortola. It was amazing how quickly the weather could change in these latitudes, thought Kinkaid, appreciating the beauty of the area, though he was suspicious of the shoreline as the boat neared it with little effort from the oarsmen, the steady breeze pushing them most of the way, the Indian crouched darkly in the bow.

They found the shoreline rough and rocky, with broken coral and driftwood piled up along the beach. After securing the boat to a stout tree along the water's edge, they made their way into the trees. There was no path, and they had to skirt around thick vegetation. The silent Monk led the way, followed by O'Toole, as the group moved single file up the embankment through the scrubby trees. Even with the moon at their backs and high above, it was difficult to see in the dark forest, and O'Toole soon came to a halt before a wall of brush.

"The Indian is gone, sir," he said.

Straining to see, Kinkaid said, "This way," motioning toward a rocky outcrop to the right of the brush. "Up we go."

As long as they continued upward, they were heading in the right direction, reasoned Kinkaid, though the going was slow and fitful, with frequent pauses to find their way up the trackless hillside. Kinkaid was beginning to wonder if Monk had become lost in the dark interior when he suddenly appeared and began pointing the way, eventually leading them to a trail that meandered along the ridge where the wind blew steadily, whispering through the branches of the low trees and rustling the dry leaves. *Swift* could be seen behind them through the swaying branches, lying at her anchor below.

Kinkaid pointed and said to Monk, "Find a way down to the bay."

Monk nodded, motioned that the group should wait, and then moved off into the jungle once again. Kinkaid and the others waited, two minutes, three minutes, five minutes. When Monk materialized again, he led them down what must have been a narrow animal trail, through a forest of taller trees and thick shrubs, where the men stumbled in the dark over roots and vines. They caught intermittent glimpses of Coral Bay through the trees, a large bay with many smaller coves and lagoons, well-sheltered from the prevailing winds.

The ground leveled off as they reached the bottom of the hill. The air was still and stagnant and great clouds of mosquitoes attacked them, the voracious swarms flying into their eyes and mouths and ears; nothing could prevent their irritating bites. It was torture, but at least the men bore their misery in silence—though Briggs started waving his saber before his face, foolishly attempting to fend off the threatening hordes with the wide blade. The Indian, crouching behind a bush along the marshy shoreline, gave Briggs a look of disgust and made a quick motion across his throat. Then he pointed in the direction of the bay. There, anchored in a narrow inlet, little more than a fetid lagoon, was the dark hulk of the schooner.

"Briggs, put that thing away before you cut your nose off," whispered Kinkaid in warning, concerned that its flashing blade might reflect the moonlight to anyone watching from the schooner or the shoreline.

He could see a clearing on the far side of the inlet, and a couple of campfires were sending off clouds of smoke, more than likely to drive away the mosquitoes. A few figures were standing around the nearest fire, and beyond it were three shacks made of bits and pieces of lumber and tarps. The middle one was the largest and most substantial, though far from palatial. Five boats were pulled up on the rough beach, long and graceful things. A bit farther out was what looked like a fish weir, made of wooden stakes where a fish might drift in and then have trouble getting out. A pirate's den if ever there was one. Now and then a peal of laughter could be heard, even the sound of women.

"I want to get closer," said Kinkaid. "O'Toole, come with me. The rest of you men remain here with Mr. Briggs."

The two moved within fifty feet of the camp, hiding behind some low bushes along the shoreline, which was well-used and nearly clear of vegetation. The beach beyond the boats was cluttered with all sorts of garbage—pieces of planking, cast-aside wooden trunks with their lids torn off or upended, a dirty blanket lying discarded on the sand, even a chair sitting askew with a leg missing. Farther up the shore, beside the last shanty, was a pile of firewood half-protected under a sagging tarp and what looked to be a veritable supply depot: spare masts and spars, coils of rope, rolls of canvas, various barrels and buckets, and wooden crates of all sizes. Beyond, on the far side of the lagoon, Kinkaid could just make out the ragged line of a half-dozen tents.

Three men and two women were sitting at a large planked table behind a roaring fire in front of the middle shack, laughing and joking. Another man, looking thin and old, and a plump woman were standing beside the fire. The woman lit a cigar from a burning twig and puffed away on it while the thin old man sipped from a mug. Kinkaid could only hear bits and pieces of what the man and woman were saying, but it was definitely English.

Monk startled Kinkaid by touching him on the shoulder, and then the Indian held up the ten fingers on his hands and pointed into the forest.

"Ten men? Behind us?" asked Kinkaid.

There was a commotion—some loud voices and a shout that sounded like Mr. Briggs. "Let's get back there," Kinkaid whispered to O'Toole as Monk disappeared into the forest.

As they turned, a group of men appeared from the underbrush, barring their way. Kinkaid brought up his pistol by instinct, but there were too many of them, all carrying heavy muskets that they pointed menacingly. Behind them stood a downcast Mr. Briggs and the others, relieved of their weapons and under guard by more than a dozen pirates.

A big man with wild, curly red hair and a long, dark-red mustache strode forward, gave Kinkaid a bold look, and asked in a deep, authoritative voice, "You are the officer in charge here?"

Kinkaid detected a Scottish accent. He stepped forward and asked, "And who am I addressing?"

The man let out a resounding laugh as he elbowed a muscular Negro in the side and said, "I believe the good man is reminding us of our manners. We do remember our manners, don't we, Gunner?"

The black man raised his head snobbishly and, mimicking an aristocrat, pretended to take a whiff of snuff and replied, "I'll have Jeeves fetch some for us, straightaway, Gov'nor," which brought rough laughter from the motley group, many fancifully dressed, most of them Negroes.

The red-haired man took off his hat and bowed elaborately with a sweeping gesture, ringlets and headscarf flying. "Captain Jack Blackstone," he boomed, "scoundrel of the seven seas, at your service, Your Highness!"

This brought more hearty laughter from his men—all but one, the short swarthy one with the big hoop earring and a jagged scar under his left eye, the eye of a man who would as soon cut your throat as look at you.

"Looks like dees men accept your invite, Captain Blackstone, just like you said dey would," said the one called Gunner, his voice deep and melodious.

"I told you we were too pretty to resist," gloated Blackstone. "Now then, who are you and where do you come from with your fancy striped flag?"

"Captain Kinkaid of the American Navy," answered Kinkaid in his strongest voice.

Blackstone, looking surprised, grinned and said, "In that case, I say welcome to Hurricane Hole, my small town in paradise, Captain. Allow me to introduce my colleagues. This is Mr. Gunner

Freeman, the best damned ship's gunner to ever sight a barrel." The big man, dressed in a red vest and dark-green, floppy hat bowed with a grin. Then Blackstone turned to the mean-looking short one standing beside him. "And this is Mr. Hawke, my, uh...master at arms."

Hawke was a study in infamy with his sharp nose and two-inch scar across his cheek where someone had tried to carve his eye out. A vaguely familiar, poorly rendered tattoo of a shark adorned his right forearm.

When Hawke merely sneered, Blackstone laughed and said, "Not exactly the sociable type." The muskets remained pointed at a deadly angle while Blackstone sized them up, then, laughing victoriously, turned and with a wave said, "Follow me."

He led them to the camp. The men and women there were not at all surprised at having guests under guard, the group scrutinizing Kinkaid and his men as Blackstone led the procession. Kinkaid could now see in the light of the campfire that the longboats on the beach were colorfully painted and bestowed with such names as *Redemption*, *Exodus*, and *Mercy*. Blackstone motioned for Kinkaid to follow him to the middle shack, where a crude sign over the door read "Chateau Blackstone."

"You come with me, Captain," said Blackstone. "Your men will stay out here. They will be well-cared for, I assure you...won't they Buttermilk?" he shouted to the stout woman smoking a cigar, who laughed as she handed a bottle of red wine to Gunner Freeman.

Not exactly sure what he had stumbled into or where it was leading, Kinkaid thought biding his time seemed the only sensible course.

Blackstone strode heavily into a large room stuffed full of furniture. A lamp burned on the table, another on a fancy dresser against the far wall. Thin, gauzelike material had been draped over the open windows, serving as mosquito netting. All of the furniture—the desk, another dresser, chairs, and a couch—was fine quality, ornate and expensive things. Oil paintings hung on the wooden walls in heavy gold-leafed frames, large and small; they were mostly European landscapes, with a few portraits and some paintings of ships at sea. Blackstone went to a side cupboard and brought out a bottle of European brandy and two glasses. He poured them, handed one to Kinkaid, and flopped down on the maroon couch with the elaborately carved legs. A low table between them held a candelabrum, a small wooden box, and a chessboard with carved ivory and ebony pieces.

"Please sit down, Captain, make yourself comfortable," Blackstone said as he reached for the wooden box, took out a couple of cigars, and tossed one to Kinkaid, who caught it in his lap.

Kinkaid could see the handsome, nutty-brown face clearly now, the quick gray-green eyes with wrinkles at the edges made by years of squinting into the bright Caribbean sunshine. His age was difficult to determine, probably mid-thirties, guessed Kinkaid, but he could as well have been a hale and hearty fifty. He wore a clean white shirt with puffy sleeves and a headscarf of blue-black silk, decorated with tiny white stars. He lit his cigar on a candle and then offered the flame to Kinkaid, who declined.

"Not a smoker?" asked Blackstone, looking at the lit cigar in his hand, rolling it appreciatively between his fingers. "Too bad. Cuban, you know." He sipped his brandy before saying, "So…you say you are in the American Navy, but even if what you say is true, some circles might deny the legitimacy of that fact." He leaned back and placed his soft brown leather boots up on the low table.

"Then those circles shall be surprised," answered Kinkaid boldly.

"And I can see that you are just the man to surprise them," said Blackstone, taunting him.

"About my ship—"

"Yes, your ship," interrupted Blackstone. "I thought to board her, take her as my own. I could have, you know, the minute you and your men were up on the hill. We saw you anchor and land. I expected as much, the moment I saw you head back for the

171

channel. Took you long enough to get here." Blackstone shot Kinkaid a challenging look, as if daring him to protest, then shifted away once again, sitting back, relaxed, confident, cigar in one hand, brandy snifter in the other.

Perhaps Blackstone was right. Perhaps he and his men were capable of boarding and taking *Swift*. At the moment any disaster seemed possible, thought Kinkaid, pondering the possibilities, which seemed few at the moment.

"I could still take her if I wanted to," boasted Blackstone.

"And why don't you?"

Jack Blackstone swirled the light-brown liquid in his glass, staring through it at the lamplight beyond. "You are an American…I am an American. We Americans should stick together, help one another."

The man couldn't possibly think Kinkaid would agree to join him. "I've orders to search out and attack pirates," said Kinkaid provocatively.

"Pirates?" asked Blackstone with a frown, eyes once more darting across the room. "In some circles, all American ships are regarded as pirates, but most especially American Navy ships."

The man had a point.

"You help the cause your way and I do it in mine…without all those regulations and uniforms and…" Blackstone was waving his cigar in the air, looking for the right words.

"Flags?" offered Kinkaid.

"Exactly." He made an exclamation point with his cigar. "And who is to say which is more effective? How many British merchants have you taken or sunk, Captain? I can tell you that my *Moondog* has taken at least three dozen of the enemy's ships, depriving them of war materials that otherwise would have gone to kill good Americans."

"For profit," Kinkaid challenged him.

"One person's cause is another's profit, but what difference does it make as long as everybody gets what they want? I sell everything I can't use in St. Eustatia, where one hopes the right supplies arrive in the right hands." The man seemed reluctant to make eye contact, preferring to stare at the ceiling, his drink, or the smoke emanating from his cigar. The quick glances Kinkaid received were cold; even the man's laughter was full of anger and malice. "Naturally, we take a few things here and there to compensate us for our troubles."

"And lives…how many innocent lives—"

"I am no murderer, Captain," said Blackstone, rising out of his slouch. "No one has been killed who has not resisted. In fact, I have been known to go to considerable lengths to return civilians to friendly shores. I have no fight with anyone. I only wish to be let alone."

"To do what?" asked a cynical Kinkaid

Blackstone sat back against the sofa, relaxed again. "To take care of my…people," he said calmly. He eyed Kinkaid a moment and then smiled. "Ah, you're concerned about beliefs…one of those fancy, idealistic words. To me, beliefs are for those who can afford them. Too often they become justifications for the sort of things you accuse me of." He took a sip from his glass.

"So you believe in nothing."

"I believe in survival. But don't misunderstand me; I take only British shipping and leave all others alone. The reasons are my own, but I tell you this in all honesty."

This big, dark man puzzled Kinkaid, normally a quick judge of character. Blackstone was loud and plainspoken but intelligent, strong and capable, shrewd and clever, seemingly more charming gentleman than murderous pirate, or was he simply a good actor as well?

As if reading his thoughts, Blackstone asked, "So what do you think of me, Captain?"

"It seems you have carved out a world for yourself," answered Kinkaid, avoiding the question. "A dangerous world, at that."

"Life is dangerous," he said, laughing. "I live by my wits and my wits tell me that I should fight tooth and claw for that which sustains me and my people, here, in my world. The rest is of no concern to me, why, even death holds no fear when all of value has been stripped from a man." Blackstone laughed as if at his own words, then asked, "But what about you, Captain, what is it that brings you here into my domain?"

A simple, half-truth would suffice. "Escorting American merchants to safe waters."

"And what now?"

"That depends," he answered, suspecting that he was being manipulated by a master.

"And what of the British? Surely your orders include making life miserable for your enemies—your enemies and mine are one and the same."

"Are they?"

"Captain, did you not just deliver an American diplomat to St. Eustatia?"

Surprised, Kinkaid managed to hide his reaction, he hoped. How could Blackstone have learned of this so quickly? The only way was if someone on St. Eustatia...of course, the entire island had been aware of Simpson's arrival.

"The enemy of your country, the threat to your diplomat's mission, would be the island of St. Kitts...not me," said Blackstone.

Kinkaid's eyes gave him away.

"Come now, Captain," said Blackstone, swirling his brandy. "I have seen those mortars on your deck. No wonder you were so slow. No ship hoping to catch pirates would carry such heavy and useless guns on her decks...useless against a moving ship, that is, but quite effective against a stationary land target. And the closest British land target in these waters, the one place most threatening to St. Eustatia and to the American dependence on trade with her, is the British-held naval base at St. Kitts."

Kinkaid sat in silence, unwilling to compliment the savvy Blackstone with a response.

"I know what you're thinking, Captain," said Blackstone with a smug smile. "That I am quite astute...for a pirate."

Kinkaid returned the smile in spite of himself. The man was a born charmer. "For a pirate."

"What do you know of St. Kitts?" asked Blackstone.

Kinkaid remained silent.

"You probably have little more than an outdated chart. Am I right?"

"Perhaps…perhaps not," said Kinkaid, hopefully sounding noncommittal.

"What if I told you that I have been there…recently? What if I told you I know how many and exactly what kinds of ships are in the harbor there? What if I could tell you the disposition of their forces?"

"Such as any shore batteries and where they were located?" asked Kinkaid, surprising himself. But after all, the man was making sense. If he did, indeed, possess recent intelligence, he would be useful, pirate or not.

"Now we're talking," said Blackstone enthusiastically.

Kinkaid lifted his unlit cigar. "About what, exactly?"

"Please, Captain, my patience is not what it used to be."

"Why would you be interested?" asked Kinkaid, incredulous that a pirate might share his intentions.

"A fair question, Captain," agreed Blackstone. "In truth I have little interest in the island itself; however, anything that will hurt the English appeals to my sense of fair play. If I stumble upon a chance to reduce or eliminate British naval presence in the Caribbean, so much the better."

"So you're telling me you'd risk your ship and your life in the name of a just cause," said Kinkaid, the cynicism apparent in his voice.

"Ha, very funny, Mr. Hero. No, that is for you to do, not me. But I could help you to your ends…for a price."

"Now I think I'm beginning to understand…"

"I doubt you will ever understand, Captain," growled Blackstone.

"Perhaps not," agreed Kinkaid. "But tell me, what is your price? If, that is, I were interested in your…help."

"There is a battery of eighteen-pound field pieces on the heights, overlooking the harbor. You give me those guns, and I will give you the island." Without waiting for an answer, Blackstone added, as if talking to himself, "With those I can defend myself against any intruders that may be foolish enough to follow me into this anchorage."

"As you hoped we would?" asked Kinkaid.

"You would never have made such a mistake," said Blackstone.

Kinkaid ignored the flattery, guessing, "You are already well-defended."

"I have a few pieces situated here and there, but nothing like those heavy guns. You might call them my security for an old age."

"And just how do you think you are going to give me St. Kitts?"

"As you well know, the guns of British ships pose the greatest danger to any attack on the harbor at Basseterre," stated Blackstone.

Kinkaid held his agreement in check.

"I can ensure that there are no ships left in the harbor when you are ready to make your move." Blackstone sat back and took a leisurely draw on his cigar, his bold proposition on the table.

"If you wish to fight for our cause, I would think a letter of marque from one of the Southern colonies—"

Blackstone laughed. "Let's not get carried away with patriotism, shall we, Captain? I said nothing about fighting."

A knock came at the door. It was Gunner Freeman with a platter of bread, fruit, and kidney pie. He wordlessly set it on the low table next to the chessboard and then left.

Blackstone stabbed a slice of melon with a dagger he pulled from his belt, saying, "We can discuss this later. Right now, let's have a drink, eat, and talk as friends. Do you play chess, Kinkaid?"

And so the two talked, drank, ate...and played chess. Kinkaid had played the game as a youth, vaguely remembered the various classic opening moves, but had never mastered the nuances of the game, and so Blackstone defeated him soundly.

"You seem to know what I'm going to do before I do," complained Kinkaid amicably, his king surrounded again.

"The secret of the game," boasted Blackstone, "is to figure out your opponent's next move and make a preemptive strike."

"Then I'd say you've learned the secret well," granted Kinkaid, checkmated again.

"Purely instinctive, part of my survival skills to be a step ahead of the next man," he said smugly, as raucous cheering and shouting erupted outside. "Sounds like a bit of fun out in the yard. Shall we join them, Captain?"

A noisy crowd had gathered around the great outdoor table, cluttered with a dozen open bottles of wine. Another half-dozen empty bottles littered the ground.

Midshipman Briggs sat across from buxom Molly Butterfield, nicknamed Buttermilk for her soft white skin, but at the moment her massive fist tightly clenched Mr. Briggs's smaller hand. They were arm wrestling, and Buttermilk had the edge.

"C'mon, Butter!" cheered a thin but winsome brunette with a scar on her chin. "Rip the young snot's arm off!"

A mighty effort from Briggs brought them back to a standoff, both arms upright, though Buttermilk was smiling hugely while Briggs had a desperate grimace on his face. She was obviously toying with the young gentleman.

O'Toole and his men cheered the straining boy while Buttermilk's cronies made the larger amount of noise, though nobody was betting because no one was dumb enough to bet on Briggs.

Rafferty had been cheering for Briggs, but now his attention had flagged. He could not take his eyes off the svelte brunette standing across the table.

Buttermilk gave Briggs a determined look and then began tilting the boy's arm back, slowly but inexorably. With beads of sweat forming on his brow, Briggs was straining hard to keep in the game.

"Hang tough, Mr. Briggs!" shouted Smith in encouragement.

"She's just a girl, after all!" Rikker reminded him.

With that, Buttermilk seemed to relent, her hand teetering backwards, which only served to provide Briggs with false hope, though it had Rafferty cheering again.

"Somebody wipe me brow! The sweat is stinging me eyes!" complained Buttermilk, whereupon the lanky brunette raised her petticoats and smeared her friend's face with the lace. "I said wipe me brow, Lucinda, not suffocate me!"

Buttermilk was riled now and, tired of toying with Briggs, looked him in the eye, gritted her teeth, and let out a bellowing cry as her massive arm came down, throwing Briggs right off his seat, making him cry out in pain and defeat as he spun backwards onto the matted grass.

"Nice try, there, pretty boy," she said with a broad smile, revealing a missing tooth. She pulled the shamed Briggs to his feet and then slapped the young midshipman on his posterior. "Maybe you'd have better luck with me a little later, eh? I could show you a few wrestling moves…in the privacy of me tent."

"Aye," came in Lucinda, "a quick learner he'd be, I fancy."

The crowd laughed uproariously at the lewd suggestion, while Briggs turned red, smiling sheepishly, but looking nonetheless interested.

A bloodcurdling scream erupted from the far side of the table, which drew everyone's attention. One of the pirates had his hand pinned to the tabletop with a dagger. Hawke, Blackstone's master-at-arms, yanked the dagger free and growled, "I told you to get your own bottle," as the pinned man fell to the lawn, clutching his bloody hand and moaning in agony.

"Hawke, get back to your camp!" ordered Blackstone, fury in his voice. "And take your brother with you."

Hawke helped the wounded man to his feet, and the two straggled off toward the tents and campfires farther down the beach.

"Sibling rivalry," explained Blackstone, playing down the violent incident. "Nothing to spoil the party." Coming over to Kinkaid, he placed a hand on his shoulder and suggested, "You and your men are welcome to spend the night, Kinkaid."

The crowd became boisterous again and began shouting its approval. Lucinda was batting her eyelashes Rafferty's way.

"I thank you for the invitation, Captain," answered Kinkaid diplomatically, though quietly, so only Blackstone heard him, the drunken throng still making enough noise, "but I believe we had better call it a night." Consorting with this wild bunch would only bring a breakdown in discipline and lead to trouble. There was no need to explain his reasoning to Blackstone.

Kinkaid made sure to have a good look around before calling the men. A ditch was being dug in front of the first building on the left, a couple of shovels poking out of the mounds of dirt, some heavy logs piled up behind—a redoubt under construction. Beyond it were some small fires blazing near the tents, dark shadows of men around them where Hawke and his wounded brother had retreated. And off in the trees across the lagoon came a reflection from those fires—the barrel of a cannon?

"All right, men," said Kinkaid after the commotion died down. "It's time we returned to the ship."

They were almost back to the trail that led up the hill and over the narrow peninsula when Monk silently rejoined them from out of the forest.

VII

Mad Doctors and Bad Cooks

The next day found *Swift* on a course for Dominica. If Kinkaid's officers and crew thought it strange that they were running with Blackstone's *Moondog*, a ship everyone considered to be a pirate vessel, they kept their doubts to themselves, with the exception of Boatswain O'Toole. Kinkaid overheard him refer to Blackstone's Hurricane Hole as "Sodom and Gomorrah combined, those immoral people in pursuit of Mammon." O'Toole suspected that any alliance with the pirate group was an unholy one at best and it irked Kinkaid somewhat that Blackstone made no attempt to allay those impressions, flying his personal flag, a white dog howling at the full moon on a black field, from the mainmast.

Kinkaid later told Major Bauer something of the conversation he'd had with Captain Blackstone, admitting that he was not sure that anything the man said had been true. But even Bauer was impressed with what Blackstone seemed to know about the island base and could readily understand why Kinkaid would want to make use of the questionable character. The knowledge gained about the four heavy artillery pieces on the high ground overlooking the town and the harbor was valuable in itself.

Blackstone's ship, with her eight nine-pounders, seemed serviceable enough for the job he had proposed for her, likely to handle well and with good speed, which was the critical factor. So it was simple, really, the reason Kinkaid had accepted Blackstone's proposal. The man seemed to know St. Kitts and was willing to help…for a price. And the price was right; even Bauer had to agree with that. But there was no explaining why Kinkaid felt he could trust the man, Captain Jack Blackstone, if that was indeed the man's true name.

Three days of easy sailing brought the two ships to the jungle island of Dominica, *Swift* arriving on her shores early in the morning, with *Moondog* trailing behind. The sky was overcast and a light shower fell on the calm sea. Kinkaid knew beforehand from the chart that it was a mountainous island, covered in thick jungle, but now, because of the clouds and rain, they could see little of the land but the tops of the trees along the shoreline, shrouded in mist. They entered the wide bay under jibs and tops, barely making headway, but that is how Kinkaid wanted it. He was suspicious of the wild, dark shore. There was a foreboding aura about the place; even the thin beach was of black sand.

Jack Blackstone in his *Moondog* remained farther out. He had made it abundantly clear that he thought little of employing the Caribs to take St. Kitts, saying simply, "Those savages are going to give you nothing but trouble, Kinkaid, and good luck to you is all I say."

"Doesn't appear to be anyone around, Captain," observed Major Bauer, looking into the wet jungle, sounding concerned. There was not a hut or a clearing to be seen. Indeed, the shore was an unbroken mass of tangled vines and overhanging palm fronds dripping with rain, the slim beach cluttered with driftwood. Not a sign of human habitation.

"I'm certain this is the right bay, sir," offered Mr. Thorne, "unless the chart is wrong."

"This is the place, Mr. Thorne. Helmsman, take us over there toward those tall trees." It made perfect sense; only a fool would bring strangers directly to one's base of operations. Yes, someone with a suspicious mind would have chosen just such a place for a rendezvous.

"And a half, four!" came the leadsman's cry from forward. At least the water was deep enough and crystal clear, though the gently falling raindrops made a constantly shifting pattern of spreading rings on the surface of the bay and prevented a transparent view of the bottom.

A large flock of blue and red parrots took off from out of the trees as *Swift* drew nearer, their squawks loud and startling in the silent bay. There, high at the top of the tallest tree, was a large, acid-green lizard, its head held proudly high like the prehistoric ruler of a primeval land. Off to the right were two more, perched at the tops of their own trees, only slightly smaller, all watching with disdain the approach of the ships.

"Iguanas, Captain," noted Weatherby. "They're harmless, actually. Their favorite foods are fruits and flowers."

"That is comforting, Mr. Weatherby. Starboard your helm, Rafferty," ordered Kinkaid quietly. "Bring us about, head us into the breeze." What little breeze there was.

"Standing by at the anchor, sir!" came the shout from O'Toole, forward.

"Let her go! Take in the sails, Mr. Lofton!" The clattering of the anchor chain seemed magnified here in the stillness of the bay, almost sacrilegious. The ship settled back against her cable with her stern toward the shore, the tide coming in.

"Anchor's holding, Captain!" shouted O'Toole.

"Sails secured, sir!" reported Lofton.

Kinkaid hesitated to dismiss the anchor detail, and so the crew waited for further orders. The shore remained silent, the humidity high, and with barely a breeze reaching inside the cove it was stifling hot. The iguanas remained perched like stone idols, their blinking eyes the only evidence of life. The flock of parrots must have found a more private roost.

Finally, Kinkaid said, "Have the crew take their breakfast, Mr. Saddler. O'Toole, lower the ship's boat so that Rafferty can finish his repairs. We'll wait. If nobody shows in an hour, we'll go ashore."

"Aye aye, Captain."

Kinkaid studied the still, dark-green trees for a moment and then said to the first lieutenant, "We'll assume a hostile shore. Set the watch accordingly. Major Bauer, I'll trouble you to provide a few of your marines on the deck as well with loaded muskets." Kinkaid was not of a mind to take any chances along this strange coast.

"I'll post a security watch, Captain," gave Bauer.

"Mr. Weatherby, will you join me for breakfast?"

"Why, thank you, sir."

Kinkaid had taken to having only a biscuit or two and some fruit for his breakfast, keeping it simple, Roach frustrating all his efforts to have a decent serving of eggs. And the coffee was still not right. But this morning, with Weatherby as his guest, he ordered a full course of eggs with fried potatoes, along with bacon, bread, and fruit. The coffee was too strong and bitter, but better too strong than too weak. Perhaps Roach was learning something after all, thought Kinkaid…until the eggs and potatoes came. The eggs were runny and the potatoes were still hard. He sent the plates back, but when they were returned the food was burnt and dried out. Kinkaid thought to fire Roach on the spot, then considered his guest.

"I'm sorry for this mess, Weatherby," said a perturbed Kinkaid. "I had hoped to serve you a hearty breakfast."

"No need to apologize, Captain," answered Weatherby, eating cheerfully. "We're quite used to the…uneven quality of meals, sir. That is, in the officers' mess, well, our cook…" Weatherby lowered his voice to a whisper, "he's not much better than your Roach, sir. And the crew's cook, Hairy Hyde, why, he's even worse."

"How is that, Weatherby?" Kinkaid wanted to know.

"Why, O'Toole had to break up a fight in the galley just yesterday, sir, when one of the crew caught Hyde spitting in the stew."

Kinkaid grimaced at the thought.

"He didn't even deny it," explained Weatherby, "said it was to add flavor. O'Toole said it was the flavor of spite, that Hyde hates everyone because he hates himself."

So no one aboard was getting better meals than the Captain. But there was a more pressing topic Kinkaid wanted to discuss with Weatherby.

"I've wanted to say something," began Kinkaid, "about Midshipman Cutler…"

"Sir, please," said Weatherby.

"Mr. Cutler was a fine, reliable officer…and a brave man," said Kinkaid uncertainly.

"And a good friend, sir," added Weatherby.

"Yes," acknowledged Kinkaid, "and…well, much too young to die…"

It was difficult, bringing back the incident, getting the words out, and he wasn't sure why he was doing this, but he felt he had to acknowledge the event somehow with Weatherby.

"I shall miss him very much…as will we all." He felt remiss enough for having waited so long to say anything, and now he thought to say something about the circumstances, the suddenness of it, maybe even to explain why he hadn't pursued the sloop. He knew that they had scored some damaging hits on her, and he suspected that Weatherby would have preferred that his captain chase her. They might have caught up with her if she had been taking on water or if her rigging had been damaged, but his purpose had been to escort and protect the merchants, not go chasing after some nebulous revenge. He thought to say all these things to Weatherby, but to what purpose? The words were said, and though Kinkaid felt they were not enough, they would have to do, recognizing that no amount of words would ever be enough.

"Hank, sir…well, he should have had the chance to live his life," said Weatherby, looking down at his plate. "I don't believe he ever danced with a girl."

The words were true, yet the bitterness with which Weatherby said them made it difficult for Kinkaid to respond.

"He said something strange, sir...before he died," continued Weatherby. "He said he didn't mind that he would be...feeding the fish." Weatherby laughed sadly, then shook his head and asked, "Why would he say such a thing?"

Kinkaid, at a loss, could only admit, "I'm not sure, Weatherby. Perhaps a revelation of some kind. Men have been known to say strange things...near the end."

Weatherby had expected no certain answer from his captain, somberly relating, "O'Toole said that Hank had made his peace with this world, that he was already crossing over into the other, better world, and knew that it was a right and proper thing for his body to remain here on earth where it belonged...that he wouldn't need it where he was going."

Kinkaid cleared his throat and said, "Perhaps O'Toole is right," and then immediately regretted the foolish statement, it ringing false in his ears, the easy, nice thing to say, but an empty, vacuous utterance, bereft of conviction.

Weatherby, understanding quite well that Kinkaid only sought to ease his sorrow, said, "Sir, I know that you have to write a letter to his parents. If you haven't done so already, I wonder if you would allow me to write that letter; the final draft, of course, left to your approval, sir."

"Of course, Weatherby."

"Thank you, sir...it's the least I can do."

An awkward silence hung in the captain's cabin for a moment, and then both men reached for their coffee.

Changing his tone, Kinkaid said, "Major Bauer tells me that you have shown an interest in the mortars."

"Of course, I am most interested in their workings, sir," answered Weatherby, relieved that the conversation was back to business, "but even more in how they are to be employed."

Kinkaid, aware that it would not do to provide Weatherby with such information before his first officer was apprised, answered, "It must be apparent that they figure largely in Major Bauer's future endeavor."

"I expected as much, sir," he answered, "but the crew was wondering when they might have the chance to, well, do something, Captain. Not that bringing Mr. Simpson down here wasn't doing something, sir, but…"

Kinkaid interrupted him. "Major Bauer believes that you are the man for the job of spotting for the mortars."

Weatherby perked up at that, asking, "Are we then to soon strike a blow against our enemies?"

Weatherby had a certain look in his eye, a look unlike any Kinkaid had ever seen in the young man: anger mixed with pleasure. It was a disturbing revelation; Weatherby was seeking some kind of revenge.

"I would be more than happy, that is, with your permission, Captain, to do what I can to help the major with…his endeavor, sir."

"I had to agree that you are certainly the best-qualified."

"The weapons present interesting problems in range and trajectory, Captain, but I've worked it all out on paper, and I'm certain I can put those bombs just where they're needed. I won't let you down, sir," he replied grimly, and then knew he had said too much.

"Of course you won't, Weatherby," said Kinkaid, unhappy with Weatherby's too serious response, suspecting that the assignment had come as no surprise, and wondering how much Weatherby had to do with it. Not that the task of killing men was not a serious one. Perhaps it could not be helped; he certainly could not blame Weatherby for his feelings. After all, how could he be expected to forever remain the same unaffected youth, especially in a time of war? But he hoped that Weatherby would keep his passion for revenge in some proportion, and not allow it to interfere with his otherwise impeccable judgment.

"Sir, there is something I'd like to ask, if I may."

"Of course, Weatherby."

"I'd like your permission to join the marines when they take their target practice, sir. I've already spoken with Major Bauer, and he is agree—"

"Mr. Weatherby, I am quite aware of the fact that you have already been joining Major Bauer's marines during their practice, along with that young drummer boy."

Weatherby could only admit, "The major agreed to allow Private Kirkpatrick to join his men if he proved a good shot, sir."

Kinkaid wanted to tell Weatherby that he thought both of them young and foolish glory seekers, but instead answered, "Well, I don't know about Kirkpatrick, but Major Bauer informs me that you are becoming quite the marksman." Weatherby sighed and was about to respond when Kinkaid added, "And you have my permission to continue." If Weatherby were to be a spotter, placing himself in harm's way, it would behoove him to at least know how to protect himself.

"Thank you, sir." said Weatherby, satisfied.

Kinkaid thought to remind Weatherby, "We will be returning to St. Eustatia when this business is concluded and a bit of liberty will be in order. Perhaps as early as a week from now."

Weatherby smiled. "I would certainly look forward to another visit, Captain."

Suddenly there came the muted sounds of muskets being fired, then shouts from above, bringing both men to the deck.

The marines were standing at the rail with their muskets, but no smoke from a recent discharge was emanating from their weapons, none visible on deck.

"Who is firing?" Kinkaid wanted to know.

"It came from the shore, Captain," said Major Bauer. "Someone fired upon two men standing at the waterline, there."

A head popped up from behind some palm fronds at the edge of the beach. Then another. Now they came, slowly, cautiously, out of hiding, two men crouching low, looking about nervously. One was a big white man wearing a filthy shirt that might have been white once. The other was a thin, elderly Negro wearing an equally dirty white shirt as well as a bright-red scarf around his neck, foolishly making himself a noticeable target. Both were covered in mud.

At first they just stood there, darting frantic glances at the ship while looking nervously behind them into the forest. Then they left the cover of the trees, crouching low across the beach, into the surf, and then cautiously began wading out, finally swimming toward the ship.

They had not swum far when five black men appeared along the shore—three were practically naked, wielding machetes, the other two wore stained pants and nondescript dark shirts and carried firearms. Spotting the men in the water, the two raised their muskets and fired almost at the same instant. One ball hit the white man in the back, the other splashed close by his head. He slumped lifeless in the water, a patch of red spreading in a large stain around him. The old Negro kept swimming madly, clumsily, churning the water with his wild strokes and exuberant kicking as the men on shore worked to reload their muskets.

"Fire over their heads!" shouted Kinkaid. "Drive them off!"

At a signal from Major Bauer, four muskets blasted the air from the deck, and the men on shore beat a hasty retreat.

The man in the water continued to thrash desperately toward the ship, gasping and shouting alternately in English and French.

"Help me, *s'il vous plais*! They want…to kill…"

Rafferty had been alongside the ship in a boat with three seamen, repairing the outer hull.

"Rafferty, pick those men up! Quickly, now!" shouted Kinkaid.

They reached the flailing black man first and hauled him up before making their way to where the white man lay face down in the water, the red stain spreading ever outward. Reaching the ship, they struggled to hoist the big man's limp body up on deck where Dr. Grafton was waiting. He placed his head against the man's chest, looked into his eyes, and pronounced, "This man's dead, sir."

Drenched and exhausted, the elderly black man feebly climbed the ladder and fell at Kinkaid's feet, coughing and spitting water.

"*Merci, Capitaine*! May the Lord bless you! You have saved me!" the man exclaimed, clinging to Kinkaid's ankles with his large hands. First Lieutenant Saddler was watching the scene with raised eyebrows, no pity there. It was embarrassing, but Kinkaid tolerated the man's anguish—for a moment, at least.

"Please, that's enough," he said, lifting one foot out of the man's grasp. "Tell me, who was going to kill you?"

"His men, *Capitaine*," said the man, still on his knees, pointing into the jungle, his terrible fright evident in his eyes. "The Doctor's men. Extremely cruel, they are, sir."

"The Doctor…Pitt-Pouliessier?" asked Major Bauer.

He must have come close to the correct pronunciation, for at the sound of the man's name the black man cringed in dreadful fright, looking toward the beach in wild terror. "Ah, the name of *abomination*, of *atrocité*! The very one! He will kill me if—"

"No one is going to kill you," said Kinkaid, trying to speak sense to the man, though he himself was glancing toward the shore. "Where is he? Is he right in-shore here? Does he know there is a ship here?"

The questions were too much for the man, overcome by terror, still trying to catch his breath. He just sat slumped on the deck, shaking his head and mumbling, "I don't know, sir. All I know is that three of us ran and kept running until we saw your mast." Then he once more reached up to clutch at Kinkaid's pant leg, crying, "Oh, thank you so much, *Capitaine*. You have saved my life. I am forever in your debt. What is it that I may do for you…only ask and I…"

Kinkaid looked to Dr. Grafton.

"Perhaps a glass of rum, sir," came the surgeon's suggestion.

"Take this man below, Rafferty," said Kinkaid. "Give him something to eat and drink; try to calm him down."

"Aye, Captain. Come along, there…"

Suddenly the man stood up, straight and tall, at attention. "Mister Cato Africanus, captain's steward, at your service, *Capitaine*, formerly of His Majesty's Ship *Sovereign*." Then he gave a military salute, which Kinkaid returned. The man seemed absolutely sane now, thought Kinkaid, no longer out of his mind with fear.

"Can you cook?" asked Kinkaid.

"More than cook, *Capitaine*. I am a chef, an *artiste*, trained in Paris. I am also a tailor. Why, I have designed and made clothes for royalty," said the man proudly.

"Well, Mr. Africanus, perhaps there are some things that you will be able to do for me, after all."

"Anything, I am at your service…"

"Right now, why don't you go with Rafferty. He'll get you a bite to eat, you can clean yourself up, and we can discuss your duties later."

"As you wish, sir," he said effusively. "Anything at all, *Capitaine*."

Rafferty heard what the man had said about being a cook, but he was skeptical. In his opinion, the man was too skinny to be a cook. Any cooks worth their pots and pans that Rafferty had known tended to be on the chubby side, not skin and bones like this one. The man continued to give thanks to Kinkaid and the Lord above until he was below.

"Look, sir," said Lofton, pointing toward *Moondog*.

Captain Blackstone was standing in his ship's boat, heading for *Swift*, probably curious about the shooting.

"Any sign of the men on shore?"

"No, Captain," answered Weatherby.

"Major Bauer, I suppose you'd like to go and find your Doctor."

"The trail of those men should be easy enough to follow, Captain."

"Would you mind very much if a few sailors joined you?" he asked, relinquishing land operations to the marine commander.

"My pleasure, Captain."

"Mr. Saddler, you will be in command of the ship in my absence."

"Aye, Captain."

"Mr. Lofton, Take a party ashore to bury that man. Make sure you're well armed."

"Aye aye, sir."

"Mr. Weatherby, I'd feel better if we had a few loaded cannons pointing at the shore."

"Coming right up, sir."

"Mr. Briggs, find yourself a musket. O'Toole, you too, and bring some water."

The deck was a flurry of activity as Kinkaid went to his cabin and took his two pistols out of their box, aware that Weatherby would be stung, left behind for the second time, yet he would get his chance soon enough. Kinkaid stuffed a handful of balls into his pocket, along with wadding and an extra flint, before returning to the deck where Mr. Lofton and the burial detail were already on their way to shore with the body. Captain Blackstone was climbing the ship's ladder.

"I thought you said the natives would be on our side," said Blackstone.

"Just a couple of men trying to get away," explained Kinkaid.

"Away from what?"

"We hope to find out, forthwith," answered Kinkaid, loading his pistols as the other men were loading their muskets.

"I'm going with you," said Blackstone, grabbing a musket out of the hands of the hard-faced Corporal Decker.

Decker was simmering while Monk reached for his hatchet.

"At ease, men," growled Sergeant Anders.

"Suit yourself," said Kinkaid, knowing that Blackstone would not be argued with, probably suspicious of being left out of something that might profit him. Kinkaid shoved the pistols into his belt. "Mr. Saddler, you know what to do if we have not returned before sunrise."

"I'll send a well-armed party to find you, Captain," Saddler assured him.

It was easy to follow the trail of broken twigs and torn leaves. Monk Chunk led the way, carrying only his hatchet. O'Toole was next and was cautious and watchful at first, his musket at the ready, not fully trusting that the armed men they were following were not hiding in ambush just ahead. Captain Blackstone brought up the rear and kept looking back to ensure they weren't attacked from behind. But it soon became apparent that the men they were following were traveling fast, interested only in getting back to wherever it was they had come from, as Monk kept indicating, always far ahead of the group.

Reaching the interior where the canopy broadened and the ground was more open, Monk led them over a trail of scuffed ground, then dead leaves, sometimes beaten-down grasses, occasionally tracked mud. They walked quickly for almost two hours until they found a well-defined trail, wide and much used. It was almost noon, and the men were tired and sweaty, the humidity intolerable, when they came to the edge of a clearing, an open area covered by waist-high grass, where Monk waited.

He pointed to an area where flies buzzed loudly. Major Bauer and Kinkaid were the first to reach the half-naked torso. It was a white man, and by the way his blood still glistened, he had been killed and mutilated recently. His hands, feet, and head were missing.

"Probably a prisoner, killed to save them time on the trail," said Bauer.

Briggs was coming up behind them with the water pouch. Kinkaid turned and put his arms on the boy's shoulder to distract him. "We'll take a water break over there," he said, indicating the tree line.

O'Toole was not so easily dissuaded, but he quickly retreated with a sour look, remarking, "Damned savages."

Blackstone noticed the flies and took note of the cadaver but ignored it, keeping his eyes on the jungle around them.

Briggs wanted to know what Kinkaid was keeping from him, and so he asked, "What was it, Boats?"

"They cut off all his important parts…they think they've taken all that makes a man a man," remarked O'Toole, wiping his sweaty brow.

"Why?" asked Briggs. He knew of the evil eye from his Sicilian grandmother and was interested in such things in spite of the fact that he was spooked.

"If they meet in the spirit world, he'll be less of an opponent, unable to exact his revenge," explained O'Toole. "But that's only what the savages believe. A man is more than flesh."

But Blackstone took issue with the remark, snarling, "A man without flesh is no man at all."

"This is no time to argue," said Kinkaid, moving between the two. The gruesome discovery had put everyone's nerves on edge. Kinkaid led them cautiously to the tree line and stopped. "We'll rest here for five minutes and check our flints and priming pans."

Monk was on the far side of the clearing and gave a signal.

"He's found the trail on the other side," explained Bauer. He returned a signal and the Indian disappeared again. "I sent him ahead."

Decker and Briggs re-primed their flash pans, finding the powder jostled out after the rough slog. The water was passed around, and the men eagerly drank their fill.

A green lizard was clinging to the leaf of a giant philodendron a few feet away, upside-down, its head darting from side to side, appraising the strangers. A second lizard was holding fast to the bark of a nearby tree, identical to the first except that it was grayish brown, the same color as the bark. They were anoles or chameleons—lizards with the magical ability to change their color to match their surroundings.

O'Toole crawled toward the green lizard, its head now immobile, eyes fixed suspiciously on its stalker. Drawing nearer, O'Toole reached his arm out slowly. His hand came within six inches of the creature when it suddenly darted up the leaf and went hurtling through the underbrush out of sight. The brown chameleon still clung to the tree trunk, watching intently.

"You'll have to be faster than that," laughed Blackstone.

"Aye, too fast for me," admitted O'Toole. Then his grin vanished as he stared open-mouthed at the jungle beyond.

Kinkaid turned to see what had caused the startled look and at first saw nothing. Then he noticed some movement, as if the bushes were walking. Then, out of the bushes, appeared the painted faces of men, perhaps thirty, all armed.

"Don't move," said Kinkaid quietly, "and for God's sake, don't raise your weapons."

These barefoot and silent brown-skinned men had been carrying bundles of tied grasses before them and now they dropped them on the ground. Armed with machetes, blowguns, or bows and arrows, they were almost naked, wearing skirts of dried grass, long shell necklaces, and headbands with brightly colored feathers. They quickly surrounded Kinkaid's party.

"Can you take us to see Doctor Pitt-Pouliessier?" asked Kinkaid, speaking slowly.

They gave no answer but merely stood there, staring back with impassive faces. Then two of them, one short and chubby, the other taller and more muscular, began talking in a strange tongue. Their voices rose, and the muscular one began vigorously waving his machete in the air. It sounded like an argument. Midshipman Briggs looked frightened and was hefting his musket nervously.

"Easy, Mr. Briggs."

Finally, the shorter, chubbier one seemed to win the argument, at the end slapping the bigger man on the arm with his bow for good measure. Then he motioned for Kinkaid's group to start moving up the trail. They still retained their weapons, but resistance was out of the question. "I believe we have met our allies," said Kinkaid, hoping he sounded more reassuring than he felt.

They crossed the grassy vale, and then skirted a marsh before the Indians took them deeper into the jungle, where giant trees spread their canopies high overhead like lace against the sky, blotting out the sun. Myriad varieties of blooming orchids, giant philodendron and ferns tall as a man lined the route and colorful birds and lizards fled at their passing. Whenever Kinkaid lost sight of the faint trail and hesitated, he would invariably earn a sharp jab from a pointed weapon, the Indians spread evenly among the group, running easily over the muddy trail in their bare feet, barely breathing hard or breaking a sweat. Soon they came to a waterfall and followed the course of its stream, crossing and re-crossing its rocky bottom many times as the hillside grew steeper and then climbing alongside one cascading waterfall after another.

A light rain began to fall and their progress up the mountain slowed as the tired men began slipping and sliding over rocks and roots that clung to the side of the mountain. The Indians seemed to take pity on them, for they waited patiently for them to catch up from time to time, and there was some relief from the oppressive heat as the air became cooler as they climbed higher and higher through the mist. Kinkaid felt near to exhaustion when the trail evened out, opening to a vista that followed along a mountain ridge. In the jungle valley below were trees filled with bright orange blossoms. Beyond the valley were more green mountains, and way off in the distance, between passing mists, rose the towering crest of a mountain, its three peaks jutting high above the clouds. Kinkaid could occasionally see the ocean through holes in the clouds off in the distance, but try as he might he could not find the bay where the *Swift* was anchored. With the sun blocked by the mist and clouds, he had lost his sense of direction.

They followed the ridge trail for almost an hour before it wound its way back down through a dark and thickly tangled jungle, the trail becoming quite narrow and steep, so that only one man at a time could pass, slipping and sliding on the wet, clay-like trail. The rain continued off and on, mostly just a light drizzle. Everyone was thoroughly soaked with water, sweat, and mud, and the air became once again oppressively hot and humid as they descended into a valley. At least the evaporation from their clothes gave some relief. They must have walked at least six or seven miles from the ship, estimated Kinkaid.

The jungle began to thin out and then opened to a barren landscape of steaming streams of bubbling waters that spewed sulfurous gases into the air, burning their nostrils with a foul odor. The valley was between two mountain ranges, obviously volcanic in origin, and Kinkaid had the strange sensation of knowing what the earth must have been like a million years before humans walked its surface. Yellow, red, and orange pools, formed from noxious mixtures of earth and chemicals, bubbled and hissed from the ground, the steaming waters flowing around places where the jungle still struggled to maintain a foothold. In some areas, entire hillsides had caved in, tumbling into the valley in a losing battle against the shifting landscape.

They came to a place where steam seemed to be rising out of a large hole in the ground. As they approached, Kinkaid realized that it was a small lake.

"Jesus, Mary and Joseph," declared an amazed O'Toole, making the sign of the cross, "it's boiling. Looks like the devil's bath, it does, sir."

All the men stopped to gape in wonder at the sight, the gray waters bubbling and foaming up from below, surrounded by a natural cauldron of yellow earth. But they had little time to study the other-worldly scene, for the chubby Indian had the others shouting and pointing toward the trail, jabbing the men with their machetes, encouraging them to keep moving.

Leaving the desolate valley and boiling lake behind, the group hiked up another narrow trail through more dense jungle until, the men thoroughly exhausted, the forest finally gave way to a level area of fields and a small settlement made up of about a dozen huts. Its inhabitants, mostly women and children, came out to see their men and the strange visitors they brought with them. A few dogs started barking, shuffling lazily over to where the men were coming through the village. Their Indian escorts did not pause, not even to recognize their families or relatives, and the dogs quickly lost interest. The Indians kept Kinkaid and the others walking through the settlement, then up a hill, and there, in front of a dilapidated wooden house, they stopped.

Three black men were sitting on the verandah, each in his own battered wicker chair, smoking under its sagging roof. A big mangy dog, half his body lying under the chair of the man in the middle, began growling through curled lips. All three had pistols in their belts and looked a murderous lot. The one in the middle, the taller one, was holding a curved Spanish saber with a jeweled handle, bouncing the flat of the broad blade against his thigh. The dog, though annoyed, seemed too lazy to move. In fact, they all just sat there, looking at Kinkaid and his group.

The two men on either side wore dirty shirts and once-white pants that would never be white again. The one on the left had a wide flat nose and smiled constantly, a cruel, vicious smile. The other looked dazed and sleepy, possibly drugged. They could have been the same two men who had fired from the shore, killing the white man. The Indians sat on the ground, forming a semi-circle around Kinkaid and the others. No one moved or spoke for a moment, and then the chubby Indian started speaking quietly, addressing the tall man in the middle, the one with the saber; a light-skinned black man with short, wiry hair, sporting a goatee, and the only one wearing clean European clothes: dark pants and a frilly, blue silk shirt. He had a long face and big ears, with a diamond stud in his left ear.

"Where you come from, mon?" he asked in a deep voice as the sword still bounced.

"Are you Doctor Pitt-Pouliessier?" Kinkaid guessed. That's when he first heard the moan from behind the house.

"Tell you what, mon," answered the man ominously, the saber still now and pointing directly at Kinkaid. "It be better for you if I be askin' de questions and you be doin' de answerin'. You get it, mon?" His two henchmen sat there puffing away, smiling maliciously.

"Very well," said Kinkaid, thinking he'd better avoid an argument with this man. "We come from Boston…in America."

The dog seemed to have lost interest in the strangers. His annoyance shifted to the flies that were buzzing around his head, and he began snapping at them, his lips curled in anger.

"I know where Boston be, mon. In de fine state of Massachusetts," he said proudly, holding the saber against his chest. "Maybe you tink I be an ignorant savage, eh? My papa come from France. I go to Catholic school in Martinique, learn everyting. Now I become Doctor of All Tings, leader of dis island." He pointed his saber at his nervous, smiling companion, saying, "Dis be General Bobo." The sleepy one he introduced as "General Pierre." Then he leaned back in his chair and propped his feet up against the banister of the verandah. Finally he asked, "You have big boat, mon?"

"Big enough," said Kinkaid warily. Once more he heard a moan from behind the house, louder this time.

Suddenly the Doctor leaped out of his chair, waving the saber over his head and raving at the men next to him. "Will you go and shut him up! Can't you see I be conducting international relations?"

The two men scrambled out of their chairs and ran to the back of the house. The ugly dog had jumped up and began growling at the commotion until the man kicked him soundly, drawing a yelp of pain. A moment later they heard a loud smack from behind the house, and the moan turned to an anguished cry, which was quickly muffled. Captain Blackstone gave Kinkaid a wary glance, eyebrows raised.

"My generals are fools!" shouted the Doctor, eyes blazing. "Damn fools, all I get!" Then he suddenly settled down again, calm, seemingly unperturbed, leaning on the railing, asking quietly, "Dis boat you got, she have de poof-poof…de cannon?"

"Twelve guns," answered Kinkaid confidently. There was no need to mention the mortars.

"Ooooo, many poof-poof. I likee poof-poof. Kill many wit big-noise poof-poof. My generals are fools, but know how to use de cannon."

The man was clearly insane, thought Kinkaid, a dangerous maniac. If this was his idea of international relations...

"You come to help Doctor of All Tings?"

"Yes," said Kinkaid, uncertainly. "We've come to assist you in—"

"You take me, my men, to St. Kitts," he said loudly, slapping his chest. "We kill all British der, fix dem good. Den I be leader of two islands." He stood there, puffing his chest out, a happy grin on his face, white teeth flashing.

The man had certainly summed up the plan, thought Kinkaid, though he made it sound like he was about to take a stroll in the park. But where were his men? He would never take St. Kitts with the few Indians sitting here and the two he called his generals.

"We leave tomorrow morning," the Doctor said, finality in his voice. Then he spoke with the chubby Indian. When the two finished talking, all the Indians got up and headed in different directions; only the chubby one remaining behind.

"You stay tonight," said the Doctor. "I have special entertainment for you. I tink you like."

Kinkaid had told the deck watch that he would be back before dark, but there seemed no chance of arguing with this insane "Doctor of All Tings." The man seemed highly unstable and could very well change his mind about anything.

"We'll remain here tonight," Kinkaid assured him. "However, I need to send a man back—"

"You need to do only what I tell you to do, mon," he said, staring at Kinkaid with wide eyes. Satisfied that he had made his point, he said, "but I will send a mon to your boat, one of your mon, I tink, telling dem you be my guest tonight. You, de old one wit de white hair." He was pointing at O'Toole. "You go and tell de boat."

"Sir?" was all O'Toole said.

"Go now, I tell you! Can you not hear, mon?" shouted the Doctor.

Kinkaid nodded in the affirmative, whereupon O'Toole gave his water pouch to Briggs before starting toward the trail.

"He be safe," stated the Doctor with certainty. Then, an instant later, "You bring rum?"

"Uh, no. Not with us," answered Kinkaid, relieved. If the man was this crazy sober…

"Go wit dis mon to de village," said the Doctor, pointing to the chubby Indian. "Dey will feed you. I come later, bring much fun."

Kinkaid and the men did as they were told, waiting patiently in the settlement, the women bringing them chunks of pork and bowls of sweet potatoes.

The children were naked and shy at first, keeping their distance, but after their meal Major Bauer soon had them coming closer. In an hour they were wrestling with him, their play becoming progressively rougher, almost out of hand; two of the boys had taken to shooting small sticks at Bauer with toy bows.

"I think they're getting the better of him, sir," observed Briggs, sounding worried.

One of the little boys had gone to fetch a blowgun and was now returning with it, the Indian men laughing their approval. Kinkaid watched as the boy drew the long weapon up to his mouth, hoping the boy did not mean to actually shoot the major, and if he did, hoping the dart did not contain a deadly poison. When the boy drew in a deep breath, Kinkaid moved forward instinctively as an old woman shouted something to the boy, whereupon the entire group of children scattered, instantly quitting their rough treatment of the major.

"Thank you, ma'am," said Major Bauer to the old woman, bowing, but she ignored him. Then, turning to Kinkaid, Bauer smiled grimly and added, "Vicious little bastards. I thought they were going to kill me."

"I think the one with the blowgun *was* going to kill you," growled Blackstone. "But we ought to bring that old woman with us."

"Perhaps you're right," agreed Kinkaid, attempting to bring some levity to the situation. "Maybe she'd have some influence with the Doctor."

Darkness was beginning to fall as the Doctor strode into the camp, his two accomplices dragging a bedraggled and semi-conscious white man behind them, bleeding from his head and mouth. A mango had been shoved into the man's mouth and was held there by a tightly bound gag of fiber rope. The women and children fled to their huts while about ten Indians gathered round.

"I bring to you de entertainment," said the Doctor. "We have played wit him enough. Now I give him to de Caribs…they know how to make a man beg."

"Our entertainment is to watch a man being tortured by the Indians?" asked Kinkaid, incredulous.

"Enemy. First dey torture," answered the Doctor happily, "den eat. A good ting, I tink."

Kinkaid balked at the thought of standing by, watching, as a man was tortured to death in front of him. Enemy or not, no man deserved such a fate. And eaten? He wished that he had obtained more information from that Africanus fellow.

"You men," said the Doctor, "you have fun, now. We go wit de women. Good trade, eh?" Whereupon he and the other two entered different huts.

The Indian men were already hauling the man toward the fire. First they cut away the gag, then they placed the man's feet into the embers to bring him back to consciousness with a terrible scream. Then they tied the squirming man face up, spread-eagled between four stakes next to the fire. He was fully awake now, his head turning from side to side, watching with wide eyes as the Indians worked. Briggs gave Kinkaid a solicitous look, which made Kinkaid feel even more helpless.

Satisfied that their victim was well-secured to the ground, one of the Indians reached down with a forked stick and picked out a coal about the size of a lemon. He dropped it onto the man's stomach, causing the man to scream once more as the skin burned, leaving a big red welt, which only made the Indians laugh in amusement. Now another Indian took his turn, finding an even larger coal. Another agonizing scream, then the next man did the same. The fourth Indian grew tired of this game, seeing that the coals would roll off the man's belly too quickly. He picked up a burning chunk of wood and held it down against the man's leg. Now the man screamed even louder, a shrill, earsplitting shriek that gave Kinkaid goose bumps and drew a hearty round of laughter from the Indians.

Major Bauer looked intensely angry, tightly clutching his musket. Briggs was actually pale and kept looking to Kinkaid for some kind of solution to the dilemma they were in. Blackstone simply looked amused. It was an untenable situation, and Kinkaid searched in vain for an answer.

Now the chubby one held up his machete, its blade gleaming in the firelight. He tested its sharpness against his thumb, and then crouched over the prone man whose eyes were watery and wide with fright, darting back and forth, desperately trying to see what fate awaited him next. An Indian crouching at the man's feet was sharpening a stick with his machete.

"Sir," said Mr. Briggs in a quavering voice.

"Easy now, Midshipman," said Kinkaid, on the verge of doing something, though he didn't know what. A man was being horribly tortured, slowly killed before their eyes, and there seemed to be nothing they could do about it. Helping these men attack St. Kitts was the only and overriding reason they were even there in the first place. He could certainly kill two of the Indians...or he could kill the poor, tortured man. Either course might result in the failure of their mission, even their own deaths. Nonetheless, he placed his hand on the butt of his pistol and slowly drew it out.

The chubby Indian with the machete dug his knee into the man's neck so that his head was pinned back firmly against the ground. Then he grabbed hold of the man's right ear and commenced to slowly slice it off. He cut halfway through and then tore the ear off with a mighty tug, causing the man's body to lurch in pain as bright-red blood flowed copiously from the wound. The Indian said something, as if satisfied with his results, and then moved lower and began slicing at the man's chest. Not deeply, but making a series of small cuts across the man's pectoral muscles while his victim groaned and closed his eyes with each swipe of the blade, not even having the energy to scream any more. Kinkaid fingered the trigger of his pistol, now resting against his knee.

The Indian with the sharpened stick was about to jab it into the sole of the man's foot when a musket roared, bringing the groans of the tortured man to an abrupt end. The entire camp became deathly silent, the Indians shocked at the sudden noise, the smoking weapon in Bauer's hand still pointed at the dead man's chest.

"You damned fool," blurted out Blackstone.

The Indians looked astonished, their eyes wide. Kinkaid cocked his pistol, ready in case they attacked.

Finally the chubby one smiled and then broke into laughter. Then the rest of them laughed their approval as well.

Briggs had turned away from the scene and was vomiting into the grass as the Indians cut the dead man loose from his bonds and dragged him away, to be hacked up into conveniently sized pieces for cooking by the women.

By then Kinkaid and the men were finding places to bed down in the jungle. It was a terrible night, sleepless, spent fighting off insects, both flying and crawling. And crabs. Land crabs and giant hermit crabs, lugging their shells around, crawled under and around the men all night long as hordes of bats flew over their heads. But the worst part was listening to the Indians as they cooked and ate their trophy and then danced and sang their strange songs into the night.

Sometime during the night Kinkaid, feeling soiled, had a conversation with Bauer. "You did the right thing, Major. That poor man—"

"You could have gotten all of us killed, pulling a stunt like that," said Blackstone angrily, behind them, waking Briggs out of a fitful sleep.

"It was taking a chance, I know, Captain," said the major uneasily, ignoring Blackstone, "but—"

"You needn't explain, Major," said Kinkaid, feeling shame and guilt for leaving the obvious action to Bauer. Would he have done what Bauer had done a split second later, he asked himself, torn between preserving his mission and ending a fellow human being's suffering?

Briggs said, barely audible, "I didn't realize these Caribs were…"

"Cannibals," finished Bauer, "and fierce warriors. A man is judged by his exploits in combat. They can be a terrible and dangerous foe, though they rarely group together, preferring to fight mostly as individuals, raiding other family groups for torture victims. They only eat men and believe that they take on the power of their victims. Women are made captive wives or slaves."

"Well, this Doctor seems to have a hold on them somehow," observed Kinkaid.

Once more Blackstone's deep voice came from out of the darkness. "A madman calling himself a doctor, with two idiot generals, leading a bunch of lunatic savages. Is this what you call an army?" he asked cynically.

Once more Bauer and Kinkaid ignored Blackstone, Bauer saying, "I doubt we could ever get them to follow us, Captain. Without the Doctor, even as crazy as he seems—"

"Of course you're right, Major. We wouldn't accomplish a thing without him."

Morning did not come fast enough. The men looked haggard and bleary-eyed. There were some long bones lying near the fire, and a scrawny dog was gnawing on one of them until Captain

Blackstone went over and kicked the dog, making it scurry away with its tail between its legs. Kinkaid had the men stay away from the area while waiting for the mad Doctor to make his appearance so they could get back to the ship.

The Doctor finally emerged from one of the huts and with a shout eight Indians came running. His two cronies also staggered out of their huts, the one still smiling idiotically, followed by a slim Carib girl. The Doctor walked over to Kinkaid and said, "We go to de boat, now."

"But where are the rest of your men?" asked Kinkaid, taking Blackstone's observation into account. Eleven men were no army.

The Doctor pointed his saber at Kinkaid and said to his men, "Dis one, he be full of worries."

His two generals were still laughing derisively as the Doctor shoved his saber in his belt and strode off down the trail.

VIII

Uneasy Passage

The Doctor led the way back, his henchmen following behind, and as they came to the bay where *Swift* was anchored, Monk stepped out of the forest, silently taking his place behind Major Bauer.

The first thing Kinkaid saw from shore was Roach sitting up on the forecastle with his canary chirping happily inside her tiny stick cage. That Africanus fellow was standing next to him and it appeared the two were having a conversation…until they noticed the party emerging from the trees, whereupon Roach gave a shout, alerting the ship. The old black man, spying the Doctor, scurried quickly below. The first lieutenant, Weatherby, and Lofton were all on the quarterdeck and they soon had the ship's boat out, O'Toole at the tiller, steering for shore.

The crazy Doctor took his place in the bow of the crowded boat, standing proudly like a conquering hero, bringing some amused sniggers from the crew watching from the deck of the *Swift*, though the man seemed not to notice or care. Blackstone sat in the back, next to Monk, shaking his head in disgust.

Reaching the top of the ladder and boarding *Swift*, the Doctor exclaimed loudly, "A fine boat, I tink, but too small." Then, noticing *Moondog* farther out in the bay, he pointed at it with his saber and asked, "Who be dey?"

"A friend…who comes to help," explained Kinkaid. Blackstone was by then taking his own ship's boat back to *Moondog*, wanting nothing further to do with the mad Doctor.

Mr. Saddler, Lofton, and Weatherby were all watching the Doctor, not knowing what to make of the scene. Kinkaid followed behind the Doctor, making a signal with his hands, hoping the men would understand its meaning. They did, and assumed a serious air around the ridiculous figure, now striding down the deck as if on an inspection, touching each and every cannon as he passed, his two flunkies following behind, totally awed by the ship and its rows of guns.

"Fine poof-poof, but also too small, I tink, for ruler of two countries," observed the Doctor to all and to no one in particular, nose in the air.

"Perhaps His Excellency will find a ship more suitable for his needs on the island of St. Kitts," offered Kinkaid diplomatically, feeling foolish for having to humor the Doctor.

"Many big boats der. All be mine soon," he said without a trace of a doubt.

When he came to the mortars, he stood before them for a moment, contemplating the squat ugly things, noticing that they were pointing skyward. "What dees be for?" he asked. "To shoot de birds?"

"For throwing a charge over obstacles, into forts, over hills," explained Kinkaid, his patience quite thin.

"I like," said the Doctor. "You give to me before you go."

"Yes," lied Kinkaid matter-of-factly, "we give to you."

"Good," proclaimed the Doctor, striding toward the forecastle, eyeing the deck with disdain.

Kinkaid signaled with a wave toward the half-dozen sailors on the forecastle, and they sidled along the bulwarks, making room for the contingent of three. Roach wisely and discreetly headed down the after hatch with his caged canary in his chunky hands.

Standing on the cleared forecastle and raising his saber, the Doctor stated with finality, "I camp here."

"O'Toole!" shouted Kinkaid, unnecessarily, for O'Toole was standing behind him, following each step of the curious inspection.

"Aye, sir," answered O'Toole, causing Kinkaid to flinch from the boatswain's unexpected nearness, his temper already aflame, having to kowtow to this maniac.

"See to it that…His Eminence, is, uh…properly cared for," said Kinkaid, trying to keep the irritation out of his voice. "Food, shelter…whatever he requires."

"Aye aye, Captain."

Kinkaid watched as the Doctor sat stoically upon the deck while his henchmen scrambled to make "camp." General Bobo spread His Eminence's blankets out while a sleepy General Pierre inspected the contents of a large and heavy bag, probably filled with food.

Turning away in disgust, Kinkaid explained curtly to the quarterdeck watch, "We may be taking aboard a number of natives. Inform me if they arrive. I'll be below."

That evening as the crew was going to supper, Kinkaid attempted to have the officers' mess bring something up for the Doctor when General Bobo came to inform him, "Hes Excellency will not eat ship's food, please. If we may have fire, we make de food for Hes Excellency."

So Kinkaid had O'Toole bring up a large bucket, half filled with sand, and a pile of sticks so that they could make their fire and cook their own food.

Later that evening, Kinkaid watched as Mr. Weatherby approached the Doctor and engaged him in conversation. Their words were low, and he could not detect even the subject of their discussion as they stood on the forecastle. Though burning with curiosity over what the two might have to say to one another, Kinkaid quickly rejected the notion of trying to eavesdrop. Having little desire to speak with the so-called Doctor, it was not a social impulse that had sparked the interest, and so he contented himself with the thought that at least someone was entertaining the man.

A half-hour later, as Kinkaid was about to turn in for a few hours of much-needed sleep—having slept little through the horror of the night before—Weatherby took his leave of the Doctor's camp, coming to the quarterdeck and halting by the railing. Kinkaid had expected some kind of a greeting, at least a word of recognition, but Weatherby simply stood there, gazing out at the dark trees along the shore. Finally, when Kinkaid could stand it no longer, Weatherby said, "That Doctor is a strange man, sir."

Kinkaid thought for a moment to tell Weatherby about the torture they had witnessed the night before, but decided against it. Instead he merely nodded and answered, "Yes, quite strange."

"You know, Captain, I don't believe he has the slightest notion that there are other human beings, equal to himself that is, on the face of the earth." Weatherby paused and then asked, "What is it, do you suppose, sir, that would make a man like that?"

"Perhaps Boatswain O'Toole would have some ideas along those lines," was the best answer Kinkaid could give his ever-curious young lieutenant.

"Hmm. Probably the same thing he said about Captain Blackstone, sir. That pride goeth before a fall," said Weatherby, guessing, "Except that we are to ensure that he does not fall, isn't that right, Captain?"

"That is correct, Mr. Weatherby," admitted Kinkaid uneasily, "In fact, we're to help raise the man up."

Weatherby, suspecting something of the turmoil that the conversation had brought up in his Captain, thought to add, "Well, O'Toole may think our alliances unholy at best, but they're to be put to a good cause, aren't they, sir?"

"I would like to think so, Mr. Weatherby."

It was still dark and Briggs had the early morning watch. He was standing on the quarterdeck, looking aft. What he saw at first was only a crescent moon, low on the horizon, barely casting its silvery reflection upon an unruffled sea, for right over the waters lay a thick mist. Then he thought he detected some movement out over the mist. Yes, there it was again, looking like a creature that Briggs had never before seen…something with long and elegant plumage. Could it be some kind of outlandish sea bird that he had never heard of? He blinked in wonder at the unexpected sight, and when he looked again, it was gone. Perhaps it could have been the fin of a large fish, maybe the fluke of a whale, basking in the moonlight, thought Briggs, as he strained his eyes into the darkness. He was about to give up, thinking that his sleepy eyes had been playing tricks on him when he distinctly saw it again...two of them. And there was another, and another...

"My God, there's a whole flock of them," said Briggs in a tremulous voice, as he watched what appeared to be strange birds barely skimming the mist-covered swells.

"A whole flock of what?" asked Weatherby, always an early riser, striding up beside Briggs at the rail.

"I'm not sure," gasped Briggs, sounding alarmed as fifty or more of the strange creatures appeared out of the mist, "but whatever they are, there are a lot of them."

"And they're heading our way," noted Weatherby.

"I think I'd better call the Captain," said Briggs with some urgency.

But as Briggs turned to give the order to Rudy, who was leaning sleepily against the starboard mortar, Weatherby reached for his arm, saying, "I don't think we need be alarmed, Mr. Briggs."

What at first appeared to be the bodies of wildly plumaged birds turned out to be the headdresses of Carib Indians emerging like ghosts from out of the mist, four to six to a boat. Their long, graceful vessels stabbed the water as the Indians paddled effortlessly, their oars making not a sound, silent as the night.

"Mr. Briggs!" shouted a frightened Rudy, pointing toward the mouth of the bay.

"It's only the savages," said Briggs, taking his cue from Mr. Weatherby, trying to sound confident. "Go tell the Captain."

"I told you dey come," said the Doctor, rising up from his blankets and standing at the rail like Hannibal or Kublai Khan.

Some of the boats drew near *Moondog*, but Weatherby could see that Jack Blackstone's men were not allowing them aboard and not so politely, at that. So they all came toward *Swift*.

The flotilla of forty dugout canoes was soon close alongside, and the dark men came swarming over the bulwarks from all directions, primitive weapons slung over their shoulders, hair festooned with colored feathers, beads and shell necklaces hanging around their necks. Some were holding live chickens by their legs; others carried mesh bags made of twisted bark, full of green bananas and sweet potatoes. Meanwhile, others were tying the boats together, forming a long chain of canoes that was then secured to the shore by a stout fiber cable produced out of one of the canoes.

As he came up on deck and found almost two hundred Indians milling about, no semblance of order apparent, it occurred to Kinkaid that if they a mind to or if the Doctor gave the word, such a force would have been able to take over the ship. One look at Major Bauer and the officers coming up on the quarterdeck told him that they must have been thinking along the same lines for they all had serious, worried looks on their faces; the only ones laughing and joking were the Doctor's generals and the Indians.

"There's no getting around it," Kinkaid announced to the deck watch. "We must deliver this...army." Then to the ship in general, "We'll get under weigh forthwith...take our breakfast later. All right, let's get these men out of the way. Take as many as you can below. O'Toole, stand by at the anch—"

Suddenly the Doctor started shouting. "No, no, no, no! Stop everyting! Nobody give de orders to de men but me!"

Kinkaid would have to call up his best diplomatic abilities, he thought, as he strode up to the big man. "Your Excellency, it is imperative that my men have room on the deck to do what they must to take the ship to sea. If you would be so kind as to have some of them go below..."

The Doctor instantly began yelling and waving his saber, kicking at some of the Indians as they scrambled to find hatches that led below. In less than a minute the deck was clear, only the Doctor and his two generals left on deck, smiling proudly.

"You see," said the Doctor, grinning. "Dey listen only to me." Then he took a few steps forward, pointed his saber in the direction of the open sea and said, "We go now!"

Kinkaid stood at the quarterdeck rail, gazing aft as the sails caught the slight sea breeze, watching as if mesmerized as the base of the island became slowly obscured, lost behind a blanket of thick fog. Above, jutting up into a clear blue sky, there remained the only evidence that the island existed: the mountain with the three peaks, the sight evocative of its primeval origins.

The regular watch was set and the ship was under easy sail, making for St. Kitts with Blackstone's *Moondog* trailing a cable's length behind, when Roach asked, "What would you like for breakfast, Captain? We've still some ham and—"

"Roach, you're fired," said Kinkaid flatly, spontaneously.

Roach looked confused for a moment, but then, as the realization hit him, he broke into a wide grin, stammering uncertainly, "Oh…thank you, sir."

"Yes, well, I'll expect you to see O'Toole about joining the deck hands."

"Thank you very much, Captain." The relieved Roach was positively joyful at the news.

"Now, where is that Africanus fellow?" asked Kinkaid of the deck. He seemed to have disappeared the moment the Doctor came aboard.

"I believe he's hiding in the orlop, Captain," Mr. Lofton informed him. "Scared to death of that big…uh, the Doctor."

"Well, go and find him. Tell him I want his best breakfast prepared right away. And if it isn't satisfactory, tell him I'll…" Then Kinkaid thought better of the threat. "No, belay that. Just tell him he's to prepare the Captain's breakfast."

The passage back up the island chain was barely tolerable because of the strange and overcrowded conditions, except that mealtime for Kinkaid was now a distinct pleasure, something to look forward to. Cato Africanus, however, when he wasn't serving Kinkaid and his guests, kept out of sight; even the mention of the Doctor's name brought him to shaking with fear.

Mr. Africanus proved himself an excellent cook, making exotic dishes out of the most ordinary fare. Partly because Kinkaid felt unable to justify his good fortune and partly because he was allowing himself to enjoy his role as captain of the ship, he had decided to make a habit of dining with his ship's officers more often. At the moment, however, he was almost regretting his decision.

For this evening Kinkaid sat with Mr. Lofton and Mr. Saddler, a not overly exuberant pair, which may have been enough in itself to depress discussion, but because the two officers seemed to share certain personality traits, there seemed very little for Kinkaid to work with, conversationally. Therefore, it seemed a good time to find out more about his new steward during their mostly silent dinner.

"Mr. Africanus," began Kinkaid uncertainly as Cato brought in a bottle of wine, a newly opened bottle that Kinkaid found himself wishing had not been opened, a bottle of rather excellent wine that would be wasted on a desultory guest list.

"Please call me Cato, sir," he answered.

"Of course, uh, Cato," began Kinkaid once more, "I wonder if you could tell me. How is it that you found yourself, you know, in the hands of—?"

"That bad, evil man," even now Cato looked nervously around. "He caught myself and three others. We were shopping for stores for the ship…in the town, Roseau. They surrounded us and took us into the hills." Cato paused as if the remembering was too awful to bear.

"Must have been a terrible ordeal," gave Mr. Saddler, unconvincingly, before shoveling a forkful of baked ham into his mouth as Cato refilled his glass. Empathy was never Mr. Saddler's forte.

But Cato took up the idea in earnest, sighing as he moved to refill Mr. Lofton's glass, as well, "And then…well, they intended to give us, one by one…to the Indians. Oh, it was horrible, sir…"

"Perhaps you will be happy to know that the Doctor and his Indians will be leaving us in a couple of days," said Kinkaid, meaning to comfort his new steward, but also because he found too much emotion distasteful in a man. Kinkaid knew very well the truth of which Cato spoke, for he had been forced to witness the barbarity with which the Caribs treated their captives. And he could see how this self-proclaimed Doctor, this megalomaniac, by providing the Caribs with victims to torture and eat, might gain their loyalty, but that was no reason to thoughtlessly feed his steward's over-excitement.

"That is good news, sir," said Cato.

"Captain, do you think it a good idea for Mr. Weatherby to be showing the Indians how the ship is run?" asked his worried first lieutenant.

"I take your point, Mr. Saddler, but I believe their leader is more interested in an island than in our *Swift*, at least for the present," answered Kinkaid. "Besides, it keeps them busy…makes them feel like part of the crew."

"Well, I for one shall be happy to be rid of them, Captain," admitted the practical and coldly efficient Mr. Lofton, ignoring Cato and the fact that Kinkaid was talking to the man, a lowly steward. "Why, that Doctor thinks he owns the ship. And those savages of his have begun starting fires all over the deck, driving Boatswain O'Toole absolutely mad."

"And relieving themselves in the corners, as if the smell of their sweating bodies wasn't horrid enough," added Mr. Saddler.

"I suppose we ought to be happy that they haven't started eating us," observed Lofton sourly.

"A frightening lot," said Saddler, "especially that General Bubo or whatever his name is. I believe he's even crazier than the Doctor. Did you see the way that maniac was flapping his arms over the bowsprit yesterday, like he could fly?"

"That other one smokes some strange smelling tobacco," observed Mr. Lofton, "that seems to make him sleepy all the time."

"At least they keep to themselves on the forecastle," intoned Saddler, reaching for another dinner roll.

"And by the way, Cato, this meal is excellent," observed Kinkaid, ignoring his two officers and taking some mild interest in the fact that they appeared unaware that he was ignoring them. "And the coffee, well, it's perfect."

"For your pleasure, Captain," replied Cato with a graceful bow.

The next morning, Kinkaid was awoken by the sound of musket fire on the deck. Less than a minute later came a knock at his door. It was Mr. Lofton with the news. "It's the Doctor, sir. He's shooting at dolphins swimming in our bow wake, forward."

"That damned fool," said Kinkaid sleepily. "I've a mind to—"

"And there's been a bit of trouble, sir."

"What kind of trouble, Mr. Lofton?"

"Well, it's Ellie, sir."

"Ellie?"

"Roach's canary, Captain."

"What about Roach's canary?"

Just then Major Bauer was at the door. "The Indians...well, they had Roach's canary for breakfast, Captain. Roach came up and saw them passing out yellow feathers amongst themselves."

"Did he do anything...?"

"O'Toole was able to stop him, sir...with the help of the Travelin' Brothers. He's...secured now, Captain, in his hammock, crying a bit."

"Thank God for that, anyway," answered Kinkaid, thankful that Roach hadn't started an incident.

Bauer agreed and offered the suggestion, "Captain, since we're coming close, perhaps we should have a meeting with the man, discuss our tactics, sir." There came the sound of another musket discharging.

Kinkaid dreaded the thought. Having a civilized conversation with the Doctor was impossible, but some kind of coordinated effort would have to be made to secure the success of their mission, and the only way to ensure that would be to make plans with the mad Doctor.

"You're right, of course," said Kinkaid. "Invite the man to have breakfast with...no, not that. Uh, just convey to him my compliments, and tell him that if he could come before breakfast, we can discuss our plans. Let's get this over with."

"Yes, sir," laughed Bauer.

The musket fire soon stopped as Kinkaid waited in his cabin for the appearance of the Doctor. But it was only Major Bauer who poked his head through the doorway a few minutes later. "He won't come, sir; says you should come to him, forward."

"I should have known. Very well, Major, let's go then...to see the dictator."

The Doctor was sitting on the base of the bowsprit, his two thugs on either side of him. The chubby Indian was also there, a couple of small yellow feathers in his hair. Seated beside him were a few of his warriors, the Indians forming a rough semi-circle around the Doctor.

Kinkaid stepped carefully through the group and knelt on the deck near the Doctor. He spread the map out and held it down with his hand and knees to keep the wind from blowing it over the side. Major Bauer crouched beside him.

"Dat be St. Kitts?" asked the Doctor, pointing his saber.

"Yes, that is the island of St. Kitts," answered Kinkaid.

"Soon to be mine," he stated matter-of-factly.

"Well, not until we do something about her defenders," said Kinkaid, hoping the Doctor would catch on to the purpose of their meeting.

"We kill dem all," came the simple reply.

"Yes, that is one way to take the island," said Kinkaid. "But first we have to form a plan to get on the island, and then we will have to work together to—"

"Plan be to attack village, kill all British," he said as he strode forward and stabbed the map with his saber, narrowly missing Kinkaid's hand.

Kinkaid kept his temper in check, however, pointing to a small bay on the northeastern side of the island. "Perhaps you would like to be debarked here," he suggested.

"No. Here," again a stab with the saber, an inch from the spot suggested.

Kinkaid realized the contrary maniac probably wouldn't know one bay from another.

"Yes, of course, here," he agreed. "And perhaps His Excellency would have some suggestions as to how best to make the attack?"

"Dis road here, how far to village?"

"About four miles," said Kinkaid, glad that the man seemed interested.

"We follow road to village…attack…kill all."

"And what time would you think—"

"Morning…very early."

"What about at night? The chances of being detected—"

"Carib no fight at night. Spirits come, take de soul away. No mon, night no good."

Kinkaid and Bauer exchanged concerned looks. It was not good news; the spotters for the mortars would be in certain danger. And *Swift* would be that much more vulnerable should enemy ships leaving the harbor spot them anchored along the shore. But if the Caribs were not going to risk death at night…

"All right, we'll make do," said Kinkaid. "Now listen here, it is important that we each understand what the other will be doing. Do you agree?"

The Doctor nodded and said, "So we can kill dem all together, yes, very good."

"You see that ship over there?" Kinkaid pointed at Jack Blackstone's *Moondog*, two hundred yards off the port beam. "That ship is going to sail by the harbor of St. Kitts very early in the morning. He is going to fire his cannons into the harbor at any ships anchored there to draw them off, to help us…so that they won't be in the harbor when we make our attack some hours later. Do you understand?"

"British ships chase red ship, den we attack."

"That's right, that's exactly right," said Kinkaid, almost ecstatically; the Doctor's seeming understanding and acquiescence had pleasantly surprised him. He looked over to see Bauer suppressing a laugh. "So we'll take you in tonight, and in the morning as the sun is rising we will expect you to be waiting with your men on the other side of town."

The Doctor nodded and said, "Kill whole town."

"Good," said Kinkaid. He wanted to tell the Doctor that he wasn't to kill the whole town, but decided to wait, since the Doctor was in an agreeable mood and he didn't want to take the chance on spoiling it.

"Now, the signal for you to begin your attack will be the first bomb that you hear or see exploding on this hill here. That is where a British battery of guns is located. Understand?"

Again the Doctor nodded, then asked, "What you do?"

"I will take my ship to the other side of the island...to this cove, here. And you see those big cannons, the ones that point at the sky?"

"I see."

"With those we are going to make sure the guns on the hill give you no trouble."

"No trouble," he repeated, and then condescended to smile and say, "Good plan...very good plan, mon. I like."

"Now, when you see or hear that first gun fired, you must take your Indians through the town and attack the garrison, here, where the British troops are quartered."

"Attack garrison. Kill all."

"But there is one thing more. You said your generals know how to operate cannons. If they could go with Major Bauer's marines, along with about a dozen Indians, to take and hold those guns—"

"No, no, no...my generals come with me. All Indians come wit me." His smile instantly turned into a snarl. "No split my forces like dis. No, no, mon. Indians not listen to you. Only me."

"What about leaving just one of your generals—"

"I tell you no, are you deaf, mon? All come wit me," he said adamantly.

Kinkaid looked at Bauer who only raised his eyebrows. There was no arguing with the Doctor, that was always apparent. First no night attack and now no Indians in the gun assault.

"Listen to me," said Kinkaid forcefully, his patience wearing thin. "Those guns are capable of turning your assault on the garrison into a slaughter, do you understand? It is imperative that they be secured as soon as possible. Major Bauer's marines will take them, of that you can be sure, but you will need to get some of your men up there to take charge of them as soon as you can. Only about ten or fifteen men should do it and of course your generals, who can handle the cannons. Can you agree to that?"

The Doctor stood there staring back at Kinkaid, seeming to take in all that he had said, and then finally he replied, "Marines take guns, den we come."

"Good," said Kinkaid, somewhat relieved. "Then we are agreed."

"You agree wit me," corrected the Doctor.

"Yes, I agree with you," said Kinkaid, suppressing a sigh of exasperation. "Now then, the garrison is here. Your Excellency, would you please look at the map? Here, there are two large buildings surrounded by a fence. Many soldiers will be coming from here. Tell your men that the people in the town are not their enemy; they will not fight you. Only the soldiers will. You need to get to the garrison compound as early as possible—"

"To kill the soldiers!" exclaimed the Doctor.

"Yes, that's right," gave Kinkaid.

"Yes, kill, kill," the word had a galvanizing effect on the Doctor. The chubby Indian and the other warriors seemed to like the word as well, and they all started chanting, "Kill, kill, kill..."

It was midnight before they found the tiny bay, and Kinkaid soon had both ship's boats put over the side, but already the Caribs were climbing over the gunwale, slipping into the water, swimming for shore, machetes and blowguns in their teeth.

"Are you sure the Indians know how to operate their muskets?" Kinkaid asked the Doctor.

The Doctor simply turned to his generals and said, "Dis mon, he be full of worries." The three laughed as they climbed into the boat.

O'Toole and his crewmen loaded all one hundred muskets into the boats with their bags of flint and shot, and then took them and the Doctor ashore. Then Kinkaid had O'Toole deliver a message to Captain Blackstone on *Moondog*, telling him that he should make his pass three hours after midnight.

As O'Toole was rowing back, Kinkaid saw Captain Blackstone standing on his quarterdeck. He gave a wave before moving his ship away, out to sea and heading south. There was nothing to do but trust that the pirate would uphold his part of the bargain. Kinkaid found himself pondering the idea of having to choose which man he trusted less and came to the unsavory conclusion that he would have been hard pressed to pick between Jack Blackstone and the Doctor, strange bedfellows all.

IX

Uprising

With the Doctor and his men ashore, Kinkaid headed *Swift* north and then around to the other side of the island, keeping far out to sea, away from any curious eyes. He had most of the night to arrive at his destination on the western side, to set up for the support of the attack.

It was a delicious relief to no longer have the mad Doctor and his Indians aboard. Cato was now lounging contentedly about the suddenly spacious deck after serving Kinkaid a marvelous dinner of roast beef and onions, potatoes, and cabbage. His new steward cooked the entire dinner in a large clay pot, making the beef moist and tender, even providing a tasty gravy. And Roach seemed a happy man now, part of the deck crew. Rikker was showing him how to use the boatswain's pipe and they made an amusing pair as Rikker taught Roach the fundamental signals that Rikker himself had barely mastered. But the fact that the Indians would only make their attack during the day gave Kinkaid worries. Not to mention that the Doctor had seemed so self-involved that Kinkaid could never be certain as to how much he actually understood of their plans.

They found the cove a little before two in the morning under an almost full moon, its bright light reflecting off a shoreline made up of precipitously rocky slopes. Kinkaid wasted no time in preparing the ship, expecting the sound of *Moondog*'s cannons in an hour. They dropped anchor fifty yards from shore and still had a few fathoms of depth beneath the keel.

"O'Toole, get both boats over the side. Take some men with axes and cut down some small trees and bushes to decorate the ship, enough to make us look like part of the shore to any vessel passing out at sea."

"I get the idea, Captain," affirmed O'Toole.

Bauer was on the quarterdeck, his scout Monk with him, wearing buckskin leggings and moccasins but otherwise naked from the waist up. He made the request, "I'd like my scout to go ashore right away, Captain."

"Very well, Major," agreed Kinkaid, "Take him ashore with you, O'Toole."

Monk leapt out of the boat as it touched the shoreline. Then he rapidly climbed the hill and disappeared over the top.

Soon the boats were heading back and forth between the shore and the ship, the entire crew pitching in to festoon the ship with vegetation, keeping most of it down low so that the mortars would be able to fire over the camouflage. The last of the shrubs and branches had been placed into the shrouds to Kinkaid's satisfaction when the dull, echoing sounds of cannon fire reached them. It had to be Blackstone. It was a little after three in the morning and the actuality of what they were about to undertake became suddenly real.

"Well, it's begun," said Kinkaid grimly. "O'Toole, we need to rig ourselves so we'll be a steady platform for the mortars. Get another anchor into one of the boats and take it out about a cable's length—half a cable from the main anchor. Try to drop it into a sandy area, away from any coral if possible. We don't want those lines chafed away or our anchors fouled."

"I've had those anchor lines prepared for some time now, Captain. They're wrapped in canvas ten feet up, but I'll make sure they're dropped in a good spot, sir."

Bauer's marines were up on deck, eager to get ashore and into position, wearing a hodgepodge of civilian clothing, looking for all the world like pirates, practically indistinguishable from Jack Blackstone's men. They were checking their weapons and discussing last minute details as Bauer brought one of his mysterious wooden boxes up on deck and started passing its contents around to his men: small, round, leather-bound objects.

"Hand grenades, Captain," said Bauer, noting Kinkaid's puzzled look. "Filled with powder and shot. Quite effective at close range."

Private Kirkpatrick was dressed in a large and flamboyant light-blue shirt, a yellow scarf tied around his head, looking happy and eager to be part of the assault team and talking with Weatherby as he took a couple of hand grenades from the box, tucking them inside his shirt.

Sergeant Anders was talking with the Travelin' Brothers, the powder monkeys, and those men who would be helping with the mortars. It came as no surprise to find that Tripp and Treadwell had been among those chosen to load and fire the weapons. And there was Weatherby and Mr. Briggs in the waist, passing muskets to the men in their party, volunteers all, Rikker and Smith among them. Soon Weatherby came to the quarterdeck and, slipping the strap of a water bag over his shoulder, reported, "We're ready, Captain."

"All right, then. Take that cable in the boat with you and attach us to the shore…around that stout tree over there. We'll draw it taut from here."

"Very good, sir," said Weatherby. He gave Rikker a nod and the boatswain's mate took up the coiled rope and hefted it on his shoulder, one end looped around the mainmast.

"Then you can take your group up the hill…but I want you to wait for the major and his men to come up, understand? Let them reconnoiter the area before you go too far. And make sure you have everything—charcoal and paper, compass, water…"

"And this, Captain," said Weatherby, hefting a heavy musket.

"Dammit, Weatherby, your job is to spot, nothing more. Make certain you stay out of sight so you won't have to use that," said Kinkaid sternly as he walked with Weatherby to the waist where the others were waiting. "O'Toole will join you as soon as they've set out the other anchor and made sure we're secure. I want

O'Toole to be the last man in your line of communications, the one passing word directly to the ship. Now, you're certain all your men are familiar with the signals?"

Weatherby looked at Briggs and the others. They all nodded in the affirmative.

"Very well, then," said Kinkaid. He stood and watched as the men went down the ladder and took up the oars. Rikker was coiling the heavy rope in the bottom of the boat. Weatherby was the last man down and took his place in the stern. He shoved the boat away from the ship's side, and Kinkaid called out the reminder, "As soon as the marines have secured those guns, you get back here right away; no delays, understand?"

"Understand perfectly, sir!" came Weatherby's reply as he took the tiller and steered for shore.

They were suddenly startled by the sound of rocks tumbling down from the hill. Looking up, Kinkaid saw three wild donkeys grazing along a ledge on the moonlit side of the steep hill. Relieved, he called out, "Good luck!" wishing he could go with them, knowing that he had little choice but to remain aboard, that he solely was responsible for the safety of his ship, that if anything happened to *Swift,* all their plans and efforts would be for naught.

Weatherby turned round in the boat and, smiling, returned a reassuring, "Be back before breakfast, Captain!"

O'Toole returned to report that the additional anchor was secured off the starboard bow, and then he went astern to supervise drawing tight the line that Weatherby had secured ashore, fixing the ship in a stable position with the triangular system of cables. Now, with both boats available, Major Bauer and his marines headed for shore and were soon scrambling up the hill. Sergeant Anders went about organizing the mortar crews and had them laying out rows of shot, bags of powder, slow match, and plenty of buckets of water to douse any errant sparks or fires.

The mortars themselves still had to be moved, positioned so that they would be pointing in the general direction of the enemy shore. Kinkaid had O'Toole rig harnesses around their trucks, then attached them to lines running through a block-and-tackle arrangement connected to the mainmast top. Anders stood patiently by, waiting for the deck hands to complete the task, believing all the while that the rigging was unnecessary, that his mortar crews, even the strong team of Tripp and Treadwell, could have manhandled the heavy guns into position. Kinkaid knew this as well and hoped the real reason for the "help" he was providing was not guessed by the tough marine.

Once Anders was satisfied that the mortars were placed exactly where he wanted them—side by side and both angled to point off the port quarter—Kinkaid joined him in the waist to ensure that their trajectory would not damage his masts or rigging. Noting that two lines of standing rigging from the top of the foremast to the port side bulwark were close enough to be grazed or burned by their discharge, he had O'Toole slack them and tie them off out of the way.

Mr. Saddler and Mr. Lofton were his only two officers left on board in case the ship had to be sailed away or defended unexpectedly. Now that most of the work had been done, the crew was allowed to turn in to get some sleep, at least until the mortars went into action. Some, not inclined to sleep, preferred to remain on deck and wait in anticipation of the attack, but a nervous Sergeant Anders appealed to Kinkaid to keep any unnecessary personnel off the main deck, away from his mortars and powder and shot especially, and so Kinkaid had the word passed that unassigned crew were to remain below. Kinkaid noticed Cato loitering at the bow, his gray head poking up from where he sat in the chains, feet dangling over the side. He decided to ignore his steward and allow him to remain where he was, since he had spent most of his time belowdecks throughout the time the Doctor had been aboard. The sky was just beginning to get light as the last of the marines made it over the top of the hill.

"What time is it?" asked Kinkaid of the watch.

"Four-thirty, Captain."

He had no idea what Weatherby was up to, and there would be little chance to influence the outcome of the action above. He could only trust that Weatherby would remain out of sight and do his job without unnecessary risk.

O'Toole, with concerns of his own and suspecting Kinkaid's, came over and stood beside him at the rail, finally saying, "That boy has the eye of the Lord upon him, Captain. He'll do right by his assignment and take care of himself as well, you'll see, sir."

"Of course he will." Then, recognizing that there was a more immediate matter, Kinkaid said, "I can't say as I like being tied down like this, Boats—loosed rigging, trees stuck in the shrouds."

"Like a pinned rat, Captain," agreed O'Toole. "If we had to leave in a hurry…"

"Let's set a couple of blocks under those cables and have some axes ready."

"I don't mind leavin' a few lines and anchors behind, Captain," allowed O'Toole, "but gettin' outta here fast, well, if we was chased, those mortars—"

Kinkaid raised a hand, stopping O'Toole in mid-sentence. Then, cupping one hand over his mouth, he said in a low voice, "We won't be taking them with us."

O'Toole nodded conspiratorially, whispering back, "I thought that might be why you wanted me to rig those tackles like that, sir. Anders ain't gonna like that one bit."

"Well, once they've served their purpose, they're worse than useless to us. But you're right, I doubt Anders is going to understand that, so you have my permission to…restrain him if he takes exception when the time comes."

O'Toole returned a wicked grin and remarked, "Right happy to be of service, Captain."

Then, with the blocks in place and axes laid handy, O'Toole made his way up to a rocky ledge high on the escarpment.

Kinkaid, with nothing to do but wait, stood at the quarterdeck rail, watching as stars winked out in the western sky and golden shafts of sunlight arced over the island, at least consoled to see only seagulls and pelicans out on the wide horizon.

"What time is it?" he asked again of the quarterdeck watch.

"Almost five, Captain."

The still air of morning promised a hot day ahead, and the men were already sweating from their climb up the hill. Weatherby had brought them along the ridge, almost a quarter of a mile from the ship, and found what he thought to be the spot marked on the map where he was supposed to wait for the marines. It was light enough to see the town, the road coming into town, and a couple of long barracks-like buildings across the valley that must be the garrison. He could see the harbor, and a row of dug-in gun emplacements where the black barrels of large-caliber guns could be seen pointing out. The mouth of the harbor was still out of sight beyond the end of the ridge before him.

"Keep down and keep quiet," he passed the word as he moved carefully through low trees and scruffy underbrush, the ground dry, hard, and rocky, Briggs, Smith, and the others close behind.

They soon came to a small rise on the escarpment; ahead was a rocky knoll. Weatherby had drawn a rough sketch of the terrain, making use of his pocket compass, and now he stopped, took the water bag from around his shoulders, and handed it and his charcoal and parchment to Briggs, telling him, "Wait here with the others."

"The Captain told you to wait for the marines, Mr. Weatherby," Briggs reminded him.

"I'm just going to have a quick look," he insisted.

Weatherby kept low and made his way to the knoll between thorny bushes. Looking over, he could see parts of a stone wall about sixty yards away, but too much scrub and low trees stood between and so he decided to get closer still. A large iguana startled him as it ran through dry leaves. Then he continued for another twenty yards to a stand of hibiscus where bees buzzed among the dark red flowers. Sweat dripped into his eyes, and an ant scampered over his hand as he crawled forward, until he felt something stab into his shoulder. He had crawled under a thorn bush. Backing away and then skirting around, he made for a high pile of rocks ahead, probably left over from the building of the berm. He took the precaution of removing his hat and then, reaching the top of the pile, peered between two jagged rocks.

There, not thirty yards away, was a man sitting on the stone wall, only a couple of low trees between them—a white man with darkly tanned skin, shirtless, his hair light in color, a blue bandana tied around his head. The inside of the berm had been nearly cleared of vegetation and the man sat in the scant shade provided by one gnarled tree growing next to the wall. Another man stood inside the wall, visible from his shoulders up, wearing the red tunic of a British soldier, unbuttoned and open at the front. On his head was a decidedly unmilitary straw hat. The two were relaxed and talking quietly. The movement of more soldiers could be seen within the enclosure. On the right, where the wall dipped down and around, was the black barrel of an artillery piece, pointing out over the bay, where a small British sloop remained anchored, the only ship in the harbor. Weatherby's heart skipped a beat as he recognized her.

Turning to leave, he was startled to find Monk Chunk behind him, hatchet in hand, a fierce look in his eyes. Then the fierce look gave way to a mischievous grin and off he went. Weatherby returned to where the others waited and found Briggs and Smith standing side by side, pissing on an anthill.

They were still buttoning up their trousers when Weatherby told them, "We'll form our line of communication from here. Rikker, you lead the way and spread yourselves back to where O'Toole is. Make sure you can see one another, and if you can't, tell O'Toole so he can send more men up. And Rikker, pass the word to the Captain that there is a battery of artillery just below and only a small sloop in the harbor. Smith, I want you right there, behind that knoll. Stay low and out of sight. You'll be taking range and elevation signals from Mr. Briggs over by that flowering bush. Understand?"

"Yassuh," whispered Smith, as the rest, led by Rikker, moved back along the ridge, spreading themselves out to form a line of communications.

"Give Smith the water, Briggs, and come with me."

Briggs followed Weatherby past the hibiscus to the rock pile, where Weatherby pointed to the space between the two rocks at the top. "Take a look at the harbor," he told him, as he removed Briggs's hat.

Briggs climbed up the rock pile and then seemed to take forever to aim and steady the glass. Finally, he sputtered, "Why it's her, Mr. Weatherby!"

"Shhhh," Weatherby warned him. "Come back down."

Weatherby filled out the details on his roughly drawn map as Briggs scrambled down, quickly adding the knoll and the battery. Then he took out his compass and estimated the direction and distance of the battery from the ship. The map finished to his satisfaction, with distances and angles figured as close to accurate as was possible over the rugged terrain, Weatherby felt his heart pounding in his chest, not so much from any discernible fear, but from anticipation. Briggs was looking nervously around.

"How do you feel, Briggs?" Weatherby asked him.

"Thirsty."

"Me too. Let's get back."

The three drank greedily from the water pouch when they arrived at the knoll where Smith crouched low. It was good having something to do, something to share, some need to fulfill. A few moments later, Bauer and his marines came trudging up, looking determined with their muskets and fixed bayonets.

"You were supposed to wait for us," complained Bauer. Kirkpatrick was suppressing a grin.

Weatherby ignored Bauer's comment, instead pointing out, "It looks good, Major. No ships in the harbor, except for a small sloop. And you'll be interested to know that there is a battery…right where Blackstone said it would be."

"Have you seen my scout?" asked Bauer, peeved that Weatherby had taken it upon himself to reconnoiter the area even before his scout reported to him.

"He went that way. C'mon, I'll show you," urged Weatherby.

Bauer followed Weatherby to the rock pile and, after taking a look, said, "That's good." He had to agree with Weatherby's assessment. "It would seem that Blackstone's ruse did the trick, after all."

"Except for that little sloop," Weatherby enjoyed pointing out.

"Yes, but I wonder why she stayed behind. She looks fast enough to catch even Blackstone's ship."

"Probably still repairing the damage we caused her that night," answered Weatherby.

"She's the same ship that—?" asked Bauer, now understanding Weatherby's perverse satisfaction.

The mirthful gleam in Weatherby's eyes was answer enough.

But Bauer had other concerns. "Do you think she can point her guns up at this angle?"

"Probably not where she lies now," judged Weatherby, "but if she was able to get farther out…I'll just have to make sure she doesn't get that far."

"You're the spotter, Weatherby, and that is all. Your orders are to return to the ship as soon as we've secured those guns," Bauer reminded him.

"I specifically informed the Captain that I would return to the ship before breakfast," corrected Weatherby.

Bauer looked skeptical. "Well, what time is breakfast?"

"Breakfast will commence after our mission is complete," answered Weatherby, scarcely concealing a smile.

"I see you insist upon playing word games with your Captain, Weatherby, and I can't say as I approve."

"You'll never hold those guns if that sloop gets your range," reasoned Weatherby. Then, to bolster his argument, he added, "Without a good artillery officer directing the battery—"

"Very well," conceded Bauer, not wishing to trust the artillery skills of the Doctor's generals. "I take your point, Weatherby."

"I knew you wouldn't want to be the cause of the crew not having their breakfast today, Major," said Weatherby jauntily, pushing his luck.

Ignoring the comment, Bauer asked, "How many men do you suppose are at those guns?"

"I've only seen about ten, but I couldn't see too well into the enclosure. If they are fully manned, I'd expect twenty or more."

Monk appeared from behind a bush. He and the major exchanged a series of signals, and then Bauer explained, "I'm going to take my men down there and work our way closer to the wall. Those rocks and trees will provide good cover; Monk thinks we should be able to get fairly close."

"Perhaps you should wait until we see where the first bomb lands," suggested Weatherby.

Bauer looked him in the eye and said, "No. We'll want to be within close musket range when they look up to see where you're spotting from. Don't worry, we'll make sure they keep their heads down."

"But the first couple of rounds—"

"We'll just have to trust you, won't we, Lieutenant?" said Bauer before he slipped away.

There was Rikker, now, at the top of the hill.

"Battery on the heights!" came the first report from O'Toole—confirming that Jack Blackstone did indeed know something of this place—followed by, "Four heavy guns! Mr. Weatherby calculates eleven hundred yards' distance, three hundred feet above, and in a southeasterly direction!"

Sergeant Anders was already making adjustments to the alignment of his mortars.

Kinkaid, frustrated and unable to see, thought to pass a request for information about shipping in the harbor when another shout from O'Toole brought, "One small sloop in the harbor!"

Only one small sloop. It would have been better, of course, if no ships were there, for some well-placed artillery from even a few guns could give the attack considerable trouble if not dealt with quickly.

After turning the guns ever so slightly and setting the quoins for a range of a little over a thousand yards, Anders began cutting fuses from a ream of slow match.

Kinkaid shouted up to the rocky ledge, "Can the marines get close to the guns?" The simple hand signals were not adequate to convey the question, so it took quite some time for each sailor to run the question to the next man and the answer to return in the same fashion, but finally, there came O'Toole's hoarse reply, "Affirmative, Captain!"

"How many men at the guns?"

Again the tedious process was repeated and again the answer came some minutes later, "Uncertain!"

"What time is it?" Kinkaid asked the first lieutenant.

"Almost five-thirty, sir," gave Saddler, looking up at the brightening sky.

The sun was well up now, and Weatherby saw three figures coming down the road on the far side of town, keeping close to the trees. The one in front wore a silky blue shirt with dark pants and was twirling that familiar gem-studded saber over his head, vigorously hacking at the air, his two generals close behind him. Now came the chubby Indian and behind him the feathered horde, all carrying muskets in addition to their primitive weapons.

The Doctor paused at the corner of the first house with his hand raised, waiting for the Indians to form up behind him, all crouching low at his signal in cautious anticipation. When a large group formed, the Doctor pointed his saber toward the town and the Indians began running down the street.

Weatherby saw them and cursed, "Damn that idiot Doctor." There was no turning back now. It was imperative to get the mortars going right away, in spite of the fact that Bauer's marines were still getting themselves into position, for as soon as the men at the battery noticed the Indians attacking the garrison, they would turn their guns upon them, causing mayhem and panic and probably bringing the Indian attack to a premature and bloody end.

Weatherby passed the word down the line of men. Rikker, at the rim, signaled to O'Toole below, and he passed the word to the ship, "Prepare to commence fire!"

Weatherby's coordinates came next, and he had added fifty yards to the range to ensure the first mortar bombs did not drop onto Bauer and his marines.

Sergeant Anders stood ready between the two guns. Kinkaid gave Anders a nod and said, "You may commence firing, Sergeant."

"Thank you, sir," acknowledged Anders, saluting. Then, turning to the mortar crews standing by their guns, he said, "Gun number one! Fire!"

Tripp lit the fuse on the charge, and then Treadwell held the match to the touchhole. A sputter and a flash and then a terrific explosion, far louder and stronger than Kinkaid had anticipated, sent a great plume of smoke into the air and rocked the ship with a powerful shudder.

O'Toole watched as the smoking projectile passed over his head like a comet, saying, "The wrath of the Lord shall smite thee, O Sodom, with fire and brimstone from on high!"

Weatherby also heard the rumble of the mortar's report, as did all the men, before they watched its smoking trail come arcing overhead. The bomb would land well down the hill and miss by a wide margin, and so Weatherby immediately began calculating his correction. It exploded too late, as well. "Right fifty. Subtract one hundred. Shorten fuses by one," Weatherby passed to Briggs, hoping he wasn't passing too much at once, confusing the information.

Frantic heads were poking up over the stone wall surrounding the battery now, the crews surprised at the sudden explosion, looking around, trying to determine where the shell had come from. They must have noticed and heard, as well, the beginning of the Doctor's attack across the valley.

And now the staccato sounds of musket fire reverberated over the hill as Bauer had his men open fire on the berm. "Shoot at any movement!" he encouraged his marines.

Kinkaid's instinct was to cover his ringing ears before Treadwell touched off the second gun, but he refrained, clasping his hands behind his back, only condescending to hold his mouth open to protect his eardrums from the concussive pressure.

Weatherby looked across the valley and watched as the Doctor's Indians began running through the town below, shouting unintelligibly in their strange language and yelling frightening war whoops. A group of about fifty was following behind the Doctor, who appeared to be leading them directly toward the garrison, where a few red-jacketed British soldiers could be seen looking over the town where the first mortar round had exploded. Another group of about twenty Indians seemed to be making their way directly toward the guns, General Bobo leading them. So far, so good, thought Weatherby.

The Indians were running between the houses, yelling and screaming their war cries, and as the people in their homes became aware of the attack, some fled toward the harbor in terror. Sporadic gunfire started as the Indians began foolishly discharging their weapons into homes they passed, then discarding their muskets after firing them once, relying instead on their bows, machetes, and blowguns. And some of them were going inside homes, becoming distracted from the main task at hand, that of subduing the British defenders.

The next two mortar rounds landed much closer but not yet on target, though the fuses were set right. Weatherby could see that the British gunners were frantically struggling to turn their guns toward the hillside, where the Doctor and his Indians were already threatening the garrison. He could also see that Bauer's marines were beginning to take sporadic but well-aimed shots at the British gun crews; so far the enemy seemed unaware of them, as no fire was as yet being directed toward the marines or where Weatherby lay.

"Left twenty, subtract ten," he calculated, and the instructions followed down the line to the ship.

Weatherby stood up for a quick look at the sloop in the harbor and saw excited men coming out on her deck, one pointing up at the hillside. He could not tell if they had spotted his position or any of Bauer's marines, now working their way ever closer to the battery, or if they were simply pointing to where the mortar bombs were landing.

The next bomb landed inside the berm, knocking the second gun off its truck and blasting two of its crew through the air in a cloud of fire, smoke, and dust. The mortars had found their mark. Weatherby restrained a whoop as he leaped back down and passed the word, "On target. Keep them coming."

In spite of the rain of death from above, the remaining three gun crews were struggling to get their weapons pointed toward the opposite hillside.

But Bauer and his men were close enough to fire upon the battery with good effect. Their volleys had the gun crews ducking behind the berm and looking in their direction, finally realizing that the musket fire was coming from the slope behind them, distracting them from making the best use of their weapons. They seemed to still be bewildered as to where the bombs were coming from.

The mortar crews had found a rhythm now and were firing the squat guns as fast as they could be reloaded. Anders quickly checking every barrel for dangerous embers before signaling a new bag of powder for the next shot.

Kinkaid could only guess at what might be happening up above, wishing that Weatherby would send some reports as to the progress of the attack as the concussions of the mortars reverberated through his body, rumbling through his tightened stomach. In between the roar of the mortars, he heard the muffled reports of muskets and even the yells of the Indians in the town. He wished that he had at least climbed to the top of the hill in view of the ship and the town below, so he could see what effect the weapons were having, though the threat of a counter-attack from the sea had always precluded that possibility.

With the mortars raining their explosives onto the gun crews and with Bauer's marines making them keep their heads down, Weatherby could see that the battery was getting off few rounds against the hillside. A mass of Indians was surging through the gate of the garrison as red-coated defenders ran from the courtyard, seeking shelter in one of two long, barracks-like buildings.

Soon the Indians were right among the stragglers, engaged in hand-to-hand combat with the retreating and terrified British soldiers, keeping the batteries from firing in that direction for fear of killing their own men. The Indians had the advantage with their primitive, short-range weapons; with no need to waste time reloading, they were overrunning the defenders of the garrison as they vainly attempted to reload their muskets. Failing that, the frantic and retreating British soldiers were defending themselves with bayonets, only to be cut down with arrows and then hacked at with machetes. A few had managed to find safety in the shelter of the barracks and were firing from the windows.

The smaller group of Indians had come through the main part of town. Led by General Bobo and the short, chubby Indian, most of them were heading up the hillside toward the guns, though some were ransacking homes and probably killing civilians, who were no threat to the attack. This caused untold confusion and made it difficult for the British gunners to pick any effective spot to point their weapons. With Bauer's marines having found good positions among the rocks and shrubs to pick off any of the gun crew who poked their heads out for a look, the guns soon went silent, while the deafening crashes of the mortar shells continued to rain down upon the battery with terrible effect.

The morning sun was well up in the sky now, a sea breeze coming into the harbor. Weatherby could see that the small sloop was getting her sails up, intending either to move farther out into the harbor so she could train her guns on where Bauer's marines were or perhaps investigate where the mortar rounds were originating from—her best guess a ship tied up exactly where *Swift* was—and attack her before the Captain would be able to maneuver in defense. Weatherby knew that he had to get to those guns and turn them on the sloop.

"Briggs, stay here and direct the fall of shot. If it veers either way, tell them to cease fire. I'm going down there with Major Bauer," he said excitedly, hefting his heavy musket in anticipation. "And keep an eye on me. When you see me wave my arms, cease fire with the mortars...'cause we'll be going in."

"But the Captain told you—"

"The Captain wants us to take those guns, Briggs," answered Weatherby forcefully, "and that is exactly what we are going to do. Just do as I say. And pass the word that the sloop is leaving the harbor."

Briggs gave Weatherby a hard look, not at all comfortable with the new set of orders that Weatherby had come up with.

Placing his hand on the worried midshipman's shoulder, Weatherby said, "I'm going to need your help with those guns, Briggs...and Smith's too." And with that he was off, scampering down the hill to where Bauer's marines were keeping up a murderous fusillade against the battery, the guns silent now, the soldiers inside worried by Bauer's marines moving ever closer, close enough to begin using their hand grenades.

Briggs could see that the Indians were overrunning the garrison, with ragged musket fire coming from the second barracks' upper windows, the soldiers making a last, desperate stand from there, a dozen or more of their dead lying bloody in the courtyard.

Bauer's marines were scattered among the rocks and brush, firing their muskets at any soldiers that dared raise their heads, the gun crews only now and again firing back, a musket barrel protruding over the berm here and there, their aim poor, their return fire frantic and ineffective. Weatherby knew that any man behind those walls must be seriously shell-shocked by now, dazed and unable to put up much of a fight.

Another round landed on the top of the wall, sending lethal shards of rock flying through the gun crews, adding to the deadly shrapnel. The next bomb landed within the enclosure itself, sending up a huge plume of rock and dust that scattered in the wind and blew over Monk, who was closest to the enclosure, lying flat behind a fallen tree trunk. Private Kirkpatrick was lying beside him, reloading his musket.

Weatherby could also see that the sloop's crew was roused, her captain recognizing immediately that the mortar attack had been concentrating on the gun position. He must have known that it would only be a matter of time before the battery changed hands. They were desperately getting their anchor up, men scrambling up her ratlines to loose her sails. They would be moving off in a few moments.

"Ready to go in, Major?" asked Weatherby breathlessly as he came up beside Major Bauer, the sharp bayonet on the end of his musket gleaming brightly in the morning sunshine. Corporal "Bull" Decker knelt next to the major, stuffing fuses into some grenades, a few lengths of smoldering slow match clenched in his teeth.

"What are you doing here?" asked a startled Bauer.

"The sloop is moving off," Weatherby informed him excitedly, "and I'll be needing those guns to get her and some of your men to help me with them. I don't believe we'll get much help from the Indians up here. Are you and your men ready to go in?"

Major Bauer could not see the sloop from his position, but he and his marines were ready to make their assault. With little or no fire coming their way, he answered resolutely, "I suppose they've taken enough punishment." He waited until the sound of the next explosion died away before shouting, "All right, men, we go to the wall on my signal!" Decker moved off, and Bauer waited for him to hand out his prepared grenades.

Weatherby stood up and waved his arms at Briggs. An instant later, Bauer put his whistle between his teeth and blew a long, shrill note. "Let's go!" he shouted.

The marines rose up from their protected positions, some carrying lit hand grenades. Before Bauer could stand and lead the attack, Weatherby was already running toward the berm, instinctively weaving his way through the low scrub, musket pointed forward, screaming like a madman. The rest of the marines were close behind, all yelling like demons, rushing toward the stone wall, a few of them firing their muskets as a couple of curious heads looked up. The last mortar shell landed dangerously close as Weatherby came up on the berm, the concussion almost knocking him down, the thick smell of sulfur burning his nostrils, the sound ringing in his ears.

"Get down, you fool!" shouted Bauer as he caught up to Weatherby. He grabbed his shoulder and forced him down behind the wall as a couple of grenades went off inside the berm. A half-dozen more grenades exploded as all the marines made it to the wall, Corporal Stockton bringing up the rear.

Weatherby found Private Kirkpatrick sitting next to him in the dirt, his face grimy with sweat and dust, and the two exchanged fearless grins.

Bauer called out down the line, "Reload!" bringing the sounds of ramrods striking home, and then reminding them, "Remember, fast and furious!"

Bauer waited until all were ready. They could hear the cries and groans of dying men on the other side of the berm. "Over we go!" he screamed and released his grip on Weatherby's shoulder. The marines went scrambling over the wall, firing at anyone inside who showed signs of resistance.

With Kirkpatrick on one side of him and Bauer on the other, Weatherby leaped up onto the berm. What he saw shocked him—dead men lying in grotesque and twisted heaps in the rubble, a few bloody body parts lying here and there, dark spots on the torn and rubble-strewn ground. At first it was hard to tell the living from the dead, but now a few red-coated soldiers turned in their direction, weapons raised.

Decker rushed forward and smashed a British soldier in the face with the butt of his musket, knocking the man backwards.

Kirkpatrick raised his musket and fired at an enemy soldier who was sitting as if wounded against the sandbagged bunker in the middle of the berm, hitting him in the arm, which he clenched in pain. A soldier on the left wore gold officer's braid and was holding a pistol in his hand. He pointed it at Major Bauer.

Weatherby raised his musket, but Kirkpatrick bumped into him as he fired and he missed, the ball blowing a dusty hole near the officer's head. Now the officer desperately turned his weapon toward Weatherby, who instinctively rushed him with his bayonet extended as the officer fired, the bullet grazing Weatherby's neck as he drove the bayonet into the man's chest, a fountain of crimson gushing out as the man moaned his last breath.

The wounded soldier sitting beside the fallen officer gazed in shock at his dead commander and Weatherby standing over him, but not for long, for Monk ran up and buried his hatchet into the top of the man's skull. Then he viciously yanked it free and ripped off a chunk of the man's scalp; brains and blood flying everywhere.

Weatherby's adrenaline was pumping, the killing frenzy upon him as he tried pulling the bayonet out of the dead officer's chest. Flesh and bone clasped the blade tightly, and no matter how he savagely twisted and turned the bayonet, it still held stubbornly. Bauer stepped up and, grabbing Weatherby's musket from him, placed his boot against the dead man's chest and wrenched the blade free before handing the musket back, saying, "I think you got him, Weatherby."

Weatherby stood there, wild-eyed and breathless in his blood-spattered shirt, his neck and bayonet dripping with blood. Most of the defenders had already been killed or wounded by the terrible carnage of the mortar barrage; the rest too dazed and confused to resist.

Major Bauer called out, "Cease fire," then had to restrain Monk from striking with his hatchet an unconscious but still-breathing soldier lying under one of the gun carriages.

Kirkpatrick stood there, his musket still smoking, mouth hanging agape at the scene before them, the very ground razed and burned. Only three enemy soldiers were left alive, their hands thrown up in surrender, their eyes wide in fright and shock. The battle for the battery was over, and Weatherby had killed a man face to face with a bayonet. Monk triumphantly raised his bloody scalp in the air and screamed a bloodcurdling war whoop.

Only now did Weatherby force himself to look at the man he had killed, the first man he had ever killed face to face, a young officer not much older than himself, his head thrown grotesquely back, his mouth rigid in agony, his eyes staring in disbelief at the clear blue sky. But there was little time to contemplate the savage action as Briggs and Smith ran up, reminding him that the battle for the island was not yet over. He dropped his empty musket and turned to his main purpose.

The guns were indeed large caliber—eighteen-pound field pieces. "Just like Blackstone said," he announced aloud. They were long range and would throw a heavy ball with terrible force. One was unusable, its truck wrecked, the heavy barrel lying on the ground.

"There's plenty of powder and shot here," announced Briggs, pointing to the sandbagged bunker.

Sounds of resistance were still coming from across the valley, puffs of smoke sporadically emanating from the second-story windows of the barracks. The sloop had pulled up her anchor and raised her sails and was moving from her position in the center of the harbor.

"Quick, get those two guns turned around!" ordered Weatherby, instinctively taking charge. "Kirkpatrick, help me! You men, too! Smith, show them what to do! Briggs, take charge of shot and powder! Major Bauer, you might want to fire that other gun into the barracks across the valley, let them know who's in control up here!"

Bauer's men hesitated for a moment as the young naval officer was ordering them about, but Bauer recognized the sense in what Weatherby was trying to accomplish. "You heard the Lieutenant! Decker, Bentkowski, each of you take a gun! Corporal Stockton, help Mr. Briggs with the ammunition!"

When Kinkaid received word that the sloop was leaving the harbor and then a moment later the order to cease fire, he knew what he had to do. He hated the thought of leaving Weatherby and the spotting party ashore, but his ship was the primary consideration. If a warship was coming to investigate, *Swift* was vulnerable in the position she was in. He could always come back to pick up the shore party later, but without a ship no one would be leaving this shore.

"O'Toole! Rikker!" he shouted. "Get down here right away!"

"On my way, Captain!" answered O'Toole. He knew what Kinkaid had in mind and immediately scrambled over the loose rocks, making his way quickly down the hill to the ship's boat, Rikker close behind him.

"Sergeant Anders, my compliments for a job well done," said Kinkaid appreciatively. "Now I'm going to have to ask you to stand aside." *Swift* was to become a brig-of-war once again. "Mr. Saddler, Mr. Lofton, prepare to take us out!"

The men needed no encouragement and came streaming out of the fore and after hatches, happy to have been released from their imposed confinement below, more than eager to get out into the open sea.

"Awful stuffy and dusty down there," said Rafferty to no one in particular, making a show of taking deep breaths of fresh air, his face and arms slick with sweat.

"And get those trees off my ship!" shouted Kinkaid.

The recently bare deck now became a scene of frantic but efficient activity as the crew took up their duties, not even minding the needless shouts and cursing from Mr. Saddler and Mr. Lofton, every man and officer only too happy to have something useful to do once again. The ties binding the limbs and bushes to the rigging were quickly cut away, the vegetation thrown over the side, and the standing rigging once more cinched tight. By then O'Toole and Rikker had returned to the ship and quickly had the ship's boat hauled aboard.

"Now the mortars," said Kinkaid.

"But sir..." Sergeant Anders began his protest, but he was in no position to force his will as First Lieutenant Saddler and Mr. Lofton roused the crew to action, pushing the Marine Sergeant, who had done his job magnificently, forcefully aside, O'Toole and Rikker standing between him and the mortars.

The pre-rigged block-and-tackle arrangement was attached to the harnesses already fixed to the mortar trucks, and with the concerted effort of the Travelin' Brothers and a half-dozen men pushing and pulling, the mortars were hauled and dragged along the deck and edged close to the bulwarks openings. The side rails were detached, and with a mighty "Heave-ho!" the heavy weapons were shoved overboard, each landing with a mighty wallop and a big splash, a few scars on the deck the only evidence that they had ever been aboard.

Sergeant Anders was still looking on in resignation as O'Toole had his deckhands winch the anchor up and Mr. Lofton directed the sail details. Everyone was sweating profusely from their exertions under the hot morning sun.

"All sail!" bellowed Kinkaid as Rikker took the helm. "Head us south."

The guns of the battery were already loaded, and with the help of Bauer's marines Weatherby had two of them pointing out over the harbor as Bauer took charge of the third.

Weatherby aimed and touched off the first gun and watched as its shot fell just yards beyond the sloop as she was heading away.

"Load her—quick!" shouted the frenzied Smith as Weatherby stepped to the second gun, aimed, and fired. This time the shot tore through her mainsail top. He had the range now as Major Bauer began firing the third gun into the second barracks, where desperate British soldiers were making their last desperate stand.

"Loaded!" came the shout from Smith. This time a direct hit amidships, sending men sprawling.

"Hurrah!" let out Smith and Briggs.

"Damned fine shooting, Weatherby!" exulted Kirkpatrick.

Weatherby was a mad fiend at the guns now, firing them as fast as they could be reloaded, Smith showing Decker and Bentkowski the rhythm of the task, Briggs directing the shot and powder from the bunker, where Stockton encouraged the constant flow of ammunition, sailors and marines working as a team. There, through the smoke, another direct hit on the sloop. Weatherby hardly noticed when Bauer turned his gun around as well, the battle for the garrison apparently over, and now three heavy guns were pounding her, tearing up her deck, smashing through her hull. Weatherby gave no thought to those men being maimed and killed aboard her, only that the vessel responsible for Cutler's death was pulling away in spite of her heavy damage and that he was determined to stop her.

Kinkaid could hear the dull booms of the artillery coming from the ridgetop as he took *Swift* down the coast toward the opening of the harbor, Mr. Lofton's crews still piling on sail. They were running with the wind, and without the considerable weight of the mortars, the shore was rushing by, the ship making good speed.

Finally they saw her, the little sloop, at the mouth of the harbor, barely moving, holes in her hull and bulwarks, with geysers of water framing her shredded sails. Somebody up above was giving her a terrible thrashing, and Kinkaid could easily guess whom.

The cannons above kept up their deadly work as *Swift* came relentlessly on, and now the sloop's mainmast top splintered in two and her topsails came crashing down, toppling into the water.

"Her stern is settling, sir," observed O'Toole as *Swift* bore down on her with broadsides ready.

Kinkaid took note of the fact, but the battered enemy sloop was still capable of delivering her own broadside. "Ready on the larboard guns, Mr. Saddler! Steady on the helm!"

There, a man on her deck was waving a white shirt. She had had enough. Weatherby's gunnery had severely damaged her, no doubt killing and wounding many of her crew, wearing down her will to fight. She was taking on water, and with *Swift* bearing down on her with gunports open, her captain had little choice but to strike. The enemy sloop that Kinkaid now recognized as the very one that had killed young Cutler had not managed to get off a single shot in her defense.

"Stand down the guns, Mr. Saddler. O'Toole, get a boat over the side. Mr. Lofton, take eight armed men and board her. Take Rafferty with you; see if you can stop her leaks. Use her own boats too and get her crew off her as quickly as you can."

Weatherby also saw the man on the deck of the sloop waving his shirt in surrender and *Swift* bearing down on her.

"Cease firing!" he yelled.

Briggs led the gun crews in a cheer. "Hip, hip, hurrah! We did it!"

Weatherby hadn't realized how thirsty he was, how dry his mouth, and how parched his lips until Kirkpatrick handed him the canteen. His bloody neck burned when he raised his head to drink, but as he gulped the warm water, his gaze rested on the town below where Indians were still shouting and running about. Handing the water back to Kirkpatrick, he said, "Major, we'd better hurry and get down there before things get ugly."

"I believe they're already getting ugly, Lieutenant," answered Bauer. He motioned for Monk, who had already tied their hands, to guard the three dazed British soldiers. Then he said, "Corporal Stockton, you and Kirkpatrick remain up here with Monk and the prisoners. The rest of you come with me."

"Briggs, you and Smith stay up here, too," ordered Weatherby, "Keep an eye out to sea. We don't need any surprises."

Weatherby followed Bauer and the marines into the town, gathering up the Indians, who were delightedly yelling and shouting in victory, some of them dressed in embroidered vests and colorful shirts, some looking ridiculous in lace petticoats. One even wore some poor bride's wedding dress, half on, half off. Others were running through the streets, palpably drunk, carrying all manner of loot: necklaces, silver candlesticks, and chalices. One Indian was dragging a heavy, ornate mirror, while another followed alongside wearing a red dress, taking obvious delight in seeing his reflection within its frame. They were easy enough to subdue, delirious in their victory, and almost all of them had discarded their muskets. Firing them once, then not knowing how to reload them, they found the heavy muskets useless.

The battle for St. Kitts was over, the town and its garrison subdued. *Swift* was dropping her anchor in the harbor while Lofton and Rafferty were boarding the sloop *Reprisal*. The second ship's boat soon made for the docks with Kinkaid and O'Toole in front, Dr. Grafton, the ship's surgeon, and a dozen armed men crammed aboard as well.

Weatherby met him at the dock, a bloody streak on his neck, his uniform collar broken. Two marines were with him, along with the crowd of Indians they had gathered.

"Where is Major Bauer?" asked Kinkaid, one of the ornate dueling pistols tucked into his belt, the other in his hand.

"Rounding up more Indians, sir," answered Weatherby. "We agreed to meet at the garrison."

"And the Doctor?"

"Still at the garrison, as far as I know."

"Dr. Grafton, I want you to set up an aid station in that building by the pier there. When more of the crew arrives on shore and after you've treated any of our wounded, make an effort to attend to any of the civilians who have been injured…and see that any medical personnel among our prisoners are free to minister to the injured on either side. O'Toole, you take the boat crew and search those warehouses along the waterfront. You two marines stay with these Indians—keep them here for now. Weatherby, come with me."

"Aye aye, sir," said Weatherby, catching up with Kinkaid, already striding up the street.

"Weatherby, you were supposed to return to the ship as soon as those damned guns were taken. What happened?" demanded Kinkaid.

"I know, sir," answered Weatherby, trying to discern his captain's mood. "But when I saw that sloop out there…well, she needed to be stopped, Captain."

"And you were the only man for the job, is that it?"

"The Doctor must have forgotten to send his men up to us and, well, sir, that sloop could have—"

"Do you realize all the work you've caused me?"

"Sir?"

"Now I'm going to have to write a long report, justifying the medal they'll have to give you," relented Kinkaid, slapping Weatherby on the back.

"Sorry, Captain," said Weatherby, happy to perceive Kinkaid's jest. And thinking his captain in an agreeable mood, he ventured,

"About Smith, sir. I've a man on number four who hopes to take Smith's place in the galley. The old guy, Helmut; always been shy around the guns, and too slow, as well…we wouldn't miss him and he gets along grandly with Hyde."

Weatherby didn't have to beg and Kinkaid knew it. Due to circumstances, he had simply forgotten about Smith's uncertain status and, feeling guilty for putting the decision off for so long, he had to say, "Very well, Weatherby."

Weatherby grinned and said, "I made him gun captain of Troubadour just yesterday, sir."

Major Bauer and his marines had combed the town, gathering up as many of the jubilant Indians as they could find and now they were coming down the street, making their way toward the garrison, joining Kinkaid and Weatherby as they arrived there.

A volley of musket fire could be heard coming from behind the first barracks building, and when Kinkaid's group rounded the corner, there was the mad Doctor and his musket-toting henchmen in the courtyard, where the flag of the British Empire still flew from the flagpole. They were lining half a dozen soldiers up against the barracks' wall. Empty wine bottles were strewn all over the ground, along with four dead British soldiers. One of them, an officer, had been decapitated, his headless body lying in a pool of blood.

"The island is ours," said Kinkaid authoritatively. "The killing is over."

"No, no, no," complained the thoroughly drunk Doctor. "I tell you before, but you not listen, mon. I kill dem all." He raised his bloody saber in the air, a signal to General Bobo, standing with a musket in his hand not five feet away.

Bobo brought the weapon up to his shoulder and aimed it at the line of soldiers, but Kinkaid fired his pistol through the man's hand, the ball lodging in the stock of the gun, which he instantly dropped, howling in pain and holding his bleeding hand. The usually sleepy eyed General Pierre now looked wide awake and promptly dropped his musket. The British soldiers, cringing in terror, looked hopeful at the unexpected development.

"As I said, the killing is over," said Kinkaid, forcing himself to sound calm, pulling out his second pistol. He strode boldly up to the Doctor and smacked the saber out of the madman's hand with the still-smoking pistol, instantly regretting the decision as he heard the stock split. "Unless you want to be the next to die...mon!"

The Doctor stood there helpless, speechless for once. A group of Indians that had been milling about were looking on, appearing confused by the sudden turn of events.

"Arrest this...madman," said Kinkaid to O'Toole. "And confine all the prisoners in the garrison. Keep the Indians here as well, except for the Doctor...we'll take him with us, for now. Major Bauer, a few of your marines to remain and guard them?"

"My pleasure, Captain."

Suddenly Smith came running around the corner. "They's a ship comin', Cap'm! Too far away to tell what she might be...but comin' this way, suh!" he exclaimed breathlessly.

"Where away is this ship, Smith?"

"Twelve, fo'teen miles, due east, Cap'm."

It seemed too early for Blackstone to return with *Moondog*. He had to think fast. "Is there anybody else up there with you?"

"Mr. Briggs sent me down, suh."

"Good, Smith. Now, I want you to go back up there and tell Mr. Briggs to keep an eye on her and send a report the minute you know exactly what kind of ship she is."

"Right away, Cap'm," said Smith, before running off.

Kinkaid looked around at the bloody scene before him. "Major, have some of your men clean this place up. Keep the Indians busy digging graves; get these bodies out of here."

"Over there behind that barracks, Captain?" asked Bauer.

"As good a place as any," decided Kinkaid, looking around at the group of Indians. "Where the hell is that fat Indian?"

"Back on the dock, sir," replied Weatherby.

Kinkaid looked up at the Union Jack still flying above. "Somebody haul that flag down and bring it along. And find another to replace it."

"Let's go," said Kinkaid, heading for the dock.

Two marines were half dragging, half carrying the stunned Doctor. O'Toole was at the harbor front, along with the group of Indians that Weatherby had gathered. The Indians looked surprised and sullen when they saw their great leader being manhandled by two of Bauer's marines and Kinkaid carrying their leader's saber.

O'Toole, however, was grinning from ear to ear. "Sir, there are four heavy cannon behind breastworks above those warehouses, eighteen-pounders. And in the warehouses are upwards of a hundred barrels of powder and all calibers of round shot. That one in the middle is filled with rice, mostly, and the others contain ship's stores, fittings, timbers and planks, canvas, and spare parts."

"We'll avail ourselves of those supplies, especially the powder and all the two- and six-pound shot we can find. The food we'll leave for the island residents. Anything we can't use, we'll burn, but later. Right now I want you to get over to that sloop and help Rafferty make her seaworthy."

"Aye, we'll make her right, Captain."

It was now obvious to all of the Indians that the Doctor was no longer in control. Kinkaid walked up to the chubby Indian and said, "Kill...no, no! Understand? No more kill!" and he made negative motions with his hands.

The chubby Indian gestured that he understood.

Satisfied, Kinkaid had a few of Bauer's marines escort the rest of the Indians back to the garrison. Some of the natives of the town could be seen peeking from behind window curtains and half-opened doors, watching the developments.

Dr. Grafton sent Boyle, one of his loblolly boys, to inform Kinkaid that they had half-a-dozen men knocking on doors in the area, informing the locals that medical help was available, "But so far we've no takers, sir. They're still frightened."

"Just as well. Inform Dr. Grafton that we may have visitors; we'll worry about the civilian population later."

The only non-crew member he took back to the ship was the mad Doctor, strangely and quietly accepting his captivity, probably surprised and thankful that Kinkaid had not killed him, which is what the Doctor would have done had the situation been reversed, thought Kinkaid. He had little time to think about the Doctor now, for Briggs had once more sent Smith down the hill.

"She be a British man-of-war, Cap'm. Mighty big, too, suh," he reported, panting hard.

It was weighty news and gave Kinkaid pause. "Very good, Smith. And I'll have someone relieve you. You must be done in, what with this heat…"

"No, suh," answered Smith without hesitation. "Ah kin run all day, Cap'm."

Taken by Smith's brash spirit, Kinkaid asked, "Where are you from, Smith?"

"Rhode Island, Cap'm."

"I wasn't aware that Rhode Island was known for its runners," Kinkaid teased him.

"Well, they's me and my pappy, Cap'm."

"Your father runs, too?"

"Fastest man in his tribe, Cap'm. Ran across Africa once," replied Smith proudly. "Pappy believes I be the fastest man in the state."

Kinkaid had to think fast, coming up with, "Some say that the diminutive state of Rhode Island is inhabited by the boastful."

"Dat may be, Cap'm," Smith readily agreed. "Like Pappy say, little men talk big."

"Hmm, fast and a diplomat too," observed Kinkaid.

"Yassuh, Cap'm."

"Smith, are you still determined to be a gunner?"

It's a lot mo' fun than peelin' spuds, Cap'm. And a man cain't hardly breave down der in da galley. Cain't see nutin', too. I much prefer the singin' and smoke that Bertha makes."

Kinkaid had to laugh. "Well, your talents are certainly wasted in the crew's mess, which is why I just told Mr. Weatherby to put you permanently on his gun teams as he sees fit."

Smith's eyes lit up and his mouth fell open. Then, collecting himself, he stood rigidly at attention and saluted, saying, "Thank you, Cap'm, suh."

"But at the moment I need you to take your fast Rhode Island arse back up that hill. Convey my compliments to Mr. Briggs, and tell him to come down to the ship. I want you to stay alert up there, Smith. Keep your eyes open and keep sending your reports."

"Yassuh, Cap'm!" Kinkaid returned Smith's salute and off he ran, back up to the gun position on the hill, happy to be a gunner's mate and free of the cruel whims of the head cook, Hyde.

X
The Prize and a Proud Name

The news of a British man-of-war heading their way filled Kinkaid's thoughts, and he found it difficult to keep away sudden and unexpected waves of anxiety and doubt, alternating with eager anticipation. Joking with Smith was one way to hide his anxiety from the men, but he needed to gain control over his racing thoughts, to decide on a course of action. This was no time to celebrate their victory. He could easily vacate the town, get his men off, and make safely out to sea before the big ship arrived; technically, they had fulfilled their mission. But leaving the island undefended from a large warship might immediately negate their efforts, and so there was only one course to consider. There was much to be done before she arrived; at least there was plenty of time in which to do it.

"See what you can do about getting the kitchen going at the garrison, Major. We have a lot of hungry Indians on our hands, and I'd prefer they eat what we give them rather than allow them to fend for themselves."

"Considering that people are at the top of their menu, a good idea, Captain," agreed Bauer. "And that should be easy enough, since it seems we interrupted breakfast preparations. The mess is full of fresh fruit, bread, and porridge."

"Good. Once you get everyone secured and fed, leave only enough men to ensure the confinement of the prisoners...and supervise the Indians; I don't want them running loose on the town. Keep the two separated and see that the Indians don't feel like prisoners."

"I'll make some of them the guards; keep the others busy in the kitchen or digging graves."

"Good idea. Oh, and you might have your men round up any British uniforms and hats they find in the barracks; you know, a nice assortment. Bring them down to the docks when you're finished here; I'll have another job for you."

Kinkaid returned to the dock area where *Reprisal* was slowly making her way back into the harbor with damaged spars and rigging, low in the water, her pumps working furiously. Lofton had her battered crew sent ashore, and they were promptly confined in the garrison. O'Toole sent along a report that she had been badly hulled but repairs were continuing. After ensuring that the crews on both ships had a late breakfast and that somebody had taken something up to Smith on the hill, Kinkaid hungrily wolfed down a few scones that Cato had thoughtfully baked the night before. They were dry but tasty and washed down just fine with two cups of coffee. Then he sent Weatherby and O'Toole ashore with a large working party that was soon bringing shot and powder aboard *Swift* from the warehouses.

By now it was noon, and Kinkaid decided that he would check on the shore and make a survey of the boats in the harbor to see which ones might best suit their purpose. Briggs had returned to the ship, and Kinkaid sent word that he was to accompany his captain ashore in ten minutes and provide him an account of what had happened on the hill. Kinkaid opened the door of his cabin, and there was Cato, holding two large groupers by their tails.

"For dinner, Captain," said Cato, grinning. Kinkaid wanted to ask Cato when he had found the time to go fishing, but here was Briggs now, coming to meet him at the ladder.

Once in the boat, Kinkaid asked, "What happened up there, Briggs?"

He listened as the young midshipman told of Weatherby's assault on the guns—how he had initiated the attack and probably saved Bauer's life by killing a British officer, before directing the marines at the guns and preventing the sloop *Reprisal* from leaving the harbor.

"You should have seen him, Captain. Like a demon from the moment he saw her, sir."

The boat no sooner touched shore than there was Weatherby, striding up to give his report. "Almost finished with the transfer, Captain." The patch of red on his torn collar had widened; his neck wound looked crusty with dried blood.

"Very good, Weatherby, and I'll have another job for you, but not until you have that wound looked after by Dr. Grafton."

"As you wish, Captain."

Kinkaid remained on the dock while the last of the munitions were taken out to *Swift*. Bauer reported that everyone in the garrison had been fed and also provided Kinkaid with a quick report of the assault on the guns, especially emphasizing the role that Weatherby had played in his accurate direction of the mortar fire, his reckless bravery in the assault, and the way he took charge of the battery against *Reprisal*.

Now here came Smith once more down from the hill to report, "Large man-of-war, forty guns or mo', Cap'm, buckin' da wind and tackin' to make da harbor, suh…'spect she be here by dark."

"Thank you, Smith," said Kinkaid, pleased to hear that headwinds would delay her. Hopefully she would not arrive until after dark; they needed every advantage against a ship of her size. "Do you have everything you need up there, Smith?"

"Could use mo' water, Cap'm."

"See you get some, then. And I'll expect another report when she's an hour out, Smith."

"Yassuh, Cap'm."

And off he went, almost bumping into a contingent of well-dressed elderly black men coming down to the docks. One carried a white tablecloth at the end of a stick.

"I be de mayor of de town of Basseterre," said the distinguished man proudly, bowing elaborately. He had a touch of gray at his temples, his eyes sharp and intelligent.

Kinkaid returned the bow. "Pleased to make your acquaintance, sir," said Kinkaid with as much patience as possible, given that his ship might soon be in mortal danger and his preparations were incomplete; there was little time for diplomacy. "However, if you have business with me, I must insist that you be as brief as possible."

The man hesitated a moment, made a scan of the docks, then, with his head held high, asked bravely, "From where do you come and what do you intend to do here?"

Instantly Kinkaid saw a way out of the dilemma that he had placed himself in by coming into the roadstead—an American ship, with orders not to be in any way linked to an Indian uprising. "You have nothing to fear from us, good sirs. Our only intention is to leave your town in peace. As an American brig-of-war on duty to chase, subdue, and punish pirates in this area, we were some miles offshore and heard the cannon fire. We saw the Indians attacking and came in to stop a certain massacre. You will find that the Indians are even now confined in the garrison."

"First de Spanish, den de English, and now dees terrible savages," exclaimed the mayor. "Their attack was frightening; we were afraid we would all be killed. I speak for de whole town when I tank you from de bottom—"

"Honored to be of service, good sirs," stated Kinkaid, relieved that the man seemed to accept his explanation, even if only half true, "but there is a British ship heading our way and there is much to be done."

"We will help you fight her," stated the Mayor.

"We will be ready for her, but perhaps you can tell me how many ships were in your harbor last night?"

"De be tree till some ship fire on dem, den two go chase; one big, one not so big."

"Thank you, sir," said Kinkaid. It was good news. The "big" one was the one they awaited and needed to neutralize. Yet, if the islanders were willing to fight and were serious about keeping their island free of British influence, they might easily drive off a single, smaller vessel. "The other may return after we are gone. Perhaps then there will come a time for you to fight."

"We will be ready for her," came the bold reply.

Taken with the man's spirit and sincerity, Kinkaid said, "Then I promise we will do everything in our power to help you prepare for her before we leave. But as of now, our ship's surgeon, Dr. Grafton, and his staff are available to treat any who are sick or injured. And there are a few tons of rice to distribute to any who need it."

"God bless you, sir…and good luck to you in your meeting with de British ship."

"Thank you, sir, and when we have dealt with her I promise to take the Indians off your hands," he added, surprised at his own sudden decision. Distributing the food was easy, but leaving the Indians would be unfair to both the townspeople and the Indians. The enemy would surely retake the island of St. Kitts in time, unless American forces were sent to defend it, which he knew was improbable. However, it would take some weeks, perhaps months, before the British could respond, offering St. Eustatia at least some period of relief from British naval presence and subsequent pressure on American trade to and from the island. He could only hope that he would be able to adequately explain in his report to the Marine Committee why he could not, in good conscience, leave this place and these innocent people in the hands of the insane Doctor.

The man bowed and walked with his group back into the town, now quiet, with curious people starting to come out into the streets again.

Weatherby was returning from his detailed survey of the harbor front after having seen the surgeon, a bandage wrapped around his neck.

"I figure we can use four of those boats there, sir. They're big enough and high-sided."

"Very good, Weatherby."

Major Bauer came around the corner, eight of his marines with him, and they brought a cart piled high with various British uniforms. "I've put Sergeant Anders in charge at the garrison, Captain," reported Bauer. "He's made a list that should keep the Indians busy for some time."

"Very good, Major, and those uniforms should do nicely. Mr. Weatherby, you might pick one out that suits you. And since Cato has two large fish that need consuming, I shall expect to see both you gentlemen in my cabin for dinner at seven."

Most of the preparations had been made by the time dinner was served and now the three of them were seated at the captain's table at the appointed hour when Cato entered, carrying a steaming platter of blackened fish swimming in Creole sauce.

"Cato, when did you find the time to go fishing?" asked Kinkaid.

"While the men were preparing the mortars this morning, Captain," he answered matter-of-factly. "And it's a good thing too, because those big guns frightened every fish within two miles of us," he scolded, as if the procurement of good things to eat was more important than military operations.

"Well, Mr. Africanus," said Kinkaid, smacking his lips, "I for one am thankful that you have your priorities in order."

"Hear, hear," put in Major Bauer, raising his wine glass to Kinkaid's steward in salute. "The cook in the officer's mess could use a few lessons from you, Cato."

Weatherby wore the red coat of a British Major and looked smart indeed as he laughed and said, "Mr. Lofton asked him the other day if he prepared our meals blindfolded."

"By the strange choice of seasoning he comes up with, I can see why one might think so," observed Bauer.

"Even worse, the man smells like a dead animal."

Bauer laughed, almost choking on the food in his mouth, before providing the information, "It's not that I mind so much the black tar he serves for coffee, but those charred deck planks he refers to as steaks…"

Kinkaid had to chuckle at the amusing banter and raised his glass as well, acknowledging, "I am indeed a lucky man to have you, Cato."

His dignified steward, finding the distinction of being compared to the officer's cook a dubious one at best, nodded politely in recognition and began refilling their glasses.

Kinkaid continued. "You might be happy to know, Cato, that those big guns will be serving as homes for the offspring of these fine fish for many generations to come." Turning to Major Bauer, Kinkaid smiled and said, "No need to remind Sergeant Anders of the fact, Major."

Bauer laughed and said, "Ah, that reminds me of something. Mr. Weatherby, why don't you tell the Captain what you overhead down in the orlop the other day?"

A grin appeared on Weatherby's face as he remembered the incident. "It was last Sunday, Captain. Sergeant Anders was regaling his marines with stories of past combat experiences. First it was heavy artillery bombardments he had endured while lying in the mud in the pouring rain with bullets flying over his head. Then he was being ambushed by an entire regiment of British regulars that he drove off with his cutlass."

Bauer chuckled and provided, "I particularly like the one about the crafty sniper that shoots everyone but him before he sneaks up on him and cuts his throat." As an aside Bauer added, "I've heard them all."

"Not to mention being attacked by mosquitoes bigger than birds," continued Weatherby. "Anyway, each story became more outlandish than the last. Combat all over the world. In Italy and France and Ireland, then against the Indians, and now the British, just going on and on. Well, then we hear somebody climbing the ladder, and there's Boatswain O'Toole coming up from the orlop…course he'd heard everything Anders had said and he says to him, 'All shore duty, huh?'"

Bauer nearly fell out of his chair laughing…which made Kinkaid laugh, and of course Weatherby caught the laughing bug too, all out of proportion to the foolish joke that only a sailor could appreciate. Soon all three were laughing and joking and enjoying the fact that they were laughing and joking, even forgetting the reason for their laughter, when there came a knock at the door.

It was Mr. Midshipman Lofton. He had been aboard *Reprisal* all afternoon with the carpenters, frantically trying to keep her afloat and was shocked to see his captain, Major Bauer, and Mr. Weatherby dining leisurely, laughing, and telling jokes while a powerful British man-of-war was expected in an hour or so. The disturbed look on Mr. Lofton's sweaty face forced Kinkaid to replace his mirth with a serious air before he asked, "How are things progressing, Mr. Lofton?"

"Rafferty has shored up the hull and we've pumped out most of the water, sir. She's floating almost normally again and now he's getting that mainmast top rigged. He says to inform you, sir, that he doesn't have time to make it work properly, but at least she'll look like she's seaworthy, Captain."

"Very good, indeed. And compliments to our fine carpenter, none better."

"I shall pass on your compliment, Captain. Oh, and the uniforms have been passed out. And here is a hat I found in the Captain's cabin."

"Why thank you, Mr. Lofton." Kinkaid took the hat and tried it on. "A bit large, but serviceable."

"Quite becoming, sir," said Weatherby.

"Yes, well, then I'd say we are quite prepared. May I interest you in a bowl of fruit salad, Mr. Lofton?"

"Uh, no thank you, sir; we've already eaten. The cooks brought us stew and sandwiches."

"Very well, then, duty calls, I know. Mr. Lofton, I'd like you to go back aboard *Reprisal*, as you shall be in command of her as our distinguished visitor arrives. I'll send word as to my orders."

"Thank you, Captain," replied Lofton, almost enthusiastically, before he left.

"And Mr. Weatherby," said Kinkaid, "you proved yourself so effective with those English field pieces that I shall have to ask you to return to those guns with two full gun crews after our fine dinner."

"It will be my pleasure to back up our hand with those ship-smashers, Captain. I take it the major will head up the boarding party, then?"

"That is correct, Weatherby."

"Too bad you'll miss out on all the fun this time, Lieutenant," Bauer teased him, but Weatherby merely grimaced, thinking of the lifeless eyes of the young British officer he had killed.

It was enough to see the look and know that Weatherby had learned a hard lesson—that vengeance came with a bitter taste— and it was with some effort to sound cheerful as he said, "But Major, don't you realize that Mr. Weatherby's idea of fun is aiming down the barrel of an eighteen-four pounder?"

"He handles cannons as precisely as he fires a musket," admitted Bauer. "Hell, Sergeant Anders believes Weatherby is as good as any of his sharpshooters."

"Now that is high praise, coming from Sergeant Anders," judged Kinkaid.

Weatherby forced a smile and modestly replied, "Practice makes perfect, sir."

Here they were, acting frivolous and eating like royalty, like it was Christmas back in Boston Harbor. The frivolity was, of course, a cover, not only for Weatherby's dark mood, but also for the feeling of enormous relief over the fact that they had actually taken the island of St. Kitts with a band of undisciplined Indians and the word of a pirate. Why, the mayor even believed that their ship was not involved in the attack, but had saved the town from certain slaughter and was responsible for preventing further violence. "Wait till the newspapers get hold of that story!" Major

Bauer had exclaimed. Finally, there was the fact that it wasn't over yet.

The golden rays of the setting sun shone through the stern windows, bathing the cabin with a warm and gentle glow as they finished the meal. As much as Kinkaid partook of the light and easy banter, pretending to be completely composed and unconcerned with the certain and inevitable meeting, his mind raced to cover all conceivable possibilities, endeavoring to leave no doubt or idea unexamined, still open to anything that would ensure their advantage. Yet he could think of nothing that he had not already put into effect, nothing that he might add to his bold yet simple plan.

There came the messenger, Smith, once again. "She'll be roundin' the headland in about an hour, Cap'm."

"Very good, Smith," said Kinkaid, dabbing his napkin at the corners of his mouth. "Gentlemen, I thank you for a most enjoyable evening, but I believe we shall soon have guests to attend to."

"Smith," said Weatherby, "I shall be requiring the assistance of you and your gun crew. Find Stevens and bring his crew along, as well."

"Right away, Mr. Weatherby," said Smith before going forward to find the men.

The ship appeared at the mouth of the harbor almost exactly when Smith said she would, an hour after the sun had gone down behind the hill. The captured sloop *Reprisal* stood out in the bay with Mr. Lofton in command and with sufficient men to man at least a few of her small-caliber guns, Rafferty among them, her mainmast top bound only with cord, her sails neatly furled. Even the slightest wind pressure on a sail rigged to that top would have torn it loose, but as Rafferty had said, "She looks seaworthy enough, so long as one don't look too closely."

Swift, with her flagstaff flying the garrison's Union Jack, was anchored close to shore, looking much like a British packet ship in a British-controlled harbor, delivering mail and orders for the fleet.

The guns on both ships were loaded and ready—ready for the word to run them out and fire should the man-of-war choose to fight. Rikker and some of his gunners had gone ashore and were manning two of the big cannons placed over the warehouses, while Bauer and his marines, along with thirty well-armed sailors under tarps, were strategically placed in four fishing shallops anchored in the harbor. And Weatherby was back up on the hill with the heavy artillery, the three guns already trained on the open space in the middle of the harbor, waiting with Smith and his gun crews and prepared to give their visitor a harsh pounding if she resisted. The town was quiet, still in shock over the morning raid and fearful of more violence to come.

The ship's ponderous bulk drifted in quietly, slowly, toward the center of the harbor, the only area left open for her by the other ships and boats, the only area suitable for a ship of her size, a third-rate double-decker, the *Isle of Wight (44)*. O'Toole waved casually to the men on her decks, her anchor detail, all fellow boatswain's mates. It was apparent that they suspected nothing as her anchor let loose with a loud clanging of chain.

Even before her sails were furled, there was Briggs on his way over in the captain's gig with a message inviting her captain to have dinner with the captain of *Swift* and informing him that the captain of *Reprisal* was already aboard and that they had mail and official dispatches for her, an invitation that was, hopefully, impossible to refuse.

Briggs had earlier volunteered to deliver the message, backing up his request by performing the best imitation of an English gentleman. Why, the boy was a natural actor. Consequently, he had been gloating over being chosen for the honor and was delighted to have found himself a rather tight-fitting British lieutenant's uniform in one of the staterooms on *Reprisal*. But donning it had brought a jolt of anxiety, and he soon began chattering away, first with Mr. Lofton, who ignored him, then with Mr. Weatherby, who humored him and joined in with a bit of British banter of his own. As the time neared, Briggs found himself becoming nervous in the extreme, suddenly fearful that he would not be able to repeat his performance, and because his uniform was too small for his frame he was having obvious difficulty breathing.

Kinkaid thought to speak with him for a moment before he got into the ship's boat, but then decided to merely smile and offer, "Break a leg, Briggs," showing he had confidence in the boy.

The oarsmen also wore outfits found aboard *Reprisal*, giving the Travelin' Brothers every appearance of sharp and disciplined English seamen in their blue jackets, neckerchiefs, and white trousers. In addition, each wore a low-crowned hat with a narrow brim decorated with a fancy ribbon, which had brought no end of teasing by their mates, quickly quelled by a stern Mr. Saddler.

Briggs stood in the bow of the boat, just managing to keep his knees from shaking too badly. Kinkaid watched him from the quarterdeck and thought his tanned, now-serious face had lost a degree or two of color.

Finally the gig pulled alongside the towering hulk of the big double-decker, and Briggs could be seen climbing her ladder to the main deck, a couple of British sailors lending him a hand up the tall ship's side. Then he headed for the stern, toward the quarterdeck, and was out of sight. Voices could be faintly heard over the water; a couple of men on her deck talking to the oarsmen in the boat, but exactly what they were saying could not be discerned from the deck of *Swift*.

"Let's just hope they're good enough actors to pull this off," said a doubtful Saddler to no one in particular, his negativity unwelcome, although saying what Kinkaid was thinking and hoping himself.

A few minutes passed, certainly time enough for Briggs to have delivered his message. Then five minutes turned into ten and then fifteen, with still no Mr. Midshipman Briggs in evidence. Perhaps he had been discovered and was even now being grilled by the master-at-arms of the British ship, her captain scheming a plan of his own to make life miserable for the Americans who thought they could trick him.

Kinkaid strolled the deck as the minutes passed, maintaining a calm appearance, and trying with difficulty to hide his anxiety. While he wore his own uniform, he could not help but keep handling the British captain's hat that Mr. Lofton had provided him from the captain's cabin of the captured *Reprisal*. Mr. Saddler and Mr. Thorne were in the waist, silent and sullen. It was nerve-rattling, with visions of those big guns on the British ship suddenly ripping through the lightly built *Swift*, tearing her and her crew asunder.

The men in the boat were still there, smoking and lounging across the seats, at least appearing to bear the wait in ease; the British crewmen had ignored them after their initial greeting.

Kinkaid worried mostly about Bauer's marines in the fishing boats—how long could they continue to remain quiet and concealed under the canvas tarps, their bodies hot and sweaty. He doubted that anyone had thought to bring any water, thinking they would only be under those tarps for fifteen minutes or so. But this was taking longer than anyone had anticipated, and now a half hour had passed with still no sign of Mr. Briggs. Added to Kinkaid's efforts at maintaining his unperturbed façade was the fact that his officers and crew, whether intentionally or not, kept shifting nervous glances his way, though he dared not let on that he noticed.

There, finally, some movement on the warship's deck. Yes, a group of men, all wearing the full dress uniform of British flag officers, came strolling toward the ladder; faint voices drifted across the water, then a loud and hearty laugh. Now an officer started down the ladder, arms of the oarsmen reaching up to lend support to a portly gentleman as he climbed ponderously down into the boat. As the larger man turned to seat himself, Kinkaid saw his hat and gold uniform trimmings, identifying him as the captain. A second officer, taller and more agile, descended next. And there was Mr. Briggs, taking his place in the bow. He gave the command to the oarsmen and the boat turned toward *Swift*.

The boat was more than halfway back now, the oarsmen pulling regularly and powerfully, and the voices were becoming distinct, the conversation intelligible.

"Well, I'll tell you, those poor men had only a keg of water to last them over two weeks on the open sea; a damned hot place this time of the year and with nary a tin of food. Why, it's a wonder any of them survived," came the deep voice of the captain of *Isle of Wight*.

"Aye, Captain," came the voice of the other officer, "they were lucky we found them."

"I'd like to get my hands on the throat of that pirate, Blackstone. I think I'd wring it myself," said the Captain.

Then Briggs came in with, "Perhapsh that would be too good for the rascal, shur." Briggs sounded every bit an English gentleman—with a slurred voice.

"Now, there's the right idea, Lieutenant. Keelhauling him first would be the better course. Say, has your ship run across the scoundrel at all? Have you been up round the Virgins yet?"

"Actually, we did see what could have been his ship, shur," said Briggs too loudly as the boat drew near. "Gave her a good shase, shur, but loshter in a rainshquall."

"Rotten luck, Lieutenant," gave the portly captain. "Perhaps working in consort we might trap that damned cutthroat."

Briggs was having too much fun with this masquerade, thought Kinkaid as he placed the British captain's hat lightly on his head so that it wouldn't fall down over his ears.

Rikker had the rowers ship their oars as the boat touched alongside.

"Drexell, you go up first, would you?" said the British captain.

"Of course, sir," said the tall officer as Treadwell helped steady the man. He stepped onto the gunwale of the boat and then climbed rapidly and powerfully up the ladder. Kinkaid, Saddler, and Mr. Thorne were on the quarterdeck, along with ten men standing at the rail. O'Toole blew his boatswain's pipe, announcing the arrival of a flag captain; his shrill whistle stabbing Kinkaid's eardrums, so close was he beside him.

The officer Drexell took a quick glance about him as he made the deck and then turned unsteadily around to give a helping hand to his captain. "Up you go, sir."

The ruddy-faced British captain joined Drexell on the quarterdeck, and there was Briggs right behind him, bounding up the ladder like a monkey, grinning too broadly and confidently for Kinkaid's pleasure, thoroughly drunk.

Drexell turned toward Kinkaid and said, "Captain, allow me to introduce Captain Heywood Woolston of His Britannic Majesty's ship, *Isle of Wight*."

"Pleased to make your acquaintance, Captain Woolston," said Kinkaid with a bow.

"I am First Officer, Lieutenant Dennis Drexell."

Kinkaid detected the unmistakable odor of alcohol on the man's breath as Drexell wobbled back on his heels, saluting the officers on the quarterdeck, Kinkaid and his officers returning the salute.

Kinkaid stepped forward and shook hands with both men before saying, "Gentlemen, I am Captain Jonathan Kinkaid of the American brig-of-war, *Swift*, and I have the distinct pleasure of informing you that you are now my prisoners of war. Run out the guns, Mr. Saddler! O'Toole! Mr. Briggs!"

The captured officers stood gap-mouthed as the gunports opened, and the trucks rumbled across the deck. O'Toole blew into his pipe, a long, high-pitched screech that carried over the harbor, and before he had quit, the guns on both *Swift* and the sloop *Reprisal* were run out, one on either side of *Isle of Wight*, poking their black snouts out through the gunports, aimed at the enemy ship. Briggs ran down the British ensign, exchanging it for their own, while the four boats filled with armed sailors and Bauer's marines rowed quickly alongside the big warship, her crew not yet even beginning to understand what was happening, although the sight of the boats filled with armed men pulling alongside soon had her deck hands scrambling madly about.

Weatherby saw this frantic activity from his position on the hill and decided to send a strong warning in case her officers attempted to man her guns or otherwise resist. He aimed his first gun just in front of the warship's bow, blew gently upon his wick, and then touched off the big artillery piece. It roared with a resounding crash that echoed off the opposite hill, spitting flame and billowing white smoke. The ball hit only yards from her bowsprit, sending a geyser of water thirty feet into the air. Rikker, at his eighteen pounder above the warehouse, touched off his gun an instant later, sending a double load of grape tearing through *Isle of Wight*'s rigging.

"I can only hope your crew has the sense to strike, Captain," said Kinkaid, tossing his overlarge hat aside. "There are two ships with loaded guns pointed at your vessel, sir, and, as you can see, my men at the shore batteries have you zeroed in. To resist will only result in the needless slaughter of your crew. The town, the garrison, all guns, and the ships in the harbor are ours. You have no chance, sir."

Without her captain or first officer on board, a subordinate would have to risk all to try and save the ship, certainly being responsible for a large loss of life and no hope of rescuing his captain, perhaps even killing him in the event. It would be a bloody and useless fight.

But Kinkaid's worries were uncalled for, as Major Bauer and his marines quickly boarded the man-of-war, and he could see that it was Major Bauer himself who brought her colors down, the men on her deck already under the guns of his marines, with armed sailors covering her hatches fore and aft. There was Major Bauer now at the rail, waving in confirmation, the British ensign bunched in his fist. Kinkaid felt almost giddy with excitement at the sudden accomplishment of taking this powerful warship with only a couple of warning shots.

Captain Woolston and his first officer were too stunned even to speak.

And Mr. Briggs could hardly stand steady.

Of course, Briggs had had little choice but to imbibe with the senior officers on the enemy ship, and so Kinkaid could not help a small smile as he said in a mock-serious tone of voice, "Mr. Briggs, I see that you have defeated our enemy single-handedly by out-drinking their captain and first officer. What have you to say for yourself, Midshipman?"

Briggs came to attention and saluted unsteadily, blurting out, "Guilty as sharged, shur!" Now he suddenly turned pale and began to waver.

"Carry on, Mr. Briggs," said Kinkaid in the nick of time, for Briggs staggered to the rail and ignominiously threw up over the side.

"Sir, I return to you your grand and beautiful island," said Kinkaid to the distinguished mayor of Basseterre on the dock the following morning. A bright and cheerful sun rose over the peninsula connecting the island with a rugged spit of land called the Scotch Bonnet, while many sacks of rice were being distributed to a long line of grateful islanders.

"Tank you so much, kind sir," said the mayor, bowing in gratitude, his happy and smiling retinue standing behind him. "You have saved many lives and returned to us our island and our heritage. For dis, we are deeply grateful."

"We have been only too glad to be of service to you, sir," answered Kinkaid, feeling both embarrassed and guilty by the profuse gratitude of these fine people. Their mission was complete here; the island of St. Eustatia at least temporarily relieved of having a British base nearby, from which it had been so convenient to harass the Dutch port.

"You and your American Navy are always welcome here."

"I doubt that you will see any American ships coming this way for some time," said Kinkaid honestly, "though I would not wager against the British returning as soon as news reaches London that their base has been lost." It was only fair to warn them that the British would be back, that their moment of independence would not last long.

The mayor stood tall and said bravely, "We will give dat British ship someting to tink about when she tries to come here again."

"Well, for the moment the island is yours," answered Kinkaid. "You should have little trouble beating off a single corvette, but remember, brave sir, that the British are a large and powerful nation, with many trained soldiers and many big ships. I understand why you would want to fight them, but doing so would only invite disaster. Many of your people would die, and the British would still have their way. I can only advise that you treat your prisoners fairly, and when the British return in force, offer no resistance; give them no reason to retaliate against you."

The proud mayor looked at Kinkaid dubiously for a moment, and then said, "My people have waited many years for dis day…a day of freedom from tyranny. We will not give it up so easily. Some of us have worked de cannon before and will show others how it is done. Do not worry about us."

Kinkaid had hoped that the man would agree to his suggestion—that non-resistance was the best policy to follow, that the British were unlikely to punish the island, since, after all, it was not their fault that the base had been taken by a band of marauding Carib Indians, led by a mad escaped slave. But these proud people would do what they could to hold on to their freedom.

"I find your courage inspiring, good sir."

"It is you who have inspired us, Captain. May God watch over you wherever you go."

Rafferty and his carpenters had worked on the busted mainmast top of the captured *Reprisal* all through that night, and now all the Indians were being transferred to its deck. The chubby Indian and the Doctor's generals were astonished to find that they were free to go, suspecting some devious trickery. Kinkaid, once satisfied that they knew enough about sailing and charts to follow the course he gave them, told them to go back to their homeland or the guns overlooking the harbor would take their revenge.

Reprisal had just cleared the harbor when the speedy Smith ran up and saluted. "They's a ship been spotted, Cap'm. Looks like *Moondog*, suh."

"Our pirate friend come to claim his guns," reckoned Kinkaid.

Moondog made the harbor around noon, and no sooner had she anchored than Captain Blackstone came aboard the captured British man-of-war.

"You've done well for yourself, Captain," said Blackstone effusively. "This warship will fetch a good price for you and your crew. Keep this up and you'll soon have your own navy," joked the arrogant Blackstone, always thinking of further power and profit.

"Thanks to you there was only the small sloop left in the harbor," gave Weatherby.

And now Kinkaid had to add something. "I understand there were two that chased you, Captain."

"Those damned British ships wouldn't let go," bragged Blackstone. "A fast corvette and this one here. She gave up first, being the slowest. I kept the corvette on a close string till it got dark, when she started heaving cannonballs at me from long range. Didn't fancy having my hair parted with steel like that...damned rude of her, so I just piled on sail and made a big circle round her during the night."

"Well, we couldn't have done it without you, Captain." Kinkaid had to say it, had to recognize the fact. The man had done exactly what he said he would do, successfully so, and now Kinkaid would keep his end of the bargain. "I hope you will agree to a slight change in our agreement, Captain."

Blackstone scowled and demanded, "I'll damn well hold you to your bargain, Kinkaid. Nothing less."

"You'll get your guns," soothed Kinkaid.

"Four eighteen-pounders, it was," he asserted forcefully.

"And four eighteens it shall be, Blackstone. Out of the hold of this ship, if that suits you."

"There's no battery on the hill?" he asked, surprised.

"There is, but I'd as soon leave it up there." With that battery and the four eighteen pounders above the warehouse, manned by the determined men of St. Kitts, the returning corvette would be in for a hot surprise if she was foolish enough to enter the harbor. She would be lucky to get back out to sea, her captain's only option to report the loss of the base.

"You think they'll protect these people from the like's 'o me, is that it?" Blackstone guessed aloud, suspicious of Kinkaid's reasoning. "But cannons are cannons," he growled agreeably, "and the nearer, the better."

"Easier than bringing them down off the hill," said Kinkaid, relieved, "and we'd better be quick about it. That corvette may return with a fleet. I'll have my boatswain…"

"I wouldn't worry about that, Captain," Blackstone assured him, "My men will have them aboard in a couple of hours." He looked around and asked, "But what did you do with the Indians?"

"You must have seen that sloop bearing off to the south as you approached."

"So, you sent them home. Good place for them. And a mad Doctor, too."

"No, he's confined in the garrison," Kinkaid told him.

Blackstone laughed. "Kinkaid, you've a heart 'o gold."

"He'd better hope the mayor doesn't realize who he is," observed Weatherby.

"Or the British, either," gave Major Bauer, coming up on deck.

"Ah, but something tells me he'll not stand to be unnoticed for long," said Kinkaid, drawing laughter all around.

Once again, Captain Blackstone was as good as his word, for the burly crew of his *Moondog* had those big guns off their trucks and hauled up from below, through the main stores hatch. By using two ship's boats at a time and balancing the barrels across their padded thwarts, all four cannons and their trucks, along with plenty of balls and barrels of powder, were stowed neatly aboard his ship in about two hours' time, an impressive feat.

"She'll be a heavy sailor until we unload those hogs," said Blackstone, "but they'll be worth their weight in gold once I get them positioned."

Kinkaid had thought much about what he might say to Blackstone, about the possibility of pardon, of giving up the pirate trade, of serving with honor a just cause, and now ventured, "Our navy could use a man with your skills and savvy, Captain Blackstone."

Blackstone stiffened in surprise, then, smiling that charming smile, said, "I'm afraid I would accept no offer of rank lower than admiral, Kinkaid."

Kinkaid brushed the joke aside. "I would be more than willing to speak on your behalf and I'm certain—"

But Blackstone would have none of it, insisting, "I've answered to no man for too long, Kinkaid. But four guns seals a friendship, Captain, and that is enough for me."

Kinkaid took the proffered hand and shook it firmly. "Then will you at least accompany us back to the Virgins?"

"Why not; its where we live," said Blackstone with a wink.

Kinkaid waited until Blackstone had taken his *Moondog* out of the harbor before getting his new forty-four gun flagship under weigh, now four guns short, but, with not enough crew to man even half her massive armament, they would not be missed. *Swift*, with Mr. Saddler in command, led the way out of the harbor.

Kinkaid, not happy with a ship named for an English island, had Gagnon, handy with a brush, hanging over the side. Between the golden lions of England, he was painting the warship's new name, to Mr. Weatherby's surprise and delight.

"The Marine Committee might insist on a different name for her once we return," said Kinkaid, standing at the stern rail, watching as Gagnon finished up his handiwork, "but as long as she is in our keep, she will be known as the *USS Cutler*."

XI

Ally to Enemy

It was a glorious sight, the three ships sailing in line over the turquoise sea, *Moondog* in front, then the monstrous *Cutler*, followed by the faithful *Swift*, all making their way to St. Eustatia. Captain Blackstone had been agreeable to sailing with Kinkaid's ships, and after picking up Mr. Simpson, they would make a sweep of the area between St. Eustatia and the Virgins, the partnership still benefiting both. Kinkaid needed to gain intelligence of what dangers might threaten American shipping leaving the island, fulfilling the final requirement of his mission.

All the while, he suspected that Blackstone was likely the most dangerous threat of all, and therefore wished Blackstone would listen to reason and apply for a letter of marque on the American side. Unfortunately, Blackstone gave no indications of taking such thinking seriously, only stating that he was hopeful that the three of them might take some British prizes. But they met not a single ship on the way back, enemy or otherwise, and when the green cone of St. Eustatia appeared over the horizon, Blackstone informed Kinkaid that he preferred to wait well offshore until Kinkaid rejoined him, that he was unwilling to go near the harbor. Blackstone's explanation was understandable enough, what with the probability of British shipping there hearing news of his predations, and Kinkaid found this agreeable as well, since it would look unseemly for an American naval vessel, especially one picking up a diplomat, to be seen consorting with a known pirate.

Cato had cleared away the breakfast dishes. Kinkaid lingered in his now spacious, even comfortable cabin, seated at the ornate desk, and was signing his name at the bottom of the report that he had mulled over for the last few days, feeling pleased and satisfied with the simple and factual account. He had made a habit of leaving his door open so that a cooling breeze could waft through the cabin unimpeded, and he could hear Cato out in the passageway, happily whistling and talking to himself as he made an inventory of his already well-stocked pantry and jotting down in his notebook what he intended to procure from the shore.

"Hmm, these coffee beans are awfully dry," Cato could be heard to say. "Low on thyme, besides. And, let's see, some shredded coconut would be nice on the dessert torte. No, I'll shred it myself, save on the expense."

"Well, thank you, Cato," called out Kinkaid through the door, "that is most thoughtful of you.

"Sorry, Captain. Didn't mean to disturb you, sir," came Cato's polite apology. Before Kinkaid could respond, Cato asked, "Would you care for some turtle soup this evening, Captain?"

"I wasn't aware that we had any turtles," said Kinkaid, noncommittally.

"I thought I'd procure a fresh one in town, sir. Fresh-caught are always better than those that have been rotting in some hold for months," he said as he checked the flour bin. "Fried in fresh butter and thyme before adding to the soup and with a glass of claret thrown in at the end, well, it's actually quite the *piece de resistance*, Captain."

It was pleasant having the domestic conversation and to see Cato so relaxed, and while he would never think of telling Cato what to cook, still it was nice to be asked.

"If you are recommending turtle soup, Cato, then of course we shall have to have it. And I'm sure Mr. Simpson will be delighted."

Mr. Briggs showed his face at the door and announced, "It's land, sir. Off the port bow."

A fine French merchant ship was departing the roadstead of St. Eustatia that morning as *Cutler* entered, followed by *Swift*. She was the *L'aigle Altier*, "The Proud Eagle," large and fancy, as

French ships tended to be. She was a luxury ship if ever there was one, with beautiful lines and brightly painted bulwarks of green and gold, even a narrow terrace around her stern, embellished with carved and painted busts of the saints.

This time there was no hesitation from the batteries of Fort Orange as they returned, once again, an eleven-gun reply to Weatherby's thirteen-gun salute. There seemed to be some interest among the shipping in the harbor as to the identity of the large British man-of-war flying American colors, the name *USS Cutler* painted on her stern. Of course, there were bound to be some British merchant ships in the harbor that likely recognized her as the former *Isle of Wight*. They anchored next to a merchant flying the flag of Portugal, and Lieutenant Saddler brought *Swift* in and anchored not far behind them.

The two ships had secured their anchor details when a white coach could be seen once more winding its way down the hill from Government House. Kinkaid had O'Toole take the captain's gig ashore to meet the coach as it arrived at the dock—taking Cato with it so that he could procure his fresh groceries—and as Kinkaid watched from the quarterdeck, out stepped a happy and suntanned Mr. Simpson, wearing a bright white suit. He must have packed his things the moment the reports reached him of ships with American flags heading toward the roadstead.

Kinkaid greeted him as he stepped aboard to Rikker's piping. "Good to see you again, Mr. Simpson."

"Welcome back, Captain Kinkaid," he answered buoyantly. After exchanging happy greetings and handshakes all around the quarterdeck, Simpson looked in awe about the spacious deck, up at the tall masts of the stately warship, and said, "You gave us quite a scare. We thought at first that the British were about to invade. My God, Kinkaid, how did you manage to take such a ship? Why, she's gigantic."

"Wait till you see your stateroom," said Kinkaid.

"Please, Captain," said Simpson, holding up his hands, "I would not dream of depriving you of your hard-won luxuries, especially after the fine time I've had while you and your men were out there waging war against the enemy…evidently with much success."

Kinkaid laughed. "You shall have the master's cabin, then. It's almost as spacious, having room even for your famously ponderous trunk."

"I'm sure it will be fine, Captain, and I look forward to hearing of your exploits."

"Over dinner, Mr. Simpson."

Mr. Simpson's dubious expression revealed the fact that he did not look forward to more of Roach's cooking.

"You will be interested to know that I have a new cook," explained Kinkaid proudly, "a chef, actually, trained in Paris."

"Did he come with the ship, then?"

"I'll explain later, but I can tell you that he looks forward to serving such a distinguished guest as yourself," said Kinkaid as the Travelin' Brothers, Rikker, and O'Toole struggled to manhandle Mr. Simpson's heavy trunk aboard.

Setting the trunk down, O'Toole wiped the sweat from his brow and Simpson observed, "Boatswain O'Toole, I see you are hale and hearty."

"Aye, the salt air does me good, Mr. Simpson. Glad to have you aboard again, sir, if you don't mind my saying so," said O'Toole truthfully, for the entire crew was aware that the ship would be heading home now that Mr. Simpson was once more with them.

"O'Toole, see that Mr. Simpson's trunk is taken to the master's quarters," said Kinkaid.

"My pleasure, Captain," answered O'Toole, motioning to the Travelin' Brothers that their task was not yet complete. "Right this way, Mr. Simpson."

"Thank you, but if you don't mind, Captain, I believe I'd like to remain up here on the open deck for awhile if I'm not in the way," said Simpson. The man suffered from seasickness at the very sight of a sailing vessel, Kinkaid recalled, and had learned that the best cure was fresh air and open spaces.

"The deck is yours, Mr. Simpson," said Kinkaid with a sweep of his arm.

"Most gracious of you, Captain."

And now there was only one thing to do, Kinkaid knew, and he decided he would have a bit of fun in the process.

"Mr. Lofton," said Kinkaid buoyantly, turning to the duty midshipman of the deck. "It seems to me that we have been at sea for an unbroken period of time and too long without liberty."

"Aye, Captain," answered Lofton in his droll way. Weatherby, however, was all ears, as was Major Bauer.

"Therefore, I wish you to make it known to the crew that the starboard watch shall partake of liberty commencing immediately," said Kinkaid. "And send someone over to *Swift* to convey my regards to Mr. Saddler and inform him that half his crew will take liberty as well, each watch in turn."

"Aye, sir. To end at what time, Captain?" asked Lofton with little enthusiasm, as if the news was not about liberty but about a working party perhaps.

"Since our rendezvous with *Moondog* isn't until this evening," said Kinkaid, rubbing his chin, "we'll give the starboard watch until noon and the larboard watch from noon to four. How does that suit you, Mr. Lofton?"

"Fine, sir," said the serious Lofton. "I would imagine an exploratory excursion of four hours' time would be more than adequate to take in the important sights of the island, Captain."

O'Toole and Rafferty were standing in the waist, having overheard the conversation. O'Toole had already taken his boatswain's pipe out to sound liberty, but before blowing into it he nudged his shipmate and in a low voice, imitating a perfect gentleman, asked him, "Will you be taking in the sights of the island, Mr. Rafferty?"

Rafferty suppressed his laughter but took up the exaggerated tone. "I doubt that I shall see much of the island, Mr. O'Toole, but you can be sure I'm prepared to find out what I *can't* do in four hours," said the ugly carpenter, thrusting his hips lewdly, whereupon both men laughed and started doing a jig, the sight of which drew laughter from Weatherby and Major Bauer.

"Belay that dancing on my deck," ordered Kinkaid with mock seriousness. "You can take that profanity ashore—and O'Toole, ensure that the men are reminded that they are representatives of the American Navy and to conduct themselves accordingly."

"Aye aye, sir," said the two with smiles and jaunty salutes to their captain. Then O'Toole held up his pipe and asked, "May I, Captain?"

"Inform the crew."

O'Toole blew on his whistle with gusto, shrilling the seldom-heard tune that every sailor recognized, calling liberty, then poked his head into the after hatch, shouting, "Liberty, now liberty! Commencing immediately, the starboard watch will turn out for liberty!" Then he and Rafferty were heading below to do whatever boatswains and carpenters do to get ready for liberty in a tropical port of call.

Weatherby had been listening and watching the antics on the deck. He had the port watch, so his liberty would not begin until noon. After Major Bauer went below to inform his marines, Weatherby took Mr. Simpson aside and asked, "Sir, I was wondering if you could tell me—"

But he already knew what Weatherby wanted to ask of him. "I'm afraid I have a bit of bad news for you, Lieutenant," said Simpson quietly. "The Marquis and his lovely daughter boarded that French ship this morning, the one that left the harbor as you were arriving."

"The *L'aigle Altier*?"

Simpson nodded. "Bad timing, I'm afraid."

Weatherby turned and looked out to sea. The regal ship's topsails were still just visible on the horizon, her canvas catching the West Indies trade winds, taking her north. "Do you know where she's headed?"

"The Marquis said something about having business in Baltimore," said Simpson, standing at the rail, also watching the departing ship in the distance. "But I have a feeling that there is more to the Marquis than what he says or appears to do."

"What do you mean, sir?" Weatherby wanted to know.

"Oh, just rumors, I suppose."

"Of?" persisted Weatherby.

"I'll only say that I have heard it from…reliable sources, that the Marquis may be involved in some sort of espionage or shady dealings with our enemies. That ship may be stopping in Baltimore, but its ultimate destination is New York. He may be dealing arms to both sides. He is known in his own country as a ruthless and unscrupulous businessman, very wealthy and powerful. But if the rumors are true, I believe he may be biting off more than he can chew this time, arrogance and greed perhaps hindering sound judgment."

"But his daughter is with him…"

"My point exactly, Mr. Weatherby. If he thinks he can deceive with such tactics as bringing an innocent girl along, then he is a bigger fool than I thought."

Weatherby had a worried look on his face, and Simpson almost wished he had not told the young man.

"I'm sorry, Mr. Weatherby, if I have distressed you. Perhaps it would have been better if—"

"No, Mr. Simpson. I'm glad that you told me."

"Well, we live in dangerous times, Lieutenant. Some will profit handsomely from the misfortunes of others. Others will overextend themselves in such pursuits, and it is the innocent who suffer because of it. An old but sad story, I'm afraid to say."

Kinkaid had not heard their conversation but noticed Weatherby looking altogether too gloomy at the quarterdeck rail. Keeping busy was one way to fight a gloomy mood.

"Mr. Weatherby, make sure the ship is in good order before the hands leave, and ensure as well that only the starboard watch goes first. I want at least half a crew aboard at any one time."

"Aye aye, sir," said Weatherby soberly. "I'll get the roster and check them off as they leave and do the same as they return, sir."

"It will be sufficient to place the list with the quarterdeck watch, Mr. Weatherby. And I'll expect you to take your liberty this afternoon," said Kinkaid. "In the meantime, I would be much pleased if you would join Mr. Simpson and I for dinner."

"Why, thank you, Captain," said Weatherby, smiling weakly.

Kinkaid waited until Weatherby left the quarterdeck before he joined Mr. Simpson at the rail. Unaware of their discussion, Kinkaid assumed, "I suppose he told you about Mr. Cutler."

"Actually, he was asking me about Marie de la Renier," answered Simpson. "But what about Mr. Cutler?"

Now he had to say it. "He was killed."

"Oh my. I'm terribly sorry," said Simpson gravely. "I assumed he was aboard *Swift*."

"It happened the night we left, escorting the merchants," he explained.

The two stood there at the rail, both men at a loss for words. Finally, Kinkaid asked, "So you had news of…"

Simpson pointed out to sea, "They left on that French ship. On bad business, I fear."

"Yes, I heard rumors about the Marquis at the party."

"From the duchess, no doubt; always full of the latest gossip and no keeper of secrets, to be sure. They were married, you know, Chester Murray and the duchess. Lovely wedding. The Marquis and his daughter were in attendance. A beautiful woman, Marie; I can well understand how young Weatherby would be taken with her. He would be interested to know that she asked me about him after you all left. I should have told him."

"Well, perhaps better not to, now," suggested Kinkaid. "Do you think she knows about her father?"

"She *seems* quite innocent," said Simpson, his brow furrowed, "yet, if subterfuge runs in the family…"

The boats were filled with seamen wearing their best, heading for shore, laughing, joking, a happy crew with weeks of discipline, hard work, and victory behind them. There was O'Toole, his hair braided in a neat queue, held by a red-and-white-striped ribbon, the end stuffed into an oiled eelskin. Kinkaid only hoped they did not overdo things with their limited amount of time, though he expected most of them would do exactly as O'Toole had said—pack a week's worth of celebrating into a few hours—and many would likely be carried back to the ship by their mates.

"Aren't you going ashore, Major Bauer?" asked Kinkaid.

"Anders is going in with the first group," he said, watching as a boatload of sailors and marines headed to the shore.

"Which means you are free to join us for dinner, then," said Kinkaid.

Bauer smiled and said, "If that Cato fellow is going to be your cook from now on, I believe I'll have to request permanent duty with whatever ship you are assigned to, Captain."

"I would be honored to have you, Major," gave Kinkaid.

It was almost an hour later, after watching the last of the starboard watch depart for their liberty, that Cato returned to the ship with a boat full of groceries and a fresh-caught sea turtle.

With the ship anchored in the peaceful harbor and in spite of Weatherby's woes, Kinkaid took a moment to reflect on his good luck, his sudden wealth, and his luxurious surroundings, and to say a silent prayer, remembering the advice of his grandfather to give thanks when blessings are bestowed. And he recalled the young Mr. Cutler, his smiling freckled face, his lively nature, and had to recognize that fortune and loss could not be reconciled.

Mr. Simpson rejoined him on the deck after having been below, unpacking his things.

"I take it your efforts on the part of our government were successful, Mr. Simpson?" Kinkaid asked him.

"Couldn't have gone better," said Simpson happily. "Though any trade agreements were naturally unofficial. And when they hear about what happened on the island of St. Kitts, well, they are going to be relieved, I can tell you that…as will a lot of American ships' captains and owners."

"Mr. Simpson, you must have spoken to many people while you were here."

"And did my share of listening, as well, Captain," said the astute Simpson.

Kinkaid smiled and asked, "What did you hear about a fellow by the name of Jack Blackstone?"

"Have you met the man?" asked Simpson, his eyebrows raised.

"Ran into him up in the Virgins," answered Kinkaid. "Led us on a merry chase through the islands, then…captured our attention, you might say. In fact, he was of some service to us in securing St. Kitts."

"You employed the services of a known pirate to help you take the island?" asked a surprised Simpson.

"He drew off the British naval presence there before the attack. Did it for the reward of a battery of eighteen-pound field pieces he knew was up on the hill."

"To defend his lair, I gather." Not expecting an answer, Simpson asked, "Am I to assume that you are aware of where this Jack Blackstone may be at the moment?"

"If he is where I left him, he is out there just over the horizon, waiting for us to join him before nightfall. He's agreed to help us scout the area to gather intelligence."

"The pirates leading the pirate hunters," said Simpson with a wry grin.

"What do you know of the man, then?"

"Well, it's difficult to separate truth from rumor, especially among frightened merchant captains—peaceful men only trying to make a living from their trade on the sea—but I have to tell you that the name Jack Blackstone strikes fear into the lot of them. I understand that his real name is McGregor, Justin McGregor, a Scotsman. They say he hates the British with a vengeance. Has to do with the loss of his family…tragic circumstances, I've heard. Moved to America at first…one of the Southern colonies…claimed some success as a privateer, then showed up down here about a year ago after some trouble with the law. What did he tell you, that he only strikes at the British?"

"That is what he told me."

"And you believed him."

"I'm not sure what to believe," said Kinkaid honestly.

"Well, I can tell you I've heard otherwise. That he recognizes no flag but his own. There have been some terrible atrocities linked to his name. But like I say, I've only heard stories, with little proof to back them up. And you know how stories become exaggerated."

"Especially about pirates," Kinkaid wanted to believe.

"Well, if the man was of help to you, then I'd say good work, Captain, and let it go at that."

The two were still talking quietly a half hour later when the ship's bell told them it was noon. Just in time, as Kinkaid's stomach was growling.

"Mr. Simpson, shall we continue our conversation over dinner?"

The massive linen-topped table in the spacious great cabin was set with fine white china with light blue trim that matched the lush blue carpeting. Slim, white, tapered candles burned in ornate silver candleholders. Shiny brass lamps hung from polished chains, and on the walls were paintings of ships at sea in gilt frames. Seven French stern windows presented a panoramic view of the harbor and revealed planters outside filled with red begonias blooming happily in the afternoon sunshine.

"A man could become accustomed to such surroundings, Captain," replied Simpson, taking his seat in one of the white leather-upholstered chairs.

Cato entered in a starched white uniform, bringing a bottle of white wine, and Kinkaid motioned for him to allow Mr. Simpson the honor of tasting it. Cato elegantly poured a small amount over his towel-draped arm and waited for Mr. Simpson to take up his glass.

Simpson gracefully swirled it about, sniffed the bouquet, and took a dainty sip before pronouncing, "Mmm, a delicate Chardonnay. Excellent choice, Cato."

Cato acknowledged the compliment with a slight nod of his head as he filled Simpson's glass before moving on to his captain. Kinkaid's new steward reveled in the large and complete kitchen he now had dominion over, and the fact that Mr. Simpson was once more aboard after the completion of their duties was reason enough to go all out.

Major Bauer soon joined Kinkaid and Simpson and the three leisurely sipped their wine until Mr. Weatherby arrived, forcing a smile and appearing unconcerned about missing by minutes a beautiful and charming woman that he had been hoping to see again for the last couple of weeks.

Cato brought in the turtle soup and fresh baked bread, "For starters," he said. Then he filled each of their bowls while proudly informing his guest, "No claret, but I found something even better to add to the soup: a fine Madeira."

The soup, of course, was pronounced excellent by all, and then came steaming platters of roasted chickens, eggplant, and stewed potatoes and gravy.

The men filled their plates and began eating, though the conversation was having trouble getting off the ground. All but Major Bauer knew of Mr. Weatherby's tale of woe, but that was not enough to explain it. Kinkaid's stomach was bothering him; he was feeling a lack of appetite in spite of his hunger, in spite of the delicious mounds of food on his plate and the promise of dessert to come, the kind of tight feeling he felt before going into battle—a nervous anticipation.

The conversation he'd had earlier with Mr. Simpson kept turning over in his mind, the bits of information gleaned from the man seeming to lead to only one conclusion: Jack Blackstone—or Justin McGregor—was not only a smooth-talking and charming man. Of course, Kinkaid had suspected Blackstone of perhaps bending the truth to suit his less-than-honorable purposes, but according to Simpson, the man possessed a reputation for violence and ruthlessness…what had Simpson said, that there were "terrible atrocities" linked to the man's name? Then there was the knowledge that a fine French ship had left the harbor, a prize any pirate would risk his life to claim, not to mention that aboard her was one of the richest men in Europe, worth a king's ransom if taken hostage. Blackstone had his artillery pieces and there would be nothing to prevent him from taking such a prize and heading back to his lair, better defended now than ever before. And wasn't that French, Spanish, and Danish furniture in his "Chateau Blackstone"? The only sound in the cabin was three forks tinkling delicately, each man seemingly lost in his own thoughts. Mr. Simpson was refilling his empty wine glass when Kinkaid made a sudden decision.

"Weatherby, I want to recall the parties that have gone ashore," he said with purpose. "Take a few men and scour the town; get them aboard as quickly as possible, especially O'Toole and Rafferty. Find as many as you can as quickly as you can, but if you can't find everyone don't worry about it. We'll return for them later."

Weatherby listened attentively, put down his fork, and rose from the table, saying, "I'll have them aboard in no time, Captain." Then he stepped out the door to follow his captain's orders.

"It's Blackstone you're worried about, isn't it?" said Simpson, stating the fact aloud.

"More that French vessel," answered Kinkaid.

"Of course," said Simpson. "Do you believe we can catch them?"

"*Swift* has a chance," he said, tossing his napkin on the table. "I'm transferring over. Major Bauer, how many marines are aboard?"

"Nine," answered Bauer.

"They will have to do, then," said Kinkaid, standing.

"I'll get them ready, Captain," said Bauer, leaving to find his marines, who were probably at that moment anticipating what they intended to do once ashore.

"I'm coming with you," said Simpson with conviction.

"I don't…"

"You will require an interpreter, Captain," added Simpson, "and I speak fluent French."

"Blackstone is a determined man and a hell of a seaman," Kinkaid warned him.

"But so are you, Captain," answered Simpson without hesitation.

"What I mean to say is he'll give us a hard time," said Kinkaid, picking up his hat.

But Simpson would not be put off, insisting, "Well, if I were him, I'd be worried."

"I hope you're right," said Kinkaid, reaching behind to take his telescope off the wall rack. "There's a box in that closet behind you, Mr. Simpson. Bring it along, would you?"

"Of course, Captain," said Simpson, quickly draining his wine glass before following Kinkaid out the door, the box of pistols tucked under his arm, leaving Cato's delicious supper unfinished on the table.

Cato was in the passageway, carrying a fancifully decorated cake on a tray. He could only blurt out as the men hurried by, "I'll save this for you, Captain…when you have time."

Mr. Lofton had the quarterdeck watch and an anxious look on his face. "Mr. Weatherby said all liberties were canceled."

"That is correct," said Kinkaid. "You will be happy to hear that we are back to serious business, Mr. Lofton. Rikker, pipe the watch out. I'll take a dozen seamen with me to *Swift*. Inform Mr. Weatherby, when he returns, that he is in command and to follow us to the Virgins as soon as he has most of our crew aboard. Tell him I suspect our Captain Blackstone of treachery, that the French ship we saw leaving this morning may be his victim."

"Aye aye, sir," said a bewildered Lofton.

Rikker roused the duty watch from belowdecks and as they came out, Kinkaid picked those who would come with him. There was Smith, stepping forward until he was practically in Kinkaid's face. "Handy gunners are welcome on this trip, Smith."

Smith grinned and returned, "Thank you, Cap'm, suh."

Then, with Rikker and Major Bauer and nine marines crammed into the captain's gig, they made their way quickly to where *Swift* was anchored, where a surprised Mr. Saddler waited on the quarterdeck. Roach stood by the ladder to pipe the Captain aboard, and the welcome sight of Tripp and Treadwell told him the starboard-side watch was aboard. There was the gun captain, Stevens, as well. Even Hairy Hyde and the old man Helmut were gazing inquisitively from out of the forward hatch, curious about the sudden activity on deck.

"Make ready to sail, Mr. Saddler," said Kinkaid without formalities as he stepped aboard to Roach's bad piping.

"Rikker, pipe out the crew and set the anchor detail," ordered Saddler.

"Where is Mr. Briggs?" asked Kinkaid.

"Ashore with the larboard watch, Captain," answered Saddler.

"How many are aboard?"

"Fourteen, sir," answered Saddler, "including Chaplain Carlton."

"Weatherby will be following, but I want us out of here in five minutes." It was unfortunate that the eager Briggs was ashore, but he would especially miss having Weatherby at the guns, though there was no helping it. Kinkaid and Lieutenant Saddler would have double duty running the deck and ship's gunnery, though he felt fortunate to have the rugged and reliable Major Bauer with him and knew that Weatherby could be relied upon to gather up the crew and get *Cutler* after them as quickly as possible.

"Let's get aloft, quickly there!" shouted Mr. Saddler. "Make ready on the topsheets!"

Mr. Simpson was already untying the binds that held the mainsheets to their booms, doing what he could to help. Men were scrambling up the ladders to their stations as Roach, Tripp, and Treadwell went forward to raise the anchor, Smith and Stevens lending a hand, as were Bauer's marines, assisting at the capstan winch. Even Chaplain Carlton was pitching in, taking his place at the mainsheet halyard. Already the unfurled jib was turning the ship into the wind, toward where the anchor lay.

"Mind your helm," Kinkaid reminded Rikker at the wheel.

They hauled in the anchor line and then winched the heavy iron cross aboard, even as the sails were braced.

"Take us out, Rikker."

The ship was heading out into the bay, toward the wide mouth of the roadstead, all in very good time.

"Compliments to your deck, Mr. Saddler," said Kinkaid appreciatively.

"Thank you, Captain."

"Steer us north by west."

"Aye aye, Captain," answered Rikker.

The headland was passing off the port beam and the ship began to pitch slightly as it met the low rollers of the Caribbean Sea.

"We'll make good time on this heading, Captain," noted Mr. Saddler.

"Yes," said Kinkaid, recognizing that Mr. Saddler was right, that the ship would make good speed on this course, for the wind was in their favor, coming out of the east, right off the starboard quarter. But would *Swift* be able to catch up with *L'aigle Altier* before it was too late? Or would they find *Moondog* just over the horizon, waiting for him as agreed, his fears proved groundless? It was something to hope for, but so far she was not in sight.

An hour passed, then two. *Moondog* was nowhere to be seen on the open ocean, confirming his suspicions, the luxurious French vessel too tempting a target. If Captain Blackstone knew that Kinkaid had brought a diplomat to St. Eustatia, then he would most certainly know about a rich man of the stature of the Marquis de la Renier. Everyone on the island seemed to know his name. Kinkaid wished the winds would blow harder, pushing his ship faster. But of course *Moondog* would then go faster, too, in spite of her heavy load.

Kinkaid anxiously paced the quarterdeck, constantly checking the direction of the wind, looking up at the set of the sails, instantly detecting any inefficiency in their position.

"Mr. Saddler, I'll trouble you to have that topsail adjusted…do you see that luffing there?"

"Right away, Captain."

"Helmsman, watch your heading."

Saddler was doing his very best to keep the braces trimmed for maximum efficiency, and he still had no information from his captain as to what they were attempting or where they were going. Finally, he guessed, "Are we in pursuit of *Moondog*, Captain?"

The question seemed to take a moment to reach Kinkaid's awareness, so deep in concentration was he with the various problems of the situation, and suddenly he felt guilty for not having the courtesy to inform his own first lieutenant of his intentions, the mission known to Mr. Simpson.

"I believe she's after that French ship we saw leaving the harbor this morning," answered Kinkaid.

"Do you think he'll take her along…the French ship?" asked Mr. Simpson, holding his question until now.

"I doubt it," answered Kinkaid, looking out to sea, thinking that taking the big ship as a prize would slow Blackstone, would give *Swift* a likely chance of catching him. The French ship was too slow and cumbersome to make a good attacking ship and was too lightly armed to defend against *Swift*, even as undermanned as she was. No, Blackstone would probably rob her of any valuables he could easily make off with and take the Marquis and his daughter for ransom.

"Well, at least we know where his base is," offered Bauer.

"Where he'll put those big guns soon enough," came Mr. Saddler's unwelcome observation.

Yet Mr. Saddler was right again, in his maddening way. Blackstone's men worked quickly and would waste no time in placing those guns—guns that Kinkaid had given him. And once placed, Kinkaid daren't go into his hole…and Blackstone knew it.

It was late afternoon when sails were sighted on the horizon. From afar, it could have been any large merchant or warship. An hour later she was hull up and Kinkaid studied her intently through his telescope for some minutes, noting her wide sails and fancy hull, before announcing, "It's her, all right."

"She seems fine, Captain," noted Mr. Simpson some time later. Indeed, she appeared to have sustained no damage and was sailing peacefully along.

"We'll see," answered a suspicious Kinkaid. When they drew nearer yet, he said, "Have the crew turned out, Mr. Saddler, and I mean everybody; I want the cooks manning the halyards…and Smith, load and man that swivel gun."

When Rikker blew his boatswain's pipe to call the crew to quarters, only Hyde and the old man Helmut had to be rousted out from below, for every other hand was already topside, keenly anticipating catching up with the French ship, which still toiled on, all sails set, not slowing at all, though it must have been obvious to her captain that *Swift* was in pursuit. Smith and the Travelin' Brothers took the lead in organizing the gun crews and by then they were drawing alongside.

"Rikker, bring us in closer," ordered Kinkaid, trying to recall what little French he knew. It didn't appear that she was going to stop for him. *Swift* was fifty yards off her starboard beam when Kinkaid brought his speaking trumpet up and bellowed, "*Excuséz moi…Plaisent bouchez!*"

A couple of men on her deck gave friendly waves.

"Try '*cessation*'," suggested Simpson.

"*Excuséz…Plaisent cessation!*" shouted Kinkaid across the gap, knowing full well he was heard. But still the men played dumb. That was obvious; they were pretending too much.

"I don't believe speaking French is helping us much," said Kinkaid. Handing the speaking trumpet to Mr. Saddler, Kinkaid gave Smith a nod and said, "Give her a shot across the bow."

Smith touched off the swivel gun with a sharp crack of fire and smoke. The shot landed just in front of her bow wave, and the men on her deck stopped waving. They seemed to be conferring. Kinkaid expected their tops to be backing at any moment, the ship slowing, but she ploughed relentlessly on. They were ignoring *Swift*.

"I don't believe she's going to heave to, sir," observed Mr. Saddler.

"Major Bauer, I'll have your marines in the tops to cover us!" bellowed Kinkaid. "Roach, take the wheel. Rikker, I want ten sailors for a boarding party. Arm them well. I'm going with them. Mr. Saddler, you'll have the deck."

The marines were scrambling up the shrouds, their bulky muskets awkwardly in tow, while Rikker picked the men who would board the French ship. It came as no surprise that every man was an eager volunteer, though he would keep Tripp and Treadwell aboard to man *Swift*'s cannon. Smith grinned happily when Rikker chose him as part of the boarding party, and now he was passing out pistols and blades to the rest.

"Take us in closer, Roach. Slowly, keep us parallel," ordered Kinkaid.

"I'd like to come aboard with you, Captain," said Mr. Simpson, handing Kinkaid one of his pistols and stuffing the other into his belt, the one with the cracked stock. "Since your French has room for improvement, I believe I may be of some service."

"Suit yourself, Mr. Simpson, though I suspect those men on her quarterdeck speak perfect English."

Those men on her quarterdeck watched intently as *Swift* drew alongside, the marines in the tops and ten sailors standing on the bulwarks with pistols and cutlasses in their hands, waiting for the two ships to come together. When they were only yards apart the French ship began to veer to port in a vain attempt to avoid the boarding. But *Swift*, true to her name, was too fast for her, her sloop-rigged sails efficiently catching the wind while the French ship lost speed with her turn.

"Ready! shouted Kinkaid. Then to the helmsman, "Steady as she goes!" When *Swift* drew to within inches of the recalcitrant French ship, Kinkaid gave the order, "Now!" and the sailors leapt across the gap, grabbing the high rail of the tall ship, scrambling over her bulwarks and onto her deck, Mr. Simpson right behind Kinkaid.

Four scruffy men stood on her quarterdeck, all holding pistols, but with a dozen armed men facing them, covered by another ten marines aiming their muskets from the tops of *Swift*, not one dared to raise his weapon at the boarding party. A half-dozen seamen were amidships, their hands raised in the air, some smiling happily, making it easy to tell which were Frenchmen and which were pirates.

Kinkaid strode boldly up to one of the worried men on the quarterdeck, the one with a scar on his left jaw, wearing the hat of a French captain, a hat too big for his head.

"*Parlaiz vous Francais*? C'mon, man, speak up!" queried Kinkaid, snatching the pistol out of the rattled man's hand as he backed away in fear, clearly at a loss for an answer, his badly mumbled French worse than Kinkaid's.

"The gambit is up," said Kinkaid, holding his pistols on the quarterdeck watch, who were relieved of their weapons by Rikker and his sailors. "Simpson, tell those men to loose sails. We'll heave to."

The relieved French seamen eagerly leapt to carry out Simpson's order, loosing the sheets and releasing the sails' grip on the wind, the ship slowly drifting to a halt. Then they began taunting the four pirates.

"Ask them where their captain is," said Kinkaid to Mr. Simpson.

Simpson queried the sailors and one with a long jaw and striped shirt stepped forward, speaking a fast French and pointing below. "He says he will take you to him, but warns you to be careful since he is guarded by a …bad one," translated Simpson.

Kinkaid turned to the man wearing the too-large captain's hat and asked, "Is it Blackstone?" But he received not even a glance of recognition. "Lead the way, sailor," said Kinkaid to the striped-shirted sailor, gesturing with his arm. Then to Rikker, "Tie their hands, Rikker, and keep an eye on them. We're going below."

They followed the French sailor down the ladder of the after hatch, pistols drawn. At the bottom was a narrow passageway, a row of doors on either side; the one straight ahead was the captain's cabin. The sailor stopped and pointed there, whispering something to Simpson.

"They're in there. The Captain and the 'bad one'," Simpson translated.

"Stay here," said Kinkaid.

"Perhaps I could do the talking," suggested Simpson.

"Very well, keep him distracted," agreed Kinkaid before moving along the port side bulkhead toward the door, tucking the captured pistol into his belt.

When Kinkaid reached the wooden door, Simpson shouted, "Give it up! We've taken the ship! You have no chance!"

No answer. Kinkaid heard scuffling and pressed himself tightly against the bulkhead as the door opened a crack and a rough voice snarled, "I'm holding the French captain, and I'll kill him if you come in!" It was not Blackstone's voice.

"As I said," answered Simpson calmly, "we've taken the ship. You don't really expect us to go away now, do you? Give it up before you get hurt. Harm the captain and you'll hang."

There was no answer from behind the door, only more scuffling movement.

Kinkaid immediately moved across the passageway, against the opposite bulkhead, which afforded him a narrow view of the interior of the cabin and what must have been the top of the French captain's balding head, a bandana covering the man's eyes. He was sitting on the deck, his back against the cot.

"I want a boat, a compass, some food and water," demanded the rough voice. "I'll take the captain with me, and I swear I'll kill him if you refuse or interfere in any way."

"No," said Simpson, simply.

"Did you hear what I just said?" he raged. "I'll kill this man!"

"Then we'll hang you," answered Simpson, maintaining his cool demeanor.

"They're gonna hang me anyway, damn your eyes!" screamed the man in frustration. Kinkaid determined that the voice was coming from the starboard side of the cabin, just opposite from where he stood.

"Then I suppose we'll hang you," said Simpson, refusing to budge, turning the conversation into an endless circle, arriving only at the same conclusion.

Boots scuffled on the floor; the man was crawling closer to the door. Now there protruded from the narrow opening the barrel of a pistol, pointing down the passageway to where Simpson and the French sailor crouched.

Kinkaid grabbed the barrel and jerked it out of its owner's hand, causing it to discharge loudly in the narrow passageway. The ball slammed into the deck and the air filled with smoke. Kinkaid stepped into the cabin and, seeing the crouched man reaching for the dagger at his belt, swung his pistol, this time with the presence of mind to use the barrel, not the stock, and slammed the hard steel alongside the man's head with a dull thud. The man moaned and sagged against Kinkaid's knee; it was Hawke, that ugly tattoo of a shark on his forearm. Kinkaid pushed against his shoulder, sending him sprawling backwards against the bulkhead, unconscious.

Kinkaid took Hawke's dagger from him before removing the bandana from the portly French captain's eyes, whereupon the man began shouting in rapid-fire French, his pale face turning red in agitation while Kinkaid untied his wrists. Released from bondage, he started for Hawke, still slumped in the corner, but Kinkaid held him back.

Simpson entered the cabin with the French sailor, who, taking orders from his captain, took the length of cord Kinkaid had removed from the captain and bound Hawke's hands behind his back, the stunned pirate reviving with a groan during the process. The angry captain made for Hawke once more, and again Kinkaid blocked his path. He spoke to Simpson and Simpson translated, "He only wants to get the keys to the hold from him."

Kinkaid stood aside as the French captain took a ring of keys from Hawke's vest pocket, all the while cursing in Hawke's face. He tossed them to the big sailor, giving orders, and the sailor scurried aft.

"He sent him to release the rest of his officers and crew locked below," explained Simpson. Then Simpson spoke to the captain before introducing him. "Captain Kinkaid, this is Captain Lavalle. He wishes to thank you for—"

The French captain interrupted Simpson with more angry words and pointing of fingers, as he wiped his sweaty brow with the bandana that had been tied over his eyes and then tossed it aside.

"He says this man murdered his quartermaster."

"Is that so?" said Kinkaid, eyeing the man Captain Blackstone had called Bloody Hawke. The swarthy pirate returned an insolent stare.

The four of them returned to the quarterdeck, Hawke safely bound, a bloody gash above his right ear. Now the French captain began shaking his finger at the man wearing the officer's hat—his hat. He angrily grabbed the hat off his head and started swatting him with it, cursing in French all the while.

"Enough of that," insisted Kinkaid, interjecting himself between the two; time was of the essence. "Mr. Simpson, ask him exactly what took place here."

Simpson once more began speaking in French to the captain, who was now placing his hat upon his own head while other French officers and crewmen were coming up on deck, thankful to have been set free. Captain Lavalle spoke excitedly, saying

Blackstone's name, and pointing to a couple of stains on the deck, probably blood. Kinkaid recognized the name of the Marquis de la Renier. Finally Simpson finished with his interrogation. The French crewmen were nodding and murmuring among themselves.

"It was Blackstone, all right," confirmed Simpson. "Two men were killed with cannon fire, three severely wounded. They boarded her and their quartermaster was killed right here on deck, by this one, murdered with his own sword after they surrendered. They then robbed everyone and took the Marquis and his daughter. In fact, they asked for him by name, seemed to know he was aboard."

"Then our Captain Blackstone had these men keep her sailing," surmised an angry and betrayed Kinkaid, "knowing we might pursue, buying him more time. And if we didn't suspect their attack, they'd eventually take her into Hurricane Hole and strip her of valuables."

Simpson translated what Kinkaid had said and Captain Lavalle spoke again, Simpson telling Kinkaid, "That seems to have been their plan, Captain."

"Then they would have sunk or sold the ship, her crew either murdered or lucky to be sold into slavery if they didn't agree to join him," concluded Kinkaid.

Captain Lavalle again started talking excitedly and then bowed to Kinkaid.

"Captain Lavalle insists that I thank you…uh, profusely sir, for saving their ship and themselves from…who knows what terrible fate," Simpson translated. "He furthermore insists that you leave these men with him…to be tried for their crimes."

Kinkaid returned Captain Lavalle's bow and then turned to the pirate with the scar, the one who had pretended to be a French captain. "Is that the story?" Kinkaid asked him.

His question brought nothing but stony silence.

"We'll leave these men with the French. I'm sure they know how to deal with pirates."

Now the frightened pretender stepped forward and said in perfect English, "Sir, I implore you. Take us with you. These Frenchies will hang us the moment you are out of sight."

"Afraid you will not get a fair trial?" asked Kinkaid menacingly. More French crewmen were coming up on deck now, all armed and looking angry.

"We will get no trial at all, of that I am certain," said the man, fear evident in his voice.

"You deserve to hang, each and every one of you, as the pirates that you are," stated Kinkaid in no uncertain terms, his face harsh and threatening.

"But sir, if you take us with you, we will show you where Blackstone's guns are located in Hurricane Hole, where he'll place those eighteen pounders," he implored.

"Shut up, you idiot," said the surly Hawke, stepping forward, his large hoop earring swinging.

Kinkaid slammed Hawke across the face with his pistol, knocking him back, drawing blood from his nose. "I'll be giving the orders here," growled Kinkaid. It gave him no pleasure to hit a man already bound, even the murderous Hawke, but the brutal act sent a strong message.

"They'll be well hidden," the begging one pleaded. "I swear, you'd never see them from the shore, Captain…until it is too late. He'll blow you and your ship out of the water."

"We'll take this one with us," Kinkaid decided. "The rest will remain with the French. They can deal with them as they please. And as for you," threatened Kinkaid, pressing his pistol against the man's chest, "If you are lying about those guns…"

"I swear to you, sir, I know exactly where they'll be," he said, eyes wide with fright. "You won't regret—"

"Mr. Simpson, explain to Captain Lavalle that we are leaving these men with him, with the exception of this one. He may be of some help to us."

"Aye aye, sir," answered Mr. Simpson like a true sailor. Simpson spoke with the French Captain again, and again it was obvious that he was thanking them profusely.

"Let's get moving... *Moondog* has a big lead on us," Kinkaid ordered.

When they were back aboard *Swift* with their prisoner, Kinkaid said, "I believe you may have missed your calling, Mr. Simpson."

"Perhaps I should have joined the Continental Navy," smiled the diplomat, thoroughly enjoying himself.

"Seems you already have."

The sun was setting by the time *Swift* was once again under weigh with all sails set, heading north by west, toward the Virgin Islands.

Mr. Saddler and Mr. Simpson had been standing at the stern rail, gazing in the direction of the French vessel that had yet to raise her sails. Mr. Saddler, who had been periodically training his telescope in her direction, handed the scope to Simpson, saying, "Captain, you might want to have a look at this."

Kinkaid approached the rail, and Simpson passed the telescope to him. At first he was unsure what he was supposed to see, but then there it was, the dark form swinging under the main spar, legs kicking spastically.

"Seems that French captain wasted no time in exacting his revenge, sir," observed Mr. Saddler.

"Revenge or justice, Mr. Saddler?" asked Simpson philosophically.

Kinkaid kept his opinion to himself, the point moot.

Simpson remained on deck with Kinkaid until late that night, talking mostly about the French and how any efforts the Americans could make toward helping the French could only help the American cause. Simpson was, of course, apprised of all the latest developments between the Colonies and France, referring to "building alliances" and "secret treaties" of a commercial and cooperative nature.

"If we could only convince them that we will win in the end, they would join us," he insisted. "And if they joined us, we would surely win this war. Britain has few friends in Europe the way it is, and with war declared with France, they would not dare send more soldiers to our shores. With the French Navy to contend with, the British would have to spread their forces too thin to maintain their blockades of our seaports…they'd be isolated. Why, with three thousand miles to send reinforcements and military supplies, not to mention the time it takes to send messages back and forth…"

But Kinkaid only half heard Mr. Simpson's impassioned monologue that evening, speaking little, nodding once in a while, giving a well-placed "ah" here, a "yes, I see" there, his thoughts occupied by the strange and varied events of the last two weeks.

As fate would have it, he had made a gentleman's agreement with a pirate. True, Blackstone had faithfully kept his bargain and helped him to win St. Kitts, but now he had just as heedlessly betrayed that trust by boarding a neutral ship, killing members of her crew, and taking innocent hostages, victimizing a potential ally.

Of course he had always known Blackstone to be a pirate, but was it too much to hope that a man might choose to redeem himself if offered the chance? Perhaps the man had committed some outrage in one of the Southern colonies and had burned his bridges there as well, negating any chance of redemption. He had seen only the man's rough charm, not his cunning or ruthlessness…until now. He had been overly trustful, too idealistic, and now he was forced to pursue and stop the man, to bring him to the same justice that his henchman, Hawke, had already received. Kinkaid contemplated these thoughts and more that evening…all the while looking to the southeast, hoping that Weatherby and the bulk of his crew were not far behind.

XII

Cannonballs Will Do

While the problem of how to deal with Blackstone kept Kinkaid's mind occupied throughout the pursuit, he kept his diminished crew busy, experimenting with various combinations of gun crews and sail-handlers until he was satisfied with their organization and then drilling them yet more.

Of course, he knew it would make Blackstone very happy if he sailed his ship straight into Hurricane Hole to be pounded to splinters by shore batteries, well-hidden by the jungle. Kinkaid had questioned the prisoner, James Porter, about the likely locations of those guns, and though the man did not hesitate, but claimed to know exactly where Blackstone had planned to place each one, Kinkaid could not be sure Porter spoke the truth. Regardless, Blackstone's lair would be better protected than ever before, and the savvy pirate would suspect any attempt to come overland, over the peninsula from Haulover Bay, just as he had anticipated and outmaneuvered Kinkaid before. Blackstone certainly had the advantage, and so Kinkaid doubted that the pirate leader would come out and fight. The only sensible solution was to simply wait, yet waiting gave Blackstone more time to prepare, a maddening dilemma.

He also did not know if Blackstone would keep his hostages at his camp or aboard ship, though Porter claimed to know that anyone held for ransom, especially someone of the Marquis's reputation and status, would be locked in Blackstone's Chateau, not aboard *Moondog*, a small and dirty ship with few comforts. As Porter explained it, "Blackstone likes to think himself a gentleman,

Captain. As long as things go his way, he'll treat them like royalty."

"And if they don't?"

"No guarantees, Captain. He'd as soon murder them both than risk getting caught."

It was the evening of the third day when there came the hail from the lookout, "Land, dead ahead!"

A long and hazy line soon appeared on the northern horizon, the large island of St. John directly to the north, the silhouette of her hills recognizable from their previous visit.

"Let's bear off a couple of points, head for that group of islands there," ordered Kinkaid as the hazy line separated itself into the same chain of small islands they had chased *Moondog* through the week before.

The sun was setting as they approached Norman Island from the south. Mr. Saddler had been standing at the rail beside Kinkaid for some time as the ship came to her new course. Finally, Saddler asked, "What are we going to do, sir?"

"We'll bide our time," snapped Kinkaid. He had slept little during the pursuit and was plainly irritated. At first that was all a peevish Kinkaid wanted to tell his first officer, but as he could see that Mr. Simpson also had a wondering look on his face, he decided to tell them.

"We'll anchor on the west side of that island in front of us. The chart shows a good sheltered bay there, The Bight, only three miles from Hurricane Hole and facing it." Hopefully, Weatherby would be arriving with *Cutler* by morning.

"Very good, Captain," gave Saddler.

The anchorage at The Bight was indeed a good one, not only providing a clear view of the opening of Hurricane Hole, but also having a nice deep harbor, well-protected from the prevailing winds. Of course Blackstone would have a lookout on the point who would report seeing *Swift* as she entered Flanagan Passage and made for The Bight.

"Have the lookouts maintain a telescope watch of the bay overnight. I want to know immediately if any sails are spotted."

"Aye aye, Captain."

Kinkaid retired to his cabin for supper, alone. Roach was once again filling in as his cook, but when he brought the food, Kinkaid paid it little heed. He had a chart of the area laid out on the table, and Roach had to place his dishes to one side. Only after the main course was cold did Kinkaid relent to absentmindedly pick at the dry roast beef. Roach dared not disturb him, finally returning to collect the half-eaten diner in silence. "Uh…more coffee, if you please," was all the notice he received, though Kinkaid did notice that Roach had made a fairly decent cup of coffee this time.

Kinkaid found himself staring at the cabin lantern before him and found himself reflecting on the night that Cutler had been killed, how he had sat where he sat now, staring numbly into its flame, thought of how deflated he had felt, how the world seemed to have changed. Of course, the loss of Cutler and the loss of Roach's bird were far from equal events, but it occurred to Kinkaid that Roach may have had some affection for his bird.

Roach soon returned to the cabin and set a second steaming cup of coffee on the table. The man's ponderous bulk was turning to leave when Kinkaid was compelled to say, "Roach…"

"Sir?" Roach turned around, a sad look on his face, as if expecting a rebuke.

Kinkaid paused and then finally got it out, "I'm sorry about your bird."

Roach stood there a moment, hunched down under the overhead. He nodded his head slightly, finally said, "Poor little Ellie."

"And the coffee…well, it's really quite good, Roach," added Kinkaid, raising his cup in salute.

Roach smiled, put out his hand as if the compliment were too much, then turned and left the cabin. Kinkaid was, for the first time, struck by how incredibly gentle this burly man was and for a moment felt vaguely ashamed that he had never noticed before.

Kinkaid returned to pondering over the chart, yet looking at it provided no more ideas as to how to approach and attack Blackstone's hideout. Any attack by land would involve moving men at least a mile or more through unfamiliar terrain. And he only had a skeleton crew the way it was. *Cutler* should be here by morning, he reasoned, if winds were favorable and Weatherby had been lucky in quickly finding most of the men.

Kinkaid's anxiety seemed to grow with the darkness. He had slept little the night before and was concerned that he might become too tired to think straight. He knew he needed to stop thinking and get some sleep, except that he also worried that by sleeping he would not think of a way to outsmart Jack Blackstone, his reasoning circular and unremitting. He had chased after Blackstone and now could only wait and worry, it seemed. For some reason that he could not fathom, except that there was some comfort in it, he found himself recalling things his grandfather had told him. He remembered some of his tales of fighting against the French and the Indians, times when his grandfather had known the terror and confusion of battle and the loneliness of command. And as the hours passed, when he could remember no more of his grandfather's words, he still stared with heavy lids at the chart. He drifted in and out of a tortured sleep, stubbornly leaning against the table as night fell. At one point he awoke with a start, overcome by a feeling of foreboding, of vulnerability, of dissatisfaction with his weakened position, and in sight of his enemy's camp, at that.

"Captain!" Mr. Saddler stood in the doorway. "A ship is coming out of the Hole, sir."

"*Moondog?*" His mind was foggy with sleep.

"Looks like her, sir, though it's hard to tell. It's awfully dark, the moon only a sliver, and it's starting to cloud up."

"What time is it?" His arm felt numb as he rose and stretched cramped muscles.

"Almost two, Captain."

Was Blackstone attempting to escape in the night? No, he rejected the idea immediately as it hit him. He mumbled something Blackstone had said to him about the game of chess: "Figure out your opponent's next move and make a preemptive strike."

"Excuse me, sir?"

"Rouse the crew, Mr. Saddler…get the anchor up. We're leaving here," he said. Of course; Blackstone wanted to fight it out while he had the advantage, before *Cutler* arrived, his *Moondog* more than an equal opponent.

"Right away, Captain," said Saddler as he rushed back up on deck, Kinkaid close behind him.

Mr. Simpson was already standing at the rail, telescope in hand, looking quite awake, the dark rings under his eyes evidence that he had probably remained on deck throughout the night. He handed the telescope to Kinkaid as he reached the quarterdeck.

Kinkaid peered through it but saw only black, his eyes not yet accustomed to the dark. Then, a momentary break in the clouds allowed the feeble light of a crescent moon to bathe the bay and, sure enough, there she was, Blackstone's two-masted schooner *Moondog*, her sails filled with the night breeze. She was making the end of the bay, coming out into Flanagan Passage, three miles' distance.

The men on *Swift* were scrambling about to Mr. Saddler's orders. They were severely short-handed, the guns only adequately manned on one side or the other, with very few sail-handlers and without Weatherby's gunnery and leadership. Blackstone was a good tactician, but this time he was luckier than even he suspected, not realizing that most of *Swift*'s crew had been left behind. Kinkaid had little choice; to remain anchored in The Bight invited certain disaster. He needed to maintain the wind advantage to outmaneuver *Moondog*, and for that he needed sea room. There was Roach again at the capstan, along with the marines, as the anchor was winched aboard.

With a full crew, Kinkaid would have chosen to close with *Moondog* and board her, Bauer's marines in the tops whittling down her gunners as they approached. But marines would be of little use in the tops in this fight; he would have to maintain his distance from Blackstone's tough and battle-hardened crew and try to damage *Moondog* with cannon fire, hopefully with his first salvos.

"Anchor detail secured," reported Saddler. "Light wind out of the northeast, and a bit more east, sir."

"Jibs and tops for now, Mr. Saddler."

"Aye, Captain."

The sails caught the breeze and the spars were braced. "Take us out, Rikker," ordered Kinkaid.

"Aye aye, Captain," came the reply as Rikker expertly spun the wheel, causing the deck to heel as the ship turned toward the mouth of the bay.

Swift was heading out of the sheltered harbor as *Moondog* turned in their direction. Kinkaid's mind was clearing with the rush of adrenaline but was shadowed with foreboding. It was bad enough that they were outnumbered; there was also the certainty that Blackstone's crew was as good and fast at firing their guns as they were at hauling them around. Kinkaid's eyes were adjusting to the dark night as *Swift* glided out of the harbor of The Bight.

"Beat to quarters, Mr. Saddler," he ordered, trying to sound calm, collected, in control. "I'll have the starboard guns loaded first…cannonballs will do. Open the ports and run them out."

"Very good, sir," answered Saddler.

The men at the guns, Saddler shouted the orders for their crews to haul them inboard, load them, and then run them out. This saved them time, with unskilled and slow men like Hairy Hyde and Helmut serving the guns, and shifted the center of gravity of the ship toward the windward side, keeping her more upright and able to catch the light breeze, moving *Swift* quickly away from the land, giving her much-needed sea room before the battle.

Smith looked up and, catching Kinkaid's eye, called out gamely, "Good to be back with Troubadour, Cap'm! We soon be makin' some mighty sweet music!"

Kinkaid returned a nod of recognition Venture Smith's way as Saddler gave his report. "Pumps manned, decks wetted and sanded. Guns loaded and run out, starboard side. Stations are manned and ready, Captain!"

Chaplain Carlton, filling in for their surgeon, informed him quietly, "Platform and instruments laid out in the afterhold, sir," reminding him that there might soon be wounded men writhing in agony down below. But this was no time to be thinking of that.

"This is as good as it gets, men!" Kinkaid announced loudly, so that all on deck heard him, courting confidence with the statement, knowing that the moment had come for decisive action, his battle plan clear in his mind, no room for doubts. "We'll keep our sails reduced for now, but be prepared to put out our mains'ls on my command."

Moondog was close-hauled with the wind over her port beam—what little there was on this peaceful, moonlit night—though she was still over two miles away. *Swift* had the weather advantage and Kinkaid meant to utilize it and keep it. His plan was to bear down on her and rake her with grape by turning to starboard, firing his portside guns first, damaging her sails and rigging. Then, passing through the wind, he would come about and give her another broadside from *Swift*'s starboard guns, this time with solid shot into her hull, hoping to knock out guns and get some hits at her waterline, before turning back again to the north to maintain his wind advantage. But first he would allow *Moondog* to clear Flanagan Island before he attacked her, to give himself room to make his turn. With land to the north of her, Blackstone had little choice but to continue on his present heading and would not be able to avoid Kinkaid's maneuver, unless she veered away to the south and the open sea, in which case he would follow and still maintain the weather gauge.

Saddler stepped closer to his captain and said, almost in a whisper, "If only the cloud cover holds, sir."

He was right, only a thick cloud cover would keep *Swift* from being silhouetted by the moon, but the negative statement immediately angered Kinkaid. It was unnecessary and something more to worry about, he thought at first. Then, reconsidering, he asked himself if he would have reacted the same way if Weatherby had made the same observation.

"Load all larboard guns with grape, Mr. Saddler. Run them out and have the crews standing by."

"Aye aye, sir," said the first lieutenant before giving his orders to the gun crews once more, who went scrambling over to the opposite side, the side that would fire first, with their buckets and gun swabs, the powder monkeys hurrying too, changing the loads they would provide from the magazine.

"Mr. Simpson, I'd be most happy if you would go below. I wouldn't want Congress asking me what happened to you when the pirates attacked." Kinkaid had to say it, to at least make an attempt to protect his high-ranking passenger. But he was not surprised at the answer he received.

"No, thank you, Captain," Simpson said matter-of-factly. "You're not going to torture me down there, not knowing what the hell is going on up here. You'll have to arrest me if you want me below."

Mr. Saddler looked at both men in turn, uncertain if Kinkaid would actually have the man arrested.

"Very well, Mr. Simpson," said Kinkaid. "I'll put you to use then, assisting Chaplain Carlton."

"I'll do my best, Captain," came the resolute answer. Turning to the chaplain, Simpson told him, "Just show me what to do."

And now Kinkaid thought of the prisoner, Porter, down in the orlop. "Mr. Saddler, I've a mind to release our prisoner, put him to use on sail detail."

"Very good, sir," said Saddler, passing the word.

The wind blew from almost directly astern *Swift*, and it seemed as if they were barely moving. But that was deceptive, for as Kinkaid watched, he saw Treasure Point pass off the port beam as the distance between the two ships closed.

"All guns loaded and run out, Captain!" came Saddler's report.

"Very good, Mr. Saddler," said Kinkaid, concentrating on the quickly approaching *Moondog*. "Stand by, larboard side guns!"

Now they had only to wait for the proper moment. There would be no surprise involved. Blackstone would expect Kinkaid to do exactly what he was doing.

The match men stood by their wicks in the buckets, the men keyed for imminent action, all eyes on the pirate vessel beating their way, a foamy bow wake evident now against the dark sea. Because of the light winds, the ships would pass slowly, giving the gun crews time to aim carefully. The seas were calm, and if Kinkaid waited for the right moment and presented the target correctly, they could deliver an effective first blow; he tried not to think that Blackstone and his crew would be having the same thoughts. So much depended upon the aim of his gunners, and he was heartened to have the likes of the Travelin' Brothers, Stevens, and Venture Smith for gun captains.

Porter came out on the deck, rubbing his eyes as if he had just been awakened, the messenger showing him to his place beside the mainsheet halyard. He squinted into the night, to where all eyes were looking across the black waters, and was startled to see *Moondog* charging their way. There was nothing he could do but accept the inevitable…like everyone else.

"We'll load those carronades as well, Mr. Saddler, though I won't need anyone to man them." Only if the Moondog came in close would they be used, but Kinkaid would do all in his power to prevent that from happening.

"Very good, sir, and she looks to be clearing Flanagan Island now, said Mr. Saddler, suspecting Kinkaid's intention to let her pass, ensuring sea room for *Swift*'s turn to starboard. "And the wind is strengthening, Captain; might be in for a blow."

"Let's have mains'ls, now," ordered Kinkaid as a sudden gust shook the sails, heeling the ship, confirming Saddler's observation that one of those sudden tropical rainsqualls might be in the offing.

"Mains'l, haul!" shouted Saddler.

With that, the men, Porter among them, drew up the mainsheets, the lines creaking in their blocks, setting fore and mainsails, and the bow of *Swift* immediately dug deeper into the trough, throwing spray, her masts leaning forward with the increased pressure as the big sails caught the wind, the ship moving ever faster toward her hostile rendezvous. The gun ports on the port side allowed some water in that washed across the deck when the ship pitched, as another gust heeled her. The clouds were a solid mass now, the black night closing in; at least the moon would not be a factor.

"She's coming left a bit, sir," noted Saddler. *Moondog* turned ever so slightly until she was on a collision course, heading directly toward them. And there was something peculiar about the way her hull was plowing through the low waves. She seemed sluggish, her bow heavy in the water, not natural on the beating course she was on. Saddler noticed it as well. "Coming right for us and…seems heavy in the bow, Captain."

Kinkaid had a bad feeling. Was her intention to board them, he wondered? Or would she try to thwart the turn he was about to make to starboard, take away his upwind advantage by forcing *Swift* to go ever farther around and bring both ships side to side? Regardless, she was only a hundred yards away now, and that heavy bow played on his mind. Suddenly, his fears were confirmed as a belch of fire and smoke roared from the bow of the pirate ship, the boom of a heavy artillery piece resounding sharply across the gulf.

Blackstone had mounted one of those massive eighteen pounders in the bow, realized Kinkaid, as the heavy ball tore a jagged hole out of *Swift*'s bow, skipped across the deck, and took off the foot of a man standing at the forward gun; Joseph Treadwell. He spun around and fell onto the deck, a look of surprise on his horrified face, gazing in shock at his bloody stump.

Then another flash of flame as a swivel gun was touched off from *Moondog*'s forecastle, sending a hail of murderous grapeshot that peppered holes in the foresail.

Aaron Tripp took a step in Treadwell's direction but Chaplain Carlton and Mr. Simpson were already there, helping the shocked Treadwell to stand on one leg, the other held before him, the stump spurting blood over the sanded deck, the man never making a sound as they helped him below.

Tripp stood watching in dazed horror until Saddler shook him and shouted in his face, "I'll have your attention, Tripp!"

Blackstone's gunners loaded quickly, and the big gun at *Moondog*'s bow roared and spat flame again as they closed to fifty yards, the shot tearing through the crew of number-three gun, killing two men instantly, blowing another over the side. It was followed by the deadly iron from the swivel gun, more accurate now and ripping across the deck, felling a number of men forward, shards of metal flying aft, narrowly missing Kinkaid and the others on the quarterdeck.

It was a terrible beginning and Kinkaid could do little but look helplessly upon the carnage of six or seven men lying dead or dying. Stevens stood dazed at number six, Nina, holding a bloody arm. And there was the prisoner, Porter, his body flung against the starboard rail, his shattered limbs bent grotesquely behind his body, dead and of no use to them now.

Already Mr. Simpson was back on deck, moving forward, his gait unsteady, slipping on the blood, gazing in horror at the scene of carnage, not sure who to help first, uncertain who was dead and who was wounded. He made for Stevens, but the wiry gunner waved him off, determined to stay with his gun. Those men screaming in pain were certainly alive, and so Simpson went to a man squirming in agony from a wound to his guts. It was a terrible shock, losing so many so soon to *Moondog*'s gunnery, and a dirty trick. He could not afford too many hits like that, thought Kinkaid, as *Moondog* bore down upon them still.

"Rudder, hard to starboard! Ready on the guns! As we come about!" ordered Kinkaid. With *Moondog* pointed straight at her like that, *Swift* could hope to repay her, rake her from stem to stern at close range before she could turn that big gun on them again.

Rikker spun the wheel and *Swift* began her turn…and just in time to avoid collision, she was so close. "Fire as you bear!" shouted Kinkaid, watching intently as the billowing sails of *Moondog* towered overhead. He looked for Captain Blackstone on the quarterdeck but spied only the big Gunner Freeman in his overlarge hat amongst the many pirates crowding her deck.

Saddler had taken Treadwell's place and was bent low over the first gun forward, sighting down the barrel as *Swift* came about. He waited until he saw the foreshortened hull of *Moondog*, allowed a moment for *Swift*'s hull to rise, and then shouted, "Fire!" followed by the next gun, then the next, each violent discharge punishing the eardrums. The dirty smoke from their muzzles billowed out over the water, hiding *Moondog* from view as the ragged volley continued all down the line from forward to aft, the crews scrambling to reload, Helmut and Hairy Hyde struggling to load the notoriously inaccurate number-two gun, Wandering Willie.

"Keep her coming round!" shouted Kinkaid, refusing to be distracted by the cries of the wounded.

Simpson stepped over a man lying on the deck as *Moondog*'s first broadside slammed into *Swift*, the ship shuddering with the impact of cannonballs that blasted splinters of wood across the deck, felling a man at Simpson's feet, Matthew Edwards, Smith's sturdy loader, his mouth agape in agony. Simpson carried him quickly below, but with others to come back for there was little time to help Chaplain Carlton, who remained below tending to the wounded.

"All crews to the starboard guns!" shouted Kinkaid.

The dwindling gun crews moved across the deck now, Stevens and Smith exhorting the men, some staggering, some bleeding, all with powder-blackened faces, all determined to fight back, ready to loose their solid shot against *Moondog*; if only they could hole her below the waterline. "Rudder amidships! A broadside this time, Mr. Saddler!"

The ship steadied and Saddler waited for the shadowy form of the pirate ship to line up in his sights, fifty yards off the starboard beam, the two ships running side by side now.

"Fire!"

A concussion of flame and smoke erupted as all six guns discharged, the deck heaving with the force, but *Moondog* touched off her own broadside an instant later, knocking Kinkaid to the deck as her nine-pound solid shot crashed home. Number-seven gun, Nina, was blasted from her truck, two of her crew lying still, Stevens standing beside them, his shirt and trousers stained with blood. Roach was on his knees on the deck, holding his hand to a splinter wound on his forehead, blood trickling between his fingers. Other fallen men added their cries to the din as Kinkaid rose. He had been stunned but untouched by shot or shrapnel. Because of the thick clouds of smoke that filled the void between the two ships, it was impossible to see if their own broadside had struck home, if *Moondog* had been damaged. Was that Mr. Saddler who cried out in pain?

"Helmsman, hard right rudder! Bring us about!" shouted Kinkaid.

"Aye aye, sir!" returned Rikker as he spun the wheel.

"Mr. Saddler, all crews to the larboard guns!"

But Saddler seemed dazed, uncomprehending. He had heard his captain's order but stood there immobile, a blank look on his grimy face, a look Kinkaid had seen on men's faces before in the heat of battle. Although Saddler had heard the order, he had immediately forgotten it, so Kinkaid repeated, "Larboard side guns!"

Now Saddler nodded vigorously to show his comprehension before shouting the orders that commenced the reloading as *Swift* continued her turn.

Heavy clouds rolling in made the night ever blacker, hiding the moon. Gusty winds drove a cold rain and heeled the ship at a sharp angle, washing water through her open starboard gunports, washing through pools of blood. Many of *Swift*'s gun crews had been killed or wounded, with the few men remaining hurrying to reload, the gaping holes in her bulwarks evidence of *Moondog*'s expert gunnery. Three guns were wrecked, sliding dangerously, threatening to crush men, their crews either dead or slumped in agony. Smith scrambled desperately about, rallying men to lash those guns down as two men carried a screaming sailor below. It was Hairy Hyde, his leg mangled by a cannonball, hanging limp at the knee, attached only by some shredded ligaments, the man's face pale with shock.

Kinkaid tore his eyes away, focused on the binnacle, and watched as *Swift* was passing south by east on the compass dial. Looking up, he could see the topsails of *Moondog* dead ahead. She was turning left, to port, to bring her big gun to bear, to finish the job. *Swift*'s gun deck was a shambles, only a dozen men left standing, most of them wounded. At least her sails were mostly intact; *Moondog*'s gunnery concentrated up till now on *Swift*'s decks, decimating her makeshift crew, the fight an unfair match from the beginning. He thought to make a run for it while the smoke hid them from further violence, to escape into the night.

"Take us due east, helm! Mr. Saddler, all sails! Take us out of here!" he shouted over the screams of the wounded.

Rikker now spun the wheel to port, and the ship stopped her turn, steadied for a moment on a course of due south, and then began turning left, toward the east…which meant they would pass the pirate ship close astern. *Moondog* was in irons, dead in the water, her bow pointed into the wind. That heavy cannon in her bow had kept her from swinging through the wind, and now her crew was backing her jibs and tops, hoping to bring her before the wind once again. Kinkaid meant to hurry off in the opposite direction, give his ship every advantage in outdistancing the enemy before she turned on them once again.

Saddler was in the waist, rallying the stunned and the wounded at their guns and keeping the men at their task of bringing the ship about. One of the carpenter's mates ran up and said something to him, whereupon Saddler glanced Kinkaid's way and then began limping toward the quarterdeck rail with a bloody wound to his upper thigh where a splinter had penetrated. He was gritting his teeth as he gamely hobbled toward the quarterdeck, finally shouting, "We're taking on water, Captain!"

"Get some men on the pumps and shore up the damage!" ordered Kinkaid. "Quickly, now!"

Moondog was drifting backward, strong gusts of wind heeling her, waves crashing over her bow as the wind and rain intensified into a steady downpour.

Swift was coming on her new course now, and Kinkaid breathed a sigh of relief when he saw that they would pass off the pirate ship's stern, her guns unable to bear. If they were lucky, they could be off into the night before she could deliver another crushing blow.

He could see Gunner Freeman standing at the wheel, helpless to fire at *Swift*, helpless to do anything except wait for *Moondog*'s rudder to bite, her sails to catch the wind.

"Smith, Stevens, rally those men there to your guns!" bellowed Kinkaid, thinking to give *Moondog* a parting blow; a lucky hit might cripple her.

Four men were roused, Roach and the old man Helmut among them, and they were standing in the driving rain by the larboard guns as *Swift* passed close astern. *Moondog* had halted her drift astern and was gathering headway now, her sharply angled rudder taking a bite. Smith and Stevens waited in anticipation for their captain's order.

"Give her your best, boys!" shouted Kinkaid, leaving it up to his gunners to fire when they thought they might do the most damage.

Stevens touched off number-three gun as *Swift* drew astern and Kinkaid could see two shadowy forms at *Moondog*'s stern rail go down as the ball tore through them.

Venture Smith waited until it was almost too late, and then, just as *Swift* was bearing away, he fired the last gun on the larboard side. As the smoke cleared, Kinkaid saw *Moondog*'s flying jib come fluttering loose, detached at the bottom where it joined the jib boom. The men on *Swift*'s deck saw it too, and Roach roused them to a cheer.

That would slow the *Moondog*'s turn considerably, and the sudden squall would hide *Swift* as they ran for their lives, thought Kinkaid with some relief. He would not dare to try and weave his way through the island chain the way *Moondog* had led them on their merry chase on that first meeting. Instead, he would simply round Norman Island before *Moondog* could get much weigh on, then head south out to the open sea into the stormy night, avoiding the possibility of running onto any reefs, negating *Moondog*'s advantage in knowing the area.

Saddler was soon hobbling back to the quarterdeck to report, "Still taking on water, Captain, but I've men at the pumps and we're shoring up the damage...I believe we're keeping up, sir."

"You've done very well, Mr. Saddler," acknowledged Kinkaid.

"Thank you, Captain," answered a pained and weary Saddler, his pant leg torn and tattered and blood-soaked.

"Steer us south by east, Rikker," said Kinkaid.

"Aye, Captain," gave Rikker, squinting doggedly through the maelstrom.

With the storm upon them, Kinkaid could feel the ship gain in speed, could hear the surge of foam along her sides. *Moondog* would likewise be heeling under the force of the fresh wind, but if that heavy gun on her forecastle slowed her as much as Kinkaid hoped it would, forcing her bow into the troughs, *Swift* stood a good chance of making her getaway into the dark, rainy night...as long as they could keep *Swift*'s flooding under control.

Aaron Tripp was tying a bandana around Roach's head wound while a blood-soaked and weary Stevens finally allowed Major Bauer to help him below. Kinkaid was about to order the men to reload the guns when he noticed that Venture Smith was already quietly taking it upon himself to ensure that all workable guns were reloaded, just in case.

Kinkaid kept watch through his telescope, trying to catch sight of *Moondog*, all the while hoping the heavy rains would keep her obscured from view. Regardless, Gunner Freeman was not the kind of man who would easily give up the chase. Just because Kinkaid couldn't see the ship didn't mean she was not out there somewhere, still following, still dangerous.

"Take us around the island, there," said Kinkaid as the black form of Norman Island appeared out of the wet and misty gloom. Then he turned to look astern once more, searching in vain for a ghostly sail, some hint of *Moondog*, hoping Freeman would think they were heading east through the island chain.

Kinkaid kept *Swift* on an eastward heading for half an hour, beyond Norman Island, before having the helmsman make his turn south, Rikker resolutely at the wheel refusing a relief as Kinkaid still anxiously watched with the telescope, straining to see through the blackness, through the rainstorm.

Major Bauer soon came back up on deck to help more of the injured below, and Mr. Saddler helped him, in spite of the nasty wound to his leg. He'd also had Roach make sandwiches in the galley and now the burly man was bringing them up to the soaked men on deck.

Kinkaid breathed easier now, yet remained ever vigilant, thankful for the rain, for the darkness of the night, feeling like an animal on the run as he hungrily chewed the crusty bread, determined to lose his pursuer, find shelter, make repairs, regroup and reorganize his battered ship and crew.

Bauer was slumped against the mainmast, bleeding from a wound to his left hand, but, like Venture Smith and Mr. Saddler, refused to go below for treatment. He had lost three of his marines; another two were below with critical injuries. *Swift* was incapable of putting up any kind of effective offense, so mauled had she been, so undermanned to begin with. Kinkaid could still hear the cries and moans of the wounded from below. He could only imagine the horror down there, the agonies of those poor men, and hoped that no more would have to die or suffer on this miserable night.

In fact, it appeared they had finally evaded *Moondog*, for no sails could be seen to the northwest; no pursuit was in evidence. Kinkaid tried to relax, to count his blessings, few though they were. Things could have been worse. Without the quick and sudden decision to turn toward *Moondog*, without the fact that *Moondog* had been forced to turn into the wind and had been stalled by her heavy bow, without Smith's lucky hit on her flying jib, without the sudden storm and the darkness of night, without all these things it was likely *Swift* would even now be settling to the bottom of Flanagan Passage.

Mr. Saddler was grimacing in pain. He had brought a couple of canteens with him from below and passed them around; the men were drinking greedily, washing down their sandwiches. With so many below either dead or having their wounds attended to by Mr. Simpson and the Chaplain, there were only a scant half-dozen men able to handle the ship, with scarcely two full gun crews unscathed by the vicious attack.

Saddler had lost his hat and was leaning heavily against the binnacle, head down, his dark hair clinging to his powder-blackened face, seemingly oblivious to the rain as it beat down upon his bare head, the red stain on his pants continuing down his leg to his shoe, blood washing over the deck where he stood. It was evident to Kinkaid that Saddler had pushed himself beyond human endurance for the good of the ship.

"Mr. Saddler, get below…have that leg tied up before you bleed to death," ordered Kinkaid, shivering uncontrollably.

Saddler seemed not to understand as he looked out at the black horizon, finally saying, "Chaplain Carlton is below, sir, tending to the wounded."

Kinkaid walked closer to where Saddler stood, so there would be no mistaking his words this time. "Mr. Saddler, you have done magnificently," said Kinkaid in all sincerity, his appreciation evident. Saddler was raising his head, smiling grimly as Kinkaid continued, "but I want you to get yourself below, have that leg—"

The cannonball tore across the transom of the quarterdeck, taking the binnacle and Mr. Saddler with it, slamming the First Lieutenant against the mainmast with horrific force, crushing his skull. His body slid down the mast, rain and blood coursing down his chin, from his nose and ears.

Rikker clung to the wheel like a statue, a stunned look on his face.

Kinkaid felt a burning sensation in his back as he spun around to see the towering sails of *Moondog* flying with the wind, bearing down on them from the starboard quarter, the smoke from her forward swivel still drifting toward them, her bow light, almost skipping over the waves. Of course; they had tossed the heavy piece overboard to gain the speed necessary to run them down and had anticipated *Swift*'s turn to the south.

It would take the gunners on *Moondog* at least a few moments to reload their swivel gun, a few moments more to come alongside and deliver a broadside, thought Kinkaid, as he remembered *Swift*'s loaded swivel gun on the stern rail.

He ran down to the gun deck, scarcely noticing the desperate looks of Major Bauer and the few seamen on the deck. He grabbed a smoldering match from a bucket, returned to the quarterdeck and, aiming the small mounted cannon at the oncoming pirate ship, blew the match to a red-hot glow and touched the gun off. He had the satisfaction of seeing at least one man on *Moondog*'s forecastle go down, others diving for cover behind the low transom. That would slow their reloading, but it would be only a matter of a few minutes before she pulled alongside and let go a devastating, perhaps fatal, broadside with all her guns. At least their own guns had been reloaded and a few men, led by Smith, were standing by to fire them. After that…

Kinkaid placed the end of the smoldering wick under his boot as he spun the gun around and reached for a bore swab. Major Bauer appeared beside him, ready with the powder, as Kinkaid struggled to reload the small-bore swivel gun, but *Moondog* was already turning, her quick pirate gunners ready with their broadside. They let go an instant later, spewing forth a deadly blizzard of flying steel, this time with grape and chain shot that ripped through the mainsail, blowing it out and slowing *Swift*.

In his haste to refill the touchhole of the gun, Kinkaid raised his boot and the wind blew the wick across the deck, sparks flying. Bauer moved to retrieve it but the wind carried it overboard. Now they were helpless to return even the measly fire of the swivel gun.

Kinkaid watched as *Moondog* bore down on them, a horde of pirates on her deck waving cutlasses in the air, jeering and shouting threats, their expert gunners preparing to deliver the coup de grace to Kinkaid's broken vessel and crew.

"C'mon, boys, let's return the favor!" came a brave shout from Venture Smith, kneeling beside his gun with a dogged grin on his face, waiting only for the chance to strike back, the old man Helmut beside him, laughing with rotting teeth and waving a pistol in the air. Roach stood beside them, a blood-soaked bandana tied around his head, grinning defiantly. And there was Major Bauer, a few of his marines beside him, and Stevens too, a rag tied around his arm. In fact, every man who could stand was there to fight the good fight—to the death if need be.

Chaplain Carlton had come up for some air, his face sweaty and pale, his shirt bloody, temporarily leaving Mr. Simpson below with the wounded, and now he stood over the men at their guns and said a prayer. "Great Liberty, inspire our souls and make our lives in thy possession happy or our deaths glorious in thy just defense."

Kinkaid's first thought was to strike, to save at least those few brave men still standing. Further slaughter was unnecessary, he reasoned, but just as soon realized that his men might be slaughtered regardless of striking, that the pirates might not honor the gesture, their bloodlust up. Even if they did, it would not help when Weatherby finally arrived to find that his captain was also being held hostage. There was one desperate chance. It would have to be done with reckless savagery, and he would have to rouse the men to it.

"Prepare to board her!" shouted Kinkaid to the men on deck.

"Hurrah!" came the roar of approval.

Major Bauer immediately understood the need for instant action and bellowed, "Fast and furious, men!" With a supreme effort, he tore into the arms locker and with Roach's help passed out cutlasses and boarding grapnels to torn and tattered men already struggling with shock and wounds, but who eagerly reached for pistols and cutlasses nonetheless.

Yet, as Kinkaid watched in pride and admiration as his exhausted crew tried as they might to come alive to his and Bauer's exhortations, he knew that these gallant but broken men would never prevail against the mad horde of pirates on *Moondog*, which outnumbered them many times over. Should he call off the attack? Should he strike their colors? Would that doom the men as well? These desperate thoughts were shattered when the deafening sound of a tremendous, rumbling explosion crashed over the water.

Surprised to find himself still alive, Kinkaid turned and watched the crowd of men on *Moondog* being mowed down like wheat, her deck swept by a blizzard of hot iron and splinters, pieces of her bulwarks blowing out in a dozen or more places, her rigging snapping, sending spars tumbling down from above, sails ripping and tearing, falling in heaps, burying the dead and maimed on her deck, instantly turning the once dangerous pirate vessel into a mangled wreck, her crew blown asunder, a few crying out in agony in the after-silence.

Beyond *Moondog*, emerging from a great cloud of smoke like an apparition, was the shadowy hull of a huge and powerful warship. The men on the deck of *Swift* stood a moment with mouths gaping in wonder and surprise, until they realized it was *Cutler*, as if sent by an avenging angel to deliver them from the very jaws of death, and they let out a cheer. Kinkaid met Bauer's eyes and saw the tough marine break into a grin.

A moment later, as *Cutler* came ever closer, her gun crews no doubt reloading under Weatherby's commands, the black flag of *Moondog* came down, the white dog howling at the moon no more. Freeman was a good sailor, an aggressive opponent, and a hell of a gunner, but he was not suicidal.

"Bring us into the wind," Kinkaid told Rikker, still clinging doggedly to the wheel. "Heave to."

There was Mr. Briggs on the quarterdeck, and Mr. Lofton and O'Toole, all peering from the waist of the high-sided man-of-war. And now there was Weatherby, waving to his captain. He said something to O'Toole and then two boats were putting out from *Cutler*.

The one with Mr. Briggs, O'Toole, Rafferty, and Dr. Grafton headed immediately for *Swift*. The other, with Mr. Lofton, Sergeant Anders, and the rest of the armed marines, headed for the shattered *Moondog*. Kinkaid made his way to the waist, where Smith sat on the deck holding his ankle.

"Someone take this man below," said Kinkaid.

Immediately the wiry Stevens stepped up and, placing Smith's arm around his shoulders, said, "Hold on to me, Venture. I'll help you below."

Kinkaid followed the two to the bottom of the ladder, and it was a haggard Mr. Simpson who met them, his face lined with horror and fatigue, his shirt stained with blood. Wounded men were lying on the deck, others leaning against the bulkheads, a few tending to their comrades, giving water or an encouraging word. One was on the table in the center, Hairy Hyde, his leg badly mangled, with a cord tied tightly around his thigh. He was moaning deliriously. At least seven were beyond help, their bodies lying still in the corner. Kinkaid went from man to man, checking on them, telling them that the battle was over, that Weatherby had found them, that *Moondog* was defeated, that they were safe.

Even the hard and steadfast Dr. Grafton was shocked when he found the terrible carnage belowdecks. He quickly had his loblolly boys working at removing splinters, amputating limbs, and sewing men up with little to quell their pain but draughts of rum, all to the relief of an overwhelmed Chaplain Carlton and Mr. Simpson, who had done their best to stop or reduce the bleeding and tie off severed limbs with tourniquets. A seaman Kinkaid knew only as Dutch had lost his forearm; another, George Wade, had a nasty splinter wound to his right eye, his head bandaged. Fortunately, due to Chaplain Carlton's efforts and Mr. Simpson's resolute action, many of the seriously wounded men would survive. Treadwell, however, was not one of them, learned Kinkaid, his wound proving mortal. His was one of the bodies in the corner, Tripp beside him in sorrowful prayer. Venture Smith had suffered a sprained ankle and though he was in pain, Mr. Simpson had bound his foot with a splint, and he was sitting quietly against the bulkhead.

As Kinkaid kneeled next to Smith, he felt a sharp pain in his back, a reminder of the splinters still lodged there. "How are you, Smith?"

Smith looked up, shaking his head. "Guess I ain't the fastest man in Rhode Island no mo', Cap'm."

"Well, maybe not for a few weeks," said Kinkaid.

Smith managed a smile, difficult with so much suffering around him.

Dr. Grafton was even now amputating the mangled remains of Hyde's leg, the man thankfully unconscious due to shock and loss of blood.

Kinkaid, while he regretted that men had to suffer and die and that there was little he could do for them, was also aware that time was of the essence, that there was much to be done, that he had to take his leave of *Swift* and take charge of three ships, repair them, and organize his crews into a fighting force. Jack Blackstone was still out there preparing his defenses against them.

Dr. Grafton was too busy staunching the flow of blood from the stump of the unconscious Hyde's leg to notice the bloodstains on Kinkaid's back when he staggered to the ladder. Gritting his teeth, Kinkaid climbed back up on deck where many had left their blood, now a scene of frantic activity. Rafferty and O'Toole were busy organizing repair crews. Rikker and Stevens were already below shoring up leaks, and Mr. Briggs and several hands were getting the deck and rigging into some semblance of order. There was Roach, asking O'Toole what he could do to help. He had proven himself an able seaman and gunner.

"Good to see you, Captain," said O'Toole. His left eye was black and blue, and there was an unfinished tattoo of a dolphin on his arm.

Kinkaid transferred over to *Cutler*, taking Mr. Simpson and Major Bauer with him, leaving Mr. Briggs and Rafferty in charge of the damaged *Swift*.

Moondog was now under the command of Mr. Lofton, with carpenters also aboard her desperately trying to keep her from sinking. Both ships had sustained considerable damage. Freeman was clapped in irons and was already aboard *Cutler*, with Sergeant Anders still transferring the rest of the crew. It was to Weatherby's credit that his preplanning and hasty action had every man in the right place at the right time.

Kinkaid climbed the high ladder slowly, doing his best not to show on his face the sharp pains he felt in his back. Finally reaching the deck, he turned stiffly and gave cursory salutes to the ensign and the quarterdeck.

"Mr. Weatherby, your timing was impeccable," said Kinkaid, happy to see his young gunnery officer again.

"We saw the flashes of the battle from quite far away, sir, but didn't think we'd get to you in time," explained Weatherby, noticing the dark rings around Kinkaid's reddened eyes, evidence that he had slept little in the last few days. "Lucky thing you turned toward us, Captain."

But Kinkaid wanted to know only one thing, "Was Blackstone aboard her?"

"No, sir. It was that Freeman fellow," answered Weatherby. "We have him below."

"I want to see him."

"Right this way, sir," said Weatherby, leading the way. Reaching the bottom of the ladder, where two marines stood guard, Weatherby parted the curtain of one of the officer's berths, saying, "Took a wound in his side, Captain. May have some busted ribs."

Compared to the cramped confines of *Swift*, *Cutler* provided a prodigious amount of space, with twice as many cabins as Kinkaid's officers needed, each with its own small table and washstand, closet, and shelves. Freeman was lying on his side in one of these cabins, a shackle around his ankle chained to the bed frame; the flame of a candle on the table revealed a pained look on his face.

"You be a lucky man, Captain," groaned Freeman, looking up.

But Kinkaid wanted to know, "Why didn't Blackstone come with you?"

"Two chances better dan one. If you beat me, you'd still have to go into de Hole," he grinned. "Besides, he still be playin' wit his new toys."

"Except for the one you brought with you."

Freeman smiled and gamely said, "Dat big blaster almost done you in. Yep, you gotta admit, Captain, I'd a sunk you or would be towin' you into da Hole by now if it weren't for dis damned ting showin' when she did."

"That was quite a trick you pulled," admitted Kinkaid, knowing full well the truth in what Freeman said: that he never came close to beating the man and his expertly handled and heavily armed vessel, that it was only luck and the propitious meeting with *Cutler* that had saved Kinkaid and *Swift*. Kinkaid saw Freeman's hat lying on the shelf over the bed and picked it up, saying, "I've a mind to borrow this, Freeman."

"Spoils of war, Captain. I used to tink she brought me luck, but now I not so sure."

"Luck can change as a man can change," ventured Kinkaid as he felt stabbing jolts of pain in his back and leaned heavily against the doorway. Wounded and worn out with fatigue and after-battle letdown, he felt a terrible desire to rest.

"What you mean, Captain?" asked Freeman, detecting the hint of an offer of some kind.

"I think you know what I mean, Freeman," said Kinkaid, gambling.

The big man looked up into Kinkaid's face, met his eyes. "You sayin' der might be time for me to change my course, Captain?"

"Depends on how cooperative you want to be," said Kinkaid evenly, locking his knees. "Like you said, Blackstone was more interested in getting his guns set up than coming out to fight, leaving all the risk to you. And now I have to risk more of my crew against those guns. Any man who saw his way to help bring down a murderous scoundrel, free kidnapped hostages, and save the lives of my crew...well, I'd say he deserved the chance to reset his sails."

Freeman gazed at the candle flame. "I will have to tink on dat, Captain."

"You have until morning; I can't wait any longer than that," Kinkaid warned, his hands gripping the beam over his head, holding himself up. He could feel drops of blood running down his back, sticking to his shirt. Before leaving, Kinkaid told him, "I'll have my surgeon take a look at you and your crew as soon as he's finished with my men."

"Tank you, sir."

It was only when he reached the top of the ladder that Weatherby noticed the bloodstains on the back of Kinkaid's shredded shirt.

"You're wounded, Captain," said Weatherby as Kinkaid wobbled and grabbed the rail for support.

"It's nothing, Weatherby. I had the surgeon look at it already," he lied. He had felt too guilty to ask Dr. Grafton to look at his few cuts when men whose lives were in danger needed immediate attention. Besides, there was simply too much to do to allow a little pain to stop him.

Kinkaid returned to the quarterdeck as the last of *Moondog*'s crew was herded below, Weatherby close beside him, watching his captain, suspecting he must be in great pain.

"We lost some good men today," said Kinkaid somberly to Weatherby, Simpson, and the men of the quarterdeck watch, feeling the need to say something, to recognize the valiant effort that had resulted in such a loss of life and limb. "And Mr. Saddler was killed. Gave his life in defense of *Swift* with honor and a fighting spirit. No man could have given more."

It hit him only now how often he had ignored the man, had spoken to his first lieutenant only as duty dictated. In truth, there was not a single man or officer aboard *Swift* who might have claimed Saddler as a friend.

No one knew quite what to say after the Captain's statement. Mr. Saddler had been their first lieutenant only because Admiral Nathanson had awarded him the assignment, a reward for bringing in the munitions transport *Nancy*, filled with badly needed war materials for Washington's army. For that reason Saddler had been pronounced a hero and promoted. But the man had been no favorite of anyone, moderately efficient in his ponderous way, supercilious in the extreme, and with an unreliable sense of judgment when it came to dealing with the men. Even so, Kinkaid could not help but admire and recognize the brave and unselfish effort that Saddler had made during the action on this night, had to appreciate his sacrifice, as well as that of the others who gave their lives or limbs.

Weatherby must have suspected something of this, for now it was he who broke the embarrassing silence. "Sad, sir. And a great loss," he managed to say.

Kinkaid heard the words and reflected that there was little truth in what Weatherby had said. Saddler's death was no sadder than his short life had been. He would not be missed, nor would his departing be a great loss to the navy, but he was glad that Weatherby had said something. And what of Hyde? This mean and petty man, who took pleasure in tormenting others, who spit in the crew's food, who would purposefully serve rotten meat, had lost a leg. And what of Treadwell and the others, men whose names would be quickly forgotten? What of them, would they be missed? Were their lives a loss to the navy or anyone else, someone on shore, a sweetheart or a mother, perhaps?

Kinkaid turned to Mr. Simpson, a man whom he could certainly call his friend, put his hand on his shoulder and said, "I must thank you for the daring service that you have rendered, Mr. Simpson, for—"

"Please, Captain," said Simpson, a tired and almost tortured look on his face. "I had no idea of the horror of battle…I am only sorry that I was not able to provide the real help that those fine men deserved."

"Nonsense, Mr. Simpson, you were indispensable," insisted Kinkaid. "Because of you, men lived who otherwise might not have."

"I did no more than any other man in the same circumstances, Captain."

Kinkaid reflected on the carnage as well as the courage, more than a dozen men lost, the sound and fury of the battle still with him. "We will have a service and burial, Mr. Weatherby, first thing in the morning. It will be easiest from *Swift*."

"I'll inform the Chaplain, sir," said Weatherby. "In the meantime, perhaps you should get some rest, Captain. There's not much left to do. Mr. Briggs and enough of a crew to sail her are aboard *Swift*, and Mr. Lofton and a boarding party have laid claim to *Moondog*. Rafferty is seeing to their repairs, and O'Toole is over there too, helping the carpenters."

"Thank you, Weatherby," said a pained and exhausted Kinkaid, thankful indeed to have men like these who took it upon themselves to do what needed to be done. Then, saving Weatherby from having to respond, Kinkaid said, "Now we will have to see if we can come up with a few good tricks of our own to play on our friend Captain Blackstone."

Kinkaid felt he was about to collapse and so turned to take the ladder down to his cabin, when Weatherby suggested, "Sir, I think we'd better have Dr. Grafton take a look."

"When he has the time," said Kinkaid unsteadily.

"I'll see you to your cabin, sir," said Weatherby. He followed Kinkaid down the ladder to the spacious cabin where red begonias bloomed cheerfully outside the stern windows.

Kinkaid slumped on the cot. It was a relief to finally sit down, to catch his breath, to ease the pain in his back. "Did you have any trouble finding the men?" he asked.

"Most of them hadn't made it much farther than the first tavern, Captain. I don't know if you noticed, but O'Toole—"

"I saw the black eye," admitted Kinkaid, "and whatever that thing is on his arm."

Weatherby laughed and said, "His new tattoo, sir...of a dolphin. He calls it his souvenir of our swim in the Sargasso Sea. Though it's unfinished."

"Interrupted by you calling back the liberty party—"

"Not by me, sir. By Sergeant Anders," explained Weatherby. "That's when he got the black eye."

"The two of them finally had it out, huh? Who won?"

"I'd say it was a tie, Captain; Anders has a black eye, too."

"So they remain a matching pair," regarded Kinkaid, giving a painful chuckle.

"Like mirror images, Captain," laughed Weatherby, explaining, "Anders has his on the other side."

"Well, I hope the two of them can put away their private war for another day or so—"

"Oh, they're fast friends now, sir," interjected Weatherby, noticing the pain and fatigue in his captain's eyes.

"So that is why O'Toole has taken up that nasty habit."

"Chewing tobacco; yes, sir. And they've been telling war stories to one another since we left the island, laughing and slapping each other on the back like old chums. Anders even mentioned to O'Toole that he has a sister his age."

"Now there is a frightening thought," observed Kinkaid, recognizing as well that there were other, more frightening thoughts trying to intrude as he slumped back onto the cot.

"Sir," said Weatherby, placing his hand on Kinkaid's shoulder as he leaned to one side. "You've been through the masher tonight and…well, it might be a wise idea to get some sleep, Captain."

Kinkaid's first impulse was to reject the idea outright, to think of what needed to be done for his ship and his crew…but then he realized that everything that needed to be done was already being done. Weatherby had the situation well in hand, the wounded men were being attended to, both damaged ships were being repaired as quickly as possible, and resting, at least for an hour or two, was a most reasonable suggestion.

"Weatherby, as always, you are right," he said as he lay down on the cot, Weatherby pulling his shoes off.

"Let me know as soon as both ships are capable of moving off," commanded Kinkaid, his eyes closing, placing his legs onto the cot, and then rolling painfully on his side, murmuring, "I don't want us within sight of Blackstone when it gets light."

"Don't worry, sir, I'll see to it we're out of here before then," said Weatherby soothingly, placing a blanket over his captain.

Then Kinkaid said, "Weatherby, I'd like our prisoner, Freeman, to know that he is to be hanged tomorrow morning, following services for our men."

It took only a moment for Weatherby to ascertain Kinkaid's true purpose and he smiled, saying, "I'll see it's done indirectly and discreetly, Captain."

Before leaving, Weatherby blew out the candle on the table, a short, stubby candle that held down a corner of the chart of Coral Bay, where inside its meandering shoreline was a narrow cove called Hurricane Hole.

Rafferty had found the damage on *Swift* significant—the bulwarks smashed through for some considerable length on the starboard side, three guns wrecked and thrown off their carriages.

She required a new mainsheet, replacement of some standing rigging, and a few cleats jury-rigged on the starboard side with which to secure their lines, at least until the bulwarks could be replaced, a major job that would have to wait. But she was still floating and sailable, her rigging not too badly damaged and her hull shored up except for a small hole in her stern still allowing in water. He left her with Mr. Briggs in command. Her wounded had been transferred over to *Cutler*.

Now the tireless Rafferty was on the *Moondog*, finding her starboard side and main deck a shambles from the terrible carnage Weatherby's gunners had unleashed upon her, though luckily only two hits were below the waterline. Over a dozen men had been killed, seven more severely injured from Weatherby's single broadside. Mr. Lofton had taken charge of her, also transferring her remaining crew to the *Cutler*, safely confined in the orlop, while unceremoniously heaving her dead over the side. She carried a minimum crew now, only enough men to help her limp along.

The weather had remained foul, although the wind abated somewhat as the storm passed off to the southeast, and the three ships continued to drift to the south away from Coral Bay. It was after four when a grimy and exhausted Rafferty reported to Weatherby that both damaged ships were seaworthy enough to get some sails up, to leave the area, though much work still remained to be done. This included making more permanent repairs to the inner hulls and bulwarks, patching the ships' boats, building entire upper-deck structures such as a new binnacle for *Swift*, as well as replacing damaged spars and rigging on both *Swift* and *Moondog*.

Dr. Grafton had also worked valiantly throughout the night, doctoring friend and foe alike, and now Weatherby found him, stooped and weary, seeing to Mr. Freeman's broken ribs, winding a large bandage around the big man's waist.

"You'll be in some pain for a while," explained the venerable doctor, finishing the job as Weatherby stood in the passageway, "but this should take some of the pressure off, keep those ribs together while they heal."

"Dr. Grafton, when you're finished here," asked Weatherby, "I'd like you to have another look at the Captain's back. He wanted to be awakened before we moved off; I was just coming down to inform him."

Dr. Grafton closed his black bag, stood up, and turned slowly around, looking exhausted and haggard. "His back?"

"Yes, those splinters…" It was immediately apparent to Weatherby that Dr. Grafton was only now apprised of any wounds that the Captain had sustained, that Kinkaid had kept the information to himself to ensure that the men were looked after first. With this realization, Weatherby gave Freeman a disdainful glance. This man had tried to kill or maim every man aboard *Swift*, including his captain, and had almost succeeded in sinking her. If Weatherby had not been led to the *Swift* by hearing the booms and seeing the flashes of fire in the night, had not made the area in time…and now here was the man responsible, bandaged and cared for by Dr. Grafton, even before his own captain was looked after.

Freeman looked up at him and, unaware of the thoughts and emotions that Weatherby was experiencing, said, "Lieutenant, I be needin' to speak to your Captain." Then, as if detecting some of what Weatherby was thinking by his look, he added, "When convenient, dat is."

Weatherby merely turned away in anger and disgust.

The marine guard pressed himself against the bulkhead as Weatherby headed for Kinkaid's cabin, where Dr. Grafton was awakening him. He helped the Captain sit up on his cot and removed his bloody shirt before opening his black bag on the table.

"What time is it?" asked Kinkaid.

"About four-thirty, Captain," Weatherby informed him, only now seeing the extent of Kinkaid's wounds. "All ships are moving off to the southwest, sir."

"Very good," replied Kinkaid with a painful grimace as Dr. Grafton investigated a bloody hole on his back. "I'll be up in a few minutes."

"Aye aye, Captain," answered Weatherby. "And Mr. Freeman asked to have a word with you, sir."

Kinkaid looked up, nodding, "Have Mr. Freeman come to my cabin, then. I'll see him directly."

"You might want to wait before seeing anyone, Captain," advised Dr. Grafton, reaching into his bag. "You've at least a dozen splinters in your back." Grafton brought a long, wicked-looking forceps out of his bag and then a small bottle of rum. "They pose no immediate mortal danger, but left unattended could lead to a dangerous infection. I see no need to put off removing them, sir," he stated matter-of-factly.

"Is this going to hurt, Doc?" asked Kinkaid.

"You might find it distracting to conversation," answered the practical ship's doctor.

"Very well, Doctor," gave Kinkaid, looking askance at the silvery instrument that Dr. Grafton was dipping into the open bottle of rum. "Tell Mr. Freeman I will see him…"

"When it is convenient, sir?" suggested Weatherby.

"Very good," agreed Kinkaid.

"I'll tell him, sir," answered Weatherby, which is exactly what he did, telling Freeman as he passed by, "He'll see you when it is convenient," before returning to the quarterdeck.

Dr. Grafton handed the bottle of rum to Kinkaid, who refused it, saying, "I'll be needing a clear head about me and—"

"If that's the way you want it, Captain," answered Dr. Grafton, extremely fatigued and not in the mood to argue with a stubborn man. "Turn around now."

Grafton felt for the end of the first splinter, lodged just under Kinkaid's left scapula. He worked the ends of the forceps into the narrow, jagged wound, Kinkaid gritting his teeth in torment. Finding the wooden splinter, he spread the tongs on either side of it, then, gripping firmly, pulled steadily, the inch-and-a-half-long piece of ship's decking coming out with a stream of blood and a long cry of pain.

Kinkaid turned around, and aware that he would have to go through the same agonizing torture many more times, demanded, "Give me that bottle, Doc."

"If you insist, Captain," said Dr. Grafton, dabbing at the bloody wound. "I'll give you a minute."

Kinkaid took a mighty swig of the burning liquid, almost gagging on its power, finally saying, "Time for the uh, medicine, to take effect, Doc?"

"That's it, Captain," said the doctor, nodding his head, his eyes closed. Might as well rest while he could.

Kinkaid took two more hearty gulps of rum in quick succession, burning his throat—and now his stomach was burning as well. After first holding back an impulse to vomit, then a few minutes later feeling his head swimming, he gave the doctor, who appeared to be falling fast asleep, a nudge, "Let's get thish over wish, shall we, Doc?"

Dr. Grafton came out of his nap, blinking his dry eyes. He found the next jagged tear in Kinkaid's back and repeated the procedure, retrieving another sliver of wood with Kinkaid once more groaning with the pain, the alcohol dulling his mind, it seemed, more than it had dulled the nerves in his back. Half-a-dozen splinters later, when Dr. Grafton asked if it hurt, Kinkaid answered, "Of coursh it hurch, Doc…though the rum makes me not mind so mush that it hurch."

Too stupid with pain and drink to care, Kinkaid emitted only an occasional grunt as the last of the splinters was removed. Finally, the operation over, Dr. Grafton bandaged the wounds and helped Kinkaid into his night shirt. Kinkaid was on the verge of passing out from the combination of alcohol and pain, the removal of the splinters almost worse than having them still in. He slumped on his cot, and Dr. Grafton put the blanket over him, telling him, "I'll be seeing you at sunrise, Captain."

Worry not letting him rest, Kinkaid rose up, saying, "Freeman…tell him I'll shee him…"

"When it's convenient, Captain," suggested Dr. Grafton.

"Yesh, that's right, Doc. When itch…convenient," mumbled Kinkaid, his eyes closing, his head falling against the pillow. It was already five o'clock in the morning when Dr. Grafton informed Mr. Weatherby on the quarterdeck that the Captain would be fine and that he was presently napping, before he himself turned in for some much-needed sleep.

The three ships were moving west in a ragged V formation, *Cutler* in front with *Moondog* off the port quarter and *Swift* still lagging to starboard, her pumps working furiously. The dark silhouette of St. John loomed barely visible to the north. The night had remained dark after a few light showers, but now the moon began peeking out from behind low, dark clouds that appeared to be breaking up and the sky was growing light in the east, promising a clear day to come.

Weatherby stood on the quarterdeck, the wind in his face as he watched *Swift* wallowing in the troughs. She was falling behind.

"No need to call out the watch, Rikker, but let's find whoever's awake and take in the main course, shall we?" Weatherby could see no reason to wake men who needed their sleep.

"Right away, Mr. Weatherby," answered Rikker, touching his brow in a quick salute. More than a few hands were still milling quietly about the ship, unable to sleep because of the excitement of recent events and the anticipation of things to come, and so Rikker had little trouble finding willing hands to help with the reduction in sail.

"Make signal to *Moondog* to maintain her station," ordered Weatherby. As the flapping sheet was hauled in and secured, he turned again to look at the struggling *Swift*, Mr. Briggs and the men on her decks sailing her by sheer determination. Then he shifted his gaze toward Coral Bay, where the ruthless Jack Blackstone kept Marie de la Renier his hostage.

XIII

Big Guns of Hurricane Hole

The rising sun shone brightly through the stern windows and awoke Kinkaid with a sense of urgency. Still groggy, he had a headache and his mouth felt as though it were filled with cotton. Rising in pain and discomfort, he unsteadily made his way to the mirror.

His face was dirty and unshaven, his eyes red, dry, and crusty, his hair poking ridiculously out to one side. He looked a hideous sight, yet stubbornly decided he had little time for vanity as he yawned and stretched, the movement bringing a groan of pain as his bandages pulled against his throbbing wounds. Making for the door, he could not help but notice that clean trousers, a shirt, and his uniform jacket were on hangers hooked over the door handle.

He agonizingly put on the trousers before opening the door to see the rotund silhouette of Corporal Stockton, the marine sentry, leaning against the bottom of the ladder, a shiny line of drool hanging from his double chin, his belly hanging over his belt, from which the dark handle of a pistol protruded.

"Sentry!" Kinkaid called out. "What time is it?"

"Almost six, sir!" blurted out the startled Stockton.

"I'll have a report from the deck, if you please."

"Aye aye, sir," gave the flustered marine.

Stockton had trudged but halfway up the ladder when Kinkaid called out, "Belay that, sentry! Come here!"

"Aye, sir!" Stockton turned awkwardly on the stairs, made his way back down, and ran huffing and puffing to stand breathlessly at attention before Kinkaid. Jerking his arm up in a rigid salute, Stockton barked out, "As ordered, sir!"

The pitiable look on the sentry's face was evidence enough that he anticipated a stern rebuke for appearing less than alert while on watch. He knew, as all sailors and marines knew, that he could expect at least a dozen strokes of the cat-o'-nine-tails for sleeping on duty, a serious offense.

Kinkaid had not intended to berate the man, but knowing he had little choice under the circumstances opted for the mild, "The ship depends upon your vigilance, Corporal."

"Quite right, Captain," gave Stockton guiltily, sounding properly repentant as he held his stiff salute.

Kinkaid returned the salute and then, giving Stockton a conspiratorial look, asked him quietly, "Has our prisoner been informed as to his fate?"

The much-relieved Stockton showed a knowing grin and answered in a whisper, "Discreetly and indirectly, Captain. Just as you ordered, sir."

Kinkaid was tempted to return Stockton's foolish grin but instead maintained a solemn tone. "Very good. Now I shall expect you to convey my regards to the officer of the quarterdeck watch, and I'll have my report…and then bring the prisoner."

"Aye aye, sir!" answered Stockton, too loudly, before turning to carry out his orders.

Kinkaid had only closed his cabin door when there came the distinctive double rap from the other side and, sure enough, there was Cato lifting a bowl of hot water from the deck, a clean white towel draped over his arm.

"How are you feeling, Captain?" asked Cato solicitously.

"Like a pin cushion," Kinkaid complained moodily.

"Dr. Grafton said he wanted to look in on you this morning, sir," Cato reminded him.

"Well, he'd better hurry," growled Kinkaid. "Little time to waste today."

"I assumed you might want to get an early start," said Cato agreeably as he crossed the cabin and placed the steaming bowl into its holder below the mirror. He picked up Kinkaid's shaving brush and expertly twirled it around in the soap dish before suggesting casually, "A nice wash and a shave, sir?"

Perhaps there was time after all, thought Kinkaid, if not for vanity, then only for what was required to begin such a day, a day likely to be full of consequence, a day not to be rushed into willy-nilly, and now he felt grateful for the simple reminder.

"Of course, Cato."

Cato helped him off with his stained nightshirt and grimaced when he saw his bandages, spotted here and there with blood.

"Cato, do you still have that red scarf you used to wear?" asked Kinkaid.

"Why yes, Captain, though it's rather tattered."

"All the better," said Kinkaid. "I'd like to borrow it today if I may."

"Of course. I'll bring it with your coffee, sir."

"And you might bring a couple of extra cups, Cato."

"As you wish, sir."

Kinkaid washed the dirt and grime from his face, lathered it, and had painfully begun to shave when there came a second knock at the door. It was the diminutive Rudy, the messenger boy.

"Mr. Weatherby's compliments, Captain. He says to inform you, uh…" began Rudy uncertainly, his head twisting involuntarily at an angle, one eye squinted tightly shut in his strained attempt to recall exactly what he was expected to convey from Mr. Weatherby to his captain, "that we are three miles to the south…of the west end…of the island of St. John."

Kinkaid knew that staring at the boy would not help Rudy to remember, so he casually returned his attention to shaving as Rudy continued his report. "The weather is clearing and…and the wind is fair…and out of the northeast, Captain," he concluded with a sigh of relief.

"Thank you, Rudy, and please inform Mr. Weatherby that we'll hold our services within the hour…and that I shall be up directly."

"Aye aye. I'll tell him, Captain," Rudy assured him.

Cato stopped Rudy in the passageway as he passed his galley. "Rudy, would you please inform Dr. Grafton that the Captain is awake?"

"Of course, Mr. Africanus."

Kinkaid had finished shaving when there came yet another knock at the door.

"Come in," said Kinkaid.

Gunner Freeman was buttoning his own torn and dirty shirt as he stepped warily into Kinkaid's cabin. His deep chest swathed tightly in bandages, he murmured a pained oath under his breath as he ducked low through the doorway. Corporal Stockton stood behind him.

"We'll be fine, sentry," said Kinkaid assuredly. "Won't we, Mr. Freeman?"

Freeman, having noted the bandage around Kinkaid's torso, nodded agreeably and said in his melodious voice, "Looks like da boaf of us not be doin' all dat fine, Captain."

"No thanks to you," answered Kinkaid, making no effort to hide his annoyance.

Another double rap on the door and there was Cato with coffee—and the red scarf. Freeman stood aside, and Cato made his way nimbly around the big gunner and placed the silver tray on the table and the neatly folded scarf on the cot, completely ignoring Freeman's subdued presence. He then poured a cup of coffee for Kinkaid and placed the cup and saucer on the table.

"Thank you, Cato," said Kinkaid, picking up the clean white shirt, "and perhaps we can spare a cup for our guest."

"Very good, sir," said Cato with an insolent sniff, his nose in the air at the mention of Blackstone's gunner even as he poured a cup for the man, adding, "There are some fresh-made scones, Captain…right out of the oven."

"Some fresh-made scones would be perfect, Cato," said Kinkaid gaily, sounding unconcerned about the fate of a captured pirate.

"My pleasure, Captain," said Cato, bowing slightly.

Dr. Grafton was at the door as Cato left, and now Gunner Freeman stood aside to allow the doctor in with his black bag.

Kinkaid had put one arm through the sleeve of the clean shirt when Dr. Grafton advised him, "I wouldn't put that on just yet, Captain."

Kinkaid obediently took off his shirt and stood as Dr. Grafton removed his bandages and checked his wounds. Kinkaid tried not to wince as the doctor touched his stitches, tried to enjoy keeping Freeman waiting, in fact hoped to extend his waiting ever longer by offering, "Would you care for a cup of coffee, Doctor?"

"Already had my breakfast, Captain," said the doctor, unaware of Kinkaid's intentions, but bringing the reminder that there were almost a dozen men down below awaiting Dr. Grafton's ministrations, men with worse wounds than his own. Dr. Grafton replaced Kinkaid's bandages with fresh ones and helped him on with his shirt. "You'll be good as new in a week, Captain, but for now, I'd suggest taking it easy," he said. Knowing his suggestion would be impossible to follow, he departed on his rounds.

Kinkaid stood looking out through the stern windows as he finished buttoning his shirt, then turned and made the airy remark, "Ah, fresh scones in the morning. A blessing to appreciate the simple things in life, don't you agree?"

"A blessing, to be sure, Captain," gave Freeman warily.

Kinkaid motioned for Freeman to take a chair, politely saying, "Please, sit down," whereupon the big man did so, heavily and with a groan of pain. Kinkaid took the time to button his top button and straighten his collar in front of the mirror before tucking the long tails of his shirt into his trousers. Satisfied, he came to the table and sat across from the gunner. Then, carefully placing an immaculate white napkin upon his lap, he looked up and said casually, "I hope you can appreciate that we won't have time for a trial."

Freeman's mouth fell open at the remark. He seemed to stare into the abyss for a moment before finally shaking his head and stammering, "I...I didn't much care for what happened back der on dat French ship, Captain Kinkaid. In fact, I—"

Kinkaid, pretending indifference, asked, "How did you find yourself...associating with Blackstone?"

"Tree year ago he give me my name, made me free man."

"To come and go as you choose," Kinkaid reminded him.

"I be grateful to him," admitted Freeman.

"Then you'll die a grateful man," said Kinkaid coldly.

Freeman's frightened eyes shifted back and forth, his defenses roused. Then his hopeless gaze came to rest on the chart on the table. "It be Hawke, Captain," he said with sudden inspiration. "A murderous bastard, dat one. Blackstone, he try keepin' him in line, but...dat one be bad. Dat's why he got left behind."

"Hmm," was all Kinkaid offered at first. Then he suggested, "You'll need a better story than that."

But Freeman persisted, "It's true, Captain. Blackstone figured you'd come along like you did, find dat French ship and...and take care of 'im."

"Blackstone figured?" Kinkaid began angrily, but there was Cato at the door with a basket of fresh-baked scones, his placid face a reminder to Kinkaid to remain calm, that revealing his anger might defeat his purpose, in spite of his annoyance that Blackstone seemed to know what he was going to do before he did. "Of course Blackstone was right," he said in a steady voice. "Your friend Hawke already found his justice with the French."

Freeman stiffened, his mind filled with the vision of himself hanging from a yardarm by the neck as he choked to death as he had seen other men do, his legs kicking uselessly, an undignified death, and with the fear of the nether regions he would warrant for a life spent free and unrepentant, the criminal life of a pirate. He wondered, as well, if "Bloody" Hawke might be waiting for him on the other side in the dark somewhere, or worse, in the eternal fires of hell.

Kinkaid kept up his easy banter as if oblivious to Freeman's fears.

"Is that why Porter was left behind?" he asked, reaching for a scone.

"Porter?" Freeman shook his head, surprised to hear the man's name. He hadn't touched his coffee and fresh scones seemed of little importance to him at the moment.

"Is he a murderer too?" asked Kinkaid, painstakingly buttering his scone.

"Porter, a murderer? Hardly, Captain. Porter wouldn't kill a snake if it bit 'im," mumbled Freeman in resignation. "Don't rightly know how dat useless man ever hook up wit us."

"I see. Harmless, therefore useless to Blackstone's operation," answered Kinkaid, taking a fastidious bite of the crumbly pastry. "I doubt that Blackstone never expected to see Hawke again. In fact, I believe Blackstone gave Hawke orders to bring that French ship in once it was determined she wasn't being chased."

Freeman stalled. Finally, looking sideways, he answered, "I wouldn't know what orders Blackstone give to Hawke."

"You're lying," said Kinkaid flatly before taking a leisurely sip of his coffee. He waited for a reaction, but when Freeman sat there mute, Kinkaid mentioned, "Did I tell you that we brought Mr. Porter along with us?"

Freeman looked up in apparent interest.

"A most helpful fellow," said Kinkaid. "Told us what happened on that French ship, where Blackstone's guns are hidden, and where he intends to place those we gave him." Seeing the confused look on Freeman's face, Kinkaid kept resolutely on, adding matter-of-factly, "You can't get Blackstone out of this one. Three men murdered, two people kidnapped, one an innocent girl, all on his authority." He paused, and then, with finality, stated, "Someone needs to pay."

Freeman sat mute for a moment. Then he began nodding his head in agreement, figuring it needn't be him if he could help it.

Pressing, Kinkaid assured him, "I intend to stop Blackstone with or without your help."

Freeman looked up, searching for the meaning in what Kinkaid said, the instinct for survival rising up, searching for a way out. "Dat's why I be talkin' to you, Captain. Like I say, dat po' girl and her father—"

"Truth is, we don't have much use for you around here, Freeman," said a relieved Kinkaid, having the man exactly where he wanted him. "After the punishment you inflicted on my ship and crew, I'm sure you can understand how there would be scant forgiveness to be wasted on the man responsible." Kinkaid waited until he saw the forlorn look of a condemned man before adding, "But let's have a look at the chart. I'd be interested to see if your information agrees with what Porter told us."

"And if it does, Captain?" asked Freeman, hope in his eyes.

Kinkaid shrugged, "Some leniency, perhaps."

"Enough to keep me off da gallows, Captain?"

"Well now, that depends."

Chaplain Carlton was on *Swift* that morning, saying some words over the bodies of Mr. Saddler and nine others committed to the deep, while *Cutler* sailed alongside in honor, all officers and crew on deck. Aaron Tripp was there in the front row, his face streaked with tears over his friend and comrade in arms, Joseph Treadwell, the other half of the Travelin' Brothers. And there stood Roach, a clean bandage on his head. Even Hairy Hyde, with his missing foot, had insisted upon being carried out on deck on a stretcher for the funeral. There, next to him, was Smith on crutches, supported between Helmut and Stevens, his ankle tightly wrapped, offering some words of consolation to the man who had before cursed and berated him in the ship's galley.

Kinkaid's back was aching and burning, the bandages making it difficult to breathe, and as the services proceeded, he felt torn between trying to properly mourn those brave men who had died in the performance of their duties and the urgent need to focus his attention on how he would rescue the Marquis and his daughter from Jack Blackstone's well-protected cove. He had been played for a fool with the result that good men had suffered and died. If he had felt any misgivings about fighting a former ally, recent events made them moot.

The three ships anchored well out in Rendezvous Bay, some six nautical miles west of the opening to Coral Bay. Kinkaid was seated at the head of the table, indicating on the chart the marks along the ins and outs of the shoreline of Hurricane Hole where Freeman had pointed out all the gun positions and strong points. Major Bauer, Mr. Weatherby, Briggs, Lofton, and Mr. Simpson were all in attendance as the crew finished an early breakfast.

"There may be fewer guns than Captain Blackstone bragged about, but counting the ones we gave him it seems he has at least eleven nine-pounders, four twelve-pounders, and the three eighteens," Kinkaid told them, "enough to give us plenty of trouble if we don't silence them quickly."

Kinkaid's wounds had stiffened and the pulling stitches sent stabbing spasms of pain across his back, but he tried not to grimace as he bent over the chart.

"Now then, it seems that Blackstone always has a lookout along this far eastern point, here. From there he can be apprised of any ships coming into the area. What we don't know is whether he has spies on the western side—which is at least three miles from his camp. But if he is expecting us, we must assume he'll post more lookouts along the shore, so Major Bauer, you and your marines will debark here at Lameshur Bay and head northeast to get behind them. This old chart indicates a road that follows the shoreline of the bay. It might be unused and overgrown by now, but it leads close to Blackstone's camp. Major, if you can get your marines to this point here, undetected…"

Kinkaid explained the plan that he had formulated in the last few hours, his officers offering some suggestions, having also thought out the possibilities. Indeed, Mr. Weatherby, Lofton, and Briggs had come up with a very good plan of their own. After all, they had not been certain of finding *Swift* or their captain upon arriving in the area and might have had to act without him, possibly having to rescue him from Blackstone's clutches as well as the Marquis and his daughter. Kinkaid listened carefully to the plan they had devised before combining it with his own ideas.

"Are we in agreement then?" he asked in conclusion, the others nodding their approval. "Good. Now then, we don't have men to spare, so this is how we shall organize ourselves…"

The sun was peeking up over The Bight at Norman Island as the marines climbed into the two boats. They were an inspiring sight in their uniforms and muskets. In addition, each marine carried a small cloth sack around his waist containing the rest of those nasty round explosive devices Bauer called "hand grenades."

"Good luck, Major," said Kinkaid to the tough marine.

"See you on the beach, Captain," replied Bauer as the crowded boats began rowing to shore.

Kinkaid had to laugh when he saw O'Toole wearing Freeman's coat and green floppy hat. O'Toole had darkened his face with grease so that from a distance he looked very much like the big black gunner; the only detail giving him away was that gap in his teeth when he smiled.

"We didn't think you looked very much like Freeman, Captain," explained Weatherby to some nervous laughter from the deck, "so O'Toole volunteered."

"It's a good thing Freeman is below. Chains or not, he'd probably strangle you for looking like that," observed Kinkaid.

Mr. Simpson laughed and said, "And who would blame him?"

"Weatherby made me do it, sir," said O'Toole, grinning foolishly, his left cheek bulging out.

The sight of O'Toole even brought a laugh from the staid Mr. Lofton, though he looked ridiculous enough himself, for Weatherby and Briggs had encouraged the lanky midshipman to wear a black suit with a black hat so he looked more like an undertaker than ever, his long legs sticking out from beneath his too-short breeches.

"Mr. Lofton," said Kinkaid, "I take it you are ready?"

"Aye, Captain," replied Mr. Lofton, climbing down the ladder where Aaron Tripp and two gun crews were waiting to take themselves to *Swift*.

"It's time, Mr. Weatherby," said Kinkaid to his trusted lieutenant. Since Weatherby would be in command of *Cutler*, he was the only naval officer wearing his uniform. Most of the best gunners would also remain aboard to man her biggest guns.

"Remember," Kinkaid told Weatherby, "give us a half mile ahead of you before you start in for Coral Bay. When we get there, we'll tack in slow enough for you to catch up to us."

"We'll make certain it looks like a chase, sir," Weatherby assured him.

"Good luck, Captain," added Mr. Simpson.

"And good timing," Kinkaid reminded them. "And make sure Mr. Simpson keeps his head down."

Kinkaid followed Briggs and O'Toole down the ladder to *Moondog*'s boat, one pistol in his hand, the other tucked into his belt. Rikker was standing at the rail, and Kinkaid placed his hand over his boatswain's whistle as Rikker brought it to his lips. "Belay that, Rikker." The high-pitched sound from the whistle would carry quite far over open water.

Rikker dropped the pipe, letting it swing from its string around his neck. "Aye, Captain."

The sight of Jack Blackstone's howling dog flag flying from the mainmast of *Moondog* brought a smile to Kinkaid's face as he was rowed toward her red and black hull, for no matter what the next few hours brought—justice or death—there was some satisfaction in knowing that he was using Blackstone's own ship against him. He had left his coat and hat behind, and he brought out the red scarf he had borrowed from Cato and tied it around his head. Briggs seemed to be enjoying himself, wearing a bright blue shirt, his hair blowing free in the breeze, looking less a dangerous pirate than a handsome actor playing the part.

The first two hundred yards beyond the beach were the roughest for Bauer and his marines, the coastline steep and rocky, the brush on the knoll thick and tough, the heat already rising. He immediately sent Monk Chunk to reconnoiter ahead, and after almost an hour of fighting the jungle, using their bayonets to hack and chop their way through, Monk returned and led the column to the road that was shown on the old chart.

The road was badly overgrown, unused for years, and after a while it dead-ended into a thick and neglected banana orchard, as if the orchard had been planted there to discourage inquisitive strangers. But Bauer waved his marines onward and in time they found the road again, a grassy road that bore off to the right around the hill in front of them—the chart exaggerating its immensity by calling it Bordeaux Mountain—and then it twisted and turned through the jungle for a mile or more beyond the hill, until finally coming to the very large Coral Bay with its meandering shoreline. In fact, the shape of its outline on the chart was reminiscent of a court jester. The lagoon on the left was one arm of the jester, raised in greeting, while the lagoon on the right looked like a squashed hand. And the one in the middle, the one called Hurricane Hole, was the head, its many narrow inlets looking like a silly star-like jester hat.

Major Bauer warned his marines to stay in the shadows and behind the trees as they made their way along the shoreline, watching for any sign that they might have been detected by lookouts along the way. In two hours the group had made its way to the top of the first lagoon. The grassy road skirted a thin beach here and offered a panoramic view of Coral Bay. Far off in the distance to the east, beyond the bay, the sun was shining high over Norman Island and The Bight. They were close now and so Major Bauer decided to halt his tired and sweaty column for five minutes, warning them to stay low and hide in the bushes.

Corporal Stockton was last in line, finding it difficult to keep up with the fast-moving column, and he was only too glad to have a chance to catch his breath as he found the resting marines. He chose a sturdy palm to sit under along the edge of the road and was leaning against it, his head back and eyes closed, enjoying the warm sunshine on his face.

"All guns are loaded, sir, and we're full and by," reported Briggs in the waist of the hastily repaired *Moondog*, her deck still ripped up in places, ragged holes in her sides, dark blotches where men had fallen. Rafferty was at the wheel and O'Toole stood beside him on the windward side of the quarterdeck, looking as he imagined Gunner Freeman might look, in command of the ship.

"Very well, Mr. Briggs," answered Kinkaid. "We'll dally out here a bit longer, make as if we're bucking the wind, allow *Cutler* to come up."

"Not hard to act that part, sir, what with the wind in our face like this," observed Briggs.

Moondog's supposed prize, *Swift*, was close behind them, the ever-grave Mr. Lofton in command, Tripp in charge of her guns. On both *Moondog* and *Swift* were sailors wearing the hats, coats, and colorful scarves of *Moondog*'s pirates.

A half-mile to the south of them, off their starboard beam, was *Cutler*, playing the chase ship, coming on with all sails set, flying the American ensign, Weatherby in command and Mr. Simpson safely aboard her, as well as the bulk of Kinkaid's crew at her biggest guns. The ponderous man-of-war was not fast or handy in a headwind, so they would have to wait for her to come much closer before the three ships could enter Coral Bay as a group.

Corporal Stockton was startled out of his reverie by the sound of twigs snapping behind him, from the very jungle he had just walked through. Someone was running along the road, heading in his direction, and so he scooted his bulk behind the tree and waited.

Stockton braced himself. When the sound of huffing and puffing reached him, he swung his heavy musket around, catching the runner on the shin and sending him sprawling—one of Blackstone's men.

The stunned pirate scrambled to his feet, saw Stockton sitting there and then dashed off down the road, running past the marines hiding in the bushes, each looking up in surprise at the speeding figure…except for Major Bauer, who promptly whipped out his knife and threw it, catching the fleeing buccaneer square in the back, the heavy weapon buried to the hilt, piercing the pirate's heart. He fell face down, dead, his legs kicking spasmodically a few times before he lay still.

The major retrieved his knife and was wiping the bloody blade on the pirate's shirt when Monk ran out of the bushes. With hand signs, the Indian scout told Bauer how far away the pirate base was, that there was a great deal of activity there, and that he had been unable to spot either Captain Blackstone or his hostages.

They pulled the body into the woods and were placing palm fronds over it when there came the dull boom of a distant cannon. There, beating around the headland, was *Moondog*, *Swift* right behind her, both ships under full sail and making for the mouth of the bay.

"Let's get moving," said Bauer, whereupon the marines blended back into the jungle, the stealthy Indian scout in the lead, heading toward the pirate base.

Mr. Lofton on *Swift* had kept the ship close astern, following with strict precision every move *Moondog* made, ever concrete in his deliberations, obsessive in following orders to the letter. Kinkaid found himself wondering if the young gentleman could appreciate the drama he was part of, wondering even if Mr. Lofton ever had a day of fun in his entire life, so unremittingly serious was he. But his pondering was soon interrupted by the sound of a cannon from the south, and when he turned he could see the puff of smoke from the forecastle of *Cutler*. Weatherby's first shot landed fifty yards off *Moondog*'s bow.

"Right on cue," noted Briggs, smiling. "May we reply, Captain?"

"You may indeed, Mr. Briggs. Just make sure you don't hit anything."

"I'll try not to, sir," answered Briggs before giving the order to fire the first gun forward, the muzzle pointing as high as the quoins would allow before it was touched off with a sharp crack. Even so, the shot landed short and in front of *Cutler*, well out of range of the nine-pounders.

"Very good shooting, Mr. Briggs, if I may say so," joked Kinkaid, both men enjoying the masquerade.

Then there came a report over the water and a puff of smoke from *Swift*, the shot also landing short of *Cutler*. The two ships were running from the big warship, acting as if they were scrambling madly for the safety of Hurricane Hole, drawing the pursuing *Cutler* ever nearer as she fired more shots and had more shots returned from the pursued, until there was little question that the sounds of those cannons were easily heard in the parlor of Blackstone's Chateau.

"Helmsman, bring us hard to larboard," ordered Kinkaid after clearing Leduck Island at the southwestern opening to the bay. "Take us in."

Moondog came deftly through the stiffening breeze, the bowlines were passed and her sails were sheeted home, and now she was entering the bay, making straight for the pirates' hideout. Ten minutes later *Swift* made her turn in *Moondog*'s wake, while *Cutler* drew ever nearer the mouth of the bay from the south, Weatherby still firing her forecastle guns, the splashes closer than Kinkaid thought necessary.

Briggs thought so too and said so. "That Weatherby, sir."

"Quite the show-off," Kinkaid had to agree.

Blackstone's pirate gunners on shore would be in their defensive positions by now, watching the dramatic chase out in the bay, waiting to see if *Cutler* would dare come into the narrow cove. They were prepared to sink her should she do so, and of course Blackstone would be hoping she would come into his protected haven so that he could put his guns to use, test his crews and the effectiveness of his defenses. His eagerness would be his downfall, hoped Kinkaid, for the pirate leader would expect both ships in the cove to join in the attack against *Cutler* as hidden shore batteries pounded her from all directions, overwhelming her formidable firepower. In actuality, the odds came to eighteen guns against eighty, give or take a couple, and if Bauer's marines could approach undetected and take them by surprise from behind...

Moondog went in first, between the two outreaches of land on either side of Hurricane Hole, *Swift* still tagging close behind, playing the battered prize. Kinkaid strained his eyes along the shoreline, but he could not detect, as yet, evidence of any guns concealed in the jungle as he stood on *Moondog*'s forecastle. The black barrels of the pirate cannons were too well-hidden behind thick foliage, but he did orient the map to the lay of the land and shoreline, pinpointing in his mind where Porter and Gunner Freeman had told him where on the map they would be. He did, however, see the dark logs and disturbed earth of the newly constructed redoubt in front of the camp.

Kinkaid stood at the bow, one foot on the bowsprit, looking into the crystal clear waters, trying to judge the depth without appearing to be doing so by anyone watching from shore. He could take no chance in having a leadsman in the chains; Freeman would not have needed such a precaution, knowing exactly where to take the ship. Fortunately, the surface of the lagoon was quite calm, which allowed him to easily see the yellow-sanded bottom that seemed to be shoaling quickly. He knew there was deeper water less than a hundred yards from the camp and hoped he could guess where that deeper water was and how to get there without running aground on a sandbar or shallow reef, to find his way to the spot where *Moondog* had been anchored the first time he saw her. Yet it had been nighttime when he'd last seen her at her anchorage, and judging the distance on this bright and sunny day was difficult as he simultaneously kept himself apprised of the tactical situation. A piece of driftwood caught his eye, and he was comforted to notice that it was moving into the bay, toward the shore, a sure sign that the tide was coming in—good to know in case any of the ships should run aground.

Kinkaid was pleased to see that Weatherby was bringing *Cutler* in fast behind *Swift*, those two forward cannons still firing sporadically, keeping the game alive. He hoped that the pirates would be paying more attention to *Cutler*, now entering the bay, than to the men on the decks of either of the smaller ships.

The bottom was shoaling precipitously on the port side so Kinkaid waved his arm to starboard, making Rafferty turn the wheel until he saw Kinkaid point ahead, taking *Moondog* into a deeper hollow and bringing the ship less than a hundred yards from the three buildings and the redoubt, to her familiar anchorage.

"Drop anchor," said Kinkaid, and seaman Decker swung the mallet that struck the holding block, releasing the anchor chain with a clatter and a rumble as it followed its anchor over the side, sending up a walloping splash as it hit the water.

An instant later, Briggs fired a cannon on the starboard quarter, missing *Cutler* by more than a safe margin, causing Kinkaid to pray that Briggs's poor marksmanship would not be noticed by Blackstone's expert gunners on shore.

As *Moondog* swung on her anchor cable with the light breeze, Kinkaid took a moment to crouch down low behind the bulwark at the bow and scan the shore with his telescope. He hoped to discern the figure of Jack Blackstone from among those few figures who showed themselves, but the pirate leader and his hostages remained out of sight. By now *Swift* had drawn near and the rattling sound of her anchor chain could be heard in the quiet backwater.

The gunners on shore would have to open up pretty soon on *Cutler*, so close was she now, her tops backing to slow her. Weatherby would be below at the guns, waiting—as all eyes on all three ships were waiting—for the pirate guns to reveal themselves, to prove Freeman right or wrong. Briggs was directing the gunners aboard *Moondog* to aim at certain spots along the shore, while Mr. Lofton was doing the same aboard *Swift* against the opposite shore.

Before Kinkaid even made his way back to the quarterdeck, the first gun from shore boomed out on the right, sending a tremendous tongue of flame and smoke leaping out of the jungle. Its concussive blast resounded loudly across the tranquil waters, echoing off the hills and leaving a long and lingering plume of white smoke hanging in the still air of the lagoon, immediately identifying the position of one of Blackstone's new eighteen pounders. Before its smoke cleared, another heavy cannon roared from the left, sending up a geyser of water in front of *Cutler*, both large caliber guns situated exactly where Freeman had said they would be. Then all of the guns hidden in the jungle added their booms and crashes to the din, the shore on either side of both anchored ships obscured by a wall of dirty white smoke as *Cutler* closed the distance.

"Signal all ships to open fire! Mr. Briggs, you may fire at will!" bellowed Kinkaid as he watched half a dozen cannonballs crash into or bounce off the hull of *Cutler*, now only a hundred yards from *Swift*, the big battleship making her turn to starboard, Weatherby preparing to loose her guns against the shore.

Briggs gave the command to fire the twelve guns on the deck of *Moondog*. The starboard double-shot loads of grape cut a deadly swath through the green underbrush along the shore, where four guns were arrayed in a line, decimating their crews with a withering wall of steel, while the port-side guns were directed against two twelve-pounders, knocking both instantly out of commission. When the smoke cleared, a few men could be seen running for cover into the jungle beyond.

Swift was getting into the action now, Lofton firing all her starboard guns against the first large-caliber cannon on the right, silencing it. Then the men ran to the opposite side, firing her port guns at the big gun there. The sound of the cannons echoed off the surrounding hills, and the thick smoke that lingered over the waters threatened to hide the shoreline from sight.

But Kinkaid could still see the redoubt in front of Blackstone's Chateau and a long curl of flame spat out from behind the heavy logs, followed by a loud boom where the third big field piece was located, its target *Swift*. Kinkaid heard the swish and whine of the ball as it sped over the midships transom, missing him by only a few yards, and sending up a towering fountain of water a hundred yards beyond the ship.

There, just to the left of the redoubt, at the edge of the jungle, Kinkaid thought he detected some of Bauer's marines. He raised his telescope. Yes, he could definitely make out two men in green throwing hand grenades toward the bunker. One grenade exploded on top, the other in front of the opening as the cannon roared again, the combined smoke obscuring the position entirely as the ball slammed into *Swift*'s aft quarter, damaging her rudder.

The pirates on shore realized the trick now as the two smaller ships in the harbor fired upon them at point-blank range, but the realization came too late. Many of Blackstone's main guns were already put out of action and the others under heavy fire or assault—and the powerful broadsides of the massively gunned *Cutler* had yet to enter the fray.

But Weatherby had her in position now, and as Kinkaid watched, a great roar filled the bay as both sides of the mighty battleship erupted in sound and fury, her broadsides crashing out with a wall of hot steel that sliced through the jungle like a giant scythe, ripping through flora and men alike.

Rows of Blackstone's gun crews were knocked down like tenpins, and Kinkaid could see a few men stumbling back into the trees through the veil of smoke and falling leaves, shocked and demoralized by the terrible power of the man-of-war. Men wounded or barely alive stumbled over their dead, hoping only to escape the next salvo, while sailors on deck were adding to the mayhem by firing double loads of grape at any retreating pirates they saw. And so went the action as the three ships methodically concentrated their fire at any signs of resistance.

In spite of heavy pressure from Bauer's marines, the big gun inside the redoubt still managed to maintain sporadic fire against the ships in the bay and so, with the batteries along the shoreline decimated and silent, Weatherby brought *Cutler* in closer until her keel touched the sandy bottom and brought her port batteries to bear on the stubborn redoubt.

"O'Toole, let's get a boat over the side!" shouted Kinkaid, tucking his pistols into his belt. "Mr. Briggs, I'm going ashore!"

Cutler's lower deck broadside crashed out, the concussions of the big guns reverberating off the side of *Moondog*. When the smoke cleared, Kinkaid could see that the logs covering the redoubt had been tossed upward, blasted asunder, the earthworks in front laid low, the few surviving pirates inside throwing up their hands in surrender. Sergeant Stockton took charge of them as Major Bauer led the others into the smoking remains of the redoubt, where they had to duck down as the popping sounds of musket fired came from the two buildings on either side of Blackstone's Chateau.

Weatherby could see, as well, that the three ships' combined gunnery had surprised and devastated the pirate's cannon defenses. He also knew that a simple and overwhelming cannon barrage could have easily blasted the three buildings into matchwood, but with Marie and her father still held hostage…

The pirate leader was yet to be found and, afraid that his captain might find himself facing Blackstone alone, Weatherby had a boat put into the water, knowing that Kinkaid would not hesitate to get ashore. Sure enough, when he looked in the direction of *Moondog,* there was Kinkaid in the bow of the ship's boat, already heading for the beach.

A hail of musket fire slammed into the boat's side. Two balls passed through the planking where Rafferty crouched.

"Let's not wait for their second volley, men," said Kinkaid. "Leave your weapons in the boat and over the side we go!"

Then he dove over the side—and none too soon, for one of the oarsmen was grazed in the arm before he could do the same. Now seven men bobbed around the boat, clinging to the sides, trying to keep it between them and the incoming musket balls that slammed into the boat with vicious thuds or skipped off the surface, zinging away with a whistling sound.

Kinkaid kicked off his shoes and began swimming toward the shore. He could hear the musket fire between Bauer's marines and the pirates in the buildings in front of them and could see that the marines were putting up a good suppressive fire and making the pirates keep their heads down. But he began to tire, his back muscles in spasm, the bandages wet and slipping against his wounds. The shore was still fifty yards away. All he could do was put his head down and continue swimming slowly, methodically, and keep pushing the heavy boat before him.

"Care for a lift?" came a familiar voice.

It was Mr. Weatherby, in a boat coming up behind him, and he was quickly dragged aboard.

"Major Bauer is making them keep their heads down," observed Weatherby, looking full of himself.

"One would think you're my mother, Weatherby," exclaimed Kinkaid.

Rafferty and the oarsmen continued to push their boat before them, heading toward shore while Weatherby's boat passed them and soon slid up on the sandy beach.

Kinkaid leaped out, Weatherby at his heels. A couple of cannons were lying just inshore, their trucks broken. They found two others abandoned, and a motley collection of arms and provisions scattered about. Kinkaid grabbed a bag of shot and a powder horn and looped them around his neck. Then he picked up two muskets, said, "Let's go," and strode resolutely toward the settlement where Bauer's marines were still firing at any pirates foolish enough to show their heads at the windows.

Kinkaid stopped the group in a shallow depression some thirty yards from the first building. He motioned for them to get down as he surveyed the scene. A few muskets were firing from both buildings on either side of Blackstone's Chateau, but the strongest defense appeared to be coming from the building on the left, directly behind the redoubt. He could see, as well, at least a couple of muskets pointing out the windows of the first shack, the one in front of them. He waited until a shadowy form appeared in a window, raised his musket, and fired.

"Spread out!" ordered Kinkaid as he knelt to reload. "Weatherby, you and Rafferty get over there along the shore, behind those fallen trees. What is your name, sailor?"

"Mills, Captain. Gunner's mate," answered the stocky blond man in the red liberty cap.

"You stay here with me, Mills, and get rid of that cap. The rest of you move into the jungle there. Keep a steady fire against that first house."

The men quickly took up their positions as Kinkaid fired again toward a musket that poked from a shattered window, and soon the various groups were pouring lead from their positions with such regularity that the return fire rapidly diminished, the flimsy wooden walls offering poor protection.

Suddenly Mr. Briggs appeared from the trees behind them, a cutlass clutched tightly in his hand. He ran up to where Kinkaid and Mills were crouched.

"Mr. Briggs, what are you doing here?" asked Kinkaid, feigning annoyance.

"There's nothing to do aboard ship, sir," said Briggs breathlessly.

Kinkaid eyed with amusement the cutlass Briggs carried. "And what do you intend to do with that pig sticker?"

Briggs turned the blade and with a sheepish look answered, "Just thought you could use some help, Captain."

"Here, take this," said Kinkaid, handing Briggs his extra musket. "Stay here and keep low. Give me covering fire."

"I'll come with you, sir," insisted Briggs.

"Did I tell you to come with me, Mr. Briggs?"

"No, sir."

"Mills, get over there and tell Weatherby to rush the house when he thinks they're reloading. Everyone will rush the place at Weatherby's signal. I'll tell the men in the jungle."

"Yes, sir," said Mills, before he started crawling on his belly to where Weatherby and Rafferty were.

"Wait for Weatherby's signal, Briggs. Until then, cover me."

"Yes, sir."

Kinkaid left the bag of shot and the powder horn with Briggs and started crawling toward the house on his hands and knees through tall grass and scrub as Briggs let loose with his musket. Dropping to his stomach, Kinkaid inched slowly forward, dragging the loaded musket with him. He went about ten yards, then waited. Mills had made it to where Weatherby and Rafferty were, and all three of them raised their muskets and fired at the window, shattering what glass was left, causing a musket in the window to withdraw quickly. Seeing his chance, Kinkaid scrambled across the open space into the jungle where the other sailors were.

"Cover me and wait for Weatherby to give the signal," he told them. "Then rush the building."

Then he made his way forward again, along the edge of the trees. Keeping low and while the men kept up a steady fire into the wooden structure, he reached the back corner of the building and peeked around.

There, coming out the back door of Blackstone's Chateau, was the Marquis, followed by Blackstone himself, a musket in one hand, the arm of the Marquis's daughter clenched in the other, a look of terror on her face. And who was that in the frumpy black suit standing behind him? Mr. Horvath, the despicable merchant who had sold them watered down rum and stale bread, looking more nervous than ever. Of course—he had been Blackstone's eyes and ears on St. Eustatia. Blackstone saw Kinkaid at the same moment and raised his musket.

Kinkaid jerked his head back even as Blackstone fired, the ball slamming into the edge of the building.

There was the shout from Weatherby, and the sailors from the jungle stood up and rushed the shack, screaming wildly.

A man with a pistol came tearing around the corner. Startled to see Kinkaid crouching there, the pirate raised his weapon, but Kinkaid pulled the trigger of his musket first, only inches from the man's face, killing him instantly and leaving a smoking hole where his left eye had been, the back of his head gone.

Peeking carefully around the corner, Kinkaid saw only an open door at the back of the chateau. They were gone. There, a white flash and a movement of leaves—Blackstone was fleeing up a jungle trail with his hostages. Kinkaid hesitated as he heard his sailors kick in the front door of the shack and waited in case any pirates ran out the back door. He realized that his musket needed to be reloaded; the pistol in his belt was likewise useless with its powder wet. With no balls for the musket and no time to reload, he hefted the musket by the barrel to use as a club. A loud scuffle was taking place inside the shack now, the sound of furniture being knocked about, the crash of crockery breaking, men grunting, and a cry of pain, then silence.

Assuming Briggs and Weatherby's assault on the shack successful, Kinkaid ran to the back door of Blackstone's Chateau, peeked quickly inside, found no one there, then ran back to find the forest trail.

The sound of musket fire from the berm was becoming sparse, the marines taking their toll. Now a series of sharp explosions—one, two, three, four—the marines close enough to use their hand grenades against the shack on the left. A man screamed. A ragged volley, then lots of men shouting, and then the firing stopped and some men cheered.

Kinkaid rushed up the narrow, dimly lit path, the jungle sweeping by, closing behind him, his unloaded musket barrel pointing the way. He dared not stop and allow Blackstone and his captives to lose themselves in the jungle. They were not far ahead of him, he was sure of it. If the Marquis and his daughter were aware that they were being pursued, they might try to slow Blackstone.

Kinkaid kept running up the hill through the thick undergrowth, unable to see more than a few yards ahead of him, breathing heavily. Finally he came to a small clearing and the path split, going off in two directions, the ground too hard to show footprints. Which way? Take the left, he guessed, but after running a ways he was unsure. He paused to listen. Nothing. Keep going was all he could think to do. There, a small shoe print in the mud. Now the trail leveled out along the top of the hill. He saw light reflecting off the water, a bay far below. There, a flash of white again. It had to be her. She screamed. There was Horvath, out of breath and panting hard, sweat running down his greasy face, holding a musket. The Marquis lay on the ground behind him, a patch of blood on his forehead. Marie knelt beside him.

Kinkaid tried to stop but slipped on the muddy trail, landing hard on his back, still holding onto his useless musket. Desperate, he threw the musket aside, gambling that Horvath would not shoot an unarmed man.

Horvath laughed, strode within six feet of Kinkaid, and leveled the musket at his chest.

"I see you still have your fancy pistol," he observed.

"Powder's wet," admitted Kinkaid.

"That is unfortunate," he mocked, a nervous twitch pulling at his cheek. "If I believed you. Toss it aside…easy now."

Kinkaid did as he was told, angry for allowing himself to get into such a predicament, fearful that Horvath might kill him at any moment. Words were his only weapon.

"My compliments, Mr. Horvath. It seems you have me at a disadvantage," he said, managing a weak smile.

"No, I have you exactly where I want you," Horvath sneered.

"I have to admit," said Kinkaid, feeling sick, "I had no idea you were involved with Blackstone."

"A business associate. Ah, but it seems you deceived us one better, after all, Kinkaid," Horvath admitted. "But I'd say I have the last laugh, wouldn't you?" He cocked back the hammer of the heavy gun and took aim at Kinkaid's head. "Good-bye Captain Hero."

A shot rang out. Horvath wavered a moment, eyes wide in shock, blood pulsing from his chest. The musket dropped and he fell with a thud, flat on his face between Kinkaid's feet.

Kinkaid stood up, turned around. No one was on the trail. He looked along the shoreline. There, perhaps fifty yards away, was Weatherby, running toward them along the narrow beach; the musket he carried was still smoking. He must have taken the trail to the right.

Weatherby passed him and went to the crying Marie, took her in his arms, and held her while she wept.

Kinkaid rolled Horvath over. He was dead, a bullet through the heart.

"That Weatherby is such a show-off, sir," said Briggs, coming up behind him, his left sleeve torn and bloody.

"I'll grant you that," agreed Kinkaid, though he could little complain, Weatherby having saved him thrice in two days.

Briggs bent over the Marquis. The man was holding his forehead where Horvath had struck him with the butt of his musket when he had refused to go on, a trickle of blood running down into his left eye. But where was Blackstone?

Kinkaid ran down the trail. It continued through the jungle, down a slight incline, and ended at a cliff over a bay far below. There, skimming through the surf in a small pinnace, was Jack Blackstone. He turned and, seeing Kinkaid standing on the cliff above him, smiled and waved as the boat rounded the headland and was lost from sight.

Kinkaid stood there, helpless, left with the realization that Blackstone had bested him again. Even so, he had to admire the crafty pirate's cunning and instinct for survival, recognize him for the estimable foe that he was, and admit that he was lucky to have survived the encounter.

Briggs came running up as he stood on the promontory, gazing out over the sparkling ocean. "The pirate base is secured, Captain."

XIV

Just Desserts

With the destruction of Blackstone's base, the pirates of St. John found themselves suddenly leaderless and without a ship. Kinkaid, badly in need of crew to man his three vessels, offered the eleven taken after the fight the chance to serve with him, with the understanding that they would never mention having once sailed under the howling dog flag. Expecting to be hung and considering their dubious fate on the wild island, all "volunteered" their services—four going to Mr. Briggs, commanding the battered *Moondog;* three to Mr. Lofton on *Swift;* and four to *Cutler,* experienced sailors all.

And of course there was the treasure. In addition to Blackstone's ship, they found crates of wine, boxes of cigars, jars and tins of jams and delicacies, boxes and chests full of jewelry, bags of coins from many countries, art and artifacts—all left behind after Blackstone's hasty departure. All were claimed as prizes of war to be divided accordingly, giving every member of Kinkaid's crew a substantial nest egg, shares of which were already being gambled away, lost, or won on the throw of the dice. After gathering all of value from Blackstone's pirate fortress, the guns were spiked and knocked from their carriages, and the place was set ablaze, leaving nothing but three piles of blackened timbers as evidence of the camp.

Finally, after spending almost two days repairing damage to the smaller vessels and transferring stores for their respective crews, all three ships left the shelter of Hurricane Hole, heading north after clearing the narrows between the towering Great Thatch Island and the west end of Tortola. And now, their duty done,

Kinkaid thought it only fitting that Cato prepare a celebratory feast.

Cato, with Roach as his industrious assistant, had turned the great captain's cabin on *Cutler* into a gala banquet hall. Tall silver candelabra graced each end of the table, covered in white linen. Each elegant place setting was of delicate china bearing the seal of the Royal Navy and was complemented with fancy silverware emblazoned with the crest of the Woolston's of Kent, the family of her former captain. In the center of the table was the very finest cuisine that Mr. Africanus and St. Eustatia could offer, tempting the palate with a wonderful variety of savory and delectable dishes. And all of Kinkaid's officers and guests were seated around the table.

"Mr. Africanus…Cato, bring us more wine," said Kinkaid expansively. "Some of that good French stuff."

"Coming right up, Captain," said the beaming Cato, energetically serving his guests, happy in his element, knowing his lavish dinner was being appreciated to its fullest.

"One thing I'll say for Blackstone," observed Mr. Simpson, "he may be a murdering pirate, but his taste is impeccable." Simpson was holding what was left in his glass up to the light coming through the windows of Kinkaid's cabin, admiring the color of the fine Chablis liberated from Blackstone's extensive stock.

"I'll drink to that," said Mr. Briggs, his arm in a sling, a souvenir of his fight with the pirates. Weatherby and Briggs had led the assault on the house and, with six sailors right behind them, had fought hand to hand with the five men inside, Briggs receiving the slashing cut to his bicep before they subdued the pirates.

They were all here at the table, all his officers and Major Bauer, Sergeant Anders, and Boatswain O'Toole as well, the latter two still sporting black eyes and without their cuds of tobacco for once, sacrificed for the formal occasion. O'Toole had his hair tied back in a ponytail, the old salt looking like a distinguished politician or perhaps a prophet. Only when he smiled, showing that missing tooth, could one recognize him for the weathered sea dog that he was. On his left arm was the outline of a dolphin, the new tattoo still unfinished, only the tail filled in with dark blue. Weatherby was sitting between Marie and her father, and Mr. Simpson sat across from him. Cato was in his glory, having served a veritable banquet to his captain and his two rich and honorable guests…well, some perhaps not so honorable, but at least rich and beautiful.

They would never know what the Marquis had been up to, leaving St. Eustatia in a French ship bound for New York, a British-held city. If the rumors were true, he was probably dealing arms to both sides, a lucrative though dangerous profession. Kinkaid found him charming, but could not feel much respect for the man for bringing his daughter into such danger.

"Sir," said Weatherby, his eyes never leaving Marie's, she returning adoring looks. "I'd like to propose a toast, if I may." Everyone was beginning to feel the effects of the excellent wine by now, and Weatherby was positively glowing with infatuation and chivalrous exuberance. Cato was scrambling to ensure that everyone had a full glass with which to toast.

"Of course, Mr. Weatherby, a toast, if you please," was the only answer to give.

Weatherby rose unsteadily, raised his glass, and waited until O'Toole's glass was filled, then said, "To life, liberty, and the pursuit of happiness."

"Hear, hear," came the chorus, everyone lifting their glasses.

"A fine toast, Lieutenant Weatherby," said the Marquis, standing. "No doubt inspired by the enlightened document recently drafted by your new government. I myself was honored to have read the Declaration of Independence brought to St. Eustatia by your esteemed diplomat Mr. Simpson, here. I would like to return the Lieutenant's fine words by proposing a toast to the courageous men in uniform of the American Navy, without whom I and my lovely daughter would not be sharing this fine dinner with you this evening. Most sincere thanks to all of you, sirs, from the bottom of my heart," said the Frenchman with a flourish.

The dinner continued for some time afterward, with many toasts coming one after the other, each more elaborate than the one before, each trying to outdo the last, until dessert was served. By now it was obvious that everyone had proposed a toast except the Captain.

All eyes were upon him now, expectant, and Kinkaid would rather have faced a murderous horde of Blackstone's pirates at the moment, in spite of the fortitude inspired by the good wine. All the appropriate and clever toasts seemed to have been taken. To life and liberty, to the American Navy, to those who had given their lives for their country (Mr. Lofton's thoughtful contribution). Then there was the black-eyed Sergeant Anders toasting to friendship, with the black-eyed O'Toole returning a hearty, "Hear, hear," and adding something about heaven smiling upon the works of justice. Others contributed toasts to beauty, to prosperity, to peace and goodwill, to love, to leadership and loyalty (Mr. Briggs's contribution, the boy seeming to mature in the last weeks), to fair seas, and more. Kinkaid could think of nothing worthy of another toast.

He found himself blankly gazing at the magnificent dessert in front of him, a light yellow cake with creamed bananas falling out of its sides, a swirl of Dutch praline chocolate delicately gracing its top, when the idea struck him. He stood up, looked at the expectant faces turned his way, cleared his throat and said, "Ladies and gentlemen…" he paused, almost choking, but his audience took it for a perfect dramatic effect. Then, raising his glass, he said simply, "To just desserts."

"Hear, hear!" Simpson rose smiling, his glass held high as all took up the simple but philosophic toast, the silence replaced by a veritable chorus of gratuitous comments and clinking glasses. Slapping Kinkaid on the back, Simpson said in his silver tongue, "A fine toast to an unforgettable evening. My sincerest congratulations, Captain."

Cato stood behind the Marquis, an ear-to-ear grin splitting his proud and happy face as he realized that his captain's toast had been inspired by none other than his very latest creation: "Torte Caribbean à la Cato."

Printed in Great Britain
by Amazon